# WRAITH

## ANGELIS SERIES
### BOOK II

## EBONY OLSON

EBANDMUSE
PUBLICATIONS

Published 2023

Published by

EbandMuse Publications

Sydney, Australia

Cover by Frina Art

Editing by Striding Ibis Editing

**http://ebonyolson.com/**

# PREFACE
## SPECTRA

I am the daughter of the Archangel Michael, and therefore, the only female Angelis walking the earth. I didn't know I was anything more than human until I was nineteen, and then assumed I was a low-ranked Nephilim.

Since Michael didn't stick around to be a daddy, I wasn't trained as a child. While I could syphon naturally without realising what I was doing, shielding has been a steep learning curve. One recently achieved by facing my greatest fear.

When I was eighteen, I died. Thankfully, the soul remains with the body for three days. Before I could convert, my best friend, Alexander Williams—sorcerer and now L'Ordre of the Nachtwelt—enlisted the help of another Angelis to save me. When he did, Alexander tied part of my soul to his, binding us in a way that draws us like magnets to be together. The only way to save me was to bring me back as a Wraith. A ghost who can take corporeal form.

I am an Angelis, a Wraith, an untrained balance, and an orphan.

That's what I am. It's not who I am.

# PROLOGUE

## FANTÔME

"IT'S THIS WAY."

Miranda led the way into the basement of the Essence safe house. Her flame-red hair had regained its luster and her face its flawless complexion after a good feed.

"I called you as soon as I got away, so it's been just over three hours," Miranda reported. "Bay's people searched the building after getting Spectra out, but they didn't take Paul Samus."

"Bay knows better," Nika grumbled.

"Bay wasn't here," Miranda clarified. "He took off when I came to get her."

Miranda looked over her shoulder at her beautiful sister. Nika's grass-green eyes were livid. Miranda needed to defuse the situation, or more blood would be spilled before the night ended. "Gina can fill us in with that later. Spectra's alive; let's just focus on keeping her that way."

Nika nodded. Miranda explained her cover had been blown by the very situation they'd set up to try and protect Spectra. Miranda's idea had been to get Spectra employed at Bay's security company, Pendant, and away from the Nachtwelt Security Intelligence Office, but Nika signed off on it.

The first clue Nika had to Spectra being anything but human, was when Spectra was eighteen, lying dead in a morgue.

*Nika stood there looking over the corpse of the person she'd vowed to protect when Spectra started exhaling everything out of her lungs in a cry of pain.*

*Nika, wide-eyed, concerned she'd been taken, checked for a pulse. Nika's eyes grew bigger when her hand passed through Spectra's skin. The loud pounding of feet stampeding the corridor forced Nika to retreat. Pulling the hood over her head, she passed Alexander Williams in the hall as he raced to reach Spectra.*

*As Nika reached the exit, another hooded cloak stood blocking the door. Nika cursed beneath her breath. She didn't need to see his face to know who it was. She knew this Angelis by his sweet sugary smell of caramel. Just like his skin and hair, and as yummy to look at. Sadly, his personality was as cold and blue as his eyes.*

*As Nika came close, he shifted to let her pass. "Was she meant to be yours?" The deep timbre of his voice vibrated every erogenous zone in her body. Death should never be this sexy.*

*"No." Nika frowned at his query. "I would never do that to her."*

*Lincoln Azangelis cocked his head. "Was I too late? Did she convert?"*

*Nika was tempted to press her hand to her chest, her heart beating harder than the day she'd been adopted. "Should she?"*

*"A balance of her level will always convert three days after death," Lincoln explained. He turned his face down the corridor. "She will be more now, not less. But first, she will need time to adapt, then I will come and find her."*

*Nika moved, ramming the Angelis against the wall before his last consonant fell from his lips. "No. Whatever you think you will use her for, the answer is no."*

*Lincoln smiled. Nika blinked, and she was against the wall, Lincoln pinning her without even touching her. "I do not use. I am not a predator. She is the only female of my kind known to exist. Had I known of her before this, I would have come for her sooner. She belongs with us."*

*"She loves Alexander," Nika gritted, fighting against the invisible restraint.*

*Lincoln smirked. He lifted his hand and traced the line of her collarbone. Nika bit her lip on the moan her body produced, all of her muscles contracting in all the right places. "The sorcerer has his part in all this."*

*Lincoln peered down the corridor. Nika followed his eyes to see Alexander carrying Spectra up the hospital corridor. Nika's eyes locked on the ghostly figure in the sorcerer's arms. Spectra barely looked like the striking and confident college student she had been a week ago. "What did you do to her?"*

*"She'll recover." Lincoln opened the egress door and stepped out. He held the door while Alexander stepped by her.*

"Nika?" Miranda's voice broke through Nika's memory.

"What?"

"This is the room," Miranda pointed to a door.

Nika stepped into the room and observed the mess, taking a deep breath. A large bed was upturned and thrown against the far wall. From beneath the bed, a pair of legs were sticking out.

"That's very Wizard of Oz," Nika said out loud.

"Ding, dong, Paul Samus is dead," Miranda said dryly. "He was missing his head before the bed landed on him."

Miranda moved to the middle of the room, where a large pool of blood was coagulating.

"This is where I found her." Miranda peered around the room. "I'll see if I can find a mop or towel to soak up most of this blood." Miranda's lean body moved gracefully out of the room.

Nika knelt by the puddle of Spectra's blood. She lowered her face and inhaled. The sweet scent of toffee and the crunch of apple filled Nika's senses. Sugary, just like every other Nephilim she'd met. Nika hadn't understood that sweetness was a way of identifying Celestial descendants until that night in the morgue, but Spectra had always smelled human. It was only now, up close with a large pool of Spectra's blood, that Nika could smell her species.

Leaning closer, Nika let the tip of her tongue dip into the blood. Lightning and fireworks flashed in her eyes. Pressing away, Nika took her feet, a snarl reverberating in her throat.

"They are wed."

"Who are?" Miranda inquired cautiously as she wheeled a mop and bucket full of bleach into the room.

"Bay and Spectra," Nika snapped. "I couldn't think of a worse match. What is he doing, putting her life at risk like this? What was she thinking? I warned her what it meant to give her body to a sorcerer, and he's immortal."

Miranda hesitated. "He loves her; I saw it in his eyes. Maybe she feels the same."

"She loves the Angelis."

"Love can be multifaceted, sister."

Nika huffed. "Let's clean this up before the Essence finds it and realizes Spectra is what they've been looking for."

Miranda used the mop to soak up the blood, then rinsed it in the bleach.

"Here, I'll do that. You call Gina and organize to meet her tonight."

"Nika, is everything okay?" Miranda worried.

"No, Miranda. Essence came after Spectra once, and someone killed to protect her. They'll want to know why, and they'll come looking for that answer."

Miranda pouted. "Just when things get interesting, you take me off her watch. I'll go call Gina." She all but stomped out of the room.

It made Nika smile slightly. Miranda needed a break from babysitting, but that didn't mean she would miss out on the fun of hunting anyone who came after Spectra.

Nika looked back at the floor and shook her head.

"Too close a call, Spec. Too close by far."

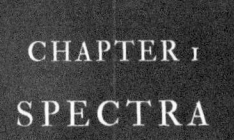

# CHAPTER 1

# SPECTRA

"YOU LOOK BEAUTIFUL." Gina smiled in the mirror behind me, golden-brown eyes sparkling behind her long black lashes. Her blond hair was falling in soft curls around her shoulders, and the dress she wore accentuated her figure in all the right places. "Hair up or down?" she asked, combing her lacquered nails through my long black tresses.

"Up would accentuate your cheekbones," a female voice declared by the door.

Gina and I turned to see the hooded figure standing in the doorway. The predator's presence ignited a ball of fear inside me. Immediately behind that alarm was an emotional upheaval too immense for words.

"Nika, you made it." Smiling, Gina assessed the predator's ripped jeans and hoodie, and she lifted a manicured brow. "Nice to see you made an effort. It's a wedding. Was a dress that impossible to come by?"

The predator closed the door securely. "You know my face can't be seen here. Formal dresses look even more conspicuous when teamed with a hoodie."

"You could have gone with a balaclava." Gina shrugged. "Ooh, what about a niqab?"

Pushing her hood back to expose her pale face, Nika rolled her grass-green eyes. "It's a Catholic Church, Gina. Can I have a few minutes with Spectra?" She shook her dead straight, pale blonde hair free from the hoodie.

When I nodded, Gina walked over and handed the predator the hairbrush. "I'll wait outside." The door closed with an audible click that made my body jolt.

"I thought de Sang presence wouldn't be so big a deal for you anymore." Nika narrowed her eyes.

"Bay is different."

"Don't I know it." Nika took a step toward me. "Powerful, strong, and moral. It didn't stop him from stealing another man's balance when the opportunity presented itself."

"It wasn't like that," I defended.

The de Sang stopped in front of me. "Explain it to me while I do your hair."

"Alexander and I had grown apart," I mourned, feeling that tug in my soul connected to his. "He strung me along letting me think I could be what he needed after he'd already decided I wasn't. But he's found someone else." Staring at my hands in my lap, my mind passed over everything that had happened over the last three weeks. I thought of how it felt when Alexander split the ether with me in his arms compared to Bay, the difference in how their raw power affected me and realized something. It didn't undo the hurt of Alexander's actions, but it relieved my guilt. "Which is good because I'm not who Alexander needs."

Nika brushed my long black hair while I talked, ensuring it was knot-free and silky smooth while I spoke.

"Bay came to me for work. He didn't know what I was. But there was a connection with him that drove me past my fear. He asked for one night. Initially, I thought it was an opportunity to become Alexander's balance that brought Bay to me, so I took it. I impassioned him and enabled him to feed himself again. In return, he exposed me to his raw power and forced me to learn my ability as a balance. That's all it was. Until it wasn't."

Lifting my topaz blue eyes, I dared to meet Nika's. The predator watched me while she sectioned and twisted my hair. "But you are here to marry the Angelis?"

"Yes. Bay agreed it was the best way forward. It was the best choice for many reasons."

"The main one being your safety," she declared.

"No. The main one is that I love Mercury. Not because our souls are connected or our bodies, but because I fell in love with him without any mystical connection forcing us. Yes, it will bring me safety, a disconnect from powerful sorcerers in a quiet war, but that was all secondary. I love Merc. We will be happy, have children—"

"Spectra"—the predator yanked my hair a little—"you wed your physical being to a sorcerer. You are his balance for the rest of your mortal existence. You will only conceive if he wants you to."

Shocked by this revelation, I blinked at her reflection in the mirror. "You didn't tell me that when you told me to hold out on Alexander."

"You were barely coherent by the time I explained my being there. Taking in your perilous existence was going to be difficult enough. I didn't want to overburden you." Placing a few pins, Nika stepped back to appraise her work. "You look stunning." She turned to leave.

"Wait," I called, standing to face her. "How did you know? That I had given my core to Bay?"

Reaching out, Nika caressed my face. "Your blood told me."

Meeting her eyes, the room I'd been held in by an Essence member flashed in my mind—a chaotic mess. The large timber bed was tossed aside like it weighed nothing and a blood pool was in the middle of the floor.

Snapping back to the here and now, peridot eyes swimming in an ocean of scarlet madness pulled me back, and I stumbled into my chair, breathless. Nika's eyes cleared to her natural beauty. "I couldn't leave your blood there for them to find. They would have forgotten Bay, forgotten the cure, after one taste of your non-existence."

Lifting her hood over her head to hide her features, Nika sighed. "Keep a low profile, Spec. They are still looking for that cure, and now that they have seen it works, they are willing to come into the light of day."

"I don't believe there is a cure," I murmured. "Not the one they are looking for, anyway."

The predator met my eyes, not directly, but I could feel them burning through the hood of her sweatshirt. "No cure comes without side effects. Just ask your Angelis."

Understanding precisely what Nika meant, I swallowed. Her hand touched the door. "Will you stay for the ceremony?" I asked quietly. Her lips tilted up at the side. "I'd like you to be there."

"I always am, Spec. Even if it's through my minions, I'll always watch over you like your own blood-thirsty guardian angel."

When Nika opened the door, Gina lifted her brow at her. "Who are you calling a minion, sweetheart?"

"Do you ever not eavesdrop?" The de Sang huffed.

"Rarely," Gina shrugged. "It is the job you recruited me for." She moved back into the room while Nika shook her head with a laugh. "Good job with the hair, but you need to make yourself scarce. The groom is growing impatient, and the boss is on his way."

"Keep her safe," Nika cautioned.

"She's a ghost. She does a pretty good job of doing that herself." Gina rolled her eyes. "But, fine."

"What was I thinking, recruiting you?"

"God knows, but you did, so stiff titties," Gina teased.

"I think the saying is stiff shit," I corrected.

Gina lifted a brow. "She gets what I meant."

"Sadly," Nika bemoaned. "I get how she is uncouth" -she gestured to Gina- "trailer trash she is. But, when did your vocabulary die a hellion's death?"

"Probably when I was dragged through hell to be brought back. Or it could be the company I keep. The Angelis are depraved souls."

The de Sang smirked. "I've noticed. None more so than that watcher you associate with."

Thinking of Tommy and how my demeanor probably had deteriorated from his education, I smiled.

"A bunch of lost souls, the lot of you," Nika sighed as she walked off.

"Takes one to know one," Gina called after her before shutting the door. "Bloody de Sangs! Even the good ones think they are above everyone."

"The more prim-and-proper they act, the more I have learned to doubt their goodness. It is a mask. The harder someone wears it, the more you know they have something to hide."

"You know, I think you are right." Looking me over, Gina teared up. "You do look beautiful."

Cheeks heating, I waggled a finger at her. "Don't you dare start to cry. I don't have time to redo my makeup."

"Please, you barely have any on," Gina scoffed. "In fact, I've never seen your eyes not smothered in black eyeliner. You make a sexy goth, but you are beautiful without all that. So why do you always wear black?"

Sighing, I looked back in the mirror. "Colour remains somewhat visible when I vanish."

Gina frowned. "Wait, so if you were wearing red and went ghost, I could still see you?"

Waggling a hand, I seesawed on the explanation. "Not so much, but there would be a red haze wherever I was standing. To humans, they'd just think their eyes were tired. Creatures of the Nachtwelt would doubt it and try to find its source, so it's safer to be black or white."

"And since it is from the Nachtwelt that you hide, you have to dress so you can do so at any time," Gina considered. "Why not white?"

"Yuck. So stereotypical Angel," I grumbled. "Plus, I'd look like a ghost with my pale skin. Connect that with hanging around churches and other sanctified ground—"

"Like graveyards," Gina inserted. "You'd scare the bejesus out of many mourners."

"Exactly!"

Gina got a cheeky grin. "I need to buy you some white slips for bed. I think the boss would love the angel stereotype."

"Bay does not need any further encouragement," I scolded. "Our bodies itch for each other as is."

"An itch, is it?" Gina grinned. I rolled my eyes which made her laugh. "You know you can talk to me about these things. I'm absolutely fascinated by these connections you have with sorcerers."

"The connections or the sex?" I debated.

"It's all research." Lifting a shoulder in half shrug, Gina snickered.

"Sure. The next time we sit down and do the girly talk about boys and braid each other's hair, I'll spill the beans," I joked.

Gina groaned. "You're so mean. Let's drink beer and watch porn instead. Way more interesting."

"Porn sucks. No one has sex like that."

"And yet, better than sitting around giggling and painting each other's toes," Gina decided.

Laughing, I liked how affable Gina was. But, thinking about what Nika revealed, about Bay getting to choose when we had babies, I wondered if he ever got clucky. "Are you and Calin going to have cubs?"

The humor dropped away from Gina's face in a blink. "No. Why would you ask that?"

Unsure why she was suddenly angry, I backed up. "Bay told me there have been cubs. I was looking forward to meeting them."

Turning her head to glare at the wall, Gina shifted uncomfortably. "Remember that graveyard that Cal and I found you freezing in?" I nodded. "You already did. I'm going to go check on my sister-wives." Opening the door, Gina walked out, leaving me staring after her.

Remembering the Angel that I huddled beneath on the night of the attack at Bay's, my mind flashed over the headstones. The one word I could remember came into focus. *Stillborn.* A single tear fell free as the reality of their curse set in.

## CHAPTER 2

## BAY

I walked through the church doors, Calin right behind me. I'd been shocked to see Calin's shoulder-length blond hair pulled back into a low ponytail and wearing a suit when he picked me up. When I commented, Calin informed me he was the best man and needed to look the part. His hair pulled back accentuated his broad nose and high cheekbones, making him look more like his brother.

Luke, Calin's older brother, stood just inside holding a suit bag, his sculptured face far from impressed as his brown eyes glanced at his watch.

"It's normally the bride who runs late," Luke snipped. Seeing Luke in a suit was standard. He looked like he did every day with his short—almost military issue—blond hair.

"Where is she?" I asked, eager to see Spectra.

"This way." Luke led the way to a side door.

I let my eyes float to the altar, where Mathew, the priest, stood talking to one of the nuns. His pale blue eyes lifted to observe me as I walked to the side door. His physical appearance was that of any middle-aged priest, but I knew him to be a Celestial half-breed. As I met his face, something about the pale skin, blue eyes, and black hair reminded me strongly of Spectra. I blinked at the similarity, then focused on the door that Luke had just walked through.

"Well, at least the groom isn't there tapping his foot at us," Calin spoke over my shoulder.

"That's because I'm here tapping my foot," Mercury Raphangelis grumbled from the hall we'd entered. He was an inch or two taller than me, his shoulders broad in his suit jacket. "Thirty minutes late, Ryder. I was about to go ahead without you." His lapis blue eyes flicked to the door he stood in front of. "Your de Viand wouldn't let my wife out till you got here."

"Our wife, Angelis. She married me first." I glared as he stepped aside so I could enter the room.

"Not legally, she didn't," Mercury sighed. He ran a strong hand through his dark hair and walked towards the church. "I'll be waiting at the altar. Don't soil our wife." Mercury walked into the church before I could respond. Calin hid a smile and turned to follow the groom.

"I'll wait in the church too," Luke excused himself and left.

With a deep breath, I knocked at the door. It opened a moment later, and big brown eyes smiled at me. Gina was one of the tallest of Calin's wives. Her blond hair was down but styled, and it was probably the first time I'd seen her with makeup since her own wedding day.

"Boss." Her red lips smiled larger as she stepped back, allowing me entry.

Across the room, Spectra stood with her back to the door. Her black hair was pulled back in a braid but hanging long and loose at the back to her waist. The wedding dress was black. It was Mercury's choice. He'd insisted Spectra wouldn't wear any color, and we both agreed white wouldn't work with her lack of pigment. The low back in the dress was unlined black lace, allowing her skin to be glimpsed to the upper curve of her backside. From the hip, the layers of black lace flowed around Spectra's long legs to brush the floor.

I noticed Spectra's pale blue eyes, accentuated by her makeup, watching me in the mirror as I took her in. When I met her eyes, she turned to face me. The black lace was unlined across her abdomen. Still, thankfully for my self-control, it was lined with black satin across her generous bust.

Gina was grinning like a Cheshire. "You definitely picked a beautiful dress, boss."

When I stayed speechless because the sight of Spectra in that dress had rendered me such, Gina laughed and stepped outside. "I'll wait out here while you change, boss. Don't take too long. The groom is waiting for his wife."

The door shut. Spectra half turned away, pretending to fuss over a bouquet of black lilies on the table as her cheeks flushed. "You're gawking at me."

"You look like an angel." I threw the suit bag over the lounge and moved closer, touching her cheek, bringing her face back to meet mine. She was only an inch shorter than me in her heels, bringing us almost eye to eye. "Granted, a very morbid one in all that black, but an angel just the same. How did I never guess what you are?"

"You were focused on getting me into bed."

I smirked. "Which is why I know just how beautiful you are out of your clothes."

Spectra's blush bloomed red across her cheeks and exposed chest. Bowing my head, I pressed her lips to mine. Instantly, my body reacted to Spectra's proximity, and I dropped my shields entirely. My senses came alive. I could feel everything around me, the air currents through the room, the moisture in the air, the press of gravity. Yet, all of that was secondary to the feel of Spectra. Her soft but firm breasts pressed to my chest, her full lips pressed to mine, her fingers threading into my hair.

I pulled her tighter to me, my body reacting like it had when I first met her.

"Bay," Spectra whispered. "Mercury." She panted his name, reminding me this dress wasn't for me.

Closing my shields, I stepped back from her, taking a deep breath. "Tonight will be hard," I admitted, wondering what I was thinking when I had Mercury move into my house with her.

Spectra watched me with concern. "You wanted this arrange-ment, Bay."

"Yes, it is for the best," I agreed. "I'm just looking forward to Mercury doing two weeks' worth of night shift."

Spectra smirked, pulling me to the lounge where my suit was waiting. "Let me help you," Spectra murmured against my mouth, her hands sliding my jacket from my shoulders. She kissed me while her fingers made quick work of my shirt buttons, sliding it down my arms before her mouth trailed south, as she knelt in front of me.

I watched as Spectra unzipped and dragged my pants down my legs to my ankles, helping me step out of the pants. She caressed one finger up the inside of my thigh, brushed it over my balls, and dragged it along the base of my erect cock.

"Get dressed, Bay," Spectra directed.

Unzipping the suit bag, I removed the pants. Spectra took them, helped me step into them, and pulled them up my legs to snug around my rear. Then, taking my balls in hand, she wrapped the other around the base of my hardness and licked the tip.

"Keep going," she murmured before sliding me into her mouth.

I moaned deep in my throat. Then, taking a moment to enjoy the wet heat of her mouth, I took my time pulling on the fresh shirt. Spectra worked her mouth skilfully, wrapping her tongue around my smooth head each time she ascended, squiggling that tongue as she descended again.

Taking a deep breath, I closed my eyes and enjoyed the sensation that only intimacy with one's balance could give. It was better than sex or a blow job. Since we wed, the connection had imbued a pure primal need in us to join our bodies. It was a perfect balance of caring and adulterated craving and desire. Acting on it was like light-ning shooting from my brainstem right down to the base of my spine.

While I wasn't keen to rush this, a warning look from Spectra forced me to finish the buttons and pull on my jacket.

Slipping her finger into her mouth, Spectra sucked it, gave me a wink, then pressed hard on that spot between my balls and ass before starting to rub there.

I gripped the back of the sofa as I swelled in her mouth. That finger moved and slipped into my rear before I could object. Momentarily, I was surprised; it wasn't comfortable. Then all of a sudden, my balls tightened, and a sensation I'd never felt before rushed through my body, causing my toes to curl. Thrusting into Spectra's mouth with a guttural groan, I forced myself deep and filled her throat with my pleasure.

Spectra removed her finger, sucked my cock clean as she pulled away from my still hard erection, and licked her lips as she stood. I stared after her, absolutely amazed as she moved into the adjoining washroom and washed her hands.

"Wow!" I muttered to myself, hanging my head back and closing my eyes as I recovered. Then, I tucked in my shirt and tidied myself, regaining my strength.

Gina stepped into the room, her face a mask of innocence. "Are you ready?"

I cleared my throat. "Yes."

"Oh, I know you are." Gina winked. "I meant the bride."

Spectra stepped out of the bathroom, fresh lipstick in place. "Yes."

Gina picked up her bouquet of flowers and led the way out. Holding my arm out, Spectra took it and blushed.

"I thought you weren't into the kinky shit," I murmured.

"Oh, I'm not. Mercury is, though. So I know that trick hurries him along when needed," Spectra answered honestly.

"You probably shouldn't have taught me that," I advised earnestly.

Spectra turned her head, worried. "Why? Didn't you like it?"

"Oh, I liked it. That's the problem. Now that I know you can make me come hard and fast when we are time poor, I might not be so well behaved when your Angelis is home."

Spectra blushed bright red. "Don't tempt him to join us, Bay."

I raised a brow. "Would he?"

Biting her lip, Spectra looked away as we reached the bottom of the aisle, and Gina started walking to the altar. I didn't pursue the answer, but I made a mental note to find out just how kinky Mercury Raphangelis was at a later date.

There was no music as Gina made her way down the aisle. Just Gina's footsteps. Calin's other wives—Cynthia, Bronwyn, and Selena—were all watching in the front pews.

On Spectra's side of the church sat the majority of the nuns from the convent, all of them crying with enormous smiles. Spectra had been kidnapped only yesterday, and one of the young nuns was murdered in the attempt. I suspected the tears were a combination of grief and joy.

Further back in the pews sat a hooded figure, and I recognized the female de Sang from the night of Spectra's vigil.

"What's wrong?" Spectra murmured.

I met her eyes and saw she was frowning at me. "What do you mean?" I asked innocently.

"You have that crease in your brow." Spectra touched a gentle finger to the center of my forehead. "You only get that look when you don't get your own way. I thought you wanted me to marry Mercury?"

"I do. I was thinking about something else entirely."

Giving her a weak smile, my eyes traveled back to the de Sang, and Spectra's followed.

Swallowing with difficulty, Spectra quickly turned her face forward to where Mercury was waiting. "It's my turn."

I squeezed Spectra's hand and walked her down the aisle. When we reached the other end, and Spectra turned to hold hands with Mercury, I saw the tears spilling down her face.

"Who presents this woman to be married?" Father Mathew asked with a smile.

"I do," I answered, offering Spectra's hand to Mercury. "I share with you, my wife. Love and adore her as I do for the rest of your days."

Mercury smiled, and I stepped back to sit with Luke for the rest of the ceremony. When Mathew pronounced them husband and wife, Luke elbowed me and indicated Calin's wives. There wasn't a dry eye amongst the four of them. As hard as those women were, they were all romantics at heart. Mercury kissed Spectra deeply, Mathew clearing his throat when the intensity of the kiss became inappropriate for church.

"When Alexander finds out she was his balance, he will go ballistic," Luke whispered to me.

"She was never his, but he will never believe she wasn't."

Alexander Williams was the only other sorcerer I'd met who came close to my power level. He and Spectra used to be lovers, but he didn't think Spectra was strong enough to be his balance and put her aside in favor of a high order Nephilim.

Raquel Nephilizza was perfect to be L'Ordre's wife. She was well-raised and part of high society already. Whether she was strong enough to be Alexander's wife was doubtful, which would usually have bothered me, until I discovered Raquel worked for Essence.

Essence was a group of purists determined to be the only predator in the Nachtwelt. The majority of members were sorcerers who were taken and condemned to hell by their lives as de Sangs. There were others, though, from the tolerant and predator arms of the Nachtwelt, who agreed with what Essence wanted to achieve and supported them.

Unfortunately for Essence, I was not one of them. An issue that put Spectra's life in danger only twenty-four hours ago. A situation I never wanted to be repeated.

Everyone was congratulating the happy couple, my eyes pulled to the de Sang still sitting further back in the church. I considered it could be Spectra's new Fantôme protector for half a second.

Saying those words together almost seemed contradictory. Fantôme was a group of elite assassins. They were explicitly recruited for Fantôme before they were even taken. I'd thought Spectra's last protector, Miranda Jackson, had planned to recruit Spectra. But, it turned out, Spectra had some powerful and very deadly friends.

"Are you thinking that is the new protector?" Luke asked, watching the de Sang. When Calin told Luke how we found Spectra, I'd had to inform him about Miranda.

"No, this one has been watching her for a while," I spoke lower than a whisper to ensure they didn't overhear. "I've seen her before."

"Maybe there was more than one," Luke proposed.

I considered it a possibility. "It would make sense. One person can't always be where she is."

Luke smiled. "They've never needed to be. She lived here and kept herself low-key. Now she lives with us and will probably leave the estate only for work. So it's not exactly going to be the hardest babysitting job."

I smirked. "Spectra can disappear at will, Luke. Think about that."

Luke grimaced. "That could prove interesting around the house."

"Bay." Mercury walked up, holding out his hand to me. I shook it. "Thank you for all you've done for Spec and helping us find a safe place," Mercury thanked sincerely. He leaned forward. "I'm currently off work, so don't panic if you don't see Spectra for a while." Mercury winked.

I took a deep breath. "Define a while?"

Mercury grinned. "Till Monday." He chuckled at whatever he saw in my eyes and turned his attention to Luke.

Spectra stepped toward me and gave me a tight hug. "Thank you," she whispered. I held her body firmly to mine. When Spectra pulled back, she looked into my eyes, and I dropped my mouth to hers. Spectra allowed my lips to brush hers before pulling away gently.

"The nuns are watching, Bay," Spectra reminded me, humoured. "Let's not kill any more of them. They'd have a heart attack if I make out with you at my wedding to Merc."

Smirking, I kissed her forehead instead. "Kissing you in front of the nuns will not be the problem if your body stays pressed to mine much longer."

Spectra blushed and stepped away, and I let her go reluctantly.

When Spectra gave Luke a hug, Luke was momentarily surprised, then he buried his nose in her neck, and I watched him take a deep breath. "Luke," I warned.

Spectra stepped back, a slight shiver vibrating through her body.

"I'm sorry. I forgot for a moment. It's nearly dinner time, isn't it?" Spectra apologized with wide eyes, her hand instinctively checking her neck.

"Yes, but I would never eat you, Spectra." Luke's smile vanished. "I was just learning your scent. It will be in our house, and I don't want to get hungry every time I smell you."

"Desensitisation?" Spectra asked.

"Something like that," Luke agreed. "Since you have raised the matter of dinner. I might steal your husband, and we can eat before meeting you at the restaurant."

Spectra's eyes came to me, a slight disappointment in them. "Of course." Spectra made her way over to where Mercury was talking with Mathew.

"She hates being apart from you for any time," Luke observed.

"The feeling is mutual," I murmured. "I suspect I now understand what it has been like for Mr. Williams all these years."

# CHAPTER 3

## SPECTRA

"T HE SIGHT of you walking towards me will forever be one of my favorite memories," Mercury murmured to my neck.

We waited in the restaurant's foyer for everyone to arrive. In other words, Bay and Luke still hadn't shown up after they took off for their diner. Mercury's nose trailed the line over my pulse point, his hands flat over my tummy.

"I've been walking the earth for over a hundred years, Spec, and you are still the most beautiful thing I've ever encountered."

I reached behind me to sink my fingers into his soft brown hair, holding his face to the heat of my neck.

"A woman is meant to be her most beautiful on her wedding day." My lips tilted up as Mercury rubbed his engorgement against my rear.

"A woman is beautiful every day that she smiles. You are stunning today, but nothing will ever take away from the beauty of you coming when I am between your thighs, Spec. I don't care who is on top. Heaven for me is being inside you. And now you're my wife."

Teeth nipped my ear. As everything in Mercury's heaven tightened and grew heavy with humidity, I bit my lip. One of Mercury's hands went to my hip, pulling me hard against him.

"Merc!" I exhaled roughly. "Too hard." I tapped his hand at my hip.

Mercury growled and released me. "Sorry."

Turning to face him, I assessed those lapis blues that enchanted me. "When was the last time you went to the club?"

Mercury shifted his eyes to avoid eye contact. "I'm fine, Spec."

My eyes focused on the crease at the side of his downturned mouth. "When, Merc?"

Mercury huffed. "The night you broke up with Williams. I should have been fine for a few more weeks, but-"

"You had to use your powers to heal me last night," I acknowledged. Then, blinking, I stared at his chest. "Right!"

A single strong finger touched under my chin and tilted my face up to meet Mercury's eyes. I swam in the blue passion of his irises.

"I can control it, Spec. You're wrong if you think I am spending my wedding night at the club. I've waited years for you to be my wife, so I'm damn well consummating this marriage. I'll control my power."

The pressure of his hand on my lower back stepped me closer to Mercury, my body melting against the contours of his fit physique. My breath rushed out, hot and eager, when his lips brushed over mine.

"At least we don't have to worry about your power rising up anytime soon. You balanced your last few weeks effectively last night."

"I would have considered every interaction with Bay to be balancing," I confessed.

Mercury grunted a confirmation. "You are wed now. He'll never hurt you." A brush of his thumb across my cheek made my eyes shutter. I lifted my eyes to his.

"That doesn't make you safe, Spec. What happened yesterday is going to be a boomerang. It will come back at some point, and if you're not prepared, it will hurt you."

My throat constricted with fear, my eyes itching with memories of Paul Samus' incisors buried in my neck. "What do you suggest, Merc?" I'd always valued Mercury's advice based on his experience.

"Let Mathew and I train you. We couldn't teach you to be a balance, but we can damn well teach you to fight like our fathers."

"Swords and holy fire?" I questioned.

"Dirty, Spec." Mercury's breath was hot against my mouth as he whispered. "The term Angels and Demons comes from the way they look, compared to the way a Celestial fights. When an Arch decides to use his power to fight, you can bet your ass it will end up a blood bath."

My heart was racing, demanding to escape the confines of my rib cage. My breath was shallow, making me light-headed.

"You make that sound so hot," I breathed.

Mercury smiled and crushed his mouth to mine. Suddenly, a wall pressed hard against my back, Mercury's body weight sandwiching me. My body ached for his touch, skin jumping as his fingers made contact.

"Whoa!" Mercury was pulled back. "Reception before consummation, folks," Mathew lectured.

My lustful eyes opened to find Mathew standing between us, gripping Mercury by the collar. One side of Mercury's mouth lifted in a smirk.

"Best we eat, Father, because I'm a starving man, and I want my wife."

Mathew shook his head, and a deep chuckle echoed around Mathew's chest. He released Mercury's collar and patted his shoulder. "I came to tell you everyone has arrived. Let's go celebrate." Mathew walked into the restaurant.

Mercury came forward and offered me his arm. "Shall we?"

I slid my hand into his elbow crease, squeezing his bicep in my grasp. My body quaked in anticipation of gripping those arms while his body pumped into mine. I looked up at Mercury. "We're not getting much sleep tonight."

Mercury smirked. "Enjoy dinner, Spec. Once we get home, we're not leaving that bedroom until I have to go back to work."

My eyes widened slightly. Since we started sleeping together, Mercury and I had spent his days off having sex marathons. Still, four days was the most we'd ignored the outside world in favor of desire. I was more concerned whether he could last another four days without going to the club or losing control of his power with me.

We entered the private dining room of one of Mercury's favorite restaurants. Our friends stood clapping as we walked in. We moved around the room, greeting everyone before taking our seats.

The food was pre-ordered banquet style. Platters of roast meats, sautéed vegetables, rice, pasta dishes, salads, and loaves of herb bread. It was a sumptuous feast. But, considering Mercury's intentions for the next few days, I ate until I thought I would explode, just in case food did become secondary.

We started the meal with our bridal party beside us. Calin beside Mercury, Gina beside me. By the time dessert was being served, Gina moved to speak with her sister-wives, and Bay opportunistically took the empty seat.

"The last wedding I attended was Calin's and Selena's. A very modern affair. Big venue, all the bells, and whistles," Bay conversed. "This is the way it used to be done. I much prefer this." Bay's eyes went to Mercury. "The Angelis and I seem to have similar tastes. Based on how easily we worked together today to organize this wedding, I believe that we can work together where it matters most."

Leaning over, I kissed Bay's cheek. He turned, eyes meeting mine, his ice-blue irises pulsing with physical need. I felt the pull towards him. This close, it was magnetic. My lips buzzed from contact with his cheek. I wanted more. I needed to taste his mouth.

Mercury's hand weighted suddenly on my left thigh, causing me to draw back from Bay with a rough inhale. Then, picking up my drink, I took a large mouthful.

Bunching my skirt enough that he could place his bare hand on my stockinged thigh, Mercury leaned in, his lips kissing just behind my ear.

"Lift your dress, and let him have your other thigh. The physical contact will calm you both and ease the pull."

Taking a deep breath, I shuffled my skirt to expose my other thigh, thankful that the dress didn't have layers of tulle underneath. Then, placing my hand on Bay's thigh, I squeezed.

Bay dropped his gaze to my hand, then casually removed his hand from the table and placed it on mine. My eyes shuttered, and my heart leaped into my throat at the contact. His fingers rubbed through mine, filling the space. I imagined him sliding into another area of my body. My breath rattled out of my chest, and my entire body shuddered.

Quiet laughter to my left brought me back from the physical connection to my right. I removed my hand from under Bay's with a forced exhale, took him by the wrist, and guided his hand to my thigh. I met Bay's ice blue eyes, a smile tempting my lips as I watched his breath come short and brutal.

Hot air breathed across my neck on my left. "The passion between you two could power a city," Mercury whispered, his body still vibrating with humor. "I always wondered about the connection between a sorcerer and his balance. Now, I get to feel it firsthand."

Mercury's palm cupped my cheek, his breath blew across my lips, and then he kissed me, slow and deep. Bay's hand firmed on my thigh, his index finger stroking the rhythm of Mercury's tongue in my mouth.

Jeers broke out around the table. "Enough of that! Get a room!" Came from all directions.

Bay stood. "I'd like to propose a toast. To the newlyweds. May their love be long lasting, may their passion never die, may the love and support they receive from us buoy them through the hard times and celebrate with them on the joyous occasions."

"They keep that kissing up, and we will be celebrating a joyous occasion nine months from now," Calin cheered.

Licking my lips, I swallowed. Gina met my eyes and looked at Bay. I followed her line of sight to see Bay holding his glass casually, not a worry on his handsome immortal face.

"To the happy newlyweds," Bay finished.

Mercury stood, helping me to rise. Placing his hand on my lower back, Mercury crowded my left while Bay adjusted his stance to put his hand just above Mercury's. Everyone raised their glasses and toasted us. The three of us. While today's ceremony was for Mercury and me, everyone knew that toast was for my new husbands—plural——and me.

Bay looked to Mercury, who smiled. Then, without a word, they both angled their bodies to mine. Mercury kissed my mouth, and Bay's lips massaged my neck. My body heated, tightened, and pulsed with life and longing.

"Enjoy your honeymoon," Bay murmured to Mercury and me a moment later. Mercury held out his hand, and Bay shook it. "We are brothers now. When you consummate your wedding, you will become part of our bond, Mercury. There will be no going back," Bay warned.

Mercury nodded. "You said before. I haven't changed my mind. I'm in this for life."

Bay nodded and released Mercury's hand. He stepped closer, pulling me into a hug, mouth to my ear.

"If you are unsure, use protection. I have my claim on you. Once Merc adds his claim, there is no going back."

Giving him a sweet smile, I kissed Bay on the lips. He grinned as Mercury took my hand, and we waved goodbye to our friends. Calin and Gina followed us out to the front of the restaurant.

"You don't have to leave with us," I laughed.

"Actually, we do," Calin contradicted and walked over to the valet.

When I frowned, Gina shrugged. "We get to double as your bodyguards tonight. Just to make sure you get home safely."

"Oh." I shivered involuntarily.

Mercury wrapped me in his arms. "Well, keep your eyes forward. The ride home is going to be the foreplay," he warned.

I blushed bright red, but Gina laughed, and Calin opened the back door for us as the valet pulled the black SUV up.

"What about Bay? How is he getting home?" I worried.

"Bay has his other car for him and Luke to get home in," Calin reminded me.

His beautiful black sports car from the night we first slept together. The night of the attack. The night my life changed entirely again. The car Bay drove when I risked everything to learn how to shield and somehow fell for Bay simultaneously. That car.

The door shut, the SUV started moving, and Mercury's hands pulled me closer. I didn't have time to think about that car or that night anymore. Mercury was ravenous, and I was his supper.

Our heavy breaths drowned out the music from the stereo in the back. Mercury was never one to waste time sitting idly, so he'd always used travel time for heavy petting between us. One arm held me to him; the other was on my bum, beneath the lace of my scanties, as we kissed continuously.

Our companions were quiet in the front of the car, so with just the music playing it felt like every other taxi ride Mercury and I had ever taken. The difference, in this case, was the location we were heading to. This was the first time we would return home to Bay's country estate together. Well, with me conscious, anyway.

I caught glimpses of the trees lining the driveway as we made our way through the dark. The same trees I ran from Bay in fear through not so long ago. Then, a week later, I became his lover. Weeks after that, his wife. I dropped my eyes to the mop of brown hair before me, almost black with the lack of light. Mercury's lips kissed and pinched across the top of my chest hungrily.

Light filled the car as we pulled into the garage. Mercury didn't wait for the ignition to turn off. Instead, Mercury pulled me out of the car and lifted me into his arms once the vehicle stopped moving.

"Thanks for the ride," Mercury called over his shoulder. "See you in a few days."

I waved at a laughing Gina and Calin as he carried me inside. Calin pulled Gina against him, whispering something which made her blush and swoon as we entered the dark hall, and I lost sight of them.

Mercury carried me to the stairs at the center of the mansion. The ground floor held most of the shared amenities, kitchen, dining, library, gym, and a large entertainment room. The first floor belonged to Calin and his wives, halls on either side leading down to rooms I'd never explored and probably never would. There was a shared lounge room in the center, off the landing for the stairs.

Mercury carried me past the open lounge room and up to the next landing. The second floor contained two wings. Luke had his suites on one side; Mercury and I were now the suite's occupants on the other side.

My eyes lifted to the third floor as Mercury opened our door. Bay lived on the third floor. There were more rooms up there, but I'd only seen his bedroom and his study so far.

"Home sweet home," Mercury chimed as he kicked the door closed behind us.

My feet touched the floor. My back was to the wall a breath later, and Mercury was kneeling before me. Gasping, I lifted my head to the ceiling as Mercury disappeared beneath my skirt. His hands quickly moved my scanties aside and pressed his mouth to the hottest part of me.

My eyes rolled into my head, toes clenching. My hands clung to the wall for dear life as Mercury's tongue delved between my lips, tasting the wetness of my arousal and burrowing into me to open the flood gates. His nose against the highly sensitive bundle of nerves of my clit initiated a countdown. Finally, I was undone when Mercury sucked the flesh around those nerves into his mouth and gave them one hard lick.

Smiling like a Cheshire cat as he stood before me, Mercury wiped the juices of my lust from his mouth. I gripped his collar, pulled that mouth close, and tasted myself on his tongue. Mercury maneuvered us into a room, his hand groping blindly for the light switch.

Mercury started undressing once the room was lit, and I had to stop and watch. Mankind was made in the Angels' image. Still, the Celestials were perfection personified, and the Angelis, the children of angels, looked just like their fathers.

Biting my lip to prevent drooling, Mercury revealed his muscled olive skin to me. It didn't matter how many times I saw it. Mercury still made my mouth water. As his pants fell to the floor, I stepped into him, hands tracing the lines of his defined torso.

Kissing over his muscled chest, I found the edge of his angel tattoo, and then my tongue traced the feathers of the wing that rose from his ribs, across his chest to end at his neck. The feathered limb led me to his nipple. I circled it, then sucked it into my mouth.

Mercury groaned, hands holding my hair, fisting it. My fingers brushed Mercury's very large, thick cock. Feather light in touch, I caressed his length, palmed the breadth, and used my thumb to massage the smooth dome until he leaked his desire. Dropping my mouth to where his tip reached his belly button, I licked the salty precum from his silky head.

Before I could suck him into my mouth, Mercury spun me around and yanked on the zip for my dress. The dress loosened around my torso and swooshed to the floor. Then, with Mercury still standing behind me, I bent at the hip and unbuckled the ankle strap of my heels. Mercury cursed behind me.

A smile pulled at my lips for the look of pure lust filling Mercury's features when I stood up. His eyes scoured my lingerie, and his tongue darted out to lick his bottom lip. Reaching behind me, I unhooked the bra, letting it fall to the floor. Mercury's cock struck his abdomen, and I licked my lips, watching the almost clear liquid seep from its eye.

"We should discuss protection before removing those panties," Mercury breathed.

My thumbs were already hooked in the lace, dragging them down. Stepping out of the lace, I threw them to Mercury. He caught them, lifted them to his nose, and inhaled.

"God, I love your smell."

Blushing, I moved over to the bed, pulled back the covers, and lay down. Mercury came to stand above me. "I'll understand if you're not ready, Spec. We can play it safe until you are ready for kids. I just want you to know I'm in this for the long haul, so being tied to you magically and legally isn't even an issue for me."

"Merc." I reached out and took his hand, moving it to my breast. "You are both my husbands. You should both have equal claims to me. I'll let fate decide when children will become a part of our lives," I decided.

Mercury rolled his shoulders, his muscles relaxing with relief. He joined me on the bed, maneuvering between my thighs. Guiding his smooth head between my moist folds, he pressed against my entrance.

"I love you, Spec. Whatever happens going forward, know that will never change for me." He pressed into me slowly, taking his time to fill me completely.

Watching Mercury's face, I bit my lip at the incredible sensation of his body fitting to mine. I loved the awe on his face as we made love the way nature intended it for the first time. No protection. We were bared to each other and to fate.

We kissed, touched, and moved with each other gently, taking our time to enjoy this moment to its fullest. We were husband and wife, a future I'd never expected even a month ago was before us. I should have been terrified, but I wasn't.

As my back arched, my breath escaping me in a cry of pleasure, I knew this was where I needed to be. All those years I'd wasted trying to be good enough for Alexander when Mercury had always wanted me for who I already was. He'd been so patient waiting for me to realize it, and I only loved him more for it.

We collapsed together, Mercury pulling me into his arms as the sun started to wake. I lay there, smiling quietly, watching a new day dawning from the safety of Mercury's arms in Bay's house.

Everything had changed in weeks, but I knew that no matter the hardship we would face going forward, the three of us would do it together, and I would be safe and loved with my new family.

# CHAPTER 4

## BAY

THE AIR WAS crisp and clean, with the smell of snow on the horizon again. I grimaced against another icy blast of wind on my face. Ice crystals formed on my eyelashes before they shattered over my cheeks in my next blink. It had been three days since Spectra married Mercury and disappeared into their suite, and the door was still closed.

What was I thinking suggesting this living arrangement? Having her this close and not being able to touch her or see her was making me itch. I found reasons to walk up and down the stairs all day yesterday—and the nights, with her sleeping just downstairs, were a tangle of sheets and provocative dreams.

Then there was the sound of Spectra's moans I'd caught on and off. They were faint, almost imperceptible, and only audible when I passed right in front of their door. I'd heard Mercury's too, but he didn't make my body crave physical pleasure. I exhaled in frustration and picked up speed.

Reaching the last corner of the running trail I'd worn through the forest around my home, I nodded at the snow leopard on guard in this area. The Changeur de corps was Graham, one of my employees and ex-military. Since the attack, Calin had tripled our standard guard on the estate, using some of his former trainees. They weren't allowed near the house but were an early defense system against intruders. Always in pairs, one on the ground and the unseen in the trees. Resisting searching for Graham's partner, I considered the fence.

A new technology alarm system invisible to the naked eye was also fitted. It surrounded the entire property, making the only way in or out via the driveway. The only creatures entering my property without my advance notice would be sorcerers who could rip through the ether, and I could sense them too.

That's how I had found Spectra the night she ran from me. The disturbance from Alexander's power was like a boulder catapulted into a lake. It was a tsunami in the air currents. I followed the power to its source and found Spectra cringing in pain from the blast.

Williams didn't pull his power in, and he didn't care that he was hurting Spectra in his anger. And yet, the fact she survived it didn't clue him in. He should have known then that Spectra was powerful enough.

Still, she was never his balance. Spectra was more powerful than Alexander needed. Spectra was always meant to be mine.

Turning the last corner, I made my way back to the house. I slowed my run as I approached the back door, then stretched out for a few minutes. When I finished, I lifted my eyes to the windows in the guest wing on the second floor. Nothing. No movement, no light, nada. I huffed, and fog blew out of my lungs.

Opening the door, I stepped directly into the kitchen. Calin sat at the meals table with Cynthia and Bronwyn, eating breakfast.

"That smells good. Tell me you made enough to share?" I teased as I started the espresso machine.

"You can have mine," Bronwyn grumbled. "I'm not hungry." Then, she stormed out of the kitchen, avoiding eye contact.

I frowned, walking over to the table and sniffing my underarm. "Do I smell that bad?"

Calin raised a brow. "I doubt anyone could sweat out there this morning and not freeze to death." His eyes went to the door Bronwyn stormed through. "She'll be okay."

Cynthia reached her hand out, putting it over her husband's in comfort. "I'll go check on her, and make sure she doesn't take that anger somewhere else."

As Cynthia rose, her eyes casually appraised my torso. It was nothing new for Cynthia. Like every other time, I didn't bother to acknowledge the interest in her eyes. None of Calin's wives appealed to me.

I took the seat Cynthia vacated and the plate of food Bronwyn abandoned. "Should I ask?"

"They've discovered Selena's affair with my brother," Calin muttered. "While Gina could accept it and was understanding, her other sister-wives have not taken the infidelity well. Bronwyn wants me to give Selena an eternal divorce for her behavior. Cynthia feels having Spectra take Selena's beast would be more fitting. If she wants to be with a de Sang, Luke can take her." Calin grimaced.

"Neither of those options is viable," I warned. "I won't interfere in your marriage, but Spectra will not be part of it, and Luke won't stand by and let you kill her. He's in love with her."

Calin's jaw tensed. "So am I. I wouldn't have married her otherwise."

"I know." I waited for a few bites of food. "How do you feel about it?" I prodded.

"I was betrayed and hurt," Calin admitted. "I still am."

"Have you discussed it with Luke?"

"No. I haven't told either of them I know, but now the others have caught on, I'm going to need to."

I assessed Calin. "She's still coming to your bed?"

Calin's shoulders set in indignation. "She's my wife. Why wouldn't she?" I held up my hands in peace. Calin shoved his plate away. "It's my pride; I'll deal with it."

I didn't argue, just nodded my head. "When you have some free time today, I need to discuss security issues at Pendant."

"Because of the hack?" Calin welcomed the change in topic.

"Because of Spectra," I revealed. "We'd never heard of someone with her ability before. If someone like her accessed the crypt..." I left it hanging. I watched Calin's jaw move side to side as he considered it.

"There can't be many like her walking around, or we would have heard of them before," Calin justified.

"Paul Samus knew what she was straight away. So we have to assume that others are out there and put defences in place," I justified.

Calin stroked his jaw. "A beast can see them," Calin pointed out. "Add a Changer de corps to the security. If a ghost walks in, the beast can alert the others."

"Agreed. We'll also push the oxygen levels up. That's what Samus did to stop Spectra ghosting on him." I finished the plate of food and sat back with my coffee.

"I'll organize it first thing tomorrow," Calin assured. He stood up. "I'm going for a run. I need a time out."

"Calin," I called. Calin looked back at me. I pointed to his plate and cup. "Clean up after yourself."

Calin smirked, came back, and fixed up his mess, then he stepped outside and started pulling his clothes off. I turned my eyes to the other window while he changed. I always felt the pain of shifting was a private thing for a Changeur.

The kitchen door swung open.

"Morning," Luke chirped, coming into the room. "We need to organize a security detail for Spectra."

I frowned. I had no intention of giving Spectra bodyguards. I'm pretty sure she'd balk at the idea anyway.

"No, we don't," I objected. "You may as well put a neon sign on her saying 'important' if we do that. Spectra already has the Fantôme watching over her. Let's not crowd the girl."

"She was taken already on their watch," Luke reminded.

"That was our fault, and let's not say taken. Abducted is better," I debated.

Luke scoffed. "She was nearly taken."

I wasn't in the mood for this today. I stood up, cleaning up my mess. "We'll discuss this later. I'm going out for the day."

"Is Calin going with you?" Luke turned to consider me.

"No, I'm going to see my family. I can't spend another day here and not see her," I explained. "The Angelis is due back to work tonight. So I'll be back in time to be available to my wife."

"She may be worn out and need sleep." Luke smirked.

"I'll let her sleep. Eventually." I winked at Luke, and he chortled.

Getting up, I went to shower and change. I slowed my steps as I passed the door for their suite on the second landing. Spectra's moans flooded the area. Soft, passionate, and a sensory stimulant to my system.

My body shivered when I heard Spectra whimper, her voice begging. Just his name, breathy and pleading, then a louder moan, a more needful whimper. Oh, how I wanted those sounds to be for me. My body quaked with the idea, and I had to physically force myself to keep walking past the door.

I went to my shower and tried to distract myself. Then, I decided not to use the stairs and ripped the ether to get to the garage. A day with my family was the perfect distraction.

The house was quiet when I returned later that night, even on the second floor. I nearly knocked to check if everything was okay but considered they may be sleeping.

Going to the lounge to watch a movie with the others, I hoped to hear when Mercury left. By midnight, I accepted Mercury had either left already or wasn't going to work. I climbed the stairs to my study and did a few hours of work before bed.

The following day, I found myself staring at the door again. There was no sound from inside their room this morning. I wondered if they'd both left, and I'd missed it.

Luke came out of his wing. "Is sex still healthy when you've gone without food and very little sleep for it?"

"What makes you think they are not sleeping?" I asked, annoyed.

"The house isn't that soundproof, and it seems Angelis are really big on praying loudly," Luke snickered. "Granted, our hearing is better than a human's. Probably better than theirs, so maybe they aren't that loud, but still. I've walked passed the door enough times to know the difference between when they are sleeping and not."

When I gripped the railing, the timber groaned beneath my hand.

"Well, Spectra is very passionate and energetic, and is left quite tired after sex."

He was smirking, trying hard not to laugh. "I've picked up on that during her visits already," Luke replied sarcastically. He stepped forward. "Shall we get to work? They'll emerge sooner or later."

"Sooner would be better for my sanity," I grumbled, following Luke down the stairs.

"You need to get used to it," Luke informed me over his shoulder. "From what I understand, Mercury barely comes home to do more than sleep when he's working. Then, when he has a few days off, those two disappear from the world, only coming out to deal with their commitments."

"Maybe we should have employed her at Pendant," I suggested. "At least I'd see her for the car ride to work every morning."

Luke stepped onto the ground floor and turned to consider me. "She wants Galaxy. If she doesn't get it, we can offer her the role with Evan. We already know he wants to hire her," he suggested.

Stopping on the last step, I considered the suggestion.

He gave me a pointed look while lowering his voice. "We can guarantee Spectra's safety more if she travels with us and works in the Pendant building. No one is going to come in there to try for her."

I took a deep breath. "Spec will get the Galaxy job. I have no doubt they'll want her. We need to think about excusing her presence in my house when others find out."

Luke nodded. "Let's get coffee and talk about it on the way in."

# CHAPTER 5

# SPECTRA

"Good morning," Gina chirped teasingly behind me. Seeing the smile on her face, I couldn't help but smile myself. "I'm surprised you can walk after four nights locked away in your room."

"I was hungry, and I needed to check my emails," I replied, picking up the glass of milk and taking a long drink.

"Wait, did you not eat anything for three days?" Gina asked, her eyebrows high and mouth falling open.

"I was sort of busy, you know." I blushed.

"For three days straight?" Gina's eyes popped. "Come on? Even Mercury must need recovery time."

"Of course. It's called sleeping, and talking, and showering."

"But not eating?"

"We intended to come down for food a couple of times," I admitted. "We'd go in to shower and not quite make it out of the room." I shrugged. "I only made it out this morning because Mercury went back to work."

Gina had the biggest grin on her face, and her eyes were alight as she looked at me. I could feel how bad I was blushing as I shut my laptop.

"You're up early."

"I'm interning at Pendant for the winter break." Gina smiled, making herself a coffee. "It's my first day, and I'm a little over-excited. When I woke up, I went for a run and didn't realize what time it was until I got back."

"I'm sure you'll be fine," I smiled.

"She will." Calin walked in with a smile, dressed, ready for work. He picked up Gina's coffee. "Thanks, G. See, you already have the intern thing down."

"Put my coffee down, or you will be walking funny at work today," Gina growled. "I'm only the intern after nine o'clock, and I'm not your intern, I'm Alfred's."

Calin lifted his eyebrow and pointedly took a sip of the coffee. Gina moved quickly. Calin tried to block it and ended up wearing the coffee. Calin swore, slammed the coffee cup down, and stormed out. Gina went to pick up the coffee cup and cursed when it fell apart and smashed on the tiled floor.

"Umm, is everything okay with you two?" I asked, concerned by what I had just witnessed.

Gina took the mug pieces to the bin and smiled at me. "Yes, why?" she asked with a tilt of her head. I gestured to what had just happened. "Oh, he was just playing with me. He didn't expect me to move that quick and spilled the coffee on himself. The breakage was accidental, though."

"That happens often?"

"The riling each other up, yes. The breaking things, less so, but we forget our strength occasionally," Gina explained.

This time, she prepared two cups of coffee. Gina turned her head as if hearing something, scoffed, and put another two cups out.

Bay walked into the kitchen a moment later, accompanied by Luke pointing to something on a tablet and discussing it. Bay was dressed in his usual suit, ready to step out of the door, when his eyes lifted from the tablet to find me at the meals table.

My face and chest heated at the smile on his face.

When Luke noticed me, he got a cheeky gleam in his eyes. "Well, look who managed to crawl out from under her husband."

Ambling over to me, Bay took the chair adjacent. "I wondered when you would come up for air," Bay simpered as he sat. "Have you eaten anything yet?"

"Some toast when I first came down and a few glasses of milk," I replied, my hand automatically reaching out to touch him.

Bay put his hand over mine on his knee; his other hand tapped my computer. "Checking your emails?" he asked as Gina put a coffee in front of him and returned to the kitchen bench where Luke was making himself breakfast. "Thanks, Gina."

I nodded. "I wanted to see if I heard from Galaxy."

"And?"

"And they've asked me to do a trial with them starting next week," I answered, barely restraining the grin on my face. "I have to fill out forms today and email them back. I also have an interview with Gims Technology on Friday. Can I get your wi-fi password? The reception out here sucks."

Bay's smile was plastered to his face. "You're still going to interview elsewhere when you are about to get your dream job?"

"I'm getting a two-week trial. I may not get the job," I answered, struggling to return my face to neutral.

"A-huh," Bay teased. "Will you join us for dinner tonight?" I hesitated at the question. Bay squeezed my hand. "Not that, Spectra. I'll feed before I come home. I'd like to see you when I get home."

"Oh." I rolled my eyes at how silly I'd been. "You should. If I'm not down here when you get home, just come and find me."

Bay looked away. "I don't think the Angelis would like me dragging you away from him."

I pulled my cardigan down further over my hands as I took my hand back. "Mercury won't be here tonight. He needs to go take care of something in the city, so he'll probably stay there the night."

Bay frowned. "He's keeping his place in the city?"

"One of them," I confirmed. "Even if Merc gets the job out here, he will still need to visit to take care of his businesses there, plus he has hobbies that will take him back."

Reaching out, Bay took my fingers in his again, his thumb

making circles across the top of my hand. As his fingers slowly crept up my hand, massaging lightly, I closed my eyes. Bay lifted my hand, pushing up my sleeve and turning my wrist as he pressed his lips to my palm. Pain stabbed through my wrist.

I grimaced and recoiled, standing as I quickly yanked my sleeve down.

"What was that?" Bay growled, standing.

"Nothing. I'll see you tonight." I took a step towards the door.

Bay's hand clamped around my upper arm, preventing my escape. "Spectra, you're injured."

When I started to exhale to escape his grasp, Bay pinched me, forcing me to inhale again. Then, before I could fathom it, he held my hand securely and lifted my sleeve to examine the black imprint of hand marks around my wrist.

A vicious snarl shook the room. I trembled and tried to retreat from the noise, but no one else was moving. Calin, Gina, and Luke all stood watching, wide-eyed and wary.

"Everyone out!" Bay snapped.

Without hesitation, the room emptied. When I tried to follow, I was yanked back to the meals table and set between the stone top and Bay. "Undress."

I blinked away the itch of tears. "This isn't the place for—"

"Now!" Bay's restrained anger vibrated through my body, shaking loose the tears and causing my heart to pound in my chest.

Swallowing with difficulty, I lifted my oversized jumper over my head. Baring my entire upper body to Bay's scrutiny.

"It's not what you think," I quickly defended as his eyes found the bruises on my breasts.

"All of it!" Bay's deep bass was barely audible as he stepped closer. Nevertheless, the sound shook my body worse than when he snapped.

My breath hitching, I released the drawstring of my pajama pants and let them fall to the floor, revealing multiple fingerprint bruises on my hips. An animalistic growl filled the space around me. Burning heat smothered me, suffocating me as it stole the air. Instinctively, my shields blocked Bay's power from harming me.

"Bay, he didn't mean to mark me. He waited too long to release his power and lost control," I defended against the rage filling the kitchen.

My sight was blurry from tears that wouldn't stop. I wasn't crying. My eyes were watering from exposure to Bay's full power. Shield or not, he was so strong.

"It is no different from every time you dropped your shields accidentally when we first started sleeping together. That hurt me too, but I knew you didn't mean it, that you couldn't control it."

Bay took a step towards me. A slow, determined action. He was dangerous right now. I naturally wanted to cower under the force of his emotions, to hide my flesh. I didn't. I stood my ground. If I showed my shame, it would make things worse.

"Does this happen often?" His voice was more contrabass than expected, a bladed edge in his words.

I shook more tears free as I shook my head. "No, just once before, in the early days of our relationship. We knew he needed to release his power, but with the wedding, it wasn't appropriate for him to go elsewhere to do it."

"So he released it on you?" Bay's voice was nearly back to bass-baritone now. Nearly. The room was still a tornado of rage.

"No, he lost control. He'll release it tonight after work. It's why he won't be coming home. He's held it in too long and will need to spend the night letting it out safely." I reached out, cupping Bay's face in my hand. "If he lets it out all at once, he could kill someone. So it needs to be released in stages. Just like you did when you fully let your shields down to me for the first time."

My thumb stroked across his cheek, my body humming with desire before I refocused my emotions.

Turning his face in my hand, Bay kissed my palm. He reached for me, and I went willingly. Tiny electric pulses struck my skin where Bay's hands connected with my waist. He pulled me tight against him and held me to him.

Bay breathed me in, his nose buried in my hair. "He ever hurts you again, and you will be down a husband, Spectra."

"And what if you lose control and hurt me?" I murmured.

"You can shield now. I won't do that."

He didn't try to contain me when I pressed away from him.

"But you just did. It's not just your power, Bay. When you make me fear you, when you threaten those I love, and when you don't trust that I'm being honest with you, that hurts me."

Wiping my nose and face with my hands, I grabbed up my clothes and turned my back on him while I dressed. When I turned around, Bay had pulled his power back in, his eyes still roaming my body.

"To be fair, Spectra. I asked you about the bruises, and you told me it was nothing." Bay stepped closer, his mouth to my ear, his breath sending a thrill of need pulsing through me. "That's not being honest with me. If you want me to trust you, be open and transparent with me."

I exhaled, holding just enough substance to be visible but see-through. "Is this transparent enough for you?" I grumbled.

Moving towards the door, I passed through Bay, electricity firing all my nerve endings and Bay cursing as his body quaked from the exposure.

"I'll see you tonight," I muttered as I became fully insubstantial and floated up to my room, only inhaling once I was safely in our bedroom.

Stopping in front of the mirror, I lifted my jumper, examining the black and purple impression of Mercury's hands on my breasts.

Mercury hadn't meant to hurt me. I knew that because he stopped as soon as I pointed out he was causing me pain. Still, it made me wonder what he did at the club when he needed a proper release. Because I was sure, the subconscious release was nothing compared to the intentional.

Closing my eyes on the imagined depravity at Havre des Damnés, I dropped my jumper back into place and decided to explore my new home.

There were two large bedrooms other than ours, plus a smaller unfurnished room right next to the main bedroom, which would make a great office. So, to keep myself occupied, I set about writing lists of furnishings we would need to make this place more homely with a smile on my face.

Once I had my list, I skipped downstairs to the kitchen to search for what I wanted. A notepad sat next to my laptop on the table with the login details to Bay's home network. I was smiling, having already hacked into it this morning, but I thought I should be polite and ask for the password anyway.

Picking up my laptop, I strode towards the stairs, stopping short of being wiped out by two women, screaming as they fell fighting down the stairs. I stopped and blinked wide-eyed as Selena fought off Bronwyn's punches.

"You slut! How dare you betray us all like this," Bronwyn screeched as she attacked.

When my instinct to protect kicked in, I stepped forward to interfere, but then Cynthia was standing in front of me, moving me away from them.

"This is pride business," Cynthia warned. "If you get involved, the boss will make it his business." She wasn't threatening me, just ensuring I didn't interfere.

My eyes went to Selena. I worried that she'd never been seen or heard from again if I walked away.

"I'll make sure it doesn't become fatal."

Selena tried to run for the stairs, but Bronwyn tackled her, which blocked me from using them.

Cynthia rolled her eyes. "Maybe use the library for now."

Swallowing the sour ball of concern lodged in my throat, I turned and headed down the hall to the library just as snarls and growls filled the hall.

Pulling out my phone, I texted Calin as I shut the library door and locked it. When Gina said they didn't always get along, I wasn't expecting literal catfights happening in the house.

I jumped when I heard something big and heavy hit the wall out in the hall, a yelp preceding a lion scream. Placing my laptop on the table, I exhaled and moved through the floors to get to my room. I hadn't had much sleep this weekend. It seemed like now was the perfect time to catch up.

# CHAPTER 6

# BAY

"I TRUST YOUR JUDGMENT, CALIN," I assured, not even looking up from the finance reports.

"I don't," Calin grumbled.

The tone and the pile of folders he dropped on my desk finally got my attention. I sat back, lifting my eyes to his.

"We weren't even married a month when she started cheating on me, boss. What if it wasn't me she wanted? I thought she loved me, but maybe that's not the case."

I exhaled, frustrated with dealing with this right now, but I understood Selena's infidelity undermined my friend's self-confidence. Calin had never had an issue with women, and he'd never had one cheat on him to his knowledge before this.

"Relationships are not the same as this situation, Calin. This is work. I've asked you to pick the guards who can be trusted in their beast form while working in the crypt. You know these people probably better than you do your wives. Make the selection. If you doubt your choice, show me who you picked afterward, and I will approve or decline as per the usual process."

Calin opened his mouth to argue when the air became charged with electricity.

"Hold that thought, Calin. L'Paix is about to visit," I warned.

My office door opened and Claire, my assistant toppled in on her heels.

"Henry Williams to see you, Mr. Ryder. He doesn't have an appointment," she announced.

"I don't need one," Henry snapped behind her.

The de Viand cowered as his power flowed into the room ahead of him.

"Thank you, Claire," I dismissed serenely. "What can I do for you, Henry?"

"Where is she?" Henry demanded. "You left a message saying she was safe, but she never went home, and no one who usually knows where to find her can tell me where she is."

"Can't, or won't, Henry?" I asked patiently. "I can assure you the nuns Spectra lived with and the priest know exactly where she is."

Henry's brows furrowed, his power diminished. Not that his radiance bothered me. Even Calin was barely affected.

"Why wouldn't they tell me? I've never hurt her."

"I doubt it's you they are protecting her from, Henry, but your son." I sighed as I sat forward. "Spectra has gone to live with her husband. She is no longer in the city and won't be returning to her previous accommodations. Essence already found her there once."

Henry took a seat on the other side of my desk. "I want to see her, Bay. I want to be able to tell Alexander that I have seen Spectra and that she is safe and happy."

My fingers fidgeted with the pen on the desk even considering letting another sorcerer near my wife.

"Is my word not good enough for you, Henry?"

"For me, yes. For Alexander?" Henry scooted forward on his seat. "You know how he feels about your kind. You started going after Spectra, and her life was put in jeopardy. He blames you for what happened, Bay. He realizes that for Spectra to be in your house that night means something happened between you two. He is angry and heartbroken that Spectra has cut him free from her life, and he is blaming you for all of that."

"Did you remind him that his relationship with the Nephilim was why she cut him out?" I queried.

"We had words about that, yes." Henry's eyes darkened. "He told me you advised he tell Spectra, so that also didn't go in your favor."

"I told him that if he believed the Nephilim was strong enough for him, he should be honest with Spectra about it," I defended. "Was I wrong, Henry? I believe she felt she owed Alexander for her life. When he released her from that debt to him, she didn't hesitate to marry the man she loved. She's happy. Let her move on."

Henry peered at me. "I want to see Spectra. She does not belong to you, so stop being obstructive and tell me where to find her."

I considered the man before me. For a middle-aged man, he still held his athletic frame well. His brown hair was cut short with a peppering of grey at the temples, his olive skin no longer as firm and smooth as his son's, but his chocolate eyes still as energized. He wasn't going to back down.

Picking up my desk phone, I turned it to face Henry. "Only Spectra's address has changed. There is nothing to stop you from calling her yourself, Henry." I collected my pen and pointed to the files on my desk. "Calin, you need these profiles. I want your selection on my desk this afternoon." Dropping my eyes, I went back to the financial reports, ignoring the two men in my office.

Calin grabbed up the candidates and left quietly. Henry took out his phone and sent a text message. I smirked, realizing even Henry didn't have Spectra's phone number. His phone buzzed in reply.

Henry stood up, moving to the window, putting his phone to his ear. With my hearing, I heard the call ring through to voicemail.

"Spectra, it's Henry. I'm worried about you. Can you call me? I'd like to meet up with you and see with my own eyes that you are safe."

Henry proceeded to leave his phone number and hung up. Then, it occurred that Henry insisted on seeing Spectra to make sure she hadn't been taken. Henry moved back to my desk and waited for me to look up. I marked where I was up to in the reports and set the pen down again. "If she hasn't returned my call within twenty-four hours, I will be back, and I won't leave until I've seen her with my own two eyes."

I raised a brow at his threat. "As you said, Henry, I am not her keeper. She's with her husband. For all we know, they may be busy doing what honeymooners do and may not wish to be disturbed by her ex's father."

Henry's jaw tensed. "I have known that girl since she was in diapers. I protected her and provided for her when her mother failed to. I am more than an ex's father to her, and Alexander is more than an ex. If there is anyone in this room who means nothing to Spectra, it is you!"

"She's married," I reminded him calmly.

"Divorces happen all the time."

The air stirred. My hand clenched in the soft flesh of Henry's throat, and my body jolted when our movement was stopped by a wall. My eyes and ears were focused on my prey as my fangs itched to rip his neck apart.

Henry's heart pounded in his chest now; sweat escaped his pores, his breath rasping where I held him by his throat against the wall. Brown eyes wide to expose the whites, set deep in a face quickly turning blue. My pupils dilated as the face of my friend registered in my mind.

Forcing my hand to release, I set Henry back on his feet and stepped back several meters, my hunger still present.

Henry bent over, gasping as he tried to regain his breath. Then, his face lifted to see me watching him, waiting patiently for his recovery and whatever words he would have to say next.

Slowly, Henry righted himself. "I care for Spectra like my own child. I want to see her and be sure no harm came to her due to her involvement with you."

"That is for Spectra to decide, not me," I answered.

Moving back to my desk, I righted the reports and other desk items blown out of the way when I moved on instinct. Henry stood watching me warily.

"I do not hold influence over Spectra any more than you do your wife, Henry. I doubt even her Angelis husband could stop

Spectra from doing something she wants to do. So don't threaten me to get to her, and don't threaten her happiness for your son's self-ishness."

"Are you willing to destroy our pact over a girl you barely know?" Henry scolded.

I sighed. "Do you remember when you met Phillipa? Fallon Lore was already trying to woo her, but the moment you touched her, you knew she was yours, and you wouldn't give her up, even for your best friend," I prompted.

Henry swallowed. Fallon had been his best friend all his child-hood. Henry taking Phillipa might have been what turned Fallon to Essence, eventually leading to his demise in the pool in my basement.

"Are you saying Spectra is yours, Bay? I wouldn't have thought her near powerful enough for you."

"I never said that. I'm saying that Spectra became something I needed to protect from the moment she first touched me. Whether she wanted more from me or not. I'm telling you, Henry, that I won't abide Spectra being hurt by anyone." I met his eyes, hoping he would see reason. "Don't let a woman's love destroy our friend-ship, Henry."

Henry's eyes were pinpricks of surprise aimed at me. After a moment, he blinked and looked down at himself. He straightened his tie and checked his phone. Henry lifted his eyes to mine with a deep breath once more and gave a short nod.

"I won't tell Alexander about this." Henry indicated the wall I'd tried to push him through. "As my friend, I'm asking you to reach out to Spectra and for her personally to assure me of her wellbeing."

"I will have someone seek her out and pass on the urgency of your request," I promised.

Henry looked out the window, inhaled, and exhaled. He took two steps forward and sat back down in the chair. "Essence has lost two men searching for the antidote, and we know at least one of their people in the NSIO now. What's our next move?"

Taking my seat, I opened my desk drawer to remove an invitation I'd received, dropping it on the other side of the desk to face Henry. "Mayer Callisie is holding a smorgasbord ball. He's invited me personally to discuss the antidote."

Henry looked over the invitation. "Mayer Callisie is an alchemist. Do you think he wants to try and synthesize the antidote?"

"He's been hiding out in Italy for forty years. For him to leave the safety of his home and travel here tells me the Essence are hoping he will be able to," I agreed. "They probably brought him here expecting to have procured a sample of the antidote."

"Do you think it wise you attend this event by yourself?" Henry worried.

"Wouldn't it be suspicious if I didn't?" I raised a brow, waiting.

Henry exhaled, his shoulders dropping as he deflated in the chair.

"I will take Calin with me if that makes you feel more secure?" I offered.

Henry nodded and stroked his chin. "Just to stir the pot, I will have blood tests ordered on our cured captive. Let's see if his curse still shows up in his body or any traces of the antidote."

"If they think they can reverse engineer the antidote from his blood, Essence will use their insiders to get to him," I warned.

Henry smirked. "Exactly. Let them bleed their own people dry for once trying to get what they want." He stood up to leave.

"Henry, that man was a Changeur. Essence used their powers to control him, but they did not respect or care for him. They will think nothing of killing him for their own needs."

One of Henry's shoulders dropped. "Well, let's cure a de Sang next and let them play with them."

I lifted a brow. "Any de Sang in particular?"

Henry smiled at me and yanked open the door. "Enjoy the smorgasbord."

Turning my desk phone back toward me, I dialed the landline in Spectra's room. She didn't answer. I tried the kitchen phone next.

"Hello?" Cynthia answered.

"Cyn, is everything okay there?"

Cynthia clucked her tongue. "Define okay?"

"No one dead or injured."

"Well, it's mostly okay."

"Spectra?"

"Was in the library last I saw her. My sister-wives got a bit rowdy for her, and the poor girl locked herself in there. Did you want me to go get her?"

"No, I just worried she wasn't answering her phone. I'll see her in a few hours."

"I'll get her to call if I see her."

"Don't have her calling the office," I cautioned. "And while it's none of my business, Selena is still one of my employees. So if she is unable to do her job, I will be just as angry about it as if you got hurt, Cyn."

"She'll be fine. Just a few bumps and bruises from a wrestle on the stairs. Calin will deal with us for it."

"Don't sound so excited," I teased.

Cynthia chuckled and hung up. Cynthia was Calin's second wife. I'd introduced them at a smorgasbord, and they'd continued seeing each other afterward. Occasionally, usually in the depth of winter when we were snowed in, Cynthia would still let me feed on her after sex with her husband. I think she would offer to do it regularly, but a Changeur's blood is never as good as a human's. It was like a vanilla sponge compared to mud cake.

My thoughts turned to the chocolate lava cake Spectra ordered me at Margareta's on our first date. Smiling to myself, I picked up the phone.

"Boss?"

"Claire, I need to order some desserts from Margareta's to be picked up for me to take home tonight."

# CHAPTER 7

# SPECTRA

"Why can I smell pizza?" Gina's voice called before she came through the lounge room door. She stopped to assess me and the slice of pizza about to pass my lips. "Did you order pizza to the estate?"

"Ah, yes," I answered, worried I'd committed a faux pas. "No one said I couldn't."

Gina threw her bag aside and came to sit on the lounge. "But no one delivers pizza out this way."

I smiled with relief. "Oh, it's a new place just opened in the village. I spotted it when you drove me to Stokes for the Galaxy interview on Thursday." Then, picking up the takeaway menu that the delivery driver gave me, I offered it to Gina.

She accepted it. "So you're not going to share?"

I peered at her. "I would offer you a slice, but Cynthia warned me you all eat a full pizza to yourselves."

"Wait!" Gina stood up. "Did they order pizza too?"

"I thought they were in the kitchen. They got enough for you and Calin."

"Bitches! They brewed extra strong coffee to cover the smell."

Gina bolted out of the room, and I went back to taking that first bite of pizza.

"Where's the fire?" Calin's voice called from outside the door.

"Your wives ordered pizza," Gina called back up the stairs. "They didn't tell us."

"Bitches!" Calin laughed. "They better save me some, or you will all be going without."

Calin stepped into the lounge and gave me a careful smile. "Thank you for the message today. My wives can be very passionate about their disputes. How was your first day here alone?"

"I wasn't alone." I covered my mouth to speak.

Calin snickered. "You weren't with people you trust," he corrected. "We know how you feel about our kind, Spectra."

"Yes, but you know I can rip the beast out of you now. So, I think your wives fear me more than I fear you." I bit off another piece of pizza.

Calin sauntered over to me, placed his hand on the back of the couch, and crowded me. I stopped mid-chew, eyes wide with concern as his breath blew over me.

"You still fear me, Spectra. You still dislike my kind. It's there in the way you look at us." His free hand traced a finger along my jaw. "Don't worry. I'll win you over in no time. Soon, you will look at me as your annoying big brother and my wives like your sisters. Then, one day, not too long from now, we will walk into the room, and you won't freeze like a rabbit in headlights. That's when you will realize we are your family."

"No one wants to be my family, Calin," I murmured. I could feel my heart pounding in my chest. I had no doubt Calin could hear it. "All my family are dead. De Sangs killed them. I don't hate your kind. I hate theirs and everything they've taken from me."

"Bay is a de Sang, Spectra. You can't cure him of that."

I lifted glassy eyes to Calin's. "Death cures us all, Calin." I dropped my face as my heart fell into my lap. "Except me. Death won't cure me."

Calin frowned as he stood straight. "You're kind of melodramatic, you know that? I think the boss needs to come home and cheer you up." Calin winked. He lifted a slice of pizza to his mouth and took a bite as he walked out.

I looked down to see the slice taken from my box. "Hey!"

"It's what horses eat," Calin dismissed. He turned at the door with a glint of mischief in his eye. "First lesson of the house, Spectra. If you don't guard your food, it will be taken from you. You live with predators now. We don't stop and pray. We eat our prey." Calin smirked wickedly. "Just some of us eat prey in a good way. The very best way." He laughed as heat filled my cheeks, and he skipped down the stairs.

Blinking away the awkward images in my head of Calin eating a woman in a good way, I clicked on the television and watched some shows while I ate. I was enjoying a cooking show - not that I could really cook - when Bay filled the doorway. Drinking in the sight of him from head to toe, my lips lifted with every inch of him until I met his eyes. I sat there smiling like a lovesick girl at her crush.

Bay's smile brightened. "I brought home dessert; if you want to join me in the kitchen?"

Turning off the television, I grabbed the pizza box. "There a few slices left if you want some?" I offered.

Bay took my spare hand in his and turned to the stairs. "Pizza is not something I ever developed a taste for."

"Since we are going to the kitchen, I'm guessing I'm not dessert."

Bay's lips twitched. "Not yet. We need to talk first."

With his hand in mine, I'd forgotten the need to talk. How my life had changed and would so again in the coming months.

Bay guided me into the kitchen, and my phone buzzed with voicemail notifications. I ignored it, setting my phone on the table, holding four takeaway containers. My heart skipped a beat when I recognized Margareta's doggy bags. I fell entirely in love with Bay when he popped the lids to expose my favorite desserts.

I looked at him, his ice-blue eyes shining with happiness. He offered me a spoon as he took the pizza box from my hand and set it in the fridge. We took our seats, and I watched Bay open the other two containers to reveal lava cake and another caramel apple pie.

"You seemed to really enjoy it on our date. So I thought I should give it a try," Bay explained.

"I would have shared."

"You would, yes. But predators do not share their food well, Spectra. Hence, why the pride all get a pizza each, even if they eat the same kind. The only person who can force those girls to share is Calin, and even then, they will only share with him."

"They share him."

"Never at the same time. It's a pride, not a harem," Bay lectured. "And Calin is not food."

"You shared your meals with Calin before we met," I debated. Bay lifted a brow. "Gina told me how you fed before."

A part of me hated that he could do the job himself now, just as I had always had a small niggle about Mercury visiting the club. Not jealousy, but a fear they may kill someone, especially Bay with his power control at pivotal moments. I wanted to ask how he was dealing with that, but the itch on my tongue made me hold it.

Bay shifted in his seat, his spork stabbing into the lava cake, spewing molten chocolate out the entry point. "I have never shared my meal. Calin doesn't feed at the same time as me. He gets off, I feed," Bay clarified. "You could see it as Calin being the chef, preparing my meal and serving it. The point is that predators don't share food except with their sire, possibly, and they take from those lesser than them."

Pausing, I frowned. "Calin took a slice of my pizza. Gina at least asked for it; Calin just stole it."

Bay's hand tightened on his spork. "Did you give Gina the slice?"

"No."

"Good." Bay's eyes looked me over, studying every bit of exposed skin. "Tomorrow morning, after I leave the house, don't shower."

"Why?" My brows furrowed at the suggestion.

"Because I'm the ruling predator in this house, and I want to make sure Calin remembers who you belong to."

I pressed my lips to prevent gawking. "Calin said he would be like an annoying big brother, that I was part of their family now."

I bit my lip waiting for Bay's reassurance that I had nothing to worry about. But instead, Bay took a spoonful of his lava cake and held it ready to consume.

"You smell like the Angelis currently, and he hasn't been accepted as a family member yet. He is an unknown male to the pride. Until they accept him as part of the coalition—what we call a pride with more than one male in it—I need you to have my scent on you when you are here alone."

I stared at my caramel apple pie. "Oh." Blinking a few times and not knowing how I could respond to that so I wouldn't seem naive, I took a spoonful of dessert and dug in.

We ate in silence, to begin with, both of us enjoying our first desserts. When Bay finished the lava cake, he ended the silence. "Do you want children, Spectra?"

I hesitated, my spoon hovering above my nearly demolished pie. "Yes. Eventually. Not yet, though."

We both sat still a moment longer.

"Do you?"

"I've already been a father," Bay sighed.

Biting my lip, I worried how children would exist in a house of predators or if this was Bay's way of telling me he didn't want kids in this house.

"I raised my son by myself. His mother died in childbirth, and I was taken a few years later. The need to care for my son was how I held on to my humanity, just as Alfred was the reason Luke kept his. I haven't desired to be a father again. That hasn't changed."

My eyes lifted to his, whites showing, worried I'd buried my chances of motherhood when I gave myself to Bay.

Bay took my free hand. "Any children you bear will not be sired by me. They will be Mercury's. However, I hold the key to your body now. You won't conceive until you tell me you are ready."

"Would they even be safe here?" I asked honestly.

Bay exhaled. "Currently, no. While Essence remains an issue, an innocent would be a bargaining chip for them. I'm risking enough having you here. Eventually, they will be dealt with. You and Mercury are immortal. Time is not something that should worry you."

"Unless Essence kills one of us," I worried. "Or worse." The last words were a whisper.

Cursing, Bay took his hand from mine. "We need to work on your siphoning ability. You do it without thinking, without realizing it. That could be dangerous if I'm hungry, Spectra."

When I frowned, confused. Bay stroked my cheek.

"The sadness you expressed for being taken was mine, Spectra. I fear your association with me will lead to your demise."

Leaning my face into his palm, I wanted to feel more of the way he made my body buzz, how he made me feel alive.

"Bay, being fed on or worse, becoming a de Sang, has been my fear since I was sixteen. Marrying you hasn't changed that."

My hand instinctively lifted to my neck, the memory of my recent encounter with Paul Samus still vivid. Shaking off the terror that raced down my spine, I sat straight and rubbed my bloated tummy.

"I don't think I can manage a second dessert right now. Maybe later."

Gracing me with a knowing smile, Bay took both our second desserts to the fridge while I cleaned up our mess and grabbed a bottle of water from the refrigerator.

"I have another present for you," Bay proclaimed as he took my hand. "It's upstairs."

My stomach rolled over in excitement. With no hesitation, I let Bay lead me to the stairs, and we walked hand in hand up to the third level. Bay frowned as we reached the top step. "You left your phone downstairs?"

"It doesn't matter; I get shit reception here," I excused. "The kitchen is the only place it picks up a signal."

"I'll get you a new phone tomorrow. I need you to be contactable no matter where you are," Bay decided as we reached his bedroom door.

"Why?"

Bay met my eyes, then his gaze flicked to the side of my neck Paul Samus had fed from only four days ago. "In case I need to warn you to get out of the house or not to come home to it. Our lives will be somewhat separate, which means you will be vulnerable when away from me. Occasionally, my paranoia will require me to reach out and know you are safe just so I can get through my day."

Thinking about what happened last Thursday, I could understand where his paranoia was coming from.

Bay opened his bedroom door, and I stepped inside. A large silver box with a white bow around it sat on his bed.

"It is tradition for a sorcerer to pay a dowry and buy his bride a present that was both needed but something she would like. So this is my wedding present to you. The dowry I paid into your account."

"Dowry? What do you mean dowry?" I asked, confused.

"Your parents are dead, Spectra. So there is no one for me to pay the dowry to other than yourself," Bay explained.

"No, that part I understood. It's why you are paying a dowry at all. This isn't the Middle Ages anymore," I challenged. "And, how did you get my account details? When you paid me for work, you did it in cash."

Bay rubbed his lips together. "I guess Alexander failed to explain this to you also. When a sorcerer finds his balance, and she survives their wedding night, proving her worth to him, he pays her a dowry of his worth."

"His worth, not hers?"

"It is both. The more powerful the sorcerer, the more valuable the woman strong enough to be his wife," Bay educated, stepping closer. "Alexander is a mighty sorcerer, Spectra. The dowry he paid you would have set you up for life." Bay licked his lips. "I am worth nearly one and a half times L'Ordre's value. I am both the most powerful sorcerer and the oldest walking this earth."

My stomach hollowed out. "How much did you pay me, Bay?"

"A modern-day King's ransom," Bay answered.

My eyes widened, and I felt my legs turn to jelly. I sat down on the side of the bed quickly.

"Due to the amount, I couldn't pay you outright without raising eyebrows with the human government and the NSIO. So, to counter that, I've opened a joint bank account in both our names, but you are the only signatory for it. It will take a few days for the paperwork to be finalized, but once it is, you will be able to access the account whenever you need. We have one hitch: you are my wife now, but we cannot disclose that for many reasons. To secure your future, I have set up some paperwork with Luke, and, should anything happen to me, he will make sure you will never need anything."

Tears welled in my eyes. "I don't even want to consider anything happening to you."

Bay cuffed my cheek. "I have no intention of ever giving you up, Spectra. You are immortal, just like me. So if we do this right, we should both be here long enough to see your great-grandchildren become parents themselves."

Bay's mouth crushed against mine, blocking out every other thought except for his taste, touch, and smell. Bay helped relieve me of my clothing while I yanked and pulled at the suit covering him. I was hot and needy, and everything I needed was right in front of me. Then, with only our skin left, Bay lifted me into his arms. My legs wrapped around his waist, clinging to him as the electricity of his touch brought my body to life.

Every smell, taste, and sensation was sharper as Bay crawled onto the bed. His arm swept back, and the silver box flew off the bed to hit the wall across the room. I caught a glimpse of blacks and whites escaping the inside, then I was lost to the feel of Bay shoving into me.

My back arched, and Bay took the offer and dropped his shields as his mouth sucked my nipple between his lips. Tropical heat bathed me and melted my insides, providing the lubrication for Bay to repeatedly bury the hilt.

Clinging to him, my body tightening, I cried out to God as I came apart in his arms. Then, as I dropped back to earth, I prayed that Bay was right. I always wanted Bay and Mercury in my life, loving me and protecting me.

While the details didn't make sense to me yet, I knew I needed them in my life. It was more than love. More than a sorcerer finding his balance. Whatever brought the three of us together, whether it be a stroke of luck or fate, I was grateful.

# CHAPTER 8

## BAY

WATCHING Spectra pull out the silk and lace slips, I smiled. "Do you like them?"

"They're beautiful."

"I wanted you to have some you could leave here in my room so you didn't have to redress just to go downstairs for a drink or back to your rooms," I explained. My eyes drifted to the clock. It was getting late. "Pick one to wear. I need you to do something for me before we go to bed." Dropping the towel from the shower we just shared, I pulled on my lounge pants, enjoying how Spectra was distracted by my naked body.

"What do you need me to do?"

Moving to where she squatted on the floor, I took her face in my hands and drew her to standing so I could kiss her again. I loved how her body melted into mine the moment I touched her.

Pulling back, I kissed her forehead and stepped away. If I didn't, I'd have her on the bed again for the fourth time tonight, and the phone call to Henry would once again be delayed.

"Meet me in my study," I murmured as I moved away.

The pout on her lips almost made me stay. Resisting, I walked to my study door and opened it. When I turned to close it, Spectra dropped her towel. The seductive smile over her shoulder told me it was timed for my eyes. With a growl of need rumbling in my chest, I shut the door and exhaled hard.

My eyes dropped to the north-pointing compass in my pants. "Down, boy. Necessity before needs."

A chuckle behind me made me curse. I turned to find Luke sitting in my study, reading through reports.

"If it's that hard, why leave her?" Luke queried cheekily.

"Because the Angelis kept her in bed for four days straight, walking is uncomfortable for her. Plus, every time my eyes find the marks he left, I want to tear his heart out," I admitted.

"She's pale. Marks show easily on her skin type," Luke reasoned. "They are probably no worse than the ones Calin leaves on his wives when things get rough. Or the ones you left her with after your first time."

My brows lowered. "I marked her up?"

"The Wednesday I took her clothes back to her, your time with her was very evident on her skin. I worried you hurt her, that something you did was why she was sick," Luke confessed. "Especially after the way you took her home."

Taking Spectra home via the ether was stupid and dangerous. Still, at that moment, I knew I'd never let her just leave me, so that was the only way I could separate myself from her.

"You're only telling me this now?" I growled as I sat at my desk.

"You're making a big deal out of her husband leaving her marked. I figured now is the time to point out that while not as bad, you too have bruised her skin during intimate moments," Luke defended. "Don't glare at me. I've always been the level-headed one."

"That's how you got taken in the first place," I scoffed.

Luke grimaced. "A hard-learned lesson for both my son and me. I have endeavoured to be a reasonable man ever since."

I couldn't fault him for that. Luke was very much a facts person. He always reserved judgment until he had all the information.

"Speaking of being reasonable, how is Selena today?"

Luke's head snapped up from the reports. "I haven't seen her. Why?"

Checking the emails on my computer, I avoided meeting his eyes. "She wasn't in the kitchen with the others for dinner."

Luke was ready to ask me something when my bedroom door opened. Spectra stepped in, the long black satin and lace robe I'd bought her tied around her pale body; a glimpse of white lace across her décolletage told me she'd gone with a white slip for bed. The thought of Spectra in white had me hard in my pants.

"You wanted me to do something for you?"

Spectra stayed by the door, her eyes flicking to Luke, keeping us both within sight. While I knew she trusted Luke to an extent, I didn't doubt the newness of this room and two predators watching made her uneasy.

Opening the drawer, I placed my hand over the biometric pad of the lockbox. When it unlocked, I withdrew one of my spare unregistered phones. Dialing the number blocking code, I then punched in Henry's number.

"L'Paix was trying to get hold of you. He's left you a voicemail, but he also came and threatened me today, giving me twenty-four hours to have you call him back."

Spectra was blinking wide eyes at me. "You want me to admit I'm here with you?"

Tossing the phone to Luke, I smiled. "Luke, can you go to Spectra and have her call L'Paix. Give her your phone if need be to make the call."

With the side of his mouth turning up, Luke set aside the reports to stand. Spectra tilted her head as she considered my words to Luke. Then, as Luke approached her, offering her the phone, Spectra's brows pulled down.

"It's called omitting, Spectra," Luke educated. "We have a problem; we need you to help us with the situation, and Bay has set it up so you can do that without lying."

Taking the phone, Spectra's throat swallowed as she pressed the call button. Luke's eyes met mine, concern flashing in them. We had no idea how good a liar Spectra was, but I knew she held secrets inside her better than my lockbox. The girl wore naivete like a second skin. She was less evasive with me since she came to live with me, but I had no doubt there was more to be discovered about this woman I'd married.

"Henry?" Spectra spoke after L'Paix answered, my hearing picking up on both ends of the conversation. "I was told you were trying to contact me?"

"You got my messages?"

"Um, no. I have no cell service where I'm staying. Bay told Luke to find me and give me the message." Clearing her throat, Spectra's eyes flicked between us.

"Good. I've been worried sick about you," Henry accepted her answer. She moved to my office window while Henry expressed his concern. "We've all been beside ourselves after what happened last Wednesday, and then I find out you married last week and didn't tell me or invite Phillipa and me to the wedding."

"I'm fine, Henry. Still a bit shaken by the experience, but I'm unharmed."

There was a moment's silence between them, Henry no doubt waiting for Spectra to address the issue of her marriage. When Spectra let the silence hang, Henry sighed. "I'd like to see you. Could you meet me for lunch tomorrow? I can come to you if you like? I'd love to see where you live, meet your husband?"

Hugging herself protectively, Spectra shook her head. "I have to come to the city and pick up the rest of my stuff from the convent. I can meet you for a coffee in the morning before I head over there."

"You can't do lunch?"

"I'm having lunch with Father Mathew."

"He must be upset not to have married you. He's known you since you were born. He probably expected to perform the ceremony, not have you run off to the registry on a spontaneous decision."

Looking down at her wedding band, Spectra sighed. "Mathew did marry us. He's good friends with my husband and has supported our relationship since it started a few years ago."

Henry was quiet on the other end.

"I'm sorry this seems out of the blue to you, Henry. I never discussed my boyfriend with any of you because of my history with Alexander. But this wasn't a spontaneous hook-up and spur-of-the-moment commitment as fallout from Alexander falling in love with someone else."

"He loves you, Spectra."

Bowing her head, Spectra gripped the window frame, her voice lowering as if she hoped to hide her words from me.

"And I, him, Henry. Alexander will always be a part of me, but he put me aside years ago, and we've each given our hearts and bodies to another since then. I love my husband. I'm grateful to Alexander for finally being honest with me so I could close that door and move on with my life. The last few years with Alexander haven't been easy for either of us. It was time we let each other go." The silent tears Spectra hoped to hide by facing away from me could be heard in her voice.

Rising from my chair, I moved to where she stood and wrapped my arms around her. Then, moving the curtain of her hair aside, I kissed her neck, letting the connection of our bodies soothe her ache.

"Henry, I have to go. Did you want me to meet you in the morning?"

"Breakfast at KK's around nine?"

"I'll see you there." Spectra exhaled.

Taking the phone from her ear, she hung up. "Can I get a lift to the city with you tomorrow?"

"I think a better idea would be for you to drive in separately with Gina. She will also go to breakfast with you," I answered, enjoying her warmth.

"Is that a good idea? Henry will know she is Calin's wife."

"I'm not letting you go to meet him unaccompanied, Spectra."

Fiddling with the phone, Spectra considered the situation. At least she hadn't allowed Henry to walk over her like a doormat. I'd wondered if they had a father-daughter relationship after Henry talked about her in my office today. Now I could see Spectra didn't look at him as the dad she never had.

"I'll have Mathew go with me. He's been friends with Henry all my life, so Henry won't cross any lines around him."

That was an acceptable compromise. Not because Mathew was a priest, but because he was an Angelis, which made Henry no match for him if he tried something. Not that I expected Henry to kidnap Spectra, but I wouldn't put it past him to bring Alexander to breakfast tomorrow to try and talk Spectra around.

"Okay. Gina will still drive you in and stay with you until the priest arrives. Why don't you go to our room to call him? I'll finish up some things here, and then we can get some sleep."

Turning in my hold, Spectra revealed her watery eyes to me. "Don't be too long."

Lifting her face, she kissed me languorously. Then, shifting her weight, she slipped from my hands and headed back into my room.

When the door clicked shut, Luke raised an eyebrow in my direction. "Is there a reason you suddenly don't trust Henry?" Luke took his seat back by the fire.

"He paid me a visit today. Besides the threat of getting Spectra to contact him, there was an implied threat of destroying her marriage."

"I bet you took that sitting down."

"Not really," I huffed.

"You think he knows?"

"He wouldn't have made the threat if he thought I was Spectra's husband. Henry is far more tactful than his son. But he now knows I'm protecting her, which will make him suspicious. It will also make his methods of getting what he wants differ from their normal approach." Sitting at the desk, I met Luke's eyes.

"You think there is more to this than his son's emotions?" Luke watched me scrub my chin. "What is your gut telling you?"

"Henry and Alexander didn't think Spectra was strong enough to be his balance. So why would they keep her on the hook? It's not like a sorcerer to keep a weak balance. They cut their loss and keep looking."

"But in this case, they were friends for years first, and Alexander hoped she'd make the cut," Luke reasoned.

"Did he?" I considered. "He ended their relationship in all but its physical form years ago and played the field openly in his search for a wife. You don't do that if you hope to marry a woman."

Luke sat forward, brows drawing down. "You're right. He should have kept Spectra thinking she was the one, worked with her to strengthen her abilities, and kept any other women the secret." Luke's gaze focused on me. "Henry and Alexander were playing her all these years, but to what end?"

"I don't know. That's what worries me. Think you can look into the reasons Spectra might be of interest to them other than her species?"

Luke picked up his tablet and made for the door. "Consider it done."

The door shut behind him, leaving me and my thoughts to silence.

Standing up, I moved to the fire and stared into the flames. Was I just being paranoid about Henry's interest? Or was there more to Miranda Jackson's warning about the NSIO than I'd first gleamed?

*"The Williams are high up in the office, yes, but in the end, they don't make all the calls. Some decisions are made higher up by people you really shouldn't trust. Even if you don't hire her, don't let her work for the NSIO."*

A pale face appeared in my periphery. Snapping my attention to the side, Spectra's pale blue eyes watched me, a wariness in them I couldn't explain. Did she worry I'd mistake her and attack her? My eyes went to the door to my room and found it open. How had I missed the lock turning?

"You're quieter than the dead."

Spectra's hand caressed my face, and I automatically leaned into her warmth.

"You were distracted. Is everything okay?"

"Did Miranda Jackson ever talk to you about working for the Nachtwelt Security and Intelligence Office?"

Spectra quirked a brow. "Yes."

Stepping closer, wanting to feel more of her. "She didn't want you to work there."

"I know."

"But you were going to interview anyway?"

Spectra dropped her hand away. "Yes. Sometimes, it's easier for me to play along with what Alexander wants."

"How far?"

Blinking, she looked at the flames. "I was still free to marry you, wasn't I?" Tilting her face so she could meet my eyes again, Spectra raised a brow. "What do you want to know, Bay?"

Something I'd started to love about Spectra was when she let her barriers down and stopped playing naive; her intelligence was mesmerizing.

"Do you know why the NSIO wants you?"

"I'm a balance. Even a weak balance can be useful to them."

"Why?"

"I was told we can be used as trackers. We can find nearly anyone in the Nachtwelt by the frequency of their power."

Spectra moved to the fireplace, holding her hands out to the flames. It looked like she was about to perform some magic, her eyes were so intent, but all she did was warm her hands.

"I've never heard of that balance ability," I admitted, putting pieces together in my head.

"I don't think it's a well-advertised job title," Spectra replied, the side of her lips turning up. "Otherwise, it wouldn't be a long-lived one. Phillipa told me about it. That's the only reason I know."

"So, it wasn't your Fantôme friends who told you?"

Spectra turned to face me, mischief lighting up her angel blue eyes. "I've never had sex by an open fire."

My brow jumped at the change of subject, but I caught on quickly to what she was asking. I grabbed Spectra up in my arms, lifting her to wrap her legs around my hips as I lay her down on the fur rug in front of the fireplace. Her feet pushed my lounge pants off my hips, my hands shifting her dressing gown and slip up, then the sound of our breaths exiting our bodies as I shoved into her.

My fingers gripped the fur pelt, body heaving forward, thrusting as deep as I could, desperate to feel her come undone beneath me. Both of us were worked up and needy. It only took minutes before Spectra shattered beneath me, her body clutching onto me for safety, knowing I'd protect her while she lost control. Holding onto the fur, gripping it for self-restraint, waiting until she was ready to take her to the next level of heaven.

Gripping that fur, I remembered how I ripped the head off the Changeur de Corps nearly a thousand years ago when it thought to hunt my grandchild. I skinned him in his fur form before ending him to make my message clear to any other. Spectra didn't know the violence of my emotions that she lay upon. She didn't need to know that, as we made love, I fisted the luxuriously soft fur and knew that the violence I showed that Changeur was nothing to what I'd do to anyone who hunted her.

As Spectra's body tightened again, I kissed her violently and pinched her hard nipple, thrusting harder and faster. Finally, as Spectra plummeted into pleasure, her body squeezed my cock until I slammed it deep inside her and roared my love for her.

Groaning as her body milked the last of my cum from me, I massaged her beautiful breast and sucked at her neck. Spectra tensed and whimpered when my mouth latched onto her but relaxed again when she realized my intentions were to show my affection, not hunger.

"Thank you, that was pretty hot," Spectra panted, perspiration from the heat and our exertion trickling from her forehead as we lay recovering by the dying fire. Despite days in bed with the Angelis, her sexual appetite was insatiable.

"You'll never have to ask twice."

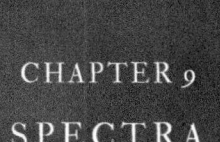

## CHAPTER 9

# SPECTRA

"You know, if you came to work at Pendant, we could do this daily," Gina suggested as she lifted the coffee to her lips. "Plus, it would make watching over you a damn sight easier."

"Putting me in a building of predators would make me safer?" I lifted a brow at her.

"The floor you'd be working on, yes. It's pretty secure."

"I don't know if my psyche could handle it, Gina."

"And you are keen for Galaxy."

"That too." We smirked at each other, both our eyes going to the door when it opened for various people keen for coffee or breakfast. My smile grew when Mathew walked in.

"Okay, shift change."

"You trust a priest to look after me?"

"I trust an Angelis who cares about you to protect you, even if I don't know his lineage. Plus, I wasn't talking about the priest." Gina stood up, emptying her seat for Mathew. Then, with a wink at me, she headed out of the cafe. "Hi, Father, bye, Father."

"Gina," Mathew greeted. Shaking off his duffle coat, Mathew put it over the back of the chair and sat down. "Morning. You look tired. Long weekend?" Mathew's eyes glinted at me.

"Exhausting, but enjoyable."

"One would hope so." Mathew appraised the menu. "Are both your husbands happy?"

"For the most part."

Mathew cocked his brow at me as he put his menu down.

Exhaling, I searched for the right words. Mathew was always easy to talk to, but I was never sure where the line became blurred between my confidante and Mercury's friend.

"Merc waited too long to balance."

Mathew's brows drew down. "He hurt you to get his release?"

"He didn't fully lose control, but he came close. I worry about how we can do this now that we live together. Sharing a bed every night he's home, even between shifts. We've only ever seen each other on his days off for the last few years. He always went to the club if he needed balancing between shifts."

"I doubt that will change, Spectra," Mathew advised. "Yes, you will be in his bed more, and he will want his wife between shifts too, but Merc is old, and he knows when he needs balancing. He'll take it to the club when he must." Mathew reached across the table and took my hand. "This is new for him too, Spec. Before now, there has been no female Angelis. Even female Nephilim are rare. So very few of us have had the temptation of a balance in our beds. Merc has coped with it this long; he will continue to employ his methods."

"Wait," I blinked. "What do you mean the temptation of a balance?"

Mathew pulled back, sitting straight. "Merc hasn't discussed this with you?"

"He only told me I was an Angelis just over a week ago," I reminded.

Mathew's lips thinned as they formed a straight line. "Right." Mathew adjusted his collar, his eyes flicking to the door. Following his gaze, I noticed Henry standing outside, finishing up a phone call. "A conversation for a better time."

"Will you and Merc ever just tell me the whole truth?" I complained.

"Yes, Spec. Now that you have ended things with Williams and

married, wedding your physical form, we will happily tell you everything. Just not right now." Mathew pointedly met my eyes before
looking back to Henry. "In fact, I think it's best Merc be there for
the conversation, since you are his wife."

"Chicken," I huffed. Mathew smirked at me.

A gust of frigid winter air blew through the busy cafe as Henry
pushed through the door and came straight to our table.

"Mathew, I didn't know you were joining us?" Henry greeted.

"It's been such a long time since we've caught up. When Spectra
mentioned you were having breakfast with her, I thought I'd meet
her here. I'll go grab some menus and order us some coffee."

Moving through the crowded cafe, Mathew stepped into line at
the register.

"Spectra, thank God you're safe!" Henry opened his arms, and I
felt doing anything other than giving him a hug would be insulting.
"Did they hurt you?"

"Nothing permanent, Henry. I was lucky that my husband was
one of the men who found me and was able to help heal the
damage." When Henry's pupils and nostrils flared, I hurried my
explanation. "My husband is a doctor."

Henry caressed my hand, fingering my wedding rings. "I heard
congratulations are in order?"

"Henry - I'm sorry."

"Are you?"

"Not for marrying the man I love, just that it wasn't the man you
hoped I would choose. But, surely you knew by now I was never
going to meet Alexander's expectations?"

"You're sure about this man, Spectra?"

"I am. We've seen each other for quite some time, and we are in
love. He's a good man, and he will love and protect me."

Frowning at his toes, Henry grimaced. "Alexander will not take
this any better than he did your ending things with him."

"That's the problem. Henry, this isn't about Alexander and what
he wants. It's about me. What did you expect to happen? Did you
think my life ambition was to be Alexander's mistress? I have tried. I
have waited and tried and loved Alexander even after he put me

aside and started searching for his balance. He gave up on me, Henry, not the other way around."

Sighing, Henry stepped back. "Of course, you're right. Forgive me. I only want what's best for you. Tell me more about your husband. He was with the team that found you. Does he work for Bay?"

"No, Bay sent Calin to get him when he realized I'd been abducted. Since Merc is a doctor, Bay thought he would be my last chance of survival if I was injured."

"Which you were?'

"Yes. My abductor tried to take me." My hand checked my neck subconsciously until I realized it and started fidgeting with my necklace to try and cover my insecurity.

"Oh, Spectra, how terrifying for you!"

"It was. Apparently, Essence found out about my computer skills and wanted to force me to work for them."

Taking our seats, Henry frowned. "Yes, I heard you got on their radar when you hacked the NSIO to gather intelligence for Bay Ryder. What were you thinking?"

"I didn't hack them for Bay; I just traced the spyware in his system back to its intruder. But, Henry, you opened the door for me when you spied on your ally. A fact I haven't shared with Bay as yet."

The wedding happened at an opportune time, and I was lucky last night that Bay was too horny to want to get into specifics about last Wednesday. Still, it would come, and I had no intention of lying to my husband.

Henry assessed me, sat back in his chair, then checked that Mathew was still at the counter. "Yet? Do you intend to? Why haven't you yet?"

"Setting up my new life with my husband, I've been able to avoid Bay and any discussion about what happened. That was until you forced Bay to send Luke after me last night. Thankfully, they were more concerned about keeping you happy, but Bay has asked to speak to me about it. Before he does, I want you to tell me why you would spy on your ally.'

Inhaling deeply, Henry straightened his shoulders. "Bay is my friend, and he does some contract work for the NSIO, but he is a de Sang, and a predator can never be trusted. You know that."

"You trust Bay with the antidote?"

Truthfully, I didn't even know if there was such a thing, but it was worth knowing if what Essence sought actually existed.

"It is not a choice, Spec. Bay created the antidote, and he doesn't trust anyone else to have it."

My eyes narrowed. "But you've seen it work?"

"I have. And, so have you."

"Which is why it worries me," I admitted. "In the wrong hands, it could hurt a lot of people. Taking away someone's free will or choice to be cured crosses so many ethical lines. But, unfortunately, there are people who would use it to do real damage. Essence comes to mind."

Henry's brows lifted. "Bay told you about Essence?"

"Samus did before he sank his fangs in me."

A natural compulsion of fear and revulsion wracked my body, visible tremors, especially my hand on the table.

"Everything alright, Spec?" Mathew took the seat next to me and placed his hand over mine.

"Just remembering Wednesday night."

Henry leaned on the table with his eyebrows dipping low, lowering his voice. "You are the last person I would expect to object to eradicating predators, Spectra?"

"But, it's not an eradication. How Essence works would be the equivalent of ethnic cleansing. It would provide an imbalance, one in which the creatures I fear most would benefit, Henry. If the item they are searching for truly exists, it should be destroyed. Look what they have already done to get hold of it. They killed an innocent young nun to get to me. They abducted and tried to take me, but I didn't know about the cure. What will they do to those who do?"

"Are you concerned for Bay's safety, Spectra?"

"I'm concerned for the safety of everyone you or Alexander are connected to in any way. They didn't find me because of my association with Bay. They found me because I looked into Raquel and sent that information to Bay. Essence knows you know about the antidote, and they tracked me from you. What happens if it's Phillipa they go after next?"

Pupils flaring, Henry gripped the table in rage. Then, studying my eyes, he took a moment to calm down. "I assure you, they found you via the spyware on Bay's computer."

"No, Henry. They want you to think that's how they found me, but I am damn good at covering my tracks. They didn't track me back to Bay. Only Bay's team could do that, and none of them had my home address at the convent. I put down the address for Ténèbres on all my paperwork at Pendant. You, however, had a file on me that Raquel accessed. It stated where I live and my computer skills, and what I do with those to help abuse victims at the local women's shelter. The more I think about it, the less I think Wednesday was any connection with Bay or my hacking the NSIO."

"You think Raquel sent them your way?" Mathew worried. "To get rid of the competition, perhaps?"

It didn't make sense. Mercury said all the Nephilim and Angelis knew who I was and who my father was. Raquel was a high-level Nephilim; she would have always known.

"No, I don't think she would have. Raquel had no reason to suspect Alexander and I still saw each other. Even if she knew we were fucking on the odd occasion..."

"Language!" Mathew scolded.

"... she wouldn't see me as a threat to Alexander's heart because she knew I'd been with Merc for years."

"She did?" Henry's brows furrowed.

"We all did," Mathew confirmed.

Henry stared at me for a moment, as if he wasn't sure he heard me right. "Your husband is an Angelis?"

Tilting his head, Mathew blinked at Henry but didn't verbally confirm.

Red flashed beneath Henry's skin at his neck and cheeks. "An Angelis seduced a balance?"

Sitting back, Mathew crossed his arms and lifted a brow. "An Angelis courted and married one of his own kind. Female Nephilim belong to our race, not yours, Henry. The females can choose to marry their own kind if they will. Your kind's inability to reproduce without a balance is not our responsibility. You are abominations according to the Celestials anyway."

Grinding his teeth, Henry held his tongue while the waitress placed our coffees on the table. "So are you, Angelis."

Smiling, Mathew bowed his head as if Henry told him a joke. "Aren't we all in our father's eyes?"

Grumbling under his breath, Henry lifted his coffee and sipped the brew, Mathew and I following suit.

"Perhaps Raquel thought I would be onboard with Essence plans?" I hypothesized. "It's no secret what happened to my family and how I feel about predators. Your file on me even states that I refuse to work for the Nachtwelt."

"That obviously needs editing," Henry complained.

"Maybe Alexander told Raquel about how I was attacked as a child, and she thought I'd happily help rid the Nachtwelt of its predators?"

"Except, they not only sent a de Sang after you, but it was also a collector," Henry debated.

Mathew turned his face to consider me and exhaled in annoyance. "We can guess all we want, but the fact is that Essence came after Spectra, and it may have had nothing to do with Bay or the antidote, which means they are likely to come again."

"We need to get you to safety," Henry offered. "If you come to work for the NSIO, we can protect you, Spectra."

"I am safe, Henry. Thank you for the offer, but you make me more interesting by protecting me. Bay is right; I need to continue on as normal, but with a safety net."

Lifting a brow, Henry considered Mathew and me. "Bay is protecting you?"

"He has organized round-the-clock protection that is subtle," Mathew confirmed.

Breathing through his nose, Henry lifted his coffee and took several gulps. I could have been wrong, but I didn't think Mathew's revelation about my safety improved Henry's mood. After the moment of quiet, Henry relaxed a little. Taking a deep breath, Henry set his coffee down.

"My apologies, Spectra. I spent the last fourteen years thinking of you as my daughter. It felt like you were already married to my son. You are right, he walked away from you first, and the way he kept you hanging on was wrong. You deserve all the happiness life can bring you. I hope your husband can give you all the love you deserve."

"I'm sure he can, Henry. I wouldn't have married him otherwise."

Bowing his head in acknowledgment, Henry continued drinking his coffee. "Bay was very accepting of your marriage. But, with how protective he is of you, I suspected he would cause an issue in any relationship you pursued."

"Strangely, the two of them seem to get along quite well. Maybe it's their age," I mused.

Mathew shrugged, setting his cup down. "Well, I can't speak for Bay, but Merc liked that Bay was always honest with you about his intentions. "

Nudging Mathew's thigh with my knee under the table, I gave him a warning look to let it go.

Not missing the subtle dig at his son, Henry glared at Mathew before collecting his vibrating phone off the table and reading the text. Then, setting his cup aside, Henry rose to stand, ready to leave.

"That may be, but I am sure Bay isn't honest about all his interests with you. He is a de Sang; he should not be trusted."

"He's given me no reason to doubt he has my best interests at heart."

"Heart, yes. Bay has quite the heart. Perhaps you should ask what led to him creating the antidote in the first place. It's a question he's never answered for me." Bowing, Henry placed a kiss on my temple. "I am happy to see you safe, Spectra. But, unfortunately, I must get to work. I will always be here for you if you need me."

Standing, I gave him a hug. "Thank you, Henry. Give Phillipa my best."

"You should visit her again soon. Perhaps she could help you learn how to better utilize your natural abilities?"

"If Alexander couldn't coax them out of me, what makes you think Phillipa can?"

Patting my cheek, Henry gave me a sympathetic smile, like I was the child who tried hard at school but never scored more than a pass.

"There is more to being a balance than being a sorcerer's wife, Spec. There is plenty for you to learn. Thank you for making the time for me today. Don't become a stranger."

Stepping away, Henry made his way out to the curb as a black town car pulled up. Mathew and I watched it pull away before we both exhaled.

"For a man who is meant to be his friend, Henry is keen for you not to trust Bay."

Searching Mathew's focused gaze, I nodded at the thinly veiled warning. Bay couldn't trust Henry, but I already knew, as much as the Williamses had been my family growing up, I couldn't trust them either.

## CHAPTER 10

## BAY

"WHAT ABOUT SPECTRA MICHAELS?"

Lifting my eyes from the screen of my tablet device, I turned my attention from staffing numbers to my head of HR, who mentioned my wife's name.

"What about her?" Luke became as still as I was suddenly.

"Well, for a start, you've not told me if we are considering her for the position or whether we should proceed to look at other candidates for the role?"

Sitting back, Luke met my eyes for a moment, then his son's. "Last week, after leaving here, Miss Michaels was abducted and nearly taken. She is still recovering from the ordeal, and we have decided to hold the position for her until such time as Miss Michaels is in a better state of mind."

Lifting a brow, Alfred made a note in his file. "Should we interview the other candidates in the meantime so that we can make a job offer if she declines?"

"Was there anyone at her skill level?" Luke considered his son. When Alfred shook his head, Luke nodded. "Leave it for now. If and when Miss Michaels is recovered and can consider our offer, we will decide whether to interview the other candidates."

"Okay, then let's discuss the new employee in the crypt security team."

"Not necessarily new, just an extra guard per shift," Calin clarified. "We need a Changeur in their beast form to guard the crypt against those we can't see."

"From creatures like Spectra Michaels, I assume?" The room was quiet as all eyes focused on Alfred. "I can't blame you. The girl is definitely unique."

"You picked up on what she was?" Luke sat forward, peering at his son.

"That she can become like a ghost, yes. Though, I don't know the term for her kind."

"She is rare, that is for certain." I sat forward, clasping my hands in patience. "Why didn't you report it after your interview? You are meant to determine a candidate's uniqueness in their files."

Sighing, Alfred set his pen down and met my eyes. "Because calling her a ghost seemed wrong. But, of course, a human didn't work either, so I decided to leave it as unknown since I didn't have the technical term."

"That's what you put in her file?" Luke queried. When Alfred nodded, Luke shook his head. "Make a note to alter it to low-level Nephilim."

"Luke," I warned.

"It's what the NSIO would have her listed as, and Henry thinks you know, so let's agree and not raise any suspicion about the girl. Now, back to the crypt." Luke nodded to Calin.

"Right. So, we are adding a guard to the roster to work in their beast for the shift. We will need one each shift. They will still need a meal break and toilet breaks. I'm not sure how we want to work those. Should we have two de Viands per shift who can swap into their beast to cover for the other?"

"We are making this too complicated," I debated with Calin. "Do we have any Changeurs who can only shift their eyes?"

"Not many. The few who can, wouldn't be able to sustain it for an entire shift. Maybe not even half a shift."

My watch buzzed on my wrist, telling me I had another meeting to attend. Turning off the tablet, I stood up and pocketed my phone.

"Well, let's push the oxygen levels up immediately and install infrared cameras throughout the crypt. As for the guard, see if we have existing guards willing to go beast for their shift on a rotation. They'll get paid a higher rate for the shifts in animal form, just like the guards at the estate. I need to go. Alfred, organize another meeting for tomorrow to finish discussing the resourcing report. Luke, see to the financial implications, Calin the logistics, and both report back to me in our strategy meeting this afternoon."

"Yes, boss," the resounding response came.

Outside the meeting room on our Human Resources level, I headed to the lift.

"Boss." Gina stepped in beside me, keeping step as I moved to the elevator. "Thought you'd want to know the priest was with Spectra when I left her this morning. I understand that there were some heated words exchanged with Henry Williams about the two of you, but everything calmed before he left. Spectra then went to the convent, packed her gear, and Mathew took her back to the estate. Cyn called ten minutes ago to tell me Mathew has her outside training."

That stopped me from walking to meet Gina's eyes. "Training?"

Continuing a few more steps, Gina pushed the lift button for me, then stepped back towards me. "To defend herself. Mathew is teaching Spectra to fight like an Angelis."

"How does an Angelis fight, exactly?"

A smirk lit up Gina's face. "According to Cyn, dirty." The elevator arrived. "That's your lift, boss." Turning on her heel, Gina marched off to her desk for the week. It was hard to believe Gina was never in the military with the way she strode across the open office.

Stepping into the elevator, I held my thumb against the scanner, smudging my print as I removed it. Then, pushing the button for the laboratory level, I watched the doors close before taking my phone from my pocket and messaging the phone I'd given Spectra last night.

The lift doors opened, and I stepped out into the foyer of the Pendant laboratory. But, really, it was just the minor lab. Gadget and gizmo developmental research and a minimal biomedical lab for blood screening. Any extensive research happened at other labs I owned around the world. Placing my palm on the gel pad, I waited for the system to scan my prints and retinas, then for the doors to slide open.

Making my way through the first set of security to the offices, I knocked on the door for my head of research. "Jacoby, any progress?"

"Boss, yes. Follow me."

Standing from his desk, Jacoby made his way towards the lab. A middle-aged empath, Jacoby's father was a warlock, or what his people referred to as a voodoo priest, and his mother human. Jacoby himself could only perform minor incantations to summon the dead, not enough to follow in his father's footsteps. However, he had strong empath abilities, making him a gentle researcher. So when his interest in alchemy led him into biomedicine engineering, my team scouted him for my lab.

"The two blood samples you provided were interesting. As you requested, we have not run any identifying tests, only a general observation of the individual samples and what happens when we combine them," Jacoby explained. He scanned his hand and eyes for his personal laboratory.

"Sample A remained in relative stasis, leading us to believe it is the sample of an immortal. Possibly a de Sang since there is minimal cell replication or death. Sample B has too many inconsistencies with regular human blood, so I believe it's a hybrid Nachtwelt creature."

"Immortal?"

"Long-lived, but not necessarily immortal," Jacoby considered as he loaded up a microscope with a slide. "This is Sample A. Notice how everything is alive and well, but there is no death and barely noticeable reproduction of cells? This suggests the body is in stasis. Nearly every de Sang presents with bloodwork similar to this. They are usually in absolute stasis. So Sample A is either de Sang or something very similar."

Changing out the slide, the video screen showed cells dividing and replicating quickly. On another microscope, Jacoby loaded another. This one was dividing at a slower rate.

"This one is Sample B. The second is human. As you can see, replication is significantly faster in sample B, but see this?" Jacoby pointed to the second screen, pointing out the dying cells. "The human cells are dying as quickly as they are replicating. Now, in the sample you provided, not only are they replicating at triple the rate of a human, the cellular death is slow. Like, it's taken twenty-four hours to see any of the cells die, slow."

"In stasis, but still alive." Watching the blood on the screen was fascinating.

"Exactly. This sample belongs to a tolerant, but not one I've ever come across. The Nephilim have increased replication, maybe twice the speed of humans, but their cells die at half the speed. So longevity, but not immortality. This is similar, but nowhere near the same."

"Do we have an Angelis whose blood we could test?"

"You think this might be a direct descendant? That would explain the replication being faster, but not the near-stasis of cells once they are created. Frankly, I'd be more inclined to believe this might be the blood of a Celestial himself. Alive, but frozen in time, if that makes sense? Still, that's not the most interesting thing."

Jacoby placed the de Sang slide in place of the human sample and put a third slide under a third scope. Peering at the screen, I noticed it was another slide with de Sang's blood.

"Keep watching the screen," Jacoby directed as he took a drop of blood from a vial and placed it on the third slide with the de Sang blood. Nothing happened. The de Sang blood was pushed to the side while the second sample protected itself and continued its quick replication.

"This was a random sample of de Sang blood I got from one of my employees," Jacoby explained as he pulled that slide off the staging platform. Then, putting up a clean slide, Jacoby took another vial and added a drop of blood. "This is Sample A that you provided. The suspected de Sang." Jacoby then took another vial and added more blood. "And this is Sample B. Our unknown species."

For a moment, the drops of blood stayed within their own bubbles, but then, in a blink, they merged, united, and the cells that had been in stasis started replicating. The change was slow at first, as if the cells of the de Sang were rediscovering how to breathe, but as the minutes ticked by, more cells divided. Then it happened faster until determining which cells belonged to which sample became impossible.

Stepping back, I blinked at the screen. My pulse was a drum beat in my head as my thoughts raced, trying to grasp what I was seeing and what it meant. "The unknown brought the de Sang back to life."

"Yes, but only for this de Sang. At first, I thought you'd brought me the blood of someone subjected to the antidote or who might have been a natural cure, but I've tried combining it with five different de Sangs. The unknown sample will not have anything to do with any others. This de Sang, it combines each and every time. Bay, I want to try combining it with a few different species, see what happens, but I'd need more of the sample."

Shaking my head, I kept watching the screens. My world was turning upside down, my mind racing with possibilities, both good and bad. Clearing my throat, I focused on not betraying my reaction and remaining as neutral to this revelation as possible. "Unfortunately, there is no more to be gathered. The scene from where the sample was taken has been cleaned. There is no more blood to be collected."

Jacoby's face fell. I knew how he felt, but there were limits to my curiosity too. "Damn, this is the most interesting thing I've seen in a long time. You don't know who the sample belonged to?"

As much as I trusted Jacoby to work on this project for me, I did not trust him with the safety of my angel.

"There is a reason they call them double-blind studies, Jacoby." Turning to the door, I pressed the exit button. "Write up your findings, then print and give them to me directly. Don't email it, okay?"

"Sure, Boss. Oh, one last thing. Henry Williams sent over a sample this morning of the prisoner who was supposedly cured of their beast."

That got my attention. "He did?"

"Yes, they wanted our lab to run it simultaneously to theirs to ensure accuracy."

"Guess they are running out of trust in that organization quickly."

Nodding, Jacoby handed me a file. Flipping it open, I read the report while Jacoby summarised.

"No indication that the man was ever anything but human. It's a better outcome than the antidote usually provides. Did you change the formula?"

"No, I changed the method of inoculation." Ignoring the frown that creased Jacoby's face, I pressed the button again and, this time, opened the door. "Just to be sure, find out what you can about the subject. Let's rule out anything to do with him as the reason for the better result."

"Yes, boss."

The door swept shut behind me with a sigh of air as I headed to the elevator, the results of Spectra's victim overtaking any thoughts about why I came down to the labs. Now, more than anything, I needed to protect Spectra. If anyone found out her method was more effective than the antidote, I wouldn't be able to protect her. I needed to find a way to make the cure a hundred percent effective before using it again.

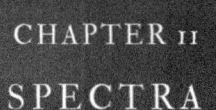

# CHAPTER 11

# SPECTRA

THE AIR WAS cold in my lungs as Mathew found an excellent place to start my training. "It will snow again this evening." Mathew stopped assessing the breeze. "Is Mercury coming home tonight?"

"He's working the night shift, but he planned to drop off some more of his stuff before heading into work. I think he slept at the church."

"Robert will be happy not to worry about walking in on you two fornicating anymore." Then, turning to face me, Mathew looked me over. "How are your injuries?"

"I'm healed."

"Good." Sweeping his leg, Mathew knocked me to the ground. "First lesson. Get me off you before I can bite you without using your Wraith abilities."

My eyes widened as Mathew swept for my neck. Years ago, when Nika first found me after my unaliving, she insisted I spend a weekend learning a few basic ways to defend myself. I was far from proficient, but I'd learned enough to escape her long enough to go Wraith and get away. I utilised that training now.

As Mathew kept me pinned to the ground, I went through every move Nika taught me and managed to stop Mathew from biting me. Still, as strong as he was, I couldn't get him off me.

"Pretend this is real, Spec. What are you going to do?"

Bucking and squirming, hitting and clawing at him, but not enough to damage him, I fought against Mathew with everything in me for several long minutes.

"Come on, Spec, what are your legs doing? What is your best defense against a man?"

Gritting my teeth in annoyance, I lifted my knee hard. Mathew jumped free from me to avoid my knee, and I rolled away on the cold ground to gain my feet. As I did, Mathew was coming at me again. There was a moment where the presence of a lioness sitting watching us lodged in my brain, then I was on the cold ground fighting Mathew off.

Over and over, Mathew knocked me to the ground, made me fight hard to get free, and he wasn't taking it easy. If I didn't earn it, he wasn't going to let me up. Balls, eyes, nails stabbing in the armpit, nails hooking inside the mouth and pulling to the side. If there was a way to get someone off me, Mathew made me learn it and use it on him over the next two hours.

By the time Mathew stood up and smiled, he wore gouge marks, and his skin was under my nails.

"Good. Much better. As good as your ability to disappear is, we now know the enemy knows how to counter it. Hence, you need to know how to get away from them without counting on that ability. Having said that, you are an Angelis. You have abilities no one can take from you that can be used to defend yourself. So we need to make them a natural instinct for you too."

"Being able to absorb their energy? I did that to get away from Paul Samus."

"More than absorbing, Spec. You can take what they are feeling and turn it into what you need them to feel. Your powers aren't there to benefit a sorcerer. Your powers are yours first and foremost. The fact you can use them to help your husband balance his moods when they create a potential danger to others is just a side effect. Do you think Raquel won Alexander's heart with her smile? That girl is

Lucifer's grandchild. Expect that she gave him her lust for him and power to seduce him."

My soul whimpered, an ache in my chest for the loss of that part of me.

"Not the best example, Father."

Observing me, Mathew shook his head. "Why he bound you to Alexander is beyond me," Mathew huffed. Then, stooping, Mathew picked up a long stick and held it out to me. "Here, draw the eternity symbol in the air for me."

Taking the stick, I started drawing the symbol.

"Lengthen your stride; keep your back straight. Keep repeating the symbol."

"What does this do?"

"It prepares you for sword work. Keep going till you can't hold your arm up anymore, then swap to your other side."

Huffing, I drew the infinity circles until my arm was so tired I thought it would fall off. Then swapping my footing, I did the same with the other arm.

Reaching the point of pain, I was distracted by the sound of a motorbike. Standing straight, I smiled. "Merc's here."

"Doesn't matter. Get back in your stance and finish."

Grumbling, I did as I was told. Finally, my arm dropped the stick as the motorbike engine cut off, and I held my arms as if I was hugging myself.

"Right, let's go for a run."

"What?" This wasn't training; it was torture.

Lifting his brows, Mathew stepped closer. "All the training in the world won't help you if you have no stamina, Spec. You are going up against Nachtwelt creatures. They have power and strength, but few build up their stamina. It will be the leverage you can use in a battle against them. Ask either of your husbands. As I understand it, even Bay runs most mornings around the perimeter of his property. Whether it be a predator patrolling his territory or to give him an edge in battle, it doesn't matter. It works for him."

Thinking of the night that I first came willingly to this house and Essence's attack, I considered how Bay had leapt into battle and how, after a good thirty minutes or so of fighting, he wasn't even breathing heavily. So, with a groan, I nodded my head and started running after Mathew.

Mathew found a trail I expected to be Bay's from the back of the mansion that took us deep into the woods surrounding the estate.

"You know, I ran for ages the night Essence attacked Bay's house. I don't know how far or long, but it took a bit of a drive to get back to the house," I conversed.

"Where did you run?"

"The graveyard."

As if that made sense, Mathew nodded and focused on the trail.

"Sanctified ground. When your soul is in agony or your emotions are unbalanced, you will seek it and find it without conscious thought. Can you find it?"

"No, it was night and snowing."

Stopping, Mathew turned to me, forcing me to a halt.

"You don't need to know where it is, Spec. Close your eyes. Feel where the graveyard is. We are deep enough in the forest that you should be able to feel the difference between newly sanctified ground like Bay's house and old ground like the graveyard." When I hesitated, Mathew's features softened. "Trust me, Spec. Close your eyes and let your need for it pull you to it."

I closed my eyes and listened to the forest, taking a deep breath. Movement in the leaves made my ears twitch in that direction.

"Ignore Bay's guards. They know who we are; we are safe. They are just curious about what we are about. Don't listen; feel, then let your feet take you to it."

Exhaling in annoyance, I took another breath and focused on how I felt. Cold. That was the first answer. Despite the training and how far we'd already run, I was freezing. I really wanted to get back to the house and enjoy a long hot shower, preferably in my husband's company.

"Stop thinking dirty thoughts and find the graveyard," Mathew scolded.

Rolling my closed eyes, I thought of the Angel I'd fallen to the feet of while running from Bay's bloody battle. Warmth brushed my left upper arm. Opening my eyes, I met Mathew's intense gaze. Lifting my left arm and pointing into the woods, I knew I was right. "That way."

"Lead the way, but stick to the trail, it's getting dark, and I don't want us getting lost in the forest," Mathew offered, a smile lifting the side of his mouth.

Stepping off, I let that warm brush of breeze lead me to the sacred land. As we closed in, the warmth grew, but so did the gloom of sunset. By the time I broke from the trail and crossed the boundary of sanctified land, it was a balm wrapped around my soul like a blanket. Stopping short of the headstones I could just make out in the forest's gloom, I whooped and spun back to Mathew, embracing him in my happiness.

"I did it."

Laughing, Mathew hugged me back. "Why so surprised, Spec? You'd already found your way here once. I never doubted you could do it again. Now, can you find your way back to the house?"

That was easy. No longer a warmth, but an itch told me which way was home.

"That way, and I think Bay is home."

Looking up, it was hard to see the sky through the trees.

"He's either home early, or it's later than I thought?"

"We've run much further than I planned. We should get back before your husbands worry."

"I fear it's too late for that," Calin's voice came from the darkness. "I was sent to find you. Luckily, the guards tracked your progress, so it didn't take too long."

Stepping into view, Calin removed his jacket, offering it to me. "Déjà vu, Spectra."

Accepting the warmth of his coat, I avoided looking at the tombstones or the way Calin pointedly ignored them as well. How many children had he buried here?

"I have the Jeep just past the tree line."

Following Calin through the trees, Mathew was suddenly very quiet.

"Bay sent you?" I asked.

"When Mercury realized you weren't with Bay, and Bay that you weren't in the house, both your husbands sent me to look for you. They are not scouring the estate in a panic because Cynthia saw you run off with the priest."

Reaching the Jeep, Calin opened the door for me while Mathew used the tire to climb into the back seat.

"No more night runs, Father. If the enemy comes, it will be after dark. It isn't safe for Spectra to be out in the forest."

"If Essence attacks, the house is the last place I would be safe. I'd be better here on sanctified ground," I argued as I sat in the passenger seat.

Meeting my eyes as he shut the door, Calin shook his head. "If they cross paths with you on the way to the house, how much chance do you think you would stand? They came with beasts last time. Even going ghost, they'd be able to track you. If Paul Samus reported what you are to them, they will be looking for you and find a way to take you. Once they have you, what wouldn't Bay give to get you back?"

"He didn't negotiate last time they took me."

Sliding into the driver's seat, Calin started the engine.

"It hurt him beyond words to do that, but it was the only way to save you. Had they known he cared, he would never have got you back. Don't give the enemy power over Bay. You have no idea what your husband will do to protect a loved one."

Turning the key, Calin started speeding through the paddock back towards the estate. My itch only grew as we got closer. My sense told me both my husbands were at the house, and as we approached, I started to feel whole again, tugging a smile at my lips. Then, looking at Calin, my smile dropped.

"I'm sorry for your heartbreak."

"How did you recover when Williams put you aside so blatantly to seek another balance?"

A pang of pain stabbed my heart.

Looking away, I searched the darkness for the right words. "I fucked Mercury's brains out until I realized I'd fallen in love with him instead."

"How long did it take?"

"To realize I no longer loved Alexander? I think I always will somehow, but the way he treated me stings still. If you're asking, how long until I realized I loved Merc? That was four years, and when Alexander ended things for good, that gave me that knowledge. If you are asking how long until you get over Selena, I doubt you ever will. The problem isn't if you can stop loving her. It's whether you can love her enough to see her happy with someone else. And if not her, how about loving your brother enough to see him find someone he loves?"

Gritting his teeth, Calin remained quiet. Mathew's hand squeezed my shoulder in reassurance.

"You'll need to come to confession soon."

Patting Mathew's hand, I nodded.

Bunching his brows as he frowned, Calin looked in the rearview at Mathew. "Why does her heartache require confession?"

"The souls of our kind can't lean too much to one side. The pain needs to be unloaded, the sins need to be forgiven, and the happiness needs to be expressed. While it is not so big a deal for a weak Nephilim, an Angelis or powerful descendent will not remain balanced if the burden of living tips us to one side or another. When that happens, we become corrupt and dangerous."

"And Spectra is the most powerful balance, so she is most at risk?"

"It is not Spectra's balance that endangers her. It is her existence as a Wraith."

"Can you explain that?"

Quirking a brow, Mathew squeezed my shoulder and withdrew. "Yes, I could, but I won't. People's confessions are mine to keep, and theirs to give."

Calin looked at me for an answer, and I shrugged. "It is not my confession to which Mathew refers. It is the one who made me a Wraith, so even I do not hold all the answers. All I know is that the closer I come to learning my power, the more chance I'll die, and unless I can get revenge on the one who killed me and made me a Wraith, I'll forever be walking a fine line."

"The man who killed you is dead."

"Exactly."

The rest of the ride took place in contemplative silence. Worrying about what I couldn't control was a waste of energy, and there was nothing to be done about my Wraith status. I would live as a vengeful ghost for the rest of my life if I could avoid converting. Which introduced a new fear.

Since my recent near-conversion—which Mercury explained that using my Wraith abilities caused—I was fearful of using more than the primary power of my kind. Shielding and siphoning didn't seem to affect me, but what was the chance that learning any of my other abilities could?

As I walked inside, my mind was wracked with the painful memories of ripping the beast from the man who was about to attack Gina and how close I came to converting.

"I don't believe you! You manipulated me into letting her go, and now she is missing. How do I know you aren't part of Essence?"

My feet stopped as that voice, and the power behind it seared over me. Lifting my eyes to the foyer, I spotted Alexander raging at Bay, his strength having no impact on my husband.

Wincing from the blow of Alexander's anger, I whimpered just before my shields closed around me, shutting off Alexander's effect.

Unfortunately, that whimper gained their attention.

Meeting Alexander's blazing hate, my presence knocking him back a step, I swallowed my fear of this moment and finished closing the distance. "Alexander."

# CHAPTER 12

## BAY

"It will be an early morning at the office tomorrow."

When my eyes stayed focused out the windows watching the trees of my driveway pass, Luke huffed. "Is the draw to see her that dominating?"

"Always. From the moment we met."

"Your impatience to return to her was obvious at dinner. You need to be careful, or people will talk."

"You think they don't already, Luke? You are not so naive. For the first time in centuries, I'm garnering my own food. That is big news within the Nachtwelt. Whispers abound that I was hexed and have somehow found my way free of an erectile dysfunction curse."

The idea made me smirk, but Calin bent over in stitches when it reached his ears. Even now, he guffawed in the driver's seat while Luke chuckled.

"They weren't exactly wrong about the erectile dysfunction, boss."

"Erectile boredom is not a dysfunction, Calin. Live a few centuries not getting to have sex, and tell me you don't become disinterested."

"I'd rather sign up for euthanasia, thanks anyway."

"Do we know if the Angelis will be home tonight?" Luke yawned, feigning boredom as he shuffled his papers.

"I understand that he is on night shift," Calin chimed. "Jealous of Spectra stealing the boss's valuable attention?"

"No, just wondering if the office will be a safe place to work tonight. I'm guessing the answer is no unless I want to listen to Spectra pray all night long."

The conversation between the brothers made me smile as the house came into sight. Checking my phone, I frowned that Spectra still hadn't replied.

"Are you sure that's the only reason?"

Looking at his brother, Luke frowned. "What's that supposed to mean?"

Calin turned into the garage with a shrug and pressed the button to shut the door.

"Maybe you like using the office while the boss is busy to cover your own misadventures."

The quiet fell between the two brothers like a bottomless well. For his part, Luke looked absolutely perplexed.

"What are you on about? Misadventures in what way."

Opening the car door, I slid out. If Calin was going to confront his brother about his relations with Selena, I'd give them the space to thrash it out.

"Forget it," Calin slammed the door and brushed past me as he entered the house.

"What's with him?" Luke asked, catching up with me in the hall.

"Best to go ask your brother."

"Boss, if you know what's upsetting him…"

"Luke, this isn't my business. We made that agreement when they moved in here. Pride business was Calin's to deal with unless it started to impact their ability to do their job for me. I've tried talking to Calin, and he's told me it's his pride and he will deal with it. I respect your brother's choice. But, if you feel you have contributed to his problems, you need to go speak to him."

Studying me at the bottom of the stairs, Luke gritted his teeth. "He knows?"

When I merely met his gaze, Luke cursed and ran up the stairs to the first level, making his way to his brother's room. Luke had more bravery than me. Walking down that corridor as the man responsible for stealing one of the sister-wives was not a target I would want on me.

Making my way to the second level, I stopped at Spectra's door and knocked. A moment later, Mercury opened the door.

"Bay, just the man I was hoping to see today. We still haven't finished our conversation about my contribution to the house."

"It's not important enough to detract from your time with your wife. We can clear it up when you have a few days off. I just wanted to see what time I could expect to have time with our wife tonight?"

Checking his watch, Mercury smiled. "I'll have to leave here by eight, so I hope Spectra gets her butt upstairs soon. Did she go to work with you today?"

Frowning, I considered Mercury. "She traveled in with Gina but spent the afternoon here training with Father Mathew. Is she not at home?"

Now it was Mercury's turn to look uneasy. "No, I haven't seen her since I arrived. I thought she must have been with you."

Leaving Mercury at his door, I traveled back down the stairs to the first floor.

"Calin!"

A scuffle down the hall sounded before a loud thump, then Calin was storming towards me.

"Spectra is missing."

"Cyn was watching her this afternoon. I'll find out where she went," Calin answered as he headed down the corridor for his wives.

"They couldn't have found her this quickly," Mercury tried to appease. "I can feel her. She's not too far away."

"Me too, but she's still a reasonable distance away after dark. If there was an attack, they'd have her away from here before we could catch them.

Limping down the hall, Luke took us both in. "I'll call the guard and see if they've seen her." Going upstairs, Luke's eyes were full of hurt.

"Should I ask?" Mercury asked once Luke was a floor up.

"Family dispute."

"Cyn said she went for a run with the priest," Calin informed us, coming back up the hall. "I'll grab my jacket and go look for her." Then, moving back to his bedroom, Calin disappeared again.

"You could just cut through the ether to her," Mercury offered, leaning against the railing with a naughty smile.

"I could, but then I come off as overprotective. If I make the people responsible for her safety catch their tails, I'm just a cautious husband."

The smirk on Mercury's face was contagious, but I wiped it clean when Calin's bedroom door slammed shut.

"The guards said the priest was teaching her to find sanctified ground," Luke offered from the top of the stairs.

Calin's sour mood only grew worse. "The graveyard. I'll go fetch them."

"Want me to come?"

"No," Calin shut his brother down as he leaped down the steps and vanished.

With a huff, Luke headed back upstairs.

"So, it's about a woman?" One of my brows lifted at Mercury. "Please, I've existed a few centuries. I know what brothers fighting over a woman looks like."

"Any input?"

"As long as it's not my woman they are fighting over, no."

"It isn't. Why sanctified ground?"

Leaning on the banister, Mercury crossed his arms. "It's in our nature to seek it out. Spec does it without thinking. Mathew would just be bringing that ability into conscious thought. It's a stepping stone to learning her other abilities."

"I thought he was training her to fight?"

"We will be doing that, but she needs to learn what her father didn't stick around to teach her."

"Do any of your fathers stay long enough to raise you?"

Lifting his eyes to the ceiling, Mercury shrugged. "They usually turn up about the age of five, and play invisible friend for a few years to train their spawn."

"Invisible friend?"

"Our dads don't usually like our mums to know they are hanging around, so they stay invisible to humans, and they think we have a make-believe friend. Some of the Archs spend a few years playing happy families until they get bored or the kid gets old enough to go it alone."

"They never have more than one child with the same human?"

Adjusting his body, the discomfort of my question radiated through Mercury. "Ah, no."

"Why?"

Inhaling deeply, Mercury assessed me before he sighed. "Human women ruin their womb giving birth to Celestial children. In some cases, the woman bleeds out during childbirth. Either way, most Celestial-human breedings result in the human woman becoming sterile. Even when a balance breeds with a sorcerer, that is usually the case. That's why they tend to be one-child families. Spectra didn't tell you her mum nearly died having her?"

Facing Mercury directly, I studied his eyes. "No. Will Spectra only be able to have the one child?"

If that was the case, I could probably relax about them starting a family. One child was better than a tribe, but then there was a chance it could harm Spectra.

"Bay, Spectra's the first of her kind. We don't know."

Turning his head to the side, Mercury stepped back. "Let's discuss this another time. You are about to have a visitor."

When I frowned at Mercury, he indicated the air around him.

"Someone is cutting through the ether, and they are coming in this direction in a rage. My guess? Alexander has some words to say."

Ready to question his assumption, the charge of electricity rose over my skin. Good to know Angelis could sense sorcerers earlier than even I could. Mercury backed up the stairs halfway and took a seat as he indicated the front door. Then in a blink, he wasn't there.

Mercury's disappearance distracted me from my annoyance at dealing with a spoilt brat like Alexander tonight.

Turning on the landing, I stepped down to the ground floor just in time for a hurricane of anger to blow through my front doors a second later. The dramatic entry made Mercury accurate in reading Alexander's temper.

Later, I'd have to sit down with Mercury and find out just what he was capable of and where our powers overlapped. As Alexander marched into my house full of his over-inflated self-importance, I focused on calming this situation without going to war with L'Ordre, the keeper of Nachtwelt law.

"Where is she?"

"Good evening, Mr. Williams. Please do come in. Can I get you a drink?"

"Don't pretend to be civil with me, Ryder. Where is Spectra? I used to be able to find her no matter where she was, but now I can barely sense her. Since you started chasing after her, Spectra has grown increasingly harder to find, and I think it's to do with you."

"Perhaps the lack of her in your heart makes finding her difficult."

"Don't even try that manipulative bullshit! I see now what you did. Since Spectra isn't strong enough for either of us, I can only assume that your seduction of her was for nefarious purposes. Maybe Essence sent you after her. Seduce her and recruit her. Is that how it went, Ryder?"

Burning rage was coming off Alexander in waves. His shields were entirely down, yet they felt like a warm breeze against my shields. The boy didn't have what it took to take me down. He'd have to use the power of his office, and without proof, he'd never get permission to do that. Not while the NSIO gained from my position and power.

Taking my phone from my pocket, I typed out a message while I replied calmly. "Alexander, Spectra's marriage to another man was inevitable once she gave up believing she could be what you needed. You are hurting, your soul is calling for the other piece of you, and Spectra has cut you off cold turkey. Maybe she did it to protect herself, but that doesn't give you the right to charge into my house making false accusations."

"I don't believe you! You manipulated me into letting her go, and now she is missing. How do I know you aren't part of Essence?"

A whimper down the hall caught our attention. Seeing Spectra grimace in pain from Alexander's power nearly made me go to her. But then she straightened herself and eased herself forward, false confidence slipping into place.

"Alexander."

Alexander's eyebrows knotted in confusion. He looked Spectra over as if he didn't believe she was there. "Spec, what are you doing here?"

"Bay sent Calin to come and get Father Mathew and me." The half-truth flowed from her tongue without hesitance. It wasn't so hard to believe with Mathew and Calin moving carefully in the hall behind her. I realized I was about to see how good my wife's poker face was.

"What are you doing here?" Spectra asked gently.

"I couldn't find you."

"So, your answer was to come here and attack Bay?"

"I haven't attacked him!"

"You barged in and are standing there yelling accusations at him."

Focusing on Spectra's left hand, Alexander spotted her wedding ring. "Why are you here?"

"I told you-"

"But why?"

"Spec?" Mercury skipped down the stairs, his hand beckoning to his wife.

Spec ran halfway up the stairs behind me and into her husband's arms without hesitation. I felt his shield encompass her and the sigh of relief that left Spectra's lips when their bodies connected.

"Mr. Williams, this is Spectra's husband. Mercury Raphangelis. He is a doctor who works the night shift. After the events of last week, he's asked that I keep Spectra here the nights he works so that she is safe."

"Safe, here? Are you insane? Why would Spectra be safe in the home of a predator?" Alexander spat his hatred for my kind across the space between us. "This de Sang is likely a member of Essence, and you trust him with her? You're a fool."

"Enough, Alexander. If Bay were Essence, he wouldn't have saved me from them last week. He could have handed me over easily. Instead, when they broke into the convent and killed Sister Kate and abducted me, Bay and his people found me and got me to safety."

"What?" Alexander scathed disbelievingly.

My eyebrows lifted at Alexander's lack of understanding. Then, looking past the boy, I met the same brown eyes in the older version. Same olive skin and brown hair, just aged an extra thirty years.

"You didn't tell him, Henry?"

"No, he was dealing with enough. Spectra was safe. There was no point worrying him."

Spinning to face his dad, Alexander clenched his fists. "Essence abducted Spec, and you didn't inform me?"

"You were away with your fiancée. It was resolved in a relative time that didn't require interrupting you," Henry justified.

"Jesus, it's fucking days of our lives," Calin chuckled.

Roaring with rage, Alexander threw his raw power at Calin. Too far away to prevent it, I was left standing wide-eyed as that power hurtled towards the Changeur.

Mathew stepped in front of Calin, a shield of white light brandished in his hands, blocking Alexander's power from touching my friend. Bending his arms in, Mathew stepped and thrust the shield forward simultaneously, using his entire body to force the power back.

L'Ordre flew across the foyer, impacting the antique clock before slumping to the ground. Rushing to his son's side, Henry checked he was okay before shaking his head.

"Was that necessary?"

Stepping down the stairs to stand beside me, keeping Spectra behind him, Mercury's lapis blue eyes spiraled like the stars were spinning within them. Mathew joined him, and then they both stepped forward, focus intent on the sorcerers before them.

"The Angelis would never align themselves with such egotistical creatures as Essence. We do not crave what we already have. We trust Ryder with my wife because he has proven himself reliable. It is not the de Sang in this room who would be easily corrupted." Mercury's words fell harshly on the marble floor by the Williamses.

"I thought she was a weak Nephilim, but if she can marry an Angelis?" Alexander muttered, eyeing the two men standing in defense of the rest of us.

The naivete of Alexander's observations made Mercury shake his head and laugh. "Sorcerers always think a balance is born for them. Yet, a balance is Nephilim and purer blood than a sorcerer. Angelis and Nephilim do not require our wives to survive our wedding night to be worthy. Even a weak balance can carry our children without our power burning them out. Only a sorcerer inflicts that hardship on his wife, and they do that because they are unstable radioactive bombs.

"My love for Spectra is exactly that. She didn't need to prove herself strong enough for me. She just had to love me. Which she does. You see, sorcerer, you may consider her too weak to be your wife, but the truth is, you were unworthy of her love. That is why she married me, and that is why your sense for her is weak."

Alexander's fists clenched as he rose to his feet.

"Don't!" Henry scolded his son. "They are direct descendants. No one fucks with the Angelis for a good reason. Bay is right. She is safer with them than she could ever be with you."

Turning his gaze to Spectra, Alexander dialed down his rage. Pure heartache masked his features. "Spec, help me."

Heartbreaking as his plea was, Spectra pushed past the barrier of Angelis and wrapped her arms around Alexander's neck, hugging him to her.

"Spec, no!" Mercury, Mathew, and I all tried to grab her back.

Smiling sinisterly over Spectra's shoulder at us a split second before electricity filled the air and thunder roared through the room. Then Alexander disappeared into the ether with our wife.

Gritting his teeth, Mercury looked up and vanished. No electricity buzzed about him, no sound of thunder where he split the ether; Mercury just dissolved on the spot. One breath later, Mathew had Henry by the throat, preventing him from vanishing.

"Mathew?"

"They planned this," Mathew accused.

"You're insane. We would never do anything to hurt that girl. Bay, tell him."

"Do you forget who you are dealing with, Henry?" Mathew wasn't even straining himself holding Henry pinned to the wall.

An explosion ripped the room apart. Bracing against the storm of angry ether that spewed around the room, I hunched over against it as Alexander fell to the floor and rolled across the marble tiles. As the ether closed, it vacuumed the storm from the room, then everything was still.

By the stairs, Mercury stood holding a hyperventilating Spectra.

"Bay," Mercury requested my presence.

Going to them, I took Spectra in my arms, trying to calm her.

"Don't let her go. She reacts badly to the damage you sorcerers cause to the ether. Keep her upright and help her calm down; I need to make sure Alexander knows better than to try that again."

Moving over to the groaning sorcerer who tried to abduct his wife, Mercury helped Alexander upright and propped him up against the wall.

"You are a watered-down want-to-be. Whatever power you think you have, I can defend. Now, I will tell you this once. Spectra is married to me. If she wishes to still be your friend, I will accept it, but if you ever try to take my wife away from me again, the NSIO will need a new L'Ordre."

Rising back to standing, Mercury backed up out of reach before tapping Mathew on the shoulder.

Releasing Henry, Mathew backed up as well.

Once back to me, Mercury took Spec in his arms again, ignoring the shocked and dishevelled sorcerers behind him.

Breathing a bit easier now, Spectra huddled into Mercury's hold. She wasn't hurt. This was more panic over the abduction than pain. Still, it hurt to see her look weak and scared.

"Henry, I believe your son may need help leaving."

"Bay, I'm sorry for the intrusion. It won't happen again."

"Make sure it doesn't. If your son invades my house and attacks a member of my household again, if he hurts Spectra in any way, I'll withdraw my support from the NSIO."

Henry's eyes bulged momentarily at my words.

"Get him home, Henry."

There was no hatred for Alexander. We all understood what was happening to him, but that didn't mean we would stand by and let him pull that shit without consequences.

"Mathew, apologies to you and your friend for the insult my son caused. He is grieving. We all know how insane a rational man can be when grief-stricken."

"I think it's Spectra you owe the apology to," Mathew groused.

All eyes turned towards her. Spectra glared at the sorcerer, who once claimed to be family, as she stepped back from her husband. Then, turning on her heel, she walked upstairs without a backward glance at them.

Swallowing the lump in his throat, Henry looked at his son and shook his head before helping him to his feet. "I'll get him home. Goodnight."

Not bothering to try walking out the door like usual, Henry split the ether and stepped into it with Alexander. Electricity and thunder filled the air around me as I lifted my gaze to the second floor. Then, it snapped like an elastic band, and everything was still again.

"I'll check on Spectra," Mercury excused and took the steps three at a time.

Remembering how hard it was to separate myself from Spectra before we wed, I understood Alexander's addiction went beyond the sharing of his soul.

"That won't be the end of it," I sighed to no one in particular.

Mathew grunted, then turned to face me. "Not a chance. I don't care what Henry said; Alexander planned to get Spectra away from her husband, and Henry was in on it. We need to keep them as far from Spectra as we can."

Lowering my eyes to meet Mathew's, I noted a knowledge in his eyes that kept secrets from me.

"Do you want to elaborate on how you know that?" When he shook his head, I gestured to the kitchen. "I need a drink."

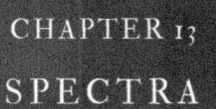

# CHAPTER 13

## SPECTRA

My body shook with the rage I'd absorbed from Alexander. Oh, he could play the broken-hearted boy better than any I'd met, and I'd fallen for it hook, line and sinker, but to his detriment. The moment I was in his arms and tried to remove his heartache, I felt the real intent, pure glee, and satisfaction of playing me. As I stormed to my bedroom as gracefully and unaffected as possible, I was sure that I'd never trust Alexander again.

"Spec," Mercury called my name tentatively from our bedroom door.

Turning from the window and the snow falling like a thousand ballet dancers outside, I met Mercury's eyes.

"I'm sorry. Alexander tricked me. I never expected him to use my emotions for him to try something like that."

It wasn't just Alexander's feelings I'd felt tonight, but the anger of both my husbands that I'd fallen for such an obvious move. Maybe it was clearly a trap to them, but I'd believed Alexander would never hurt me in my heart.

"Is the lesson learned?"

"Yes."

"Then that's the important thing. Are you okay? You're trembling." Mercury gripped my upper arms gently, looking over me with concern.

"I siphoned off some of all your emotions accidentally. I was stealing Alexander's rage when you grabbed me from him, so the draw instantly transferred to you and then to Bay." Licking my lips, I met my husband's beautiful lapis blue eyes. "How did you do that? How did you grab me from him in the ether?"

"Celestials have traveled between realms long before their mongrel great-grandchildren started ripping it apart. When we travel, it's nowhere near as violent."

"Can I learn to do that?"

"Eventually. It will be one of the last things we teach you because it can be one of the more dangerous of our abilities. The control and power it takes to travel that way is more than most Nephilim ever master. Even amongst the sorcerers, very few succeed." Eyes focused on me, Mercury looked me over. "You need to expel that energy you absorbed. Bay has a boxing bag in his gym if you want to take all that hate out on it?"

"No, boxing isn't really my thing."

"I'll change that soon enough."

Glaring through my brows at the smirk on his face, I realized the anger wasn't mine, and it wasn't with Mercury. Taking a deep breath, I closed my eyes.

"I'm supposed to be able to turn someone else's energy into something they or I need."

"What do you need, Spec?"

"Comfort. Reassurance that I'm safe here. That you love me."

Mercury gazed at me with love and devotion that could never be faked when I opened my eyes.

"You. I need you and Bay."

Jumping his brows, Mercury smirked wickedly. "Are you asking me to invite Bay to join us for a threesome? Because I never thought that was your thing. In fact, you've been very adamant that is not your scene."

Smacking his chest, I shoved him away. "No, I just want you both, but not like that."

"Are you sure?"

Contemplating the idea, I wasn't strictly opposed to it. Still, at the same time, the fantasy of taking all this energy out on both of them was probably a direct correlation to my fear.

Sighing, Mercury pushed Calin's jacket from my shoulders. "I need a shower before I head to work. Join me?"

Taking my hand, Mercury led me into the bathroom. After turning on the taps, Mercury undressed, eyes intent on me as I removed my exercise gear.

"Mathew really roughed you up."

Eyes flicking to the mirror, I noted the bruises now blooming inky lessons learned across my pale skin.

"God, we should invite Bay to observe so he knows you didn't do this to me. He flipped his lid when he saw the marks you left on Monday."

Pressing his lips, Mercury took my hand and stepped back into the warm water, pulling me against him under the spray.

"I'm sorry for hurting you, Spec. It just kept getting away from me."

Placing a finger over his lips, I waited for Mercury's lips to still.

"Enough apology. Do you still have some of it in you?"

The look on Mercury's face when he shrugged was cute. "Some, it was tempting to use it all up on your ex while we were in the ether, but part of me understood where he was coming from. You house a piece of his soul. He's always going to yearn for it."

"Did you use any of it on Alexander? I noticed he was barely conscious when you threw him out of there."

Lifting his hand, Mercury looked super cute as he held his thumb and index finger an inch apart.

"A little bitty bit."

Mercury snickered when I raised a brow and made the gap bigger between his fingers.

"Okay, maybe more than a little bit, but I didn't unleash it all. Why do you ask?"

Licking my lips, I went up on my tiptoes, keeping eye contact as I stroked Mercury's growing engorgement. "I want it."

Trying to pull away, Mercury instantly started shaking his head. "No, Spec."

"Hear me out, Merc. I think it's what I need to deal with this rage. Hate sex. That's a thing, right. It's gritty and aggressive?"

"Spec, I'm not the guy you want to fuck you hard and fast, angry. Why don't I call Bay in, and I'll watch him pound you senseless. Hell, I'll hold you down for him."

Tempting. Too tempting, considering my usual feelings on the kinky shit.

"Please, Merc. I trust you not to hurt me too badly."

Considering me, Merc slowly stepped back into me. "If it gets too much, you just say the word, and I'll stop. I'm in control enough to pull it back fast."

"You know I will."

Mercury lowered his lips to mine, brushing stray hairs from my braid off my face. When he shoved me back into the wall and took my hands above my head, pinning them, the whimper was one of shock and liking what I was getting. Lifting my thighs straight to his waist, Merc took no time niching his hard-on in my folds and shoving into me.

My inside passage burned as Mercury thrust into me. There was a reason we'd always spent quality time on foreplay. But, today, with the energy shifting beneath my skin, not fitting with my usual self, I could feel it seeping out of me, into Mercury. He played my body to the tune of that disturbing energy perfectly.

Hard, angry thrusts hammered my back into the wall. Jolts of pain lashed across my spine and shoulder blades, stealing cries for more and whimpers from my lips. His huge cock rammed deep, eliciting curls of discomfort amongst the pleasure.

This was an entirely new experience for me with Mercury. But, as much as I hated it, I loved every second of it. Feeding him this energy, being able to be his whipping boy for once, was more than the sex; it was everything.

When Mercury came hard and grimacing like he was in pain, I'd given all the foreign rage energy to him and was happy to fall on his shoulder and sleep. It wasn't until Mercury set me down gently that I realized how sore and tired I was from my day of training. Everything ached—muscles, bruises, my womb, and my heart.

As if sensing my exhaustion, Mercury washed me off, towelled me down, then carried me to our bed and tucked me beneath the blankets.

"Bay will come to you tonight. I'll see you when I get home in the morning."

"Okay. I love you," I sighed as I cuddled down.

Smirking, Mercury kissed my temple. "Love you too, Angel."

Catching a glimpse of Mercury's bare backside as he moved back to the bathroom, I let my eyes fall over my smile and drifted off to sleep.

*Something heavy was weighing me down, preventing me from getting up. Pain pierced my neck, a mouth latching on like a lover, but this one was sucking. Then, the letdown began, the feeling of someone pulling a plug on a sink; my sink, and now life was leaching from me mouthful-by-mouthful. Clawing, pushing, I was helpless. A weak and pathetic excuse who didn't deserve to live, wouldn't live.*

*As my mortal vessel reached the level on the gauge marked fatal, my head started to ache, my eyes throbbing. This sensation wasn't new. It was the start of one of my migraines, and this one was going to be a doozie.*

*Finally free to move, I made my way to the bathroom downstairs. It was night in the convent, the sisters all asleep. The cold floor seeped into the soles of my feet, creeping up the bones in my legs, slowing my steps, making it painful to walk.*

*Turning on the light, I grimaced from the sudden brightness against my retinas, ramping the migraine up another level. My pulse thudded in my temples like there was a vice slowly tightening and crushing my skull as I drew closer to the sink.*

*Washing my face helped. The cool water refreshed and cleansed my mind of the nightmare. Not the pain, but the sluggishness dissipated. Feeling better, I opened my eyes to the reflection. Sapphire irises greeted me.*

*My breath caught in my throat, and tears filled my eyes as the mirror's reflection revealed all their bodies. The sisters of the convent. Twisted and deformed, their blood drained from their bodies, and the girl in the mirror who looked just like me smiled in satisfaction.*

*"Why?" I pleaded with the angel in the mirror.*

*Looking down, she caressed her swollen belly. "They would have killed it."*

*A shadow passed behind the reflection. Startling, I turned to find Alexander standing there, tears in his eyes.*

*"Spec." He reached out and caressed my jaw. Barely a brush of his fingers.*

*"What's happening?" I sobbed.*

*"I'm sorry, Spec. My child, they would have allowed. Not theirs. It can't be theirs."*

*Burning agony arced across my belly. I couldn't breathe. Blinking, I stared down to where Alexander had sliced open my stomach. The baby fell to the floor, covered in fluid and blood. Stumbling backward, I fell, helpless as Alexander readied to kill my child.*

*"No, no, no. Bay! Mercury! Help us!" I cried out.*

*A second man squatted before me and sliced his wrist, moving it towards my mouth. My horrifying scream of betrayal echoed through the silence.*

"Spectra!"

Eyes snapping open, I found Bay holding my shoulders, his face creased, eyes searching the darkness for danger.

"Bay. They killed my baby. They're going to kill me." Then, falling into his arms, I cried.

"Boss? Everything alright?" Luke inquired from the other side of my bedroom door.

"What's happening?" Calin worried.

"Nightmares. Spectra was having a nightmare. It's okay, I've got it. Thank you."

Waiting for the suite door to click shut, Bay adjusted himself to lean against the headboard while he held me, caressing my hair and rubbing my back.

"Mercury told me your mother nearly died having you. Do you fear childbirth, Spec?"

Shaking my head, I clung to Bay. Truthfully, I'd never really thought about it.

"In the dream, it wasn't me."

"The woman they killed?"

"A de Sang attacked me, then I got one of my migraines, and when I looked in the mirror, my eyes had changed color. I'd converted. The Angel was pregnant, but they killed me trying to get to her."

Bay's hands firmed their grip and held me tighter. "It was just your mind coping with everything, Spec. The attack, your marriage, last night with Alexander. You're just trying to deal with all the change and trauma. It was just a bad dream."

"I know. It just felt so real."

Taking my hand and placing it on his bare chest, Bay lifted my face to see my eyes.

"This is real, Spec. Focus on being here with me. That dream will never happen because I won't let anyone harm you. Neither will the Angelis. You are safe with us."

Tilting forward, Bay pressed his lips to mine.

Gentle pinches, soft caresses, our breath joining together in the silence. Gripping my thigh, Bay pulled my leg across him until I straddled his craving for me. Itching to be filled by him, to feel the connection of our bodies tingling through me, I moved my hips and slid over him, cringing with the rawness of my sheath.

Fingers gripping me, Bay moaned as I took him within me. I felt suddenly so alive even as our connection grounded me and brought me clear of the nightmare.

Rocking my hips slowly, we kissed and touched and made love in the silence and darkness. By the time we fell sated in each other's arms, I'd forgotten most of the dream. Not all of it.

"Will my child be dangerous or an abomination?"

"If and when you decide to start a family, your child will be the first of its kind, Spec. That is why they will fear it. The unknown. But you and Merc are both tolerant. Nothing dangerous could come from your union. I promise you, I won't let anything happen to you or your son."

"It could be a girl."

"Celestials don't breed females. Even for the Angelis and Nephilim, girls are rare. The male decides the sex, so I will assume until proven otherwise that it will be a son."

"It's not going to be anything anytime soon. Not until I know it's safe."

"Plus, it's always nice to enjoy being married before bringing more people into a relationship."

Nibbling across my shoulder, Bay rolled me onto my back. "A husband should practice a lot to make sure he gets it right when the time comes."

Laughing, I was grateful that Bay came into my life. As he smiled at me, I caressed the angles of his jaw and admired the light in his eyes. Bay was part of me, and I felt his happiness deep within, but I also felt a tendril of fear connected to it.

Pushing that away as Bay thrust into me, I drowned in his lust and love. That's what I needed to feel.

# CHAPTER 14

## BAY

SHE LOOKED ANGELIC. Asleep curled into the nook of my shoulder, hair sprawled across the sheets behind her, and her pale luminous arm wrapped across my torso. Pulling the blanket higher around her, not cold myself, but sensing the chill on her skin, I adored how her lips curled up as a sigh of peace escaped them. In a matter of weeks, she'd become my everything.

Holding Spectra settled her in her sleep. The dream she had was haunting me still as the sun rose above the horizon. Soon, I would need to leave her and go to work, but after last night, I didn't trust leaving Spectra alone. Slipping from beneath the softness of her warm body, I pulled on my tracksuit pants and shirt and went to find Calin. At this time of the morning, Calin would be running or in the arms of one of his wives.

Calin came out of the hallway for his suites as I headed for the lower level.

"Didn't expect you to be running this morning after last night," he said.

"We need to arrange things. So getting a run in while we talk will be beneficial."

"Energy to burn?"

"Something like that."

Waiting until we'd exited the back door and headed for the forest run track, I got comfortable in my stride.

"Leaving Spectra alone isn't doable. It would have been hard to do before last night, but knowing Alexander is willing to risk my wrath to get her makes it even more important to keep her safe."

"Did the priest explain why Henry and Alexander would want her?"

"No, but he knows. So does Mercury. The Williamses think Spectra is a low-order Nephilim, so whatever they want her for isn't power. Spec told me that the NSIO uses a balance to track those in the Nachtwelt. That even the weakest Nephilim can be used as a tracker."

"Do you think that's what it is?"

"I believe a fair bit of what we saw last night is an obsession. But yes, I believe Henry had Alexander seduce Spec at a young age, ready to draw her in for their purposes. They probably hoped she'd become more powerful than she seemed, but they kept her hanging on all these years when she didn't, so there was a plan in play before that ever came about. Despite all that, we now have the NSIO and Essence looking to get their hands on Spec. So, I need something in place which allows me to leave her side each day. Because right now, taking her to work with me is the only way I'm going into the office today."

"Did you have something in mind, or are you hoping for me to come up with something?"

"Throwing ideas around."

"Spec isn't going to come into Pendant offices again willingly. If she's staying at the house, she's fairly safe with the pride."

"Alexander can get past the pride effortlessly."

"Is Merc coming home today?"

"Yes. But he'll need to sleep, and Spectra will be up and moving around."

"What about the priest?"

"He has things he needs to work on at the church this morning but said he would come out at lunchtime to continue training Spectra."

"Should we discuss her training?"

"Later. Protection is the priority."

"That's fine, but could we request they stay away from my children? It's heartbreaking to go there to fetch her."

"It's a place of peace for her."

"She finds peace in my misery? That alone pisses me off, and it rubs my wives the wrong way."

"I'll talk to Spec. Can we get back to the protection issue?"

Passing one of the guards in the forest, Calin nodded his head in greeting, then they rounded the bend to run along the road boundary, the trees and fence hiding them from view.

"So, we need something in place until Mathew can get here at lunchtime? What about her Fantôme protector? What do we know about their capabilities? Could we bring them into play with this?"

"That would be possible if we knew who it was or how to find Miranda Jackson again. She told me last we spoke they'd replace her. So, there must be someone new, but I haven't seen anyone, and I'd have no idea how to find them."

"Would Spec know how to find them?"

"She's never even mentioned them, so I can't be sure she knows."

"She knows. Miranda was recruiting her for Pendant to get her away from the NSIO. She must have told her why."

"You're right. Spectra told me as much. I'll ask when we get back. Maybe we can bring the Fantôme in on the roster for her protection. But if we can't, we still need another option."

"Something that can protect against ether-jumping sorcerers."

Stopping, I leaned forward on my knees and cursed. But, of course, the issue was that Alexander could cut through the ether. The Angelis could sense someone moving their way long before I could. In that case, Spectra should be able to feel someone coming and take precautionary action.

"Bay?"

Shaking my head, I started running again. "I need to talk to

Merc. If I'm right, Spectra should be able to protect against Alexander or his father before they ever step foot in my place. Or any other sorcerer, for that matter. I just need Merc to help Spectra learn what to do. In the meantime, let's work up some ideas for protecting against Essence. I don't want another home invasion to catch us unawares. We need a way for our guards to alert us, which doesn't put them at risk, and also gives us a heads up earlier than when they are halfway up the stairs."

"We need more guards closer to the house to which the boundary guards can communicate."

"Essence will expect that. I think what we need is to go old school."

"How old school?"

"I need to do some spell work."

Lifting his eyebrows almost into his hair, Calin nearly tripped over. "When was the last time you conjured?"

"About two hundred years ago. I can do most of what I need without needing to conjure anymore, but I'll need to spill some blood for this."

"Human or animal?"

"Nachtwelt. To protect against predators, I need to use their own strength against them."

Cursing beneath his breath, Calin averted his eyes. "It's not like you to take that line. Are you sure you want to cross it for Spec? I'm not sure she's going to be understanding on this. She's a pacifist if ever there was one."

"Two predators went missing when they tried to force Spec to work for them in the past, Calin. She's not averse to getting her hands dirty regarding her life and principles or protecting another. Still, it's only a few drops of blood, not a soul I need. No one will die to make this happen. Only a weak sorcerer would need to perform a sacrifice to conjure the elements."

"So, we upgrade our defenses and add a bit of sorcery. That works when Spec's home. Essence is not stupid. Once they find her, they will just wait until Spec leaves the estate to take her."

Cringing at his choice of words, a shiver passed through my body.

"Sorry, wrong word. Still, if Essence gets their hands on her, it could be the outcome. She's worth a lot to them with her skills."

"Even without her skills. They would never let her go if they ever discover what she can do."

"Spec would not allow them to keep her. Even if they took her, she'd find a way to escape, and then she'd have Merc kill her."

My heart hammered in my chest at the idea of Spec ever asking the men she loved to end her to prevent her from having to live as the thing she hated most. A de Sang. The creatures that killed her sister, attacked Spectra and took her life from her.

Spectra may not talk about her family, but the time she mentioned her, it was apparent she'd adored her big sister and missed her. The fact that Spectra's sister's demise instigated her mother's eventual downfall didn't help. If I ever found the de Sang that hunted her mother and attacked Spec instead, I'd rip his carotid out.

Approaching the house, we slowed from our run to a jog to cool down.

"You get started organizing the upgrade of the systems and find extra guards to add to the rotation when we get in the office this morning. I'll organize what I need to do my part. We may need to find a way to have Spec leave the estate while I conjure. The magic will more than likely irk her."

"Merc should be able to tell us what her limits are when it comes to that sort of thing. My wives will need to take time out as well. They've never been exposed to you conjuring before. I remember how much it itches my ruff."

"It will probably be best to clear the property while I conjure, but I will need at least a hair strand of all the residents and guards for the spell."

"So the spell doesn't see us as intruders."

"You did pay attention when I talked magics all that time ago?"

"I was young and dumb and eager to know how bad you could fuck someone up."

Laughing, we approached the back door. "Before we go in, I'm going to be attending an event that will likely be a trap for me."

Stopping, Calin considered me. "Why?"

"I want to know what Mayer Callisie knows and why he is here."

Sweeping his hand through his hair, Calin shook his head. "This isn't a good idea, Boss. You are newly married, and that girl takes risks. With her current situation, you will be putting her in peril. If they use you as bait to get to Spectra, you will never forgive yourself, and Mercury will kill you. He's still not okay that we put Spectra on Essence's radar in the first place."

"Spectra won't be going with me. And if anything happens to me, you will ensure her safety. You won't allow her to come looking for me, and you will protect her from the knowledge that I'm in any danger."

"You know that won't work. You two have a connection I couldn't hope to understand. Spec will feel if something is wrong, and she will act on it."

"Make sure she doesn't. Keep her life on an even keel and below the radar. I'm making you responsible for her, Calin. Keep my wife safe."

Chewing his cheek, Calin scanned the property. "You shouldn't be going alone. I'll go with you. Luke can take care of Spec."

"Luke is a de Sang. Spectra will only let him so close. She tolerates Changeurs better. Merc has befriended you. Calin, like it or not, you are the best option I have in this situation. Luke will attend the ball with me. He offers no value to them. If they want me, they more than likely will let Luke walk. I want you here that night just in case they intend to try for the cure again."

"But they think Henry has it at the NSIO."

"Now that we know Alexander's girlfriend is Essence, we have to assume she may know that was a ploy to mislead them. If that's the case, they'll try for the estate again."

Inhaling deeply, Calin clenched his jaw and pushed the kitchen door open. "This has all the makings of an epic fuck up."

"Your technical terminology might be on point, but sometimes getting inside the enemy's camp will give better insight into their plans."

Opening the fridge, Calin took out the milk and poured us both glasses. "Again, are you factoring Spectra into this plan of yours? And I don't mean protecting her or keeping her naive to it. I mean if something happens to you. You've been married just over a week now. You yearn for each other in a way I've never witnessed before. She's in love with you. What will it do to her if they kill you? Or worse? What pain will it cause Spec if they take you away? Have you calculated that risk to her?"

Scrubbing my chin, I sighed. I picked up the milk, skulled it, then took the glass to the sink.

"I'll make this work. Mayer Callisie is my best chance at finding out what Essence is planning."

Pushing through the door, I started for the second level. Mercury would be home from work in a few hours, and before I left, I wanted my wife one more time.

When I entered her bedroom, the bed was empty. Instead, following the sound of running water, I found Spectra enjoying a morning shower. Dropping my clothes to the floor, I stepped into the recess with her, Spectra jumping a little when my hands took hold of her naked hips.

"You're up early."

"Nightmares."

She didn't need to explain. Her anxiety was heightened after the fight with Alexander last night. Losing trust in someone you once loved was hard on your subconscious as well as the heart. Kissing her shoulder, I took inventory of all the new bruises and marks on her pale skin from yesterday's training.

"Are you sore?"

"A little. Hopefully, Mathew won't expect me to do sword training today. I don't think I can even hold my toothbrush for an hour, let alone a stick."

Taking her arm, I lifted the long limb and placed my lips to the pulse at her wrist.

"Do you know how to contact the Fantôme protector assigned to you?"

"Why?"

"That's a yes."

"Is it?"

"You would have just said no if it was the case. You hedge when you hide things from me."

"I don't want to hide anything from you, Bay. Tell me why you need the information, and I will be honest."

"I don't want you alone. The pride can only protect you from external enemies. Someone like Alexander could bypass them, and you would disappear without anyone knowing. While Essence and the NSIO are hunting you, I want someone with a higher set of skills protecting you."

"De Sang assassins."

"Like it or not, Fantôme are the most skilled assassins in the Nachtwelt. None ever get caught. That's how good they are."

"You caught Miranda."

"That was a fluke. How long was she embedded in my company without us knowing?"

"Years."

"Exactly."

"So, you want me to pass along a message that you want them to show their face and guard me publicly?"

"I'd like to discuss them being on the rotation at the very least, so I feel better about leaving you."

Turning to face me, Spectra wrapped her arms around my neck. My hands pulled her close on autopilot, and my mouth dropped to hers. Lips twitching, Spectra brushed her mouth across mine.

"I'll pass them the message. Then, if they want to be involved, you'll hear from them."

"How?"

Smirking, Spectra lifted a shoulder and dropped it again. "They just show up when I'm least expecting it."

Lifting her, I put her back against the wall while she wrapped her legs around my waist.

"Do that with me, and they'll likely end up dead."

Squinting, Spectra kissed my chin. "Try not to piss them off. I kind of like you in my life."

Thrusting into her, I pressed my forehead to hers while we caught our breath.

"I'll do my best."

All chance of Spectra responding disappeared as I worked her body to our absolute pleasure.

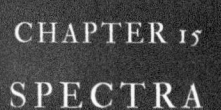

# CHAPTER 15

# SPECTRA

WHILE BAY WAS UPSTAIRS DRESSING for work, I went to the kitchen and made myself breakfast. Gina came in and started making coffee. "How are you? I heard last night was a bit much for you?"

"There were nightmares."

"I meant the sorcerer ex who tried to abduct you."

"Which probably caused the nightmares."

Stepping closer, I lowered my voice, unsure how good Bay's hearing was. Still, I knew predators were akin to animals, if not better.

"I need to go to church and read the four Beatitudes according to Luke."

Stilling, Gina checked the door then kept making her coffee, really clanging things now. "Why?"

"Bay doesn't want me alone, even here after last night. Sorcerers can bypass coming through the front door, so he doesn't think being here with your sister-wives is enough."

"God, soon he'll have you locked away in the crypt."

"Crypt?"

Shrugging off the question, Gina poured the coffee before facing me. "So, you need to go to church?"

"Mathew is going to train me this afternoon. Could you give me a lift in, and then he can bring me home? It doubles up because at least I'll be with Mathew this morning."

"What about Merc? Isn't he going to want his wife when he gets home?"

"Nah, he's more interested in sleeping. We never used to see each other when he was working, only when he had a couple of days break."

"Does a shift impact his powers that much?"

Chewing my lip, I wasn't sure what Gina knew of the Angelis and their powers, so I decided to keep it vague.

"No. But healing can be exhausting. Merc can go days without sleep if he needs to, but why put his body under that strain?"

Smirking, Gina sipped her coffee. "Better to save it up for his days with you?"

Warmth flushed across my chest and cheeks. Glancing over my head, Gina grabbed another mug, stopped and listened, then grabbed two more and filled them with coffee.

"I was going in with Bay today. Just get a lift with us. He'll understand."

"What will I understand?"

Turning to watch Bay push through the kitchen door, I swallowed the spit that filled my mouth. He was gorgeous, and with him in his suit, ready for work, I finally understood the obsession with men in suits.

Lost in my lust, Bay was standing in front of me, watching me with a smirk when I blinked back to cleaner thoughts.

"Ah, I asked Gina to give me a lift to the church this morning."

Bay lowered his brows severely, taking the coffee Gina poured for him and shaking his head. "No. Essence already found you there once, and Alexander knows the place too well."

Sucking in a breath, I chewed my cheek.

"I thought, if I was there with Mathew, it would be better than here for the morning."

Considering me, Bay took a seat at the table. When he held his hand out to me, I went to him without hesitation and straddled his lap. Slipping his hand into my loose hair, Bay pecked my lips. Hungry for him, I took the offer and kissed him as I wrapped myself around him.

"Are they fucking in here?" Calin's voice filled the silence.

"Shh, not yet, but we might get a show."

Pulling away at Gina's humor, Bay stared into my eyes. Then, falling into the blue of his irises, I saw myself praying while Mathew took confessions at the church.

*Lighting a candle in the lady's chapel, I prayed for God to watch over my husbands and keep us all safe while whatever fate was doing played out. Then, asking for guidance and help in learning my abilities, I grieved how I always walked the line of conversion, and the pain using my powers sometimes caused me.*

Blinking, I returned to the kitchen and the intense way my husband watched me.

With a sigh, Bay kissed my mouth lightly.

"Go get dressed. We'll need to leave twenty minutes early to drop you off. I have an early meeting today."

Surprised by his change in opinion, I slid from his lap and headed for the door.

Smirking, Calin sipped his coffee and gave me a wink before his eyes went to Bay. "You right there, boss. Sure you don't want to go help your wife get ready?"

"I said we'll need to leave earlier, so joining Spec would not prove efficient."

"Unless we drop you at the office first, and then I take Spec to church and take some time to get her inside safely. It would be better for me to walk her inside rather than just dropping her at the door."

Glancing over my shoulder, I watched Bay lift a brow and the side of his mouth. When his eyes met mine, I couldn't help but smile. A moment later, I was in his arms and having the air kissed from my lungs as we went upstairs.

After dropping Bay and the others at Pendant, Calin drove me to the church. Parking out front, Calin made me wait to get out of the car until he opened my door.

"Chivalrous."

"Not really. It looks it to anyone watching, but it means you aren't out in the open until I'm beside you. Try not to get more than a meter from your protective detail. The older de Sangs can jump long distances, so it's almost like flying, and the Changeurs they enslave can move fast when motivated."

"Great!"

Uncomfortable for the first time on church ground, I started watching all around me as we walked inside. The church was always open after the first service of the morning. The doors were usually unlocked either for confession, other rites, or just for cleaning. Since Tuesday was confession after mass, a few bodies were lining the pews already doing penance.

Soon, I would need to go to confession to unleash the weight on my soul, but today wasn't the day for that. I didn't know if God considered my relationship with Bay marriage or infidelity now that I was married to Mercury. Something I needed to check with one of the Angelis before I could truthfully shed my sins. You really needed to know what constituted a trespass before asking forgiveness for it.

"Where's the Angelis?"

"Probably call him a priest here," I suggested to Calin, checking to make sure no one heard him. "Not all predators can pick his kind and realize they need to be wary of him."

Bobbing his head, Calin gazed around the church. "Still doesn't answer my question."

"The confessional is set up in the North transept. They aren't allowed to have closed-door confessions anymore, so it almost gets to be a bit of entertainment around here for the nuns to guess what everyone has done. It also halved the number of people who come since they lost their anonymity."

"What do you confess?"

"That's personal."

"At an overarching level."

"Well, minor stuff like a fib or thinking badly of someone, I can ask God directly for forgiveness. So, it's only the grave or mortal sins like lust, taking the Lord's name in vain—usually during sex—and wrath."

"Wrath?"

"I'm a vengeful spirit raised from the dead to seek out wrath before I can have my life back. So it's a constant niggle under my ribs to find the guy who killed me and swap his life for mine."

Calin frowned, dropping his eyes to where my fingers scratched at my lower left ribs. "Shouldn't that have come undone when he died?"

"You would think that would be how it worked, but it seems I had to be the one to extract the life. So, I guess I'm doomed to always have this seed of murderous hate incubating inside me."

Jumping his eyebrow, Calin peered around the church again. "And I thought the Angelis were pure souls."

It made me laugh. "The fallen didn't riot because they were good little soldiers of God. Even the Archs lose themselves in lust with human women to sire the Angelis and Nephilim."

"Then how are they heavenly?"

"I guess that depends on what constitutes your theory of heaven and goodness. The truth is, they are a species of balance. Whatever good they do, they have to counter somehow. They don't get a choice in that. It's what caused the fall. Free will was never the Angels. Humans could choose to be all good, all evil, or shades therein. If an Angel heals, he must harm. If he watches, he must exhibit. If he gives peace to dying souls, he must torment the living."

"If they protect the innocent...?" Staring down at me, Calin waited for me to complete the sentence.

*They hunt the guilty.*

Swallowing the truth, I met his gaze. "Risk. I balance by doing risky things. Balance must always be found for the Angels whether they want it or not."

Eyes narrowing, Calin considered me longer before rechecking the church's occupants.

"Let's find the priest. Then, I can get back to work."

Rubbing my lips together, I led Calin towards the transept. A couple of nuns were waiting for their turn, so I stayed in the nave to catch Mathew's eye. He sat listening to whoever sat on the other side of the curtained seat holding the bible in hand.

As if he sensed my presence, or maybe it was Calin's predatory nature, Mathew lifted his eyes only. Still, on seeing us, his entire face came up. Giving him a wave, I pointed to the door for the lady chapel and put my hands in front of me in prayer.

Nodding his head, Mathew returned his focus to his parishioner's words.

Walking back down the aisle, I spied the de Sang coming in and taking a seat in a back pew, hood pulled up over her hair, hiding her face as she went to her knees and bowed her head.

Eyes on the hooded predator, Calin stayed beside me. "I told you to stay close to your protector; why are we moving away from Mathew?"

"He knows I'm here. He'll be listening for me now. He'll know and sense if anyone enters the church and approaches me. He will also feel a sorcerer splitting the ether long before getting here. I'm safe now."

"The Angelis can sense predators?"

"We can recognize you no matter how old or new. It's a sixth sense all the descendants of Angels have. Even the weakest Nephilim know when they share air with one of the Nachtwelt. It's an ability I've always had, even before I knew I was something other."

"What do we feel like?"

Shrugging a shoulder, I tried to think of a way to describe the disturbance they created around them.

"Static, or white noise maybe. It's not really a sound, but a sense like a thunderstorm on the horizon."

"I get it. My fur stands on end when lightning charges the air. That sort of thing."

Liking the comparison, I nodded. "The point being, this is

Mathew's congregation. Nothing can come in here without his awareness. I'm safe once he knows I'm here."

"You had to tell him you were here. He didn't sense you; he sensed me, didn't he? You used my presence to get his attention?"

Smirking, I gave Calin a wink as I walked by him to the Lady chapel.

"Not many predators come to church, let alone approach the confessional. Reconciliation isn't really a predator's ritual. I'll see you tonight."

Making my way to the statue of Mary, I dropped a coin in the box and took a candle.

Lighting it, I set it in the holder and kneeled to pray.

Once I'd asked for God's blessing for those I loved, I crossed myself and sat to the side. The hooded figure entered the chapel and took a seat at the other end of the pew.

"Gina let me know you wanted to meet. What's wrong?"

"Alexander tried to kidnap me last night."

"Tried?"

"He came to Bay's and took me into the ether in front of my husbands."

"He's either insane or stupid."

"Desperate and jealous were the emotions I absorbed. Henry was there. Mercury told me I can't trust them now. Bay wants me under twenty-four-seven guard with someone who can defend against Alexander should he try and steal me into the ether again."

"So, he brought you to the Angelis. Clever sorcerer."

"Actually, he wants to meet with my Fantôme protector to organize a roster. Not that I agree with this. Next week, I start my new job, and I can't have Mathew or one of your sisters coming to work and just sitting there to watch me like a bodyguard."

"Bay wants to liaise with Fantôme?"

"He thinks they are protecting me after he discovered Miranda. I don't think he realizes that's not the case."

"What he knows is more than he should. He'd be dead for knowing that much if he were anyone else. But, of course, Bay Ryder has been a font of knowledge and secrets, not always his own.

His second in command is also a sponge of information. So be careful what you reveal to them."

"Bay is my husband. I don't want to have secrets from him."

Despite the hood covering her eyes, I felt the glare of her green eyes.

"Just be sure it is your secrets you reveal and not anyone else's."

Standing, Nika crossed herself before blowing a kiss to the statue of Mary. Then, pausing, she glanced my way again.

"She was a mortal woman. So what good does praying to her do us?"

"She gave birth to the son of God but was a virgin. Why is your assumption she was mortal and not God in her physical form?"

"Because you told me once about Yahweh wanting to be the only God, and that's why he created the garden of Eden and his own people to worship him. That sounds like every egotistical power-hungry male I've ever met, and I've met many in my second life."

Smirking, I turned my eyes to the statue of Mary. "The pagans pray to the lady and lord. An entity for each, but they venerate the goddess. Even in their faith, she lays with the male God and gives birth to a son. Their beliefs supersede Christianity, yet we are taught the same story."

"Except the Christians make their goddess a mortal, so she is powerless and not worthy of adoration. But why a virgin?"

"Because it was a miracle. How could a woman be with child and still a virgin?"

"Um, by letting a guy blow his load on her pussy and the little buggers swimming."

Smirking, I demurred. "Virgins are considered sacrosanct and worthy of a man's adoration in all religions and cultures. Men desire virgins. They see them as pure and uncorrupted. Women are meant to look up to her. We are meant to believe that by staying pure and chaste, she was worthy of a God's attention and giving birth to his son."

"Uh, huh. That really rubbed off on you."

"Well, unlike fifty years ago, where women were uneducated

purely to keep them under thumb, I was raised in a time that sees value in educating its females. It allowed me to realize it was all representative and not fact. For example, the church believed sexual pleasure belongs to men and is merely to propagate the species. Hence, women used to be told to lay back and think of Mary."

"I thought it was 'think of England?'"

Chuckling, I shrugged. "The English were protestants, so it makes sense they wouldn't think of Mary."

"And their god was a rapist, but no one wants to acknowledge that." Shaking her head, Nika genuflected. "This religion thing is seriously fucked up sometimes."

"It's not meant to be about the religion. It's your belief and what you hold true in your heart. Praying and preaching does not effect change. Your actions will. Mathew's job is to guide his parishioners with morals, and he uses a book of stories representative of those morals. Men twist and pervert the teachings of Jesus to their own values and use it as a mechanism of control."

Standing quietly for several breaths, Nika stared at the statue of Mary. Then, finally, she took a breath and turned away.

"I'll arrange something."

Leaving the chapel, Nika disappeared into the open space of the church.

Sighing, I lifted my eyes to the empathic face of Mary watching over me. "Bless her too. She needs it more than any of us."

# CHAPTER 16

# BAY

Pushing through the door, I stalked towards my desk, my assistant hot on my heels with her notepad.

"I need to speak to accounts. Get Jack up here as soon as you can. When Calin gets back, I want a report on the recruitment for the Gatesbury job."

"Yes, boss. How did the meeting with Lycin go?"

"Your sire is a bastard, but we may negotiate."

"No arguments from me about his personality. I did warn you he'd try and screw you."

"Well, gratefully, he didn't do it literally, or things would have gotten much more awkward."

Snickering, Claudia turned for the door. "I sent the memos of missed calls to your computer. L'Paix also wanted to meet with you today, but I told him you were busy. Should I make time for him?"

Placing my digital tablet from my morning meeting on the desk, I slipped my jacket and hung it up before dropping into my seat.

"No. I've seen Henry enough this week. He can stew on his actions for a while."

Eyebrows jumping, Claudia didn't question my annoyance with

the local NSIO. Instead, bowing her head, she closed the door and left to chase what I'd requested on the ride up the elevator.

Clicking my computer to life, I typed my password and scanned my hand to access the system. Security was beefed up since Spectra found the leak. Not as good a job as I'm sure she could do, but Elias guaranteed it would keep Essence out.

Honestly, they only got access last time by having someone inside. Essence could do the same again, but Elias had isolated my system from the rest of the companies, something Spectra suggested. Technically, I didn't understand any of it, but Elias did, and he could make it work.

After checking the messages, I got stuck into the high number of emails in my inbox. I needed to read and approve reports, requests, invitations to meetings, and other work-related items that would keep me busy. Yet today, my mind was distracted with thoughts of Henry and Alexander's behavior last night.

Pieces of the puzzle were floating around my mind but not making any connections. So far, the only two I could get close to were Spectra's ability and the Williamses trying to recruit her for NSIO. What Spectra mentioned about the tracking would make sense, except I'd never heard of that ability before, and I was pretty knowledgeable about all things Celestials and their offspring.

The intercom buzzed an hour into a report on Spectra's cyber-security breach. "Boss, Jack is here."

"Send him in."

Looking at the time, I wondered where Calin got to. He should have been back from dropping Spectra off a half-hour ago. My fingers itched to pick up the phone and check on her.

Something wasn't sitting right with me about her going to the church today. It felt clumsy after Essence found her there and Alexander's behavior last night.

"Claudia, check in with Calin. Find out where he is."

"Yes, boss."

The door swung open as my CFO entered the office and took the seat opposite my desk. "Boss, you wanted to see me?"

"What would be the financial impact of separating ourselves from the NSIO?"

"Separating?"

"Not providing teams for them anymore. No training, nothing."

Eyes widening, Jack stopped for a second as his mouth fell open. "What's happened?"

"Nothing yet."

"Nothing yet?"

"As in to say, there was an incident that I'd rather not discuss. But the outcome of the insult is that I may need to pull my support from the NSIO. So, I want you to tell me what financial impact that would have on my company and its employees."

"Right. I can already tell you that it would have a minimal financial impact."

"None? How can that be? Over fifty percent of our resources are contracted to them."

"Yes, which prevents us from considering all the private contracts we are contacted about. Private contracts pay more, so the loss wouldn't impact us for more than a year while we picked up those other clients. We'd take an initial hit, but it would be a financial benefit."

Sitting back in my chair, I considered Jack.

"You haven't needed to look at any reports about this."

"I've been trying to extend our resources to take on more private contracts for years. The profit we make is substantial enough that you haven't felt the need to add much beyond the NSIO, but they are holding the potential of this company back."

"That contract may also be why others seek us out, so I want a full analysis. Financial impact, but also, let's look at the reputational side of things. Are private clients coming to us because of the government contract? Who else could we lose if we broke that contract?"

"A full risk analysis?"

"How long will it take you?"

"Is the threat to depart from the NSIO that pressing?"

"As of yesterday, it became imminent. If another offense occurs soon, it will not be a discussion but action."

Standing, he headed for the door. "I'll get on it straight away."

"Tell Claudia I need to see Jeff from legal on your way out."

"Yes, Boss."

As the door opened and he passed through, Calin stepped in, shutting the door.

"Where have you been?"

"Making sure your wife was safe. Did you tell her to make contact with her protectors today?"

"Yes. Is that what Spec went to church for?"

"Maybe. The hooded de Sang arrived and took a pew as I was leaving. Spectra didn't approach her, but it couldn't be a coincidence."

"Unlikely. Spectra said if they agree, they will make contact with me. However, she did warn that they don't tend to announce their presence or call for an appointment."

Sighing, Calin sank into the chair with a file in his hands.

"That's unfortunate. Think Fantôme will put a rose in their lapel or something to warn us?"

"Unlikely. Try not to snap the neck of any random women to approach me for the next few days."

Tilting his head, Calin smirked. "You know where the easiest way for a woman to make unquestionable contact with you is, don't you?"

"Dinner."

"A smorgasbord. I believe there is one at Catalina tonight. Should I have Claudia call and request your name at the door?"

Shaking my head, I considered. Catalina would be too obvious. Many eyes and ears and not much privacy without raising suspicion.

"It's been a while since I visited the Dungeon."

Nearly swallowing his tongue, Calin sat forward.

"For good reason. The cost of a meal there is ridiculous."

"They secure premium specimens that are all tested and prepped for service. The cost is worthwhile if you want that sort of experience. The presentation alone is not something you'd get anywhere else. Plus, it will be cheaper now that you don't need to participate in the meal prep."

"Typical. You choose the Dungeon and cut me out of the experience."

Lifting a brow, I smirked. "Don't your wives burn your energy enough? Here I thought preparing my meals for the last two centuries was sufferance."

"If I hated it that much, I would have been the one with the erectile dysfunction. The Dungeon has the sweetest morsels. Please, boss? Don't deny me from enjoying one of those sweet delicacies."

Chuckling under my breath at the pleading look on Calin's face, I picked up the phone and pressed the button to connect me with my assistant.

"Claudia, I need you to book the Dungeon for tomorrow night."

"Just you, boss?"

"No, Calin and Luke will come with me. Get me a private room for four."

"Four?"

"I'm allowing for a plus one. Find out what's on the menu. I'll select in advance." Disconnecting, I shook my head at the happiness radiating from my friend. "You have that report for me?"

Grinning, Calin opened the file, and we discussed the Gatesbury job. By the time we finished, Claudia had emailed through the menu for tonight at the Dungeon.

"Anything good?"

"The usual human varieties and a few Nachtwelt. What are you in the mood for?"

"Human. I miss the meat taste now that all my wives have chosen to become pride."

Gina held out the longest, waiting for years after dating to take the beast. While Calin was honored, he'd also been disappointed to lose her.

Not that I'd noticed a change, but Calin assured me there was a part of them that was lost when they changed, and that had been something he'd loved most about Gina.

Frankly, she'd stayed the most human out of all his wives. Gina's wants and needs were still the same as when they met.

Scanning the list, I licked my lips at one option. Highlighting my selection, I replied to Claudia and told her to check with Luke.

"Well, that should make it easier for Fantôme to approach me to help protect Spec."

"Did you choose de Sang?"

Screwing up my nose, I shook my head. While fun during sex, the blood of another de Sang was never as satisfying as a human.

"Tolerant."

"You're fucking me? They got tolerant? What sort?"

"Elemental."

"Holy shit! You could have told me. That's human and Nachtwelt. We could have shared and saved some money."

"We are. She's a petite blonde. Exactly your type. You fuck, I'll eat just like before. I'd rather wait to see my wife anyway."

A message from Claudia popped up on the screen.

"Now that that is sorted, my legal team is waiting to advise me on how painful it will be to renege on a contract."

"NSIO?"

"Yes. The fact that I signed in my blood will make cancelling that contract difficult."

"I thought you were just threatening."

"I was. But Henry and Alexander are not going to give Spectra up easily. So I need to be prepared to act if they try something like last night again."

Getting up, Calin considered me. "You're not telling me something about that mess."

"I'm still trying to puzzle it out. Once I do, I will brief you. Mathew and Mercury know even more and could probably clear everything for me, but they won't."

"Which means whatever it is will reveal something about them that they don't want you to know."

"Or about Spectra. They've kept her in the dark. Why? What good does that do her? They only decided to train her now that she is aware of her origins, and her life was put in peril. Merc made out that they kept it from her because of her involvement with Alexander."

Hand on the door, Calin considered me. "To me, that means she's more special than we think, and they didn't want Williams knowing."

"Spectra is still an enigma. There is much more I need to learn about my wife, but to do that, I need time. Something that I don't exactly have in spades right now."

"About that. Spec was telling me about their natures today. How a balance must keep their power and the scale of them steady. Every time she uses her power to protect someone, it puts her life in the balance. So let's consider just how many women Spec protected with her illegal business?"

"You think the scales are out of balance still? Even after last week?"

"We don't know how long she went without balancing."

Tapping my fingers on the desk, I stared out the window over the city. "Last week was a huge hit. She nearly died and was nearly taken."

"Before that, she saved Gina. We know she helped at least one other woman in the weeks you seduced her. So it may have evened out, but I worry, and I think Merc and Mathew know that wasn't enough."

"Thank you. I'll try and talk to Merc about it tonight."

Bowing his head, Calin left. Grabbing my mobile, I sent Mercury a message asking to catch up tonight. Then, as the legal team came in the door, I sent a list to Claudia of items I would need for the protection spell. She loved shopping, so it was better to leave that sort of thing to the experts.

"Boss, you wanted our advice?"

"I'm blood bound on a contract. How do I get out of it with minimal damage?"

# CHAPTER 17

# SPECTRA

"Don't kill my wife, Mathew."

Panting, I lowered my arm and the wooden sword it held and almost fell into my husband's arms.

"Save me!"

"Always."

Lifting my chin, Mercury claimed me with a kiss so intense it breathed life back into me, stealing away the ache of hours of wrestling and sword practice.

"Oh, enough of that! She needs to know how to tap her own energy resources, not rely on you for replenishment."

Chuckling, Mercury stepped back. "She'll get there. She taught herself to siphon and shield; otherwise, Ryder would have killed her when he married her."

Huffing, Mathew grabbed a water bottle from the ground and took several mouthfuls. He stood shirtless despite the ankle-deep snow we were training in today. His jumper and shirt had come away as the swordplay became more physical.

"If that's your attitude, we should just switch to live blades and see if instinct kicks in for her like our fathers did with us."

Tilting his head, Mercury assessed me. Then, holding his hand out to the side, he blinked, and a blade covered in fire flared into being.

"Let's try."

"What?! I was joking, Merc. You can't expect her to just kick into Celestial memory."

"Why not? We did. We may have got hurt a few times to start, but each time we got a lick, we ensured we didn't get it again."

Looking between the two Angelis with my eyes wide, I shook my head.

"You're joking, right?"

Mathew glared at Mercury, but when Merc simply shook his head, Mathew closed his eyes and, tucking the practice sword into his belt, put his hands in the air, and took five steps back.

Eyeing Mercury's flaming weapon, I lifted my training sword and swallowed. "Um, I don't have one of those. How is this fair?"

"You are Michael's daughter, Spec. Protecting yourself, and protecting others, will be second nature to you in whatever form that takes. If a fallen comes at you with a flaming sword, you will find a way to protect yourself. Until you learn to generate a shield and sword, I suggest you get very good at dodging."

As Mercury stepped toward me, I backed up.

"Wait, you mean I don't even get a weapon? Isn't that going to hurt if it hits me?"

"Yes. So, don't get hit."

Twirling his wrist, Mercury sent the sword into a spiral of flame, and then it was coming my way. Yelping, I dodged, the fire singeing the hair on my arm when I lifted it to protect me.

"Fuck!"

"Spectra!" Standing off to the side, Mathew scolded me, but Mercury was swinging his sword again before I could apologize.

Ducking left, then back and right, Mathew stood with his arms folded while Mercury swung his sword in my general direction.

"You're not even trying to hit her. If you're going to go at her like this, we should just go back to the training sword. She was doing better with it. Either make her react or let me get back on with the training."

Lifting a brow at Mathew, Mercury turned those raised eyebrows my way. "I'll heal you if you get too hurt."

"Too hurt? How about we just don't hurt me?"

"That's not how this works, Spec. You either protect yourself, or you get hurt."

"Um, sorry for butting in, but the boss may have an issue with this approach," Bronwyn perked up from the bench she'd been sitting on to watch.

Mathew kept his arms crossed and merely looked down at his shoulder, not bothering to turn around. "He's not here. She's ours to train. The de Sang doesn't get a say in this."

Peering at Mathew's back, Bronwyn scowled. "She's his wife."

"Either sit and watch or leave, but stop distracting us. It's too easy for duelling Angelis to lose control."

Sinking her brows low over her eyes, Bronwyn dropped her voice to a hiss. "But it's his wife?"

Holding a hand up to indicate she shut up, Mathew nodded his head at me. "You have always learned your ability best under stress, Spectra. Mercury is right. This is the best way for you to learn. I'm sorry."

Blinking at Mathew, I glanced at Mercury to see the sword coming straight for me. Jumping back, I slapped the flat of the blade to the right to avoid it stabbing me, yelping when the flames burned my hand. Thinking I could nurse my injury was wrong. Mercury came straight back at me and slashed at my side, burning a hole in my loose flowing top and caressing my skin with the fire before the sword swung over his head and came towards mine.

Ducking, I fell to the ground and rolled to distance us. Getting to my feet again, Mercury was on me. All of his strikes now aimed to connect. Ducking and swerving, I did my best not to feel those flames again.

There were a few close calls, material singeing on contact, and my skin breaking out in a sweat. Not only from exertion but the heat building around me as the sword surrounded me with quick thrusts and swings. Exhausting quickly, I twisted away from a lunge, only for Mercury to pull back and the sword to catch me behind the thigh with the blade. Crying out, I fell to the ground.

Eyes glowing, Mercury brought the sword down towards me, instinct telling me he wouldn't pull up.

"Merc, no!" Mathew called as the sword's heat swept towards my stomach.

Exhaling quickly, heat radiated through my midsection as the sword passed into my incorporeal being.

Despite being in ghost form, the fire swept through me, filling my non-being, burning my soul just like Alexander and Bay's power attacked me. Recognizing what I was experiencing, I pulled together my shields quickly and imagined pushing the sword and its inferno out and away from me.

Light flashed. Mercury's sword flew out of his hand and landed on the ground several meters away. Rolling to the side, my hands went to the area that still hurt as I sucked in a deep breath coming back into my body with a scream.

"Spec."

Mercury was beside me, rolling me to look at the area I held tight, but I couldn't unfold my body to let him see. "Mathew!"

More hands. I stared up at the snow falling from the sky, my insides still burning from exposure to that fire, my eyes filled with tears, and my vision blurring.

"Celestial swords cross the corporeal veil, Spec. Turning invisible doesn't protect you from the eternal flame." Cupping my face, Mathew checked my eyes while Mercury tended the wound. "You shielded, though. That's good, Spec. You got there in the end."

"What the…? Are you kidding me? He chopped her near in two with a fiery sword, and you're saying it's good?"

"You're overreacting, Changeur. There is no blood. She was incorporeal. The pain she feels is the remnants of soul fire."

"I don't care that there's no blood. She's crying and in obvious pain, and you caused it."

Gritting his jaw above me, Mathew glared up at Bronwyn, who was wringing her hands in my peripheral. "And now he's fixing it. This is Celestial business, so stay out of it."

Shaking her head, Bronwyn backed up. "No. I'm calling the boss."

Taking her phone out of her pocket, Bronwyn was lifting it to her ear, but then the phone was gone.

Standing next to her, Mathew threw the phone, and it disappeared into the trees.

"We would never harm her. So don't start trouble where it doesn't need to be, or I'll start trouble with you."

Whatever Bronwyn saw in Mathew's eyes, she backed up a step, her astonishment making her slack jawed and taking a few tries to get her mouth to close.

"Merc?" Mathew growled.

"Spec's fine. The pain is gone."

Blinking, I realized he was right. I was so caught up in watching the showdown with Bronwyn and Mathew that I'd not noticed that the pain had dissipated.

Frowning, I crunched up and touched the area I'd been hurt. The shirt was cut and singed, but my skin was white and untouched. I pressed my hand over the exposed flesh and sighed when nothing pained.

"I'm okay."

Squatting beside me, Mercury caressed my cheek. "What happened? How did you throw my sword?"

"Ah, your sword reminded me of Bay's power when I let my shields down, so I pulled them together and focused on pushing the burning pain out."

"Do you think you could do it again without letting it get so far this time?"

Chewing my lip, I lifted onto my elbows to consider where his sword still stuck out of the ground. It was no longer burning, just shining steel now that it was out of his hands.

"I don't know."

Thumb wiping away remnants of my tears, Mercury considered me. "Another time."

Lifting his eyes to Mathew, Mercury took my hand as he helped me to stand. "Is that enough for today? I think you need to go balance yourself."

Still not looking at us, Mathew bowed his head. "I'll be hunting."

Without another word, Mathew stalked to where his shirt and jumper were, grabbed them, and in the next step, disappeared.

Dusting snow off, I checked on Bronwyn. "Are you okay?"

"Yes, of course. I've just never challenged one of your kind before. Everyone warns not to, but I didn't think he'd get that angry about me calling the boss."

Mercury collected his sword before slipping an arm around my shoulders as we walked back inside.

"He was in protection mode. Spectra is in Mathew's care. Has been since birth. He already feels like he has failed her too many times. At the same time, Spec needs to learn. Because she is female, Mathew is worried about approaching her training the way our fathers taught us. Still, it will probably be the best way for her to learn."

"It didn't look like she learned much in that session."

Lifting a brow at Bronwyn, Mercury squeezed my shoulder. "To an outsider, it wouldn't. To Spec, it was invaluable."

"How?"

Licking my lips, I pushed open the kitchen door. "I know that going ghost won't protect me from a Celestial now. That's not something I knew beforehand. So, yes. I learned something important."

"Oh. That's not something he could have told you?"

"He did, once. A long time ago. I forgot. I doubt I'll ever forget that again."

There was no chance I was going to forget that pain anytime soon. Yet, I knew it should have been worse. My mind turned to Mathew and how he wouldn't look at me and his need to balance.

"Mathew protected me from the worst of it. He let me feel enough to remember but kept me safe." Then, turning to Mercury, I met his eyes. "That's why he needed to hunt."

With a bow of his head, Mercury wrapped me in his arms and put his mouth to my ear. "Let's go upstairs. I've got an hour until I need to look at getting ready for work."

Kissing me languorously, Mercury waited for me to sough before taking my hand and leading me upstairs.

When we got to our room, Mercury turned me to face him and took my cheeks in his hands. "What else did you learn?"

"I can shield. Not just to protect me from another's power, but I can throw a light shield to ward off weapons."

Lips pulling up on the side, Mercury nibbled my lower lip. "That's just the start, Spec. By the end of the week, you'll be able to hold and wield that shield to protect against an attack. Practice forming it when I go to work. Work on making it big enough to cover your torso. Tomorrow afternoon, we're going to do that again, and I expect you to be using your shield to fend me off."

"What if I can't?"

Mercury smiled, twisting his hands to hold my face and cuff the back of my head in his fingers. "Oh, my dear, sweet angel. What if you can?"

His mouth crushed down on mine, and all thoughts of shields of light were stolen away.

Lifting me, Mercury carried me to our bed and relieved me of my singed and torn clothes.

"I love you," I murmured. The words eased the tightness in my chest.

Mercury held his body ready, stopping above me, his eyes lighting up at my words. "And I love you. Never forget that."

His lips and body on mine were my everything. Soothing away any lingering tightness from today's training, leaving me floating on a cloud of pleasure and belonging when he left for work.

CHAPTER 18

BAY

THE DOOR to Spectra and Mercury's suite finally opened. Mercury emerged, noting how I leaned against the banister waiting.

"Bay? Are you stalking our wife?"

"You. Do you have time for a talk before you go to work?"

Brow pinching, Mercury shut the door to their suite. "Sure. Can I get something to eat while we talk?"

"Of course."

Following Mercury to the kitchen, it was apparent it was the first time he'd eaten here.

Once he was in the kitchen, he struggled to find anything, and I found myself opening cupboards handing him a bowl and spoon for his cereal and then a mug for his coffee.

"Tell me about the balancing."

"It's not that difficult to understand. If we use our powers to benefit people, we need to do the opposite to bring our souls back into balance."

"And this can put you at risk?"

"Spec. You want to know if it puts our wife at risk, and the answer is yes, but only because her nature is to protect, and so the opposite puts her at risk."

"Couldn't she just not protect, and that would balance it?"

"You expect Spec to stand back and allow someone innocent to be badly hurt or murdered and do nothing? Could you do that? I know I couldn't, and that's not my nature."

Mercury switched on the coffee machine and crossed his arms as he leaned against the counter.

"As far as powers go, Spec drew the short straw. Maybe Michael has so few children because their power will always put their lives in danger. It doesn't matter. Training here is the best way to ensure she can balance without risking her life. Once she is suitably trained, Mathew will teach her methods to balance out safely. Well, as safe as a Michangelis can."

When the machine clicked, Mercury picked up his coffee and cereal and took them to the table. Grabbing a water bottle, I followed him and sat opposite him.

"Shouldn't what happened last week have balanced her?"

Muttering under his breath, Mercury dropped into a chair and looked at me. "I didn't say risking her life balances her. I said balancing puts her at risk, in many ways. When she uses her power to protect, it is others she uses her power for. Therefore, it is in putting other lives at risk that she balances. When Essence came for Spectra, the nun who died took some weight out of Spec's scales."

My ass dropped into the chair at the table. The nun's life was put in danger because of Spectra, and so it balanced out the others that Spectra protected. Gods! No wonder Spectra didn't balance. She'd struggle with the ethical dilemma of doing so.

"What else do I need to know about our wife that you haven't told me?"

Peering at me over his cereal, Mercury assessed me before he shrugged. "Can you be more specific? There is probably a very long list of things you don't know."

That was something I was starting to realize.

"Why does Henry want her?"

Gritting his teeth, Mercury cracked his neck. "Female Nephilim, even the weakest of balances, have a capability the NSIO discovered some years ago and have been using them for it since. The problem is that exploiting that ability puts their lives at risk and leaves them constantly out of balance. Now that I've explained that issue specific to Spec, you'll understand why that would be detrimental to our wife's health."

"How does it put them out of balance? By tracking someone, the NSIO wants to be found, it would put that life at risk and allow Spectra to balance her need to protect."

"Bay, that's not... Yes, if she was doing it for personal satisfaction or to help someone, it would counter. But, doing it because she gets paid or because they force her to would throw her balance to the point she could die. Imagine she's tracking a de Sang, and she sees it stalking its prey, a young, innocent woman. And this de Sang is a feral, maybe. You and I both know Spec would have no choice but to get between them, and we know what the feral would do to her."

A feral de Sang killed its food. While not frowned upon, leaving a litany of dead bodies invited the NSIO to take your head and heart. The feral de Sangs were without self-control or survival instinct. The taste of blood was all they craved. They hunted in packs and couldn't be reasoned with. Even other de Sang killed them if they found them.

Over the centuries, I'd encountered the odd feral pack and put them out of their misery, but they could be real fighters and hard to put down. They usually lived on the streets because they had the intellect of a caveman. No one knew why some that were taken went feral. It was no different from the humans who randomly became sociopaths or serial killers. Some just turned bad.

"Please don't take this the wrong way, Merc, but I feel there is more to it that you aren't telling me."

Finishing his cereal, Mercury sat back with his coffee.

"Nothing personal, Bay. You love her, and I respect that. But you are a de Sang, a predator, and other than the fact we love the same woman, I have no reason to trust you."

Annoying as it was, Mercury had a point.

"Are you working tomorrow night?"

"Yes."

"Spectra needs to be off the property for a couple of hours. Any suggestion of a safe place she could bide her time?"

Smirking, Mercury finished his coffee.

"Ténèbres. The Watcher will keep her safe."

Chewing my cheek, I considered that might not be the best situation.

"You have a problem with sending her there?"

"Spectra made a deal with him to get us access to your restaurant and club."

Lifting a brow, Mercury tilted his head. "What sort of deal?"

"He got to watch us together. Spectra and me. I've delayed using the incident last week to keep his debit card at bay, but if she goes there, he will want his payment."

"Tommy has a special interest in Spec. But he's not the one you need to be worried about. He likes to watch, that's all. He's not taking that information anywhere. The benefit of the watchers is that they see all but never gossip or trade in secrets. Everything they see is used only for the purpose of final judgment."

"So your suggestion is…?"

"Pay the debt. Put on a real show for Tommy, and the Watcher will be an ally. If you refuse to pay, he will collect his debt another way. Remember that Watchers balance by exhibiting. You might find a homemade porno of Tommy and one of Calin's wives or your human great-great-granddaughter making the rounds of the internet if you refuse."

Mercury took his bowl and cup to the sink to clean up, leaving me blinking at the space he'd just vacated.

"Spec got a little hurt during training today."

"I felt it." If Mathew hadn't messaged me straight away, I would have split the ether to get back to her.

"I took care of it. If I have a bad night at work tonight, I'll need to balance tomorrow. So if I'm late home in the morning, send her to the church again. It's a safe place for her to go if Mathew is there. If he has to do rounds, the graveyard is the next best place."

"The graveyard?"

"It's sanctified ground, and not many Nachtwelt hang out there."

"But it leaves her unprotected."

"There is always a Celestial in the graveyard when Spec is there. He just doesn't talk to her."

"Are you always so cryptic?"

Laughing, Mercury grabbed his keys. "When it comes to Celestial business, I will tell you only what you need to know, and I only tell you that much because our wife needs you. I'll see you tomorrow evening."

Heading through the door, Mercury started whistling.

I could guarantee that I knew everything and more than Mercury when it came to Celestials, but how it related and impacted my wife was where my ignorance lay. Mercury and Mathew had years of experience with her that I didn't want to have to wait to discover on my own.

Annoyed with the dribs and drabs of information I was getting about Spectra, I made my way upstairs. The supplies that my assistant bought me needed to be cleansed tonight and left out on the window in the full moon to be ready for the true full moon tomorrow.

The full moon was used to bring things into your life, and the new moon removed. This spell was about protecting and keeping loved ones safe while keeping enemies out, so it needed to be done at the moon's pinnacle just as it turned to wane.

Turning left at the top of the stairs, I unlocked the door to my workrooms. The upper level had been my private space since I'd moved into the manor when it was first built nearly ninety years ago. I oversaw the construction, making additions that never found their way to the blueprints. In fact, the entire back hall and the rooms coming off it, above and below, weren't on the plans, and nearly every internal wall was moved or altered. Hell, the garage was a ballroom until the eighties.

Making my way down the hall, I bypassed my research room and the room where I conducted the occasional alchemy. Instead, I made my way into the open area at the far end of the house, my sacred space.

I placed out the items I would need for the conjure, set them out in readiness, then went to the bathroom and showered. I washed with a salt and sugar scrub infused with sandalwood. Body cleansed, I walked naked out to the space and collected the jar of salt, creating a circle of protection around my workspace.

The power of the circle swept over me as it sealed, holding out any contaminants that could damage my work.

Kneeling down with filtered water and salt, I cleansed all the items I would use in the conjure and set them aside. I sat back on my heels and lifted my face to the roof when I finished. Above me, the glass skylight showed me the moon already high above, the clouds circling but not covering as the snow fell.

Inhaling deeply, I picked up the tray of cleansed items, covering them with black silk before breaking the circle.

Crossing the room, I climbed the spiral stair to the large oculus skylight and set the tray on the top step before removing the protective cloth.

After setting up the cleanse, I made my way back down to the workroom, sorted the herbs I'd need tomorrow night, gathered the gemstones to conduct the correct elements from the storage drawers, and finally checked my book of shadows for any contradictions that were necessary to note. Once happy everything was prepared, I redressed and went to find my wife.

Knocking on her bedroom door, I could hear Spectra shuffling around as she came towards the door. Opening the door as she pulled her jumper over her head, Spectra smiled up at me.

"Bay. I was going to head down and fix some dinner. Are you hungry?"

Loaded question. Eyes cataloguing the new bruises visible as Spectra's jumper fell into place, I licked my lips. "How about we order pizza on our way upstairs?"

Tilting her head, Spectra frowned. "Why are we going upstairs?"

Stepping closer, my hand encircled her waist and pulled her

tight to me. "Because this is your place with your husband, and I don't want to smell him while I'm inside you."

"Oh!" Pulling her door closed, Spectra looked over her clothes. "Um, should I shower before we go upstairs then?"

Putting my nose to her neck, I inhaled and realized she hadn't washed since Mercury had her this afternoon. I was still covered in sandalwood.

"We'll shower in my bathroom."

Taking her hand, I led her upstairs, loving the shy smile and how she bit her lip as we climbed the stairs.

"Tomorrow night, I'll be conjuring. Have you ever been around Alexander when he did that sort of thing?"

"Not really. It was dangerous being around Alexander with his shields down."

Nodding my head, I squeezed her hand, sensing the melancholy that thinking about Alexander caused her.

"It could be an experience you might not enjoy, much like when we split the ether. Perhaps you could go for a drink at Ténèbres or something. Calin and his wives will also need to leave. They don't like feeling my magic flowing over them. I can come to get you when it's all over and done."

"Tommy will want his payment if you and I are there."

"Then we should pay him. I don't like to have outstanding debts. But, Spec, you need to have safe places to go that won't hinder your lifestyle. If you want to continue helping abused women, I won't complain, but I will suggest you continue to work out of the Watcher's bar."

"Okay. Maybe we can all go to Ténèbres then, or to Mercury's club to get dinner. Anywhere there are Nephilim or Angelis should be safe."

"I would have thought that myself a week ago, but you discovered Alexander's fiancée is one of Essence. If she has been corrupted, is it such a big leap to believe others may also have sided with them?"

Biting her lip beside me, Spectra lowered her head.

"I'm sorry. I've just made your world even smaller, haven't I?"

"It's okay. I really only ever went to the Reins de Tombées with Merc. I love the food there, but I can live without it."

"Or, you can suggest dinner with your husband tomorrow, and then he can take you to Ténèbres afterward."

The way Spectra smiled up at me was my everything. Squeezing her hand, I pulled her closer to me and stopped on the landing to kiss her deeply. Yes, she carried the scent of the Angelis and the priest, but it was nothing to her lips on mine. Realizing the jealousy was not going to be as big an issue as I thought, I smirked.

"What?"

Shaking my head, I cupped her neck and pressed my mouth back to hers. When her body relaxed into mine, I couldn't wait. On the landing to the third level, I took my wife and made her mine again.

Pressing her up against the wall, I slotted my knee between her thighs and rocked against her. I tugged at her leggings, the material ripping due to the ferocity of my need. My shirt and jacket fell to the floor as Spectra's fingers made light work of my belt and zipper. When her hand gripped me, I growled. It was the only warning she got.

Turning her, I shoved Spectra against the wall roughly. Then slid my hands under the material of her jumper. Molding my hands to her beautiful breasts, I used my leg to force her to spread her legs wider.

The first brush of my fingers over her erect nipples made Spectra gasp and throw her head back on my shoulder. Then, how she exposed her elegant neck to me and rubbed against my hard cock made me close my eyes and focus on controlling myself.

"Fuck, what you do to me. The way your body calls to me, Spec," I murmured as I kissed her where the jumper had fallen off to expose one shoulder.

Pulling her hips back, I slid my hand between her cheeks and rubbed my fingers through the wetness of her slit.

The sounds that came from Spectra's mouth were heaven to my ears. Then, thrusting two of my fingers inside her, I groaned at how wet and ready she was, the way her pussy clenched my digits tight.

Pressing my mouth to the prominence of where her neck met her back, I scraped her skin with my teeth, loving the shivers that wracked her body right before I licked right up her spine.

"Bay! Oh, god!"

Spectra tensed and cried out as she came, clenching my fingers and praying to her god for mercy as she shattered for me. Grabbing my cock with my free hand, I gritted my teeth, holding my need for her from erupting all over her back. That's how much she affected me. Just the feel of her coming for me was enough to make me want to do the same. Spectra didn't even have to touch me.

As Spectra panted against the wall, I bent my knees, using her hips to tilt her ass back a little more until I could rub the seeping head of my cock through her folds. Spectra cursed as my thickness found her slick opening, and then I thrust into her.

"Fuck! Bay!" Spectra cried, panting and scratching at the wall as I pounded her beautiful body from behind.

Grabbing her jaw, I turned her face and kissed her furiously, loving how her tight body gripped me as I thrust into her repeatedly. Nothing had ever felt this good. Spectra was worth waiting a million lifetimes to find. She was mine now. Always would be. My wife. My ghost. My angel.

I already knew if anything were to happen to her, I'd have to use my own cure and follow her, or I'd go mad over how she would haunt me.

Spectra broke from my mouth, grabbed my arm, and directed it between her legs.

"Please?"

There was no hesitation as I rubbed her clit, slamming her from behind, my balls tight and ready. But I wanted Spectra to come undone for me again while I was balls deep inside her. It was an effort to fight the temptation to try and knock her up right now. Wrong time or not. The instinct to put my child in her was as primal as the need to feed. Luckily for both of us, that, at least, was out of my control.

My cock grew thicker and harder at the thought, and the need sent a zing down my spine, straight to my balls. Spectra took the All-

Father's name in vain and shattered on my hardness, the slickness of her audible as my hips pumped faster. My entire body seized as I lost myself to her. Our voices rang through the stairwell, echoing into the levels below.

As we stood there panting, my body still holding Spectra against the wall, laughter reached us from two floors below, feminine and sweet. Holding Spectra's half-naked body to mine, I swept her hair back from her face to watch the heat of embarrassment rise across her chest and cheeks.

Sweeping my hand under her jumper, I weighed her breasts gently as I kissed along her jaw. "So, about that shower."

# CHAPTER 19

## SPECTRA

"ARE YOU READY TO GO?"

Mercury looked tired, coming out of the bathroom, but he gave me a smile that made my heart beat faster.

"Oh, you meant to church?" His grin was wicked. Mercury winked and pulled on his shirt. "Let's go. We both need confession, and then I believe my beautiful wife requested dinner before I leave her in the care of a kinky watcher."

When Mercury got home in the morning and I passed on Bay's suggestion of dinner, Mercury agreed, but he needed to sleep first. He'd been home late, and I had the feeling by the fact he barely kissed me that he'd visited one of his clubs after finishing work or even during the night.

Grabbing his helmet, Mercury took my hand and led me downstairs to his bike. Bay wasn't home yet, and possibly wouldn't be for hours, so it was just Selena and Cynthia wandering around. As long as I told them where we were going, they were okay with it.

Mercury and I walked in hand-in-hand at the church, heading to the north transept together. "Are you first today?" Mercury asked when we got to the chairs to wait for our turn.

"You can go. I think you need it more."

Meeting my eyes, Mercury swallowed and took the first chair. "If you were interested in-"

"I'm not. And I'm not jealous, so you don't need to be weird about it suddenly because we live together. You never made a big deal out of it before."

"We weren't married."

"So, having sex outside of our marriage is something I need to treat as a sin and confess to Mathew?"

"Not for you, no. You have two husbands, and that is all you are entertaining, to my knowledge. If you and Alexander were still fucking, you would be stepping out on your marriage bed and need to repent. So, in this situation, only I am the sinner."

"I don't see it like that. Your need to balance requires those actions. Yes, you could find a way to do it without sex, but you are making the hurt pleasurable for you and your masochist. I'd much prefer that than you hunting and torturing people. Therefore, you do not sin; you follow your nature. A nature God designed and Angels were punished for wanting the free will to avoid."

Side-eyeing me, Mercury clasped his hands together. "I love you, Spec. It's not just our marriage bed I step out on when I go to the club; it's my heart. That's why I need this confession, and it's why coming home to see you smile at me was uncomfortable this morning."

Blinking, I assessed Mercury. Then, slipping my hand into his, I squeezed his hand.

"This isn't about another woman. The look on your face this morning was about yesterday and the sword. Are you worried I am angry about it?"

Mercury put his other hand over mine, sandwiching it in his grasp. "Angry, no. You have never been the sort to harbor a grudge. But, I worried I'd walk in, and you would fear me or flinch away from my touch. You didn't. You acted like you do every other time we see each other. You smiled and kissed me like I was the only man in the world. It made me feel worse, Spec. I hurt you yesterday, and you didn't even get angry at me about it."

"It was a lesson I needed to learn."

"But—"

"Merc, Alexander told me he loved me, wanted to marry me, but I had to prove myself worthy of him. That he'd date others to see if anyone else would be his right woman until I proved I was good enough. That hurt. You have never promised me more than your love. That's all I ask, Merc. Never make me feel unworthy of you. Never hurt me in that way. Then, just like you have to accept Bay as part of my life, I can accept you as you are."

Staring into my eyes, Mercury reached for me abruptly, his hand cuffed the back of my head as he kissed me deeply. A throat clearing pulled us apart. Mercury got up and headed into the confessional, grinning, Mathew shaking his head. Still, the side of his mouth tipped up as he followed Mercury.

Sighing, I sat back in my seat and closed my eyes, already deciding in my head on my confession. It wasn't until a body took the seat beside me that I opened them. Brown eyes watched me from beneath a mop of brown hair in olive skin, the body clothed in an expensive-looking business suit.

"Alexander." Sitting up straight, I looked around.

"We need to talk."

"I don't think we do. You made your intentions clear the other night."

"That wasn't meant to happen. I reacted badly to seeing you there, Spec. Seeing you with your husband."

"He's here, Alexander, and Mathew and Mercury are still angry about the stunt you pulled. I'm livid that you would do that to me. You know how the ether hurts me and your power, but you didn't care. It was all about you, as usual."

Eyebrows jumping, Alexander considered me.

"You think I'm selfish? Spec, our souls are tied. So who is the selfish one trying to hurt the other by walking away from me?"

His finger caressed my arm. A tendril of need followed his caress, but it wasn't enough to tempt me anymore.

"You should never have tied our souls. That was on you from the start. You could have let me go, but you brought me back to spend the rest of my life as a ghost. Don't blame me for this. You knew by then I wasn't going to be the one you chose."

"I didn't. Not back then. It took my mother years. I thought…" Sighing, Alexander shook his head. "It doesn't matter. That's not why I'm here. Can we go outside to talk? There's something important we need to discuss."

"Not a chance."

"Spec-"

"Alexander, you broke my heart, and I endured it for years. You kept me on a hook dangling, reeling me in whenever it suited you, and you would have kept on doing it. Maybe you planned to marry and never let me know. I don't know. I will never know. What I do know is that despite it all, I'd always trusted you as my friend. Now, we don't even have that."

Standing up, I stepped away to put distance between us.

"Find the one who tied us together and get it undone. Whatever that means for me, I'll deal with it, but it is all that remains between us anymore, and it should never have existed in the first place."

Sighing, Alexander propped his elbows on his knees to support him. "I won't be doing that."

"Why not?"

Rising out of the chair, Alexander inhaled deeply as he met my eyes. "The tie didn't just benefit you. Not that I knew that at first, but after it was done, I felt the change in me as you grew more stable. I won't be giving that up."

Realization pulsed inside me. Even without the bond of a balance and sorcerer, the tie of our souls benefitted Alexander my power. That's why he never gave me up. Yet, he never realized that for that to happen meant I was more than some weak Nephilim.

Alexander closed the gap between us and hovered over me. His fingers caught some strands of my hair and caressed along them, his eyelids fluttering as if the sensation was a high for him. Then, opening his eyes, he met mine, and his lips turned up in a cruel smile.

"I won't give you up."

"You have no choice. I am married. Not just by law, but in heart and body."

Snapping his wrist, Alexander caught the back of my neck in his hand, yanking me to him until our breaths mingled in the space between our lips.

"You better hope you are wrong about that, Spec. I don't care if he has your heart, but you belong to me, body and soul. You're just too naive to realize it."

I was damn sure that wasn't the case, but I saw an entirely new side to Alexander right now, and it made me realize why most feared him. How had I missed this all these years?

"My only naivete was that I believed you loved me and that you were the kind of man I wanted to love. But I see the real you now, Alexander, and how you treated me these last few years is why you lost me. It had nothing to do with any other man in my life. You need to realize your actions are to blame for where we are and that behaving like this will never win me back." Exhaling enough to lose my physical presence, my lips curled up in a feral snarl. "You can't own what you can't hold, Alexander."

Stepping backward through his hand, leaving him grasping air, I stayed unsubstantial but visible.

"We're done."

"No!"

Trying to grab me, Alexander's arm swept through the air, a chill echoing in my soul as he passed through me. Floating back, he gave chase, still trying to grab me until he tripped on a pew.

A gasp sounded. My head turned to see the parishioner cross herself and scamper out of the church, no doubt freaking about the ghost girl hovering in the pews.

Tropical heat poured over me as Alexander got to his feet, his shields dropping.

"Oh, Spec, you're messing with the wrong sorcerer. I told you, you're mine." Closing his eyes, Alexander twitched.

A fire raged through me, lighting up the ties between us, burning the coiled tethers that bound our souls. Sucking in a breath,

I screamed loud enough to cause it to reverberate through the church.

Clinging to my stomach, I fell between the pews, trying to smother the fire within. Instead, the fire cut off as a crashing sound filled the church, echoing violence, shattering the peace.

"By all that's holy!" Strong arms turned me, but I couldn't uncurl from the ball my body had curled into. "Merc, I need you here!" Mathew called, trying to hold me.

The agony of the tether was twisting into barbed fingers, gripping around my gut, bleeding my energy, hurting me. Tears streaked down my cheeks, my vision blurry through the suffering of my soul.

"Merc!"

"I'm here. You go deal with the sorcerer."

Taking me in his arms, Merc peered down at me. His hand felt my forehead, then checked my pulse. Closing his eyes, Merc moved his touch to my stomach, maneuvering his arm amongst my curled body and limbs to lay a cooling hand against the fire in my belly.

White light filled my vision, surrounded Mercury, and pushed into me like ice on a hot saucepan. Fire sucked the air from the room as if the ether ripped open around me. Merc held me tight, throwing his body over me, protecting me from the storm that raged around us.

Merc clung to me for several minutes while he pushed cooling gel into my soul, murmuring a language I didn't know to understand under his breath.

A tornado swept around us, and peace filled the church again in its wake.

Panting, I stared up at Mercury, blinking wide eyes at him. There was no need to ask; I could feel where that power came from. "That was me."

Pressing his lips into a thin line, Mercury stroked my cheek before putting his finger to my lips. "Shh, let him think it was Mathew."

Lifting his gaze to take in the church, Mercury cursed beneath his breath. "Mathew, you okay?"

"I'm fine. How's Spec?"

"Breathing. The sorcerer?"

"He'll live. I'm going to dump him somewhere else, then come back and deal with this mess."

"I think one of your parishioners got a lot more than they planned." Then, bringing his eyes back to me, Mercury stroked my cheek. "Ghosts in a church. That's one way to scare faith into people, Spec."

"Wasn't exactly thinking about the witnesses."

"Obviously, or you would have noticed us approaching and let me deal with Alexander instead of starting an incident."

Helping me sit up, Mercury brushed my hair out of my face and peered into my eyes.

"How do you feel?"

"Drained. What did Alexander do to me?"

Still helping me to look somewhat decent, Mercury sighed. "He used your bond against you. Alexander wanted you to know that he could hurt you with that soul tie, that the ability to harm each other worked two ways. You have strangled the bond for years now, trying to close it off, which has hurt him. Not in the same way he hurt you just now, but he felt it just as much as you did."

"Did you know he could do that?"

"It's not about knowing he could; we never thought he would. The bonus is that he needs to be within close proximity to hurt you like that, so if we can keep you away from him, he shouldn't be able to hurt you again."

"Do you know who did this to me? Who tied me to Alexander?"

Averting his eyes, Mercury nodded. "Yeah, Spec, there is only one who it could be."

"Can you contact him and ask him to undo the bond? I don't want to be tied to Alexander. I never did. Being tied to someone like that, yearning to be near them and with them, it's not natural."

Sweeping his hand across my forehead, Mercury sighed. "It is no different from the bond you have with Ryder. You will always yearn for him physically."

"Desire, I can handle. Even unquenchable as it is. But the

yearning of your soul is agonizing, Merc, especially with someone who broke your heart. I want it undone if it can be."

Jaw tense, Mercury stood up, then he helped me to my feet. "I'll ask. Come on. I doubt you'll be getting to make your confession today. Let's get you back to safety."

A siren sounded outside. Looking around the overturned pews, I grimaced. "I was meant to be safe here."

"You are. It was everyone else who wasn't safe from you. But, on the upside, I think you just balanced."

# CHAPTER 20

# BAY

THE DUNGEON WAS a former torture chamber beneath an old Victorian Manor house. It came complete with rusted shackles and chains hanging from the ceiling and bloodstained walls and floors. The rest of the establishment had been cleaned and refurbished for luxury, but not those walls and chains.

The chains and stains were reminders of the atrocities of history and a warning of the ghosts that haunted this place, still screaming for mercy and begging for death.

It wasn't just a myth either. Even as my party of three sat at the bar waiting for our private dining room to be ready, a female wailed and thrashed against invisible chains, naked and bloody.

Depressing enough to put most off their meals if they weren't accustomed. It wasn't that I enjoyed the atmosphere of the Dungeon, no one did, but it served a particular purpose. You see, this place had belonged to human hunters, and the ghosts of the tortured were Nachtwelt citizens lured and trapped by these evil men.

Eventually, the souls were liberated by Kendrick, the current owner. Still, he wanted it to serve as a reminder, even after the

Treaty of Otherworlds was formed with the human government, that we should always be wary of the evil within them.

It was one thing to kill for food or survival, but doing it for plea-sure, torturing and maiming in the name of research, should never be accepted and, worse, ignored.

"Do you know what I always think of when we come here?"

Turning my focus to Luke, I waited for him to continue.

"Even with the Treaty of Otherworlds, the human and animal ethics laws still don't prevent this from happening again. Calin is protected as an animal, so he has some rights, but not as a human being. De Sangs are not classified as living beings, so we have the same rights as a corpse."

"In the human world, but only if we are discovered by the right authorities."

"Yes, by the human government. This place always reminds me what they are capable of."

"That's what Kendrick wanted."

"Gentlemen, your table is ready."

Standing to follow the Hostess into the private dining area, which formerly served as cells, I looked around for any sign of a lurker, but there were just the regular patrons.

The rule with the Dungeon was that all meals must be aware and consenting. For this reason, humans were rare to have on a menu. For predators, it was also a case of the price. Why pay a fortune for a meal you can get for free at the local nightclub?

Since the Dungeon's appeal wasn't the atmosphere—unless the screams of tortured souls were your thing. Those who it was usually just booked a seat at the bar—Kendrick started preparing his food in a unique way to entice predators to his restaurant.

A week of pure organic foods, orgasms three times a day, and only water or the best wine could be consumed by the de Sang menu items. For the Changeurs, it was the most tender, organically farmed, and grass and clover fed animals that you could get. Always raw or cooked to the customer's liking. Even syphons could feed here, as long as everyone followed one rule. No harm and no killing.

"Gentlemen," the waitress paused at an open doorway.

Stepping in, we found ourselves in a small room. On a chaise sofa along the far wall sat a stunning blonde with legs that went forever and a day. On the adjacent wall was a claw foot bath, half full and currently occupied by a petite blonde I already recognized as my elemental.

"Enjoy your meal. Please ring the bell if you require anything." Closing the door, the waitress left, us to it.

The blonde on the chase frowned. "Three of you, but only two of us?"

Slipping out of his jacket, Luke sauntered toward her. "They are sharing. You are all mine."

Taking Luke in, the Changeur smiled and untied her robe. "Lucky me!"

As Luke hoisted her up and laid her back on the chaise, I took a seat in the reading chair in the corner by the door.

"Your bath looks relaxing. May I join you?" Calin asked the elemental.

"What's he going to do?"

"He's going to watch until it's time to feed." Toeing off his shoes, Calin unbuttoned his shirt.

The elemental watched, her lip catching in her teeth as she admired his body. "I've never been with a Changeur. Do you bite?"

"Only my wives."

"Wives? Plural?"

"Plural."

"They don't mind sharing?"

"As long as I don't leave them wanting, they don't mind me dating. Don't worry, I have the stamina."

"Wow!"

Pushing his pants to the ground, Calin climbed into the tub. The elemental's focus got caught on Calin's pride and widened. Her mouth fell open as she repeated her last word.

Taking out my phone as Calin sank into the bath, I checked my emails while my dinner was warmed up. Then, fire swept through my veins out of nowhere, and a sweat broke out on my brow. My phone fell to the ground as a scream echoed in my head.

Without thinking, I dropped my shields, tasted the power assaulting me from afar, traced it, and my heart stammered. "Spec!"

"Bay!" Calin called in alarm.

White light surrounded the fire, and then a pulse of...

"Bay!" Calin's voice freed me from the chaos.

In the bath, Calin used his body to shield the elemental, gritting his teeth as he called my name.

Throwing my shields up, I searched the floor for my phone while the others recovered.

"What happened?" Luke asked as he checked on the unconscious Changeur.

"Spectra was attacked."

"Are you sure she didn't just get hurt at training again?"

Yesterday, I'd felt her pain, but it was short-lived, and when I messaged Mathew, he came straight back with reassurances that Spectra was safe, just training.

"I know Alexander's power when I feel it."

Dialing Mercury on my phone, I waited, growing annoyed when the phone rang out.

Taking it away from my ear, I checked the messages between Spec and me earlier today.

BAY

What are the plans today?

SPECTRA:

When Merc wakes, we are going to confession.

BAY

I don't think Mathew really wants to hear about what you are doing with your husbands.

SPECTRA

Not for that!

BAY

Plans for the rest of the evening?

SPECTRA

After confession, we will meet Calin and his
wives at Merc's club and then dance at
Ténèbres.

BAY

I should be there by one. Wait for me. Don't
leave until I get there.

Other than agreeing, there hadn't been anything since. Trying Spectra on her cell and waiting for it to ring out, I tried Mercury again. Finally, he answered.

"Bay."

"What happened?"

"Alexander showed up and tried to talk to Spec. When she refused to go with him, things got volatile. Spec is okay; she's just a bit shaken."

"Put her on the phone."

Waiting a moment, I listened as Mercury gave Spec the phone, but it took another few seconds before she spoke.

"Bay. I'm okay. I'm sorry, I just-"

"What happened?"

"I made a scene. There were witnesses, and we sort of trashed the church. I'll have to help clean up before we can meet the others. Can you let them know we are running late?"

"Where is Alexander?"

"I don't know. Mathew was dealing with him."

"That isn't a safe place for you anymore."

Over the phone, Spectra sighed, her voice softening in defeat. "I know. Can we discuss this tonight? I need to help Merc clean up my mess."

"You're sure you're okay?"

"Yes. Just a bit jittery."

There was more to it, but I wasn't going to press it over the phone. Tonight though, we'd be talking about what just happened. Hopefully, it wouldn't finish with me needing to hunt and kill her ex.

"Bay, I still need to go to church."

"We'll talk tonight." Hanging up, I had to resist stepping through the ether to reach her, to steal her away from the pain I could hear in her voice.

"Everything okay?" Calin asked, standing with a towel around his waist.

"Do we need to go?" Luke followed.

"No. We'll finish our meal. There's no urgency there."

Giving me a nod, Luke returned to seducing his meal. Calin stood watching me another moment.

"I'm going to step outside for some air."

The Hostess who escorted us earlier was pinned against the wall by a fit-looking redhead in the hallway. The waitress' knee hooked over the redhead's black miniskirt clad hip, and the redhead worked the woman to a quick orgasm.

While it didn't do anything for me, I knew that all Dungeon staff were off-limits. But, before I could say anything, the Hostess was coming, and the redhead sank her fangs into her neck.

"Hey, wait!"

A glint of silver was all I caught before the redhead jammed a dagger beneath the Hostess' ribs. The woman cried out and tried to fight, but the redhead was quick. She spun as she pulled the blade free, the steel glinting in the low light and the waitress's head separating from her body to land with a thunk on the stone floor.

Emerald green eyes shined out at me as the redhead met my eyes. "Essence scum," Miranda huffed as she wiped her blade clean and eased it back into her minimal clothing. The hint of a cloaking spell was the only warning she was probably armed to the teeth. "I hope you didn't eat anything she served up?"

Turning, I threw open the door to the room. "Stop!"

For the second time tonight, my best friends were interrupted by my sudden outburst.

"Let's go. Now!"

Not even hesitating, Calin was out of the bath. The elemental still blinking and confused. The Changeur with Luke was faster to react, and as Luke stepped away, she shifted her arm and attempted to go for Luke's heart.

Unfortunately for the Changeur, Luke was an absolute scrapper before becoming the refined academic he is now. She was thrown across the room and landed in a heap a second later. Shrinking into her bath, the elemental whimpered.

"What's happening?" Calin asked, his eyes wide.

"Essence plants," I answered Calin as he dressed.

"Do we know what they wanted?" Luke growled.

"Should we ask the one still breathing?" Calin indicated the elemental. All eyes turned to the petite blonde.

Shrinking lower, the elemental had almost submerged herself in the water when Miranda's pale hand grabbed her around the throat and threw her onto the love seat.

"Wait, aren't you that-" Luke's eyes widened.

"Assassin," Calin finished.

"She's also the only reason we still have Spectra, Luke," I reminded.

"I'm also the only reason you still have your librarian friend," Miranda smiled coyly as she addressed me. "Do you want to do the honors? She was meant to be your dinner after all."

"Is she safe to drink?" I stepped forward.

"This one, yes. She'd be dead if Essence gave her anything dangerous to you. Plus, you weren't their target tonight."

"Why are they trying to kill me?" Luke asked, insulted.

Sitting beside the trembling elemental, I caressed her cheek. "Let's find out, shall we?"

Firming my hand on her neck, I pulled her close, kissed her pulse, then sank into her. Images and words flashed behind my eyes as her blood flowed.

Taking enough to feed before pulling away, I licked my lips and eased her to lie back on the chaise, her eyes fluttering, barely conscious.

"They wanted me to know they can get to me if they want to." Sighing, I stood up. "It wasn't just Luke. She was going to drown Calin while I fed. Only I was meant to survive this meal. Eyes lifting to Miranda, I raised a brow. "How did you know?'

"Oh, I didn't. I was sent to meet with you. Kendrick and I have history. So it was weird he hadn't answered my calls to get access. Then, when I got here, the Hostess avoided giving me a straight answer to his whereabouts, so I fucked her to get the truth."

"Which is?"

"Essence killed Kendrick the same way they planned to kill Luke. Tainted food. They wanted the diet under their control, and Kendrick wouldn't join their cause. The Hostess was willing to betray her own kind for Essence. She took over the run of the place and made everyone think Kendrick was still the man."

"Damn, Kendrick was a long-time friend."

Miranda stayed silent, her red lips drawn into a thin line. Emotion lurked in the depth of her eyes, but she didn't voice what Kendrick's death meant to her. He could have been a mentor, the de Sang who took her, or even a lover. Whatever it was, the discovery of his demise caused this kickass assassin to feel emotions.

While I would miss a friend, the downside to immortality is that death becomes a ritual; the loss is no longer substantial, and being alone is expected. Except now, after so long, there was Spectra.

"Should we go to the bar to talk?" I suggested.

"Not here. I don't relax in this place. Plus, I need to get some scouting done tonight. There's a quaint little human pub not far from your place."

"That almost sounds like a pickup line."

"You're married, and while that wouldn't necessarily stop me, it does when who your wife is comes into consideration."

"Your protection is more than just keeping her alive."

Shifting her weight. Miranda considered me. "Bay, Spectra is dead. She's a vengeful spirit trapped here for eternity in her living form. Had she been able to take her vengeance, she could have returned, but she can't. So our involvement has never been about keeping her alive. Our job is to keep Spectra as she is because the alternative is fucking horrifying. Now, I have some things to do here first. I'll meet you at the pub in thirty minutes. We can discuss how we are willing to help when I get there."

Following Miranda's eyes to the elemental, I understood her

meaning. The woman worked for Essence, and she'd heard too much as it was. She wouldn't be walking out of here alive.

"Can I order you a wine?" I asked, straightening the cuffs of my suit jacket.

"Beer. I like a good beer."

# CHAPTER 21

# SPECTRA

Reins de Tombées was packed by the time Mercury and I arrived. Calin and his wives stood against the wall outside, looking rather annoyed.

"Finally," Gina growled. "They won't let us in."

Letting go of my hand, Mercury nodded. "I'll take care of it."

While Mercury cleared the de Viands to come inside, Calin pulled me into a hug. "Are you okay? Bay said Alexander hurt you!"

Suddenly overcome, I clung to Calin and hid my face against his chest. There was no telling him I was okay because I wasn't. The people I once trusted most were now the last people I could turn to. Well, maybe not the last, but the distinction between the Williamses and any other Nachtwelt citizen no longer existed.

"Spectra?" Calin worried. After a moment, he held me tighter and rubbed my back.

A year ago, I'd been certain who was good and evil, right and wrong, but from the moment Bay Ryder entered my life, it had all turned on its head.

I was married to two men, one an Angelis and the other everything I'd hated. I lived in a house full of predators, shared my bed and body with one, trusted another to keep me safe, and had come to look at the man who held me like a kind-of brother.

"Spec," Mercury's voice was low as he placed his hand on my neck and turned me from Calin's chest to his own. "Shh, I know!" Then, slowly tilting my face up, Mercury met my eyes. "Let's go inside. Food will do you good."

Taking the hankie Merc offered, I cleaned up my face as best I could. Inside, we passed the dance floor to the restaurant stairs. Unlike when I brought Bay here, we were taken straight to our table away from the window.

The Changeurs were the talk of the gossip vine as we passed, many unhappy that Mercury would let them into their sanctuary. First, I'd brought a de Sang, now de Viands. Could I sink any lower?

"I think we've really pissed off your clientele," Calin muttered to Mercury as we took our seats.

"They'll get over it. Just don't go telling your friends about it."

"Seriously? I'd already posted it to my social media account."

Smirking, Mercury crooked his finger, and a waiter came running. "Entrees. Four of everything. We need tea, Spectra needs coke, I need vodka, and whatever the Changeurs want. Spectra is also going to need sweet corn soup and orange juice. Start with that. We'll order mains once entrees arrive."

"Yes, Sir." The waiter took the drink orders for everyone and ran.

"Why are you ordering for Spectra?" Gina glared.

"She needs food to recover from Alexander's attack, or her body goes into shock. So if she uses her abilities, make sure she eats. It won't stop the aftershock, but it should minimize it. The more power, the more food she'll need."

"I'm not even hungry," I grumbled. "Just tired."

"You need energy," Mercury firmed his voice.

Knowing better than to argue, I rested my head on his shoulder. "Fine."

"Ah, ah, no going to sleep. Eat first." Shifting his shoulder from beneath my head, Mercury made me keep myself upright.

"Meanie."

"Would you prefer another hospital visit?" When I hissed at him, Mercury put his arms around my shoulder and his mouth to my ear. "If you're struggling, do something to keep you awake."

When I turned to look at Mercury, his eyebrow jumped several times.

Shaking my head at his smirk, I elbowed him playfully. "We have guests."

"We can entertain ourselves if you two need to do the honeymoon thing and find the coat closet," Calin offered cheekily. "It's not like we haven't been newlyweds before." Calin's wives snickered.

Plates of food slid on the table. Clicking his fingers, Mercury mock pouted. "Saved by the food, Spec." Putting a plate directly in front of me, Mercury kissed my cheek. "Eat."

Suddenly ravenous, I picked up my chopsticks and dug in. After a few mouthfuls, I realized Mercury was right. I was starving and thirsty. I all but skulled the coke, and after another plate of mixed entrees, the orange juice disappeared too.

Even after the main meal, which would have filled Calin, I was still hungry. For every cup of water I drank, Mercury would refill my glass until I crawled over him to get out of our booth and raced to the toilet, unsure if my bladder would burst or I'd puke first.

"Spec? Are you okay?" Gina called from outside the toilet cubicle.

"Yeah," I groaned.

"Left it too long?" Gina asked with a chuckle.

"Nearly." Honestly, I hadn't noticed the need until it became desperate. Still, I always felt disconnected from my body after using my power. Mathew said it was my Wraith existence that caused it. That I threw my soul out of my body whenever I powered up. Whatever that meant.

Making my way out to the sink, I washed my hands and gazed at myself in the mirror. Black circles were deep under my eyes. "Argh. I look like I'm dead."

Turning to consider my reflection, Gina tilted her head. "I mean, you are, but the lighting in here makes it look worse than it is. You do look like a week's sleep would be beneficial, though. Maybe get the guys to give training a rest for the remainder of the week. Let you recover properly."

"I start my trial at Galaxy next week. I'll have less time to train, and Mathew wants me to have the basics honed by then." Wiping my hands on a paper towel, I winced at how tender my wrists still were. "If I have to do anymore figure eights with a stick, I'll be limp-wristed by next week."

Gina dried her hands with a smirk, and we returned to the restaurant.

"Spectra?" A tall, beautiful brunette stepped in front of me. Her eyes were round, as if she was surprised to see me.

"Raquel," I forced a polite smile for Alexander's girlfriend.

"Are you okay? You don't look well," Raquel continued as if we were friends. When she tried to touch me, a growl alerted her to Gina's presence behind me, causing Raquel to snap her hand back to herself and look between us.

"I never took you to be the kind to hang with de Viands."

"Gina was my maid of honor at my wedding. Her husband Calin was Merc's best man," I gave the most straightforward explanation.

"Calin Abernathy?"

"Yes. Do you know him?" I moved a step closer, to which Raquel backed up and side-stepped out of my way.

"By name only." Raquel gave me a forced smile. Her eyes flicked between Gina and me before settling back on me. "I didn't realize you and Merc had married?"

"Last week," I answered, offering the least amount of information possible. "We're having dinner to celebrate tonight with our bridal party." I indicated to the table where Mercury was watching us with narrowed eyes.

Raquel glanced at our table and swallowed visibly at the shade Mercury was throwing her, but the smile on her face seemed more genuine now. "How lovely. I heard there was some kafuffle at the convent last week. I hope everyone is okay?"

Gina growled close to my shoulder, but I ignored her in favor of studying Raquel. She held her clutch tight in her hands, tiny beads of sweat dotted her hairline, and her shoulders and jaw were tense.

"Unfortunately, no. A de Sang attacked us. One of the sisters was murdered, and I barely escaped alive."

Raquel's jaw fell open, and the blood drained from her face. "He tried to kill you?"

"The de Sang apparently has a penchant for taking women of a certain appearance. Bay Ryder told me he was a collector. If it wasn't for Bay, Calin, and Mercury, I'd likely be in a terrible place right now."

"Spectra, I'm so sorry. I know how you feel about their kind. That must have been... no wonder you look so drawn."

"Ladies," Mercury interrupted. "Everything okay here?"

"Yes. Raquel was just asking about the attack at the convent last week," I informed Mercury, leaning into him as he slipped his arm around my waist protectively.

"It sounded truly terrible. De Sangs know no bounds, do they?"

"I wouldn't blame all de Sangs for the whim of a few fanatics, Raquel," Mercury responded. "There are those who desire power at the loss of their morals in all species. Even the Celestials aren't immune. Just take your grandfather, for instance."

Pursing her lips, Raquel looked like she'd sucked on a sour lemon. "A valid point."

"Anyway. We should get back to our guests," Mercury excused, using his arm around my waist to turn our backs to Raquel and walk away. Halfway back to our table, Mercury glanced over his shoulder. "Apple doesn't fall far from the tree with that one."

"She was surprised to see Spectra here," Gina offered. "I don't think they told her it all went wrong."

"By the look on her face when I told her I was nearly taken, she didn't know what they planned past abducting me to work for them. So she might rethink trusting that alliance again."

"Or at least handing one of her own over to them without being sure what they planned first," Gina said.

"I doubt it." Mercury stopped by our table, turning his head, so his eyes followed Raquel to the stairs down to the dance floor. "You were more than a hacker, Spec. You're a threat to her future plans to be Alexander's bride."

Scoffing, I dropped back into my seat. "Well, she knows we are married now. Hopefully, that puts her concerns at ease."

Mercury exchanged a look with Calin as he slid into his seat beside me. Deciding not to read into it, I picked up my full glass and chugged the water again.

"So, are we going to go dancing now?" Cynthia chirped.

"Not here," Mercury answered, checking his watch and gesturing to our waiter to bring the bill. "I'll see you to Ténèbres, and then I need to head to work."

"Oh, we're going to the goth club?" Bronwyn asked.

"Hence why I told you to wear all black," Gina chuckled. "What, did you think we were going on a mission on the way home?"

Lifting a shoulder, Bronwyn sucked her straw until the glass was dry. "We're here as Spec's muscle tonight, so black made sense."

"You're not my bodyguards," I argued. "We're here as friends and... family?" I hesitated over the last, eyeing Gina before looking to Mercury.

Giving me an easy smile, Mercury wrapped an arm around my shoulders and hugged me to his side, placing a kiss on my head. Sinking into him, I sighed, loving the warmth of being in his arms.

The waiter placed the bill on the table. After a small discussion where Calin offered to pay, Mercury refused, then signed it before standing.

"Let's get you girls to your next port of call so you can start dancing up a storm."

Taking my hand, Mercury helped me out of the booth and led the way out. We walked the ten minutes towards the harbor where Ténèbres was located near the old warehouse district.

Leading us inside, Mercury saw me to the bar where Tommy was serving. His eyes came to us, and his brow lifted when Mercury knocked his knuckles on the counter to get his attention. Grabbing a bottle of water, Tommy placed it in front of me without asking, studying my eyes.

"Drink that. You're still depleted," Tommy instructed, then turned his gaze on Mercury.

"You heard about the church today?" Mercury asked.

"Amongst other things." Tommy widened his stance and crossed his arms. "She's safe here, Raphi. I won't let anyone harm your wife. Congrats, by the way."

"How far has the news travelled?" Mercury huffed.

"He knows. He's pissed. Don't be surprised if he comes for her anyway."

Huffing out a laugh, Mercury rapped his knuckles on the bar again. "That's what we're hoping for. Give me a heads up if you see him coming?"

"That's not my job, but I'll see what I can do," Tommy assured.

"Should I know who we are talking about?" I asked before finishing my water.

Pulling me close, Mercury cupped my face. "We'll talk about it later. It's not important tonight." Turning to Tommy, Mercury slid a few notes across the bar to him. "Keep her safe until Ryder gets here. I have to go to work. This should cover anything she needs tonight. Call me if she drops."

Lifting his pierced eyebrow, Tommy's pale blue eyes came to me as he took the money. Swallowing, I nodded. The side of Tommy's mouth lifted before he gave Mercury a confirmation and turned back to his paying customers.

Caressing my jaw, Mercury stared into my eyes. "Don't leave with anyone but Ryder, Spec."

"I won't."

Mercury's lips brushed mine, once, twice, and then he stole my breath in the sweetest kiss, which ended too quickly. When I opened my eyes, Mercury was chuckling. "It's been a long time since you disappeared on me from a kiss, Spec."

*Oh.*

Breathing in, I checked around me as I did to see if anyone saw me suddenly fade in. My cheeks heated at the laughter in Mercury's eyes.

"Sorry." Tucking my long, dark hair behind my ear, I laughed a little too.

Shaking his head, Mercury threaded his fingers into my hair to hold my head, then pressed his mouth to mine quickly. "Enjoy your night out. I'll see you tomorrow. Love you."

I felt those words all the way to my core. "Love you."

One last kiss, and then I watched Mercury take one step and disappear. I seriously needed to learn how to travel the ether like that.

A presence beside me drew my attention to a smirking Calin leaning against the bar watching his wives on the dance floor. "You two can be really intense. Have you always been like that?"

Thinking about it, I nodded as I finished my water and put the empty on the bar.

Calin chuckled quietly. Lifting his bottle of beer to his lips, he paused. "The sex must be mind-blowing."

Heat rushed through my veins at the vivid recall of how hot things could get with Mercury. It must have shown because Calin watched me a moment, then gave me a saucy wink and turned his eyes to his wives. Though, I noted the way he somehow took in the entire room at the same time.

Tingles broke out in my extremities. Frowning, I turned my gaze to my hands and wiggled my toes in my boots. "Weird."

"What?" Calin was suddenly standing straight next to me, eyes scanning the room.

"I feel like I just put my hands and feet into a bath with lemonade fizzing all around them," I answered honestly. The sensation crept up my legs and arms towards my torso.

"Like a bad fizz?"

"No, it's..." The tingles rushed over my entire body all of a sudden. My nipples hardened, and my sex clenched and became slick. "Oh!"

It was like an entire post-orgasmic high. As if I'd just had the best sex of my life, but instead of coming down from the high, it just kept getting better.

"Oh?" Calin was still looking around for a threat.

"Oh, yeah!" I moaned as the room washed away, and there was just this incredible energy crawling over my skin and the music playing through the club. The vibrations thrummed through my body, making me move to the beat, winding my hips and body. The more I danced, the better I felt.

I was vaguely aware of a presence on the other end of the sensation. Of chanting underlying the pounding beats in the club. Swinging my body in time with the music, I danced out to join the crowd of revellers. I basked in their energy, drawing it into me, building the euphoria, and giving it and myself over to the presence demanding it.

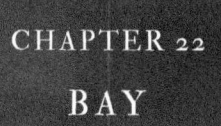

## CHAPTER 22

## BAY

SITTING DOWN OPPOSITE ME, the red-headed assassin beauty picked up the pint of beer I'd ordered for her and skulled it while she got comfortable. Once it was empty, she placed the glass, licked the head off her top lip, and gained the server's attention to order two more.

"Is the way you swallowed that beer an indication of how your night is going or preparation for dealing with me?"

"The former," Miranda answered before chugging the second beer as it was placed in front of her.

Even the server lifted a brow before turning to me and asking with her eyes if I needed a refill. I declined. Alcohol and high magic never mixed well.

Placing the second empty on the table for the server to collect, Miranda settled back in her seat and took the third beer in hand but didn't lift it to drink. Instead, Miranda waited for the server to clear off before talking.

"Spec is a homebody. Your only real risk is in her traveling to and from the Watcher's bar, or when she starts her new job," Miranda stated. "Eventually, the travel won't be an issue if she can learn to walk between the here and now like all Celestial descendants can. So we will leave her travel and safety at home in your hands. We'll take the new job."

Intrigued by how quickly they'd deduced a plan, I sat back and crossed my arms over my chest. "How?"

"Spectra already knows me and is comfortable with me. So, I'll be planted in her new workplace as a colleague. I'll share the cubicle with her and eat lunch with her. Hell, we might even carpool to remove one less item from your list of protection duties."

"You can pull that off?"

Miranda smirked. "I got into Pendant, didn't I?"

When I failed to be thrilled with that reminder, Miranda opened her purse and threw a Galaxy lanyard and staff swipe card on the table. Picking it up, it had Miranda's photo and name on the card.

"I'm in already. Don't fret." Sitting back, Miranda took a few large mouthfuls of her beer.

"It's a concern how quickly and easily your lot can infiltrate what others consider a secure location."

Shrugging a shoulder, Miranda just took another drink.

"So that is your addition to Spectra's security. You'll watch her at work and drive her to and from?"

"Yes. We can renegotiate if and when it's needed. But for now, that is all we feel is needed."

"How do I contact you?"

Finishing her beer, Miranda sat forward as she placed the glass down. "You don't. We don't work for you. But." Miranda put a card on the table. It was blank except for one of those modern QR codes. In the center was a lily, like the one tattooed on Miranda's wrist.

"If you have a question or problem pertaining to Spectra, you can leave a message using that. Don't expect a return call, so make sure the message is detailed. We'll action on our end as we feel is needed."

Miranda got up from the table and headed to the bathroom without even a goodbye. I doubted she'd reappear, and I still had work to do before I went to collect Spectra and paid the Watcher our debt.

STANDING BAREFOOT, I STARTED TO DRAW IN THE MAGIC, PULLING into my toes and fingers and slowly into my body. I didn't take it too quickly; otherwise, the violence of my absorption could cause a backlash.

Over the years, I had perfected the drawing up of magic to exactly its purpose. I knew that if I needed a small amount of magic, I just had to fill my hands. If I required more, then I would fill my extremities. More still? Limbs and torso. But for casting high magic like today, it would be a whole body experience, all the way to the head, giving me a euphoric feeling at the end of it. It's why high magics became addictive for wielders and could lead to corruption.

As the magic filled my body, I felt like I had never before. Almost as if it was being echoed throughout my body.

Filling my entire body with the magic, I held on to it. Letting it build. Allowing it to become what I needed it to become. In the circle before me, I had samples of hair from everyone who had permission to step onto the property. All of the family. All of the pride. Spectra, Mercury, and all of our guards. In a bowl beside that was the blood of one of the Nachtwelt that I would need to help activate the spell. They had to be unwilling, and not one of the bodies permitted entry. Luckily, I had a vault with several Nachtwelt I was keeping captive.

Once my body was full to the brim with the power I needed, I focused on building the protection spell. I imagined the boundary clicking into place like a dome over my property. But it wasn't just going to be a shield. This needed to be more. It needed something that could stand even if the safeguard was taken down.

When this spell was finished, a barely-visible mist would seep through the property seeking out any who passed through, making sure that they belonged. And if someone didn't, it would slow the intruder down. It would give us time to react before they were on us.

Once I had built the protection spell to what I wanted, I opened my arms up to the ceiling and let it out. The room lit up with a flash of light, and then a thrumming pulsed around the magic circle as the dome shield encompassed the property. The invisible mist slowly bled from the house into the surrounding forest.

The magic dropped from my body. A sudden emptiness, but the euphoria caused by the high endorphins still fizzed against my skin, and my cock stood tall and stiff.

With the magic-fade came the echo again. As if the magic euphoria was felt elsewhere by many. I could feel Spectra tethered to me by our bond, and I wondered if she'd felt the magic even that far away. If our bond somehow brought her into the spell without me knowing it? It would be a question I could ask later when I saw her again. For now, I had to clean up, get dressed, and go find my wife.

FORTY MINUTES LATER, I SCANNED THE CLUB AS I CROSSED TO THE bar. There was an energy about the place tonight that was uplifting but unsettling. Narrowing my gaze, I focused on finding Spectra. The sense of her bounced all over the club, like every breath she took created an echo making it impossible to locate her that way.

Turning my gaze into the small group of writhing bodies, I only found Spectra by looking for Calin's wives' blonde hair. But once I saw her, I wondered how she didn't have my attention when I walked inside.

Dancing dead center in the middle of the floor, Spectra was a sight to behold. The sleeveless black velvet longline dress hugged her body until it flared at her hips. Swishing around those slender pale thighs in time to the heavy beat of the music. Perspiration glistened on her skin, and her eyes shone as the club lights bounced off them.

My wife was mesmerizing. The club lights reflected off her skin as if they came from her. I stood there watching her, my skin tingling with her presence as if I was still beneath the oculus with the lingering touch of magic flowing around me.

"She's been dancing for hours now."

Turning my head, surprised that someone had sidled up to me without my knowledge, I noted Calin, then quickly scanned the rest of the club again. Lots of female and a few male eyes were on me in a way that should have made me blush. I'd dressed down for the club, so I could fit in.

Calin turned his head to the dance floor and jutted his chin. "We were standing and talking, then she mentioned a fizzing sensation before sashaying out onto the dance floor and losing herself to the music. The entire club was caught up in whatever it was with her for a while. We were all high from the dancing. Tommy was the only one immune."

My eyes went back to Spectra. "I felt her when I was casting. I must have sucked her into it."

"Well, Spec hasn't stopped. Everyone else got free of it but her, though Tommy thinks at this point, she is just burning off whatever happened at the church today. He's been making me take Spec bottles of water twice every hour. He said it's important to keep her hydrated, or the power drop will worsen."

"Power drop?"

"Tommy likened it to sub-drop."

"From the endorphin high. Sorcerers and witches get it too, but we call it magic-fade. It makes sense the half-breed Celestials suffer it too." Glancing at Tommy, I gave him a nod which he returned before he went back to serving.

"Do you constantly feel like these angels' bastards keep important information from you?" Calin asked.

"Yes." But I wouldn't care what they thought they were keeping from me if it didn't potentially impact my wife. She was the only unknown in every scenario I ran.

"I like Mercury. But I worry the secrets he's keeping will put us in danger or worse, her." Calin's eyes moved from Spectra to mine. "My wives are warriors. We can all take care of ourselves. Your wife is the most vulnerable out of us."

"Only until she's trained. Then, she will be the most dangerous in our house."

Huffing, Calin finished his drink. "As long as she doesn't become a danger to us." Turning, Calin headed back to the bar.

Striding into the crowd, I made it to Spectra without issue and took her hand in mine. The sensation of our contact passed through me, my dick growing hard with the same need I'd had for this woman since we met.

Spectra's eyes cleared, her focus falling entirely on me, bringing her back from wherever the magic I'd called had taken her. "We have a business deal to uphold," I reminded the beauty before me.

I wanted to take her in my arms and kiss her with all the longing riding my body, but for her safety, the world should see us as a work arrangement, maybe friends.

Dragging Spectra away from the dance floor, her practical boots making it easy for her to keep stride, I headed towards the bar. Still meters from it, I held up the key Spectra had given me the night of our second date. Meeting my eyes, Tommy tilted his head to the end of the bar and a door signed as staff only.

Changing direction, I pushed through the door and waited for it to close behind Spec. Further down the hallway was another entry marked 'Private.' Taking the key, I unlocked the door and entered what appeared to be Tommy's subterranean apartment.

Lightwells running along the street side of the open living area made the entire space visible. It was luxurious and opulent. Leather furnishings in dark shades, parquetry floors, and the black kitchen cabinetry with a wine-red herringbone butcher block for the counter.

Off the living area was an indoor enclosure. Walking to the open stacker doors of the courtyard, Spectra admired the wall of plants, the fountain in the center, and the small seating area amongst the flowering garden beds. There was a high peaked glass roof over the area protecting it, so that despite it being the depth of winter, and pouring rain outside, nothing about the space felt cold.

When Spectra moved through the doors on the other side of the courtyard, I followed and found myself standing in a master bedroom. The king-sized bed was on a small dais with a leather headboard and wine-colored coverings. There was a luxurious bath-room off to one side, a cozy sitting chair beside a cigar table in the corner, which had a perfect view of the bed.

Stopping at the foot of the bed, Spectra turned to face me. Her nervousness was evident in how she fidgeted as she glanced around the room. Finally having her alone, I caressed her cheek, bringing her focus to me, and dropped my mouth to hers.

"Don't we have to wait?" Spectra whispered a breath from connecting.

"Did he specify he had to be in the room while we were together in the original deal?"

Shaking her head, Spectra licked her lips. "Just that we spend a night in his bed together."

"Then I think we're covered. Tommy may not need to be present to watch, or maybe he just wants the smell of us on his sheets."

Or he had a camera in here, but that wouldn't make Spectra relax, so I wasn't going to mention that possibility.

The side of Spectra's mouth lifted. "The feel of you doing magic was post-orgasmic bliss. You don't have to send me away next time."

Cupping her cheek, I kissed her heatedly. The idea of being able to cast and then head straight out to my room and make love to my wife affected me the same way as Spectra playing with my balls. Damn, my lust for her was all-encompassing. The moment I thought of her, I needed to be inside her.

"I've been hard for you since I saw you dancing," I murmured as the straining bulge in my pants pressed against her.

Catching her lip between her teeth, Spectra swept her hands up my body to grab my collar. "Bay, I need you."

*Thank the gods!*

# CHAPTER 23

# SPECTRA

OUR MOUTHS COLLIDED in wanton need. Pleasure, love, and lust radiated through me, opening my pores, relaxing my muscles, easing my anxiety until the where and why didn't matter. I was with Bay; that was all that was important.

Wrapping my arms around Bay's neck, I pushed up on my toes to deepen the kiss. Gripping my ass, Bay tugged me tight to the front of him, grinding the hardness of his desire against me, causing my back to arch and our mouths to break apart as I gasped for breath.

Bay's lips found mine again as his hand swept under my dress, and his fingers delved into my scanties, finding my clit and pressing hard against it. The latent fizz of Bay's magic grew again in my fingers and toes, making me moan as it reached to join Bay's fingers. Wetness flooded my core. The sound of Bay's fingers moving through my slickness reached my ears in the silence of this space.

A grin filled Bay's face when he pulled back. Nipping at my neck, he turned me to face the bed and used his hands to bend me over until my palms were resting on the mattress. Kneeling behind me, Bay ran his hands up the back of my thighs, circling my rump before caressing back down and over my calves.

Unzipping my boots, Bay eased my feet out one at a time, sliding his fingers down over the back of my ankle to remove the socks. Once I was barefoot, Bay slowly massaged up again. The tingles of skin-to-skin contact raced along my nervous system, firing signals that melted my body and mind.

When Bay flipped my dress up to pool around my waist, I had no doubt the effect he had on me was evident in the dampness of the gusset of my black lace scanties. The press of his thumb to the soaked material covering me, landing right where my entrance would be as he applied pressure, had me squirming and moaning. My sex clenched, the lingering tingle of his magic reaching me there and almost making my knees collapse.

"Your body is my heaven. The beat of your heart, my reason for being. Your eyes are my world. I have waited a long time for you, and now that you are mine, I can't deny my need for you."

"I don't want you to," I whispered back, grinding over his thumb, yearning to have him inside me.

"I'm not going to hold back, Spec. Tell me now if you can't take it because I won't stop once I let go."

Moaning in need, I was sure my wetness was answer enough. Still, I twisted my body to meet Bay's bright blue eyes, the dilated pupils thrumming with his energy and need. The look in his eyes, the way his magic tickled beneath my skin, was a warning that this was more than just a sorcerer and his balance making love. Still, my brain was too hazed to understand.

"I love you, Bay. Whatever you need, I'll give you."

A gasp escaped my lips as he yanked my knickers down my legs. My back arched, pushing my sex back to meet him, and my hands fisted into the bedding as his hungry mouth latched onto me, sucking and licking me in a frenzy. I cried out from the over-whelming sensation and surrendered to his power.

Caressing his hand over my smooth rump, Bay squeezed it in a way that tilted my pelvis automatically to expose me further to him. It was getting harder to keep my legs under me as Bay's hunger assaulted my clit, driving me quickly to the pinnacle of pleasure. He placed the pad of a thumb against my heat. He didn't push in, just covered my entrance and applied intermittent pressure.

It took seconds until I was cursing, my knees buckling, but Bay used his spare hand to hold me up. I'd forgotten how strong de Sangs were until he held me effortlessly in place with that single hand. Usually, that would strike fear in my heart. But tonight, it only added to whatever wanton need was passing between us.

Despite it being winter and rain pouring down outside, it felt like the middle of summer. Kisses, sucks, nibbles, bites, and Bay touching my flesh. I couldn't stay still in his hold as the itch and need for him reached its breaking point, and I prayed loudly to Bay and God as I fell apart in his grasp.

Easing me onto the bed, Bay rose to his feet as I rolled to face him. Pure animalistic hunger looked back at me as Bay shoved his black jeans over his hips, boxers and all. The sight of him naked and hard made me lick my lips. Sitting up as Bay moved towards me, I rose to meet him, then I was in his arms, legs wrapped around his waist as he carried me to the middle of the bed and dropped to his knees.

His kisses fed me, heating me from the inside out. "So, beautiful," Bay muttered as he yanked the straps from my shoulder and tugged the material covering my chest out of his way. Dropping his head, Bay pressed into my spine to arch my body for him, making me moan again, and hug his head as his mouth latched over my nipple.

He did the same to the other side, holding me in his strong arms, rubbing my dripping sex against his rigid cock. My dress pooled at my waist as I begged Bay to do things I'd never given voice to before.

Groaning, Bay pitched forward, pinned me down as he settled his bodyweight between my thighs and slid the bulging slick dome of his cock between the folds of my sex. My nails gripped his biceps as Bay thrust into me, stealing my breath with a cry of surprise.

I was lost to our bodies moving together, to the hard thrusts of Bay's body, the bruising grip of his fingers as he held me where he wanted me. Our bodies were slick with sweat, our chests heaving and gasping for breath between lip locks. The fizz of his power encompassed me entirely now, inside and out.

I'd never felt this way. Staring up at the oculus and the stars in the sky overhead, it was like I was flying. Turning my head, the circle of magic we lay in glowed and danced around us. If it wasn't for me recognizing that it was Bay's power, I'd have probably freaked out. But as Bay slowed his thrusts, circling his hips to change the pleasure, all that mattered was the absolute rightness of being with him like this.

Bay's weight grinding me into the hard wooden floor was all that could hold me down. I felt the most alive I ever had. Sitting back on his ankles, Bay took me with him, hooked my knees over his elbows, opening me to him, finding the deepest part of me and claiming it as his. The position tilted my pelvis perfectly to meet his fast, forceful grind. Pain from his depth merged with the pleasure. My body clamped tight around him, and the glow of the magic circle filled my peripheral vision.

Bay cursed, grabbing my ass and raising it as he pounded my body. My eyes opened wide, my breath rushed out, and a long, tortured moan with it. The pain was barely noticeable while my entire being was encapsulated in being with Bay.

My body grew tighter with every thrust. The magic fizzed around me, causing sensory overload as lust flooded my core, and Bay filled me entirely. Then pleasure exploded outward, nerves firing, muscles tightening, air rushing from my lungs as I cried out in sweet agony.

Grimacing, Bay groaned loudly. He put all his strength into dragging out my pleasure before thrusting one last time, his cock swelling and throbbing as he unloaded his need and power inside me.

Magic swept around us like a cyclone, reaching up to the oculus. Then it speared into the sky, penetrating the dome of protection, adding to it, and reinforcing it. There was the heavy breathing of a third person, the grunt of their pleasure adding to the magic we created.

Closing my eyes, I moaned as Bay lifted me into his arms,

holding me against his chest, so I sat wrapped around him. He was still buried deep inside me when a mouth pinched mine. The strange sensation of metal brushed over my lips and clinked against my teeth. Bay tensed against me as a hand wrapped in my hair and forced the kiss deeper.

With a moan, they pulled away, and I opened my eyes to take in Tommy, shirtless, jeans open. His abs were coated with the pleasure of his massive spent cock, which was slowly relaxing.

"Magical," Tommy whispered before he gave me a naughty wink and moved into the bathroom.

"He watched us," I whispered as Bay relaxed but tightened his hold on me.

"He did." Bay kissed the length of my neck, making me moan as he pressed a firm hand up my spine, seeming to massage any remaining tension out of me as he did. I wonder how long he knew Tommy was there.

"Are you okay?" Bay asked quietly.

"I think so. It was very intense."

Bay kept touching me. Small intimate gestures of affection. "Did I hurt you?"

As my brain fog cleared, I could feel the slight twinges of my body where Bay went too deep and where his grip had bruised. It was nothing I wasn't used to. Mercury always left me a little tender afterward.

"Not in any way I didn't enjoy," I answered. "Just don't ask me to move or do anything for a little bit. I kind of feel like a rag doll. That was some heady sex. I totally spaced out and was seeing things."

Bay tensed. "What things?"

"A room full of magic. It had a circle on the timber floor and an oculus in the roof that the stars shined through."

Threading his fingers through my hair, Bay used it to help tilt my head back so he could see my eyes. His forehead bunched at whatever he saw, but Tommy was beside the bed before he could say anything, drawing our attention. Tommy looked the two of us over, a massive smile on his face as he rubbed his hands together.

"It appears you have the same recovery rate as us angels, Bay. So, shall we go again?"

"Spec needs a few minutes," Bay huffed. And he was worried about me, because I could feel he was ready to go again inside me.

Tommy's pale blue gaze came to me, and his pierced brow jumped. "Of course. First time exposed to magic and all that. I'll grab you some water, but I have a request. I'd like you to consider it while I do."

Bay's eyes dropped to Tommy's loose jeans. He'd tucked himself away, but it did little to hide his hard length. "You can't fuck my wife."

Tommy smirked. "That would be Spectra's decision and hers alone, but it is not what I'm requesting tonight. I'll keep my dick to myself, but I want to taste both of you."

"The both of us?" Bay blinked, seeming a bit lost. Admittedly, I was too.

"When you remove yourself from Spectra's body, your combined pleasure will seep out of her. I want the honor to lick her clean if you will. To taste the power of the two of you together."

Bay balked. "You want to..." Glancing at my wide-eyed gaze, then back to Tommy, Bay scoffed. "Are all Angelis kinky fucks?"

Tommy's lopsided grin spread across his face. "We are true to our natures. Observing is what I do best; I am usually satiated by that alone. But watching the two of you was..." Tommy sucked in a sharp breath, bit his lip, and ran his eyes over the two of us. "Hmmm, the sort of power you two have together would make anyone greedy for a taste."

"Greed corrupts," Bay warned.

Snorting a laugh, Tommy shook his head. "I am a creature born of the original magic, sorcerer. We cannot be corrupted. That is the balance of what we are." Eyes coming to me, Tommy reached out and caressed my face as he swept my hair back behind my ear. His fingers played the strands as he followed their length, the ease of his touch creating a yearning in me. "Angelis are not monogamous like humans. We can't be. Our natures demand that we give to receive and take to give. You understand, don't you, Spec?"

"Yes," I breathed. Because I did. Tommy's touch caused a similar sensation in me that Mercury healing me had. It was different, but in essence, the same.

Losing the cheeky smile, Tommy met my eyes with the most gentle expression I'd ever seen on him. "I'll get you some water while you discuss my request."

Waiting until Tommy crossed the courtyard, Bay met my eyes. "We agreed to a night in his bed. Did you ixnay his joining us when you agreed to the deal?"

Chewing my lip, I shook my head. Caressing Bay's face as he dropped it to my chest, I forced it back to meet mine. "This isn't about sex for him."

"I saw evidence to the contrary before he went to the bathroom."

Nodding, I ran my thumb along Bay's jaw. "When I first met Tommy, he recognized me immediately. If he wanted me, he's had years to come onto me, so I know this isn't about fucking me."

Tilting his head, Bay considered me. "You want to do it?"

Blinking, unsure if that's what this was, I couldn't deny there was an appetite in me to give Tommy what he required. Frowning, I played with that sensation and considered the mechanics and how it would play out in my head. If Tommy went down on me, Bay would have to watch it, and I don't know if that was fair on him. "Oh."

"Oh?"

"Mathew told me that there has been no female Angelis before now. Even female Nephilim are rare. So very few of the male Angelis have had the temptation of a balance in their beds."

"What does that mean?" Bay asked, loosening his grip on me.

"I don't know, and when I asked Mathew to explain, he said it's something Mercury should be present to discuss. It was right before I met with Henry, so the timing meant I couldn't push him on it, and we haven't circled back to it, but I think Tommy's request is connected to it. I think we overloaded him. By tasting me, you'll have to watch him with me, which will balance him," I explained.

"The temptation of a balance in their beds," Bay mused.

Shifting forward, Bay laid me on my back and hovered above me, staring into my eyes. "Actually, I think I understand exactly what Mathew meant."

The sound of Tommy placing glasses on the bedside table brought our attention to the side. Tommy stood there, looking gorgeous like all the other Angelis I'd laid eyes on.

"So, what was the decision?"

## CHAPTER 24

## BAY

C OMBING my fingers through Spectra's long hair, I watched her sleep soundly on my chest. It was already midday, but we only got home at sunrise, and we certainly didn't get any sleep last night at the watcher's. True to his word, Tommy kept his dick in his pants. He didn't even rub up against Spectra in a sexual way. Still, there was no missing how turned on he'd been either.

I was still processing my feelings about everything that happened last night. Having sex while someone watched was almost a standard of de Sang society. As was observing others. Smorgasbords were effectively a voyeur or exhibitionist playground. Watching two people fuck and feed did nothing for me. Usually.

Watching Tommy bring Spectra to orgasm with his mouth turned me on and made me want to rip his head from his body. It was both a lesson in self-restraint and a total mind-fuck. And not just for me. I'd watched Spectra try to resist the pleasure, and then I'd encouraged her to let go when her eyes came to me, fearing my anger.

I'd kissed her with the desire I always felt for her. Then I'd whispered my love in her ear before taking her body with mine, only for

Tommy to feast on our pleasure again. It was a merry-go-round of satisfaction for all of us, and we didn't stop until Spectra slumped exhausted in my arms and begged no more.

"I think we've done enough to stop any backlash now. Get Spec home and let her sleep it off," Tommy told me before taking himself off to the bathroom to clean his spend from his stomach again.

Caressing my wife's silken hair, I opened my shields just enough to wash over her and get a read on her physical and mental state. She was exhausted physically and emotionally, but happy. Lifting my head, I placed a tender kiss on her head, then rolled her gently, snuggling her in the blankets before climbing out of bed.

Pulling on my sweatpants and a shirt, I laced up my joggers and went for a run. When I returned to the kitchen, the priest sat at the dining room table with a coffee. Grabbing a drink of water, I joined him.

"Is Spectra okay? I expected her to be up by now," Mathew asked straight away.

"She's exhausted but well. Tell me about the temptation for you Angelis having a balance in your beds."

Mathew muttered a curse in Angelise. Probably not expecting me to know it. Even if I didn't understand, the tone suggested he was swearing before he met my eyes and asked, "Tommy?"

When I lifted my glass to my mouth and drank, keeping my eyes on the priest, he huffed a breath and set his coffee cup down. "We didn't know it was a thing until Mercury and Spectra became intimate. Obviously, since she's the first female of our kind, it's not something any of us could have expected."

Sitting forward, Mathew leaned his elbows on the table and sighed. "The first time Mercury was with Spectra, he realized that the benefit sorcerers gain from our daughters was the same for Spectra and her own kind. We don't get the benefit from Nephilim. Neither do other Nephilim. We couldn't have known that a female Angelis could act as a balancing board for us." Mathew swallowed with difficulty. "Even if she's not willing."

Holding up his hand before I could react to what he was

suggesting, Mathew met my eyes. "Mercury stopped as soon as he realized. He was terrified by what happened, Bay. He'd never felt the need to balance like that before. To unleash his need so ferociously. And what little Spectra took for him, despite it not being something she'd ever willingly do, it unloaded her scales too."

Frowning, I considered Mathew. "Because the balance of protection is to be harmed?"

Mathew licked his lips. "There are two ways a Michangelis can balance, Bay. It would make Mercury and Spectra perfect for each other if she had even an ounce of masochistic tendencies, but she doesn't."

I wouldn't say she had none. Spectra loved being with me with my shields down, even though it initially caused her discomfort. And she'd left my bed satisfied after I'd pinned her down and taken her hard in our short time as lovers that there was no doubt in my mind she loved being dominated. Still, I wasn't about to correct Mathew because I'd heard Spectra cry out when Mercury got too rough. I could only imagine it was a much different level from mine.

"It took some vigilance on Mercury's part to learn how to cope because Spectra has never controlled her powers," Mathew explained. "She siphons the need of others, and then she converts that need into what they or she needs, without conscious thought. Their wedding weekend was the only other time since that first time, and only because Mercury didn't have the opportunity to balance after saving her. Still, he feels the temptation if he's even slightly off balance."

Titling my head, I considered what I knew about Mercury and Spectra's relationship. "That's why they only saw each other when he had time off. He'd go to the club on the way home, knowing he'd spend several days with her."

"Yes. Living together will tempt Merc more than ever, but he assures me he will cope. It's not like he can go to the club daily. His playthings take time to recover."

Watching Mathew, I considered what he had just revealed. "What is the second way Spectra can balance?"

Nose flaring as he inhaled, Mathew averted his eyes. "You need to understand that Spec has spent most of her adult life unbalanced because she hasn't learned how to do it, or is unwilling to fulfil that need. Admittedly, her desire has been worse since her transition to a Wraith. Until now, opportunities have presented themselves every few years. Almost as if her need to balance draws her prey to her."

"Prey?"

"The Nachtwelt predators who tried to force Spectra to work for them."

My next question got stuck in my throat. "My wife's only two ways to balance are to let someone hurt her or to harm others?"

"Not hurt them, per se. Hunt them is the correct ideology. It needs to match her actions. If protecting someone just prevents them from harm, then to balance, she must be hurt or hunt her prey until they injure themselves. If protecting someone saves their lives like she did for Calin's wife, then it has to cost hers, or she needs to be the cause of another losing theirs."

Silence. I'm not sure I was breathing as the weight of Mathew's words fell like sand scattered across the table between us. A million tiny silica quartz crystals bouncing and rolling across the timber top, each the potential for me to lose my wife or her to lose herself.

Don't get me wrong. I suspected Spectra killed those predators who crossed her. Still, there is a difference between self-defense and hunting someone intending to harm. "How did she kill them?"

"Did you think Spectra randomly discovered her ability to pull a beast from a Changeur to protect Calin's wife? It never hurt her before because she did it to balance, not to save a life. While she didn't kill them directly, her actions drove one to suicide, and another to be killed by its masters."

Mathew wet his lips. "I'm Spectra's confidant. Mercury didn't even know she did that. When she admitted what nearly converted her last time, he made her promise never to do it again. He unknowingly took her best non-violent ability to balance away from her."

"How off-kilter are her scales now?" After everything that had occurred these past two weeks, I found it hard to believe Spectra was still unbalanced.

Refusing to meet my gaze, Mathew scratched the back of his neck before sighing. "Yesterday, Spectra balanced out or came very close to it. Alexander hunted her and hurt her, and then Spectra's actions scared one of my parishioners to the point she raced from the church straight out into traffic. Spectra isn't aware that her actions yesterday stole a life. Mercury and I would prefer her to remain unaware. The power she used against Alexander was a lot for her. We needed to focus on the physical repercussions without adding guilt to the mix."

That must have been what Tommy implied about the backlash. That's why he was keen to keep going until Spectra almost passed out from pleasure. Which meant Tommy was working with Mathew and Mercury to protect Spectra in more than just his capacity as a watcher. It made me wonder how many other Angelis were working in the shadows to care for my wife, but that wasn't my biggest concern. If Spectra drew prey to her when she needed to balance, then having Essence suddenly interested in her could be fatal for her.

Studying Mathew, I suspected part of his training was preparing Spectra for what she would need to do to survive. Especially now that Mercury had taken her previous tactic away from her. Not that it would have worked on Paul Samus.

"When Spectra wakes, we will teach her how to slay de Sang, and we will make sure she can do it without fail before the weekend is done."

"Bay," Mathew worried, watching me.

"Essence is hunting her, Mathew. If hunting predators balances her and the universe sends them her way when she needs them, then she needs to know how to kill my kind. Luckily, you have two ancient and powerful de Sangs in the house for her to learn on. I can assure you, if Spec can come close to taking either Luke or me down, then she will be successful with nearly every other de Sang who threatens her."

Leaning forward, I eyed the priest. "Now, tell me what happened with Alexander at the church yesterday. And I want the truth, Mathew. No more hiding my wife from me."

Clearing his throat, Mathew sat back in his seat. "What do you know about Celestials? About their origins?"

Frowning at the question but understanding it was relevant, I shook my head. Time to play naive. "The only story about angels come from religious texts. They were God's creation."

The side of Mathew's mouth lifted slightly, but it was too quick for me to determine if it was a smirk or sneer. "It is only something the Celestials know the truth of because for all others, angels just always were."

Considering his words, Mathew nodded to himself before continuing. "In all texts that cover the subject, men were made of clay and given life by a god. Women were made of earth, and their life force was drawn from the combined essence of a god and the great Goddess most humans call mother nature.

"Human men treat their women as lesser because of physical strength. Yet, in all literature, women are imbued with the energy of the most powerful force on this planet, backed up by a minor god. If you want to debate physical strength, women endure childbirth, a pain that modern medicine claims would cause a mortal man's heart to stop in his chest from the strain it places on the body."

"I come from a time when women were exalted as the vessels of the Goddess herself. Before Christianity reduced them to the origin of sin," I reminded Mathew.

Nodding his head, Mathew sat forward again, placing his elbows on the table. "Celestials were the first creatures born of magic. They come from the pure source. The same well of power that some corrupted elementals misused and were punished for by the great Goddess, becoming the first de Sangs or Changeurs."

Taking a moment, Mathew tilted his head as he met my eyes. "The same source you can still touch as a result of your Celestial ancestors, but sorcerers usually only have minimal access to it. You've always been a strong magic user, Bay. I dare say your ancestor was a powerful Celestial. But Spectra is only one generation away from the pure source. She can access and wield that power beyond your limited comprehension."

Focusing on his words, I thought back to last night. "When I did the casting last night, I drew more magic faster than I've ever done before." Not that it had ever been difficult for me.

Staring into my eyes, I almost felt like Mathew could see and feel my experience. That turned my mind to when Spectra and I first joined our bodies after the casting, and she added to it.

"Sorcerers always find they have better control when they find a balance and bond with them. It's because those females are closer to the power they wield. You are now physically bonded with a creature only one step away from the pure source. Spec will act as a direct conduit for you. You are now the most powerful sorcerer the world has ever seen."

I used magic so rarely now, relying on my power as a de Sang instead, that I hadn't noticed any change to my capabilities. Knowing my bond with Spectra catalyzed any magic I performed made last night make sense. She was the embodiment of magic, slightly watered down by the genes of her human mother.

"How does this relate to what happened in the church yesterday?"

Rubbing his thumb across his bottom lip, Mathew assessed me. "You're not going to like this, but you should know. You are not the only sorcerer bonded to Spectra. You wedded your bodies, so the physical connection between you and the source is cemented for you. The fact she is falling in love with you will only give you more power. But you're not the only one."

My hands clenched into fists. "Alexander. She loved him, and their souls are joined."

"Not joined," Mathew protested quickly. "Tethered."

"Same thing," I argued.

"No. Your bond is permanent. Until you die, Spectra will be yours. What was done to prevent Spectra from converting is as permanent as the knot of a shoelace. The years have made it tight and difficult to unravel, but it can be undone."

Mathew's jaw tensed as he considered his next words, cracking his knuckles as he stretched, then slowly curled his fingers into fists. "When that tether formed, Alexander experienced the same benefits you have of being wedded to a female Angelis. His power stabilized, and he had greater access. Alexander is not as powerful as everyone thinks. His connection to Spectra makes him the most powerful sorcerer of his time. Before you married Spec, he probably could have rivaled you, which is why he feared you two finding each other."

"Does Alexander know his tie to Spec makes him so powerful?"

Mathew's adam apple jolted. "He's aware the tether made him more stable. It's one of the reasons he is desperate to have her back. You heard him the other night. His sense of her is fading. That's because she's lost trust in him, and her love for him has shifted. It's impacted his capabilities. Not drastically, but enough he's noticed."

Sitting back, I cursed, suddenly understanding.

Mathew nodded. "When Spectra told Alexander she's going to have their souls untethered, he threatened her, and then he used their tie to hurt her. As I explained, Spectra has access to great power but has always used it subconsciously. When Alexander hurt her, Spec shielded herself."

"Like you did two nights ago to protect Calin from Alexander's temper?" I asked.

"Yes. Except Spectra has no control. So when she pushed Alexander's power back at him, she multiplied it exponentially. The result was the equivalent of a neutron bomb exploding in the church."

Staring at Mathew, I knew my eyes were wide. Slowly, I blinked, imagining what that must have felt like, but another worry formed in my mind. "Did Alexander realize?"

"No. It had Alexander's power signature, so there was no reason for him to suspect Spectra threw that at him. Since I'd done it to him the night before, he probably thinks I did it again."

"Are you certain of that?" I checked. The last thing we needed was Alexander to realize how potent Spectra was.

"Absolutely," Mathew assured.

Accepting that answer, I sat back, a tingle racing up my spine and across my shoulders, drawing my attention. "Spec's awake and about to join us," I warned.

"Then you best call Luke so we can start training her how to kill you." The smirk on Mathew's face drew one of my own as I stood up to greet my wife in the kitchen. She would need a big breakfast, so she had the energy for what I was about to demand of her.

# CHAPTER 25

## SPECTRA

"It looks like you had a rough weekend." Mercury's voice drew my focus from applying my eyeliner to his reflection in the bathroom mirror.

Bruises and scrapes covered my body from a weekend of fending off two de Sangs until I could defend myself to their satisfaction. "Thank God it's winter, or finding a work-appropriate outfit would have been difficult," I answered and returned to applying my light makeup.

So far, I'd only put my underwear on, so Mercury had an unfettered view of the training impact. It also meant when he used his hands to explore some of the darker bruises, it was skin-to-skin contact. My breath caught in my chest as heat gathered between my thighs wantonly. Being married to Bay and Mercury was turning me into a nymphomaniac. If they were in the room, I needed them inside me.

"Merc, I can't. I don't want to be late on my first day."

Mercury frowned when touching the skin around an especially painful bruise on my right shoulder blade. "I haven't balanced." That was Mercury's way of telling me it wouldn't be safe for us to be together right now. "Do you want me to heal any of these? You'll be feeling them all day."

"I don't want to tax you."

Meeting my gaze in the mirror, Mercury placed a kiss on the bruise. The sun's warmth spread from his lips across my shoulder blade as white heat flashed where our flesh met. These injuries were minor and required little of Mercury's power.

The sun touched me wherever his lips found all of the most painful spots. When Mercury finished, he stood and met my eyes in the mirror. A smirk pulled at the side of his mouth as his thumb brushed the damp gusset of my panties.

"It's a pity you need to leave soon. I would love to wrap my arm with your hair and fuck you hard like this right now." Giving me a wicked wink, Mercury gave my bottom a spank, just hard enough to make me jump but not hurt, then he turned on the shower and stripped.

Blowing out a breath, I used my fear of him accidentally hurting me to temper my lust. The sight of Mercury naked and wet did nothing to help. "Will you be home for dinner tonight?"

"Yes, but I intend to sleep until I have to leave for my next shift. I worked forty-eight hours straight." Turning his head toward me, Mercury wiped the water out of his eyes and then swept it back through his wet hair before meeting my gaze. I was going to need to change my panties before I dressed. "Tell Bay we still need to discuss this living arrangement. I'm unhappy with us living here and not contributing to the household expenses."

"Gina told me there is a joint account they all pay an agreed amount into to cover food and utilities. I got the account number, and what she pays so I can set up autopayments. I'll leave the details on the bedside table for you."

Mercury's smirk was back. "Bay wouldn't tell you either?"

"He said I was his wife and, therefore, his responsibility. I argued that wasn't acceptable to me, but he distracted me. So, I asked Gina instead." Giving him a wink, I headed for the bathroom door. "Sweet dreams."

"Good luck today."

"Thanks."

"Spec?" Mercury waited for me to stop at the door and look back at him. "I love you. Stay safe."

My heart fluttered in my chest at his words. "I love you too."

Once dressed, I put my hair in a chignon at the base of my neck and headed downstairs. Bay was already in the kitchen plating up a vegetarian frittata for me. "Morning," he greeted, handing me the plate while dropping a sweet, leisurely kiss on my lips. "How did you sleep?"

Bay was out on his run this morning when I woke up and went downstairs to prepare for my first day at Galaxy. "I always sleep well in your arms. You didn't have to do this." I held up the plate of food before heading to the table.

"I enjoy taking care of you. It's not like I'll do it daily. Some mornings I have early meetings, and you'll have to fend for yourself," Bay assured. Joining me with his coffee.

"You're not eating?"

"I don't really need a lot of solid food sustenance. I can eat for the joy of it, but it's not necessary to my survival," Bay informed me, reminding me subtly that I'd married a de Sang.

"We're kind of more alike than I realized," I replied, considering our habits. "I eat regularly out of habit more than hunger. I haven't exactly tried going without to see what would happen. Still, on occasion, I have been too busy to think about food and gone a day or two without eating and not been hungry or any worse for it."

"Interesting. Is that the same for all Angelis?" Watching me, Bay sipped his coffee.

"I don't know. I always got hungry before I died, so I was attributing this to us both being undead, or whatever you consider a de Sang and a Wraith to be."

"You seem very alive to me, Spec."

"You do too, but I know I'm not. It's like suspended animation, maybe. We are neither alive nor dead. Perhaps the same thing that makes a de Sang is part of what makes Wraith?" I theorized.

Bay's brows lifted as he considered. "Perhaps. Although I would hypothesize that they are quite different, but maybe sit on the same plane of existence. After all, there is no coming back for me. A Wraith, however, is held in stasis until their vengeance is achieved, then they become one of the living again."

"That's never going to happen for me," I muttered unhappily.

"But it was still your purpose. No matter what, a Wraith is meant to be a temporary existence. Mine is permanent until I make the final pass to the Summerlands."

Admiring the handsome de Sang across from me, I didn't want to think about him never being here. "Just don't make that final pass without me, okay? I don't think I could handle losing you, Bay."

Leaning forward, Bay cupped my face in his palm and caressed his thumb across my cheek. "I will never leave you while it's in my power to stay." His mouth came close to mine, but a phone ringing drew us apart.

Pulling out his cell phone, Bay answered it. "Yes? Of Course. Yes, let her through." Hanging up, Bay sat back with his coffee just as Calin and Gina entered the kitchen. "Your ride to work is here. Eat up."

Focusing on the delicious frittata, I listened to Bay and Calin discuss their day until their phones buzzed. They pulled up the camera feed for the front stairs.

"While I appreciate your friends helping to keep you safe, Spec, they are not welcome in our home," Bay warned.

Taking the hint. I stood up, cleaned my plate, and put it in the dishwasher before using Bay's tie to tug him to me and kiss him—in a way that was unacceptable for company. "I'll see you tonight."

"You will," Bay confirmed.

"God, you two are adorable," Gina laughed. "I'll walk you out, Spec. Let these two keep talking work."

Grabbing my bag, I headed out the front with Gina. When we got to the car where Miranda rolled down the window on her red vintage sports car. "Morning. Jump in, Ghost."

Rolling my eyes at the nickname Miranda always used for me, I headed to the passenger seat. "Want me to order pizza for dinner?" I asked Gina.

"I'll send you the order and the time we are heading home,"

Gina confirmed before moving closer to Miranda's window. "Be careful. L'Ordre has made a few grabs for her last week. The priest thinks the NSIO will try and take her now that she is refusing to work there."

"I was briefed last night. My intel suggests that L'Ordre's actions are personal. Still, his father's are not," Miranda answered, keeping her voice down.

"Any news on her other problem?" Gina also dropped her voice until I could barely hear her as I closed the passenger door.

"Some unusual activity but with multiple plays happening simultaneously, we have no way of knowing which they might be targeting currently."

Gina's eyes flicked to me. "Stay close to Miranda. No ghosting her." When I saluted mockingly, Gina snorted a laugh and waved us off as she turned and headed inside.

"She's worried," I noted.

"With good reason," Miranda acknowledged as she put the car in gear and headed back out to the gate in a hurry.

Once we passed the estate boundary, Miranda blew a breath and rolled her shoulders while giving her body a bit of a shake. "Damn, that's a good repelling shield he's put on the estate. Made breathing hard for me, and I don't even need oxygen to survive."

"We probably should have got you added as a permitted person," I said, realizing it was too late.

"I am. Well, at least Bay took a hair so I could come to pick you up. He said he'd add me as a passing guest and that I could come up the driveway but not inside the house," Miranda explained.

In the back of my mind, I saw a bowl full of different hair strands sitting on a photo of the house laid over an aerial view of the estate. More hair and the same aerial photograph with the house cut out in another bowl. Then over a picture of the driveway was the third bowl with very few strands.

"The casting only allowed you to drive the length of the driveway, not use the Porte-cochere or circular drive," I realized. "Next time, pull up by the garage doors, and I'll come out that way. It should stop the shield from affecting you."

Lifting a brow at me, Miranda smirked. "Learning some magic from your lover, are you?"

"No, I figured it out by his tools to determine who could go where." How I knew what tools he used was a mystery.

As we cruised towards Stokes Industrial Park, where Galaxy was located, I thought about Friday night and the vision of Bay and me in a magic circle while we were intimate. It felt so real. The timber floor beneath me, the stars through the glass roof in the oculus above us.

"Are you nervous about today?" Miranda asked.

"Yes. I worried Galaxy wouldn't want to bother with a fresh graduate. Do you think you'll be able to handle the expectations of your role?"

"Of course. I would have been happy with an admin role."

"Except those roles were all taken. Plus, admin doesn't sit near where I will be in the building," I explained. Luckily, one of the IT project manager assistants for a team sitting adjacent to my trial team handed in their resignation last week. So, I added Miranda as a preferred candidate to the list they'd interviewed only two months ago.

"So, what do I need to do for this role?"

"You'll be responsible for supporting the resource management, scheduling, prioritization, and task coordination for specific projects. They have three project managers in IT, and you're one of six assistants. Though reading the exit interviews for your new boss's last three assistants, he's a sleazy asshole who has been cited twice already for sexual harassment. Just so you know."

"Ooh, just the type I like for dinner," Miranda chirped.

I smirked, knowing exactly the kind of guy Miranda liked to feed on.

"And don't stress. You hacked them before you ever set foot in the building. You know you can do this job with your eyes shut. What's on the cards today?"

"I assigned the same person to induct us, so we'll be together all day. That will explain our friendship going forward. From tomorrow, we will have different meetings and places to be during work hours, but that shouldn't be a problem."

"Just don't leave the building without me," Miranda warned. "Stokes is a long way out. I won't have any backup during the work day."

Giving Miranda the guarantee I'd stay inside unless she was with me, I turned our conversation to the training I'd done over the weekend. Miranda was excited to hear about me having to fight Bay and Luke and started giving me tips for the next time I trained with Bay.

Galaxy was a large facility made up of three E-shaped buildings connecting together. None of the buildings were more than three stories, and I understood that one of the wings was entirely taken up with server rooms.

There were cafes and restaurants all around the industrial park. Galaxy had a handful on the ground floor outside of each building, plus one in each of the six indoor courtyards just to cater to the amount of staff who worked there.

Our first meeting for the morning took place in one such cafe. After checking in at the front reception, we were met by the HR member assigned to take us through our orientation. He started by taking us to the cafe for coffee and casually introducing the policies and expectations of working at Galaxy. That was followed by a tour of the different Galaxy departments, suggestions on which cafes are best to eat at, and all that other organizational-level stuff.

After lunch, we were taken to a meeting room, where we sat through the formal orientation. Employment paperwork, occupational health and safety, and all the other mandatory workplace safety learning modules. I got a bit of a chuckle when we had to complete the one on cyber security.

Even though I was only here for a trial, the HR rep put me through all the same things as Miranda. His idea was that it saved me from having to do it all again if I was offered a position, and it was a requirement of working in the building in most cases. So our first day was spent on required learning and paperwork. At three in the afternoon, we finished early. Since we weren't due to meet our new team for another half hour, we went to security and had our passes issued instead.

Finally, we were taken to the second floor in the middle of the building and introduced to our individual new managers. Miranda was handed off to her senior manager for introductions to the project management team. I was taken to the Information Assurance team and handed off to my temporary manager, Jack Ardley.

"It's nice to meet you, Spectra." Jack shook my hand with a big smile. "My good friend Professor Gibbons has been singing your praises since you first walked into his Foundations in Digital Forensics seminar."

That was a surprise. I'd had to apply to Galaxy, but they'd been watching my education journey. Jack swiped me into the secure office wing, an area even HR couldn't access.

Walking into the small corridor in the middle of the Galaxy building, I realized there weren't cubicles here despite the explanation in the employment system I'd hacked. Offices took up both sides of the corridor down to the next security door.

"Because of the nature of our work, each team is allocated their own space," Jack explained. "We're spread out over four offices and share meeting space with the Project Management team. Now you scored well in most areas of cyber security, so during your two-week trial, I want to rotate you around the seven different areas of IA."

Halfway down the hall, Jack pushed through a black tinted glass door. It was transparent, but the black tint stopped you from reading anything showing on the screens inside. "This is the office of our Firewall, IDS/IPS Administrators, and our penetration testers."

Jack then spent the next few minutes introducing me to the five guys—they were all men—in that office area. Their desks circled the room, and then in the center was a small meeting table where they could all roll their chairs for group discussions. I noticed a large screen on one of the glass interior walls in the office for displaying anything they needed to while in a group meeting.

Moving into the next office, I was introduced to the four people who made up the Incidence Response Team and the one SIEM analyst. At least there was one other female in this office. The layout was precisely the same as the first.

The last office was smaller and was where Jack and the systems architect sat. Despite the room being half the size, they still managed a small meeting table due to desks only taking up the exterior window and one side wall of the space.

After that, I was shown the two small online meeting rooms next door that could fit maybe four people max. Across the hall was the large meeting room we shared with the IT project team, which was the same size as Jack's office.

"I'm going to start you off with me tomorrow. Then for the rest of the week, you'll be in with IR. Shadow Jenny Wednesday and Thursday, and I've got you working with Gavin on Friday." The SIEM Analyst. "Next week, you'll spend three days with the Firewall and penetration guys, then Thursday with Samual—the architect—and Friday with me. How does that sound?"

"Like a great learning experience," I answered, excited by the opportunity.

Jack smiled and checked his watch. "Well, you have only thirty minutes left in the workday. How about we get a coffee and discuss where you currently want to specialize?"

"Sure. Do you mind if I just let Miranda know? She started with the IT project team today. We spent the day together in orientation and got along. So, we decided to meet when we finished the day to arrange to carpool."

Glancing into the office where Miranda was sitting with her new manager and his other assistant, Jack cringed. "Harvey isn't the most approachable guy. I'd hate to get the new girl in his bad books on her first day. Can you send her a message?"

"Oh, sure," I answered as we headed for the doors out of the restricted area. Taking out my mobile, I kept a happy expression. "Which cafe? I'll let her know where to meet me."

Jack told me the name and even explained which courtyard since Miranda was new. I sent her the message and kept cautious watch while Jack led the way, but we stayed in the building. Jack, true to his word, was keen to hear where I thought I wanted to specialize and why.

On the drive home, I was excited by the prospect of getting a permanent role with my dream company. Miranda was plotting how to drain Harvey, the pervy pig, dry.

"I think I'm going to like this new job," Miranda informed me, full of mirth as we pulled up by the garage of Bay's house.

"Me too."

"I'll see you tomorrow morning," Miranda sang as I gave her a wave and shut the door.

Before I could head to the door, Miranda called out, "Spec, don't forget you promised the beasts pizza."

Crap, I nearly had. As Miranda drove off, I pulled out my phone and ordered dinner. Then I sent Bay and Mercury a message letting them know I was home safe.

I was two steps into the kitchen when I sensed another Angelis. Lifting my head, I felt all my joy drain away.

"Good, you're home." Mathew stood up. "Go get changed. We're training in the gym tonight."

I kept my thoughts to myself lest I spend the rest of the night saying Hail Marys for the profanity.

# CHAPTER 26

# BAY

It started with the delicate flutter in the middle of my chest, followed by the sharp sting of Spectra's pain.

"Pull the car over, now!" I demanded. We were only five minutes from the house, but it was five minutes too long.

"What's going on?"

"Spectra."

That's all Calin needed to hear. He swerved off the road instantly. Jumping out, I took one step and was cutting through the ether a second later. In a matter of breaths, I was striding into the kitchen where I could feel my wife. I didn't expect to find her crouched on the floor, one of her hands shaking above a broken glass, her blood dripping and pooling on the floor already. The smell of toffee apple filled my nose.

"What the hell happened?" I asked.

"I don't know." Cynthia stood wide-eyed. "We were talking, and Spectra was yanked sideways all of a sudden. She stumbled and tripped, and the glass she was drinking from smashed in her hand."

Spectra stayed where she was, panting, pressing the center of her chest with her uninjured hand. Crouching by her, I smoothed the hair away from her face, concerned by the panic in her eyes. "Spec, what happened?"

"I... I don't know. My world shifted sideways all of a sudden. Like my spirit tried to leave my body, or something forced me to go Wraith. I've never felt that before."

The way she was trembling concerned me. I'd not seen Spectra this terrified before. But there was a more immediate problem I needed to deal with before we could address the potential of Spectra losing control of her gifts. Maybe she wasn't as balanced as Mathew perceived her to be.

Taking my wife's hand that still hovered over the broken glass, I turned it over and observed the deep lacerations. Shrugging out of my jacket, I ripped my button-down over my head, then balled some of it in her hand and wrapped the rest around her arm to stop it from bleeding everywhere.

"These are very deep, you'd need stitches normally, but you are lucky enough to have two other choices. I can heal these for you with my saliva, but it means tasting you. Or, we can call Mercury and get him to come home straight away."

"It's not that bad." Spectra tried to take her hand away, but I kept hold of it. "I can just put Band-aids on them."

Yeah, that wasn't going to work. The scent of a toffee apple was overwhelming and made my mouth water. I could only imagine what it would do to Luke. "Stop it, Spectra. You live in a house of predators, and you're bleeding. Luke will be home soon, so we need to clean this up now. You have a choice. I either use my saliva to heal you or call Mercury."

Still blinking quickly from whatever affected her, Spectra bowed her head and simply muttered, "Mercury."

I understood her choice. Spectra's fear of de Sangs was not overridden just because she had married one. I hadn't tasted her blood nor sunk fang into her, so licking her wounds would cross a line for her.

Acknowledging her request, I pulled out my phone and called Mercury.

"Bay, I felt it. What happened?"

"Spectra is injured. I need you to come home straight away. We'll discuss the cause when you're here."

"I'll be there in a few minutes," Mercury responded.

Putting my phone away, I eased Spectra to standing just as Calin and Luke pushed through the kitchen door. "What happened?" Calin took in the room, looking for any threat. Luke's focus came immediately to the pool of blood.

"Luke, get out. Cyn, I need you to take Spectra to her room. Mercury will be home to heal her in a moment."

Luke turned on a dime and was out of the kitchen before I finished talking. Elevating Spectra's hand, I moved her closer to me, lowering my voice for just her ears. "Do you know what it was?"

"No. I've never felt that before." Spectra looked just as uneasy as I felt about this. Maybe she just stumbled, but Cyn and Spectra were both too freaked out for that to be the case.

"Okay. If it happens again, you'll call Mercury or me instantly. Whatever this is, I need to be concerned about it if it can affect you like this."

"I'm sure it was nothing." Spectra tried to shrug it off. "Maybe all the training sessions I've been doing."

"Maybe. Go with Cyn. I'll be up in a moment."

Waiting for Cynthia to lead Spectra out, I turned my eyes to Calin. "Go get the kit from the car." Calin's eyes drifted to the pool of blood on the kitchen floor, then he left the room.

Grabbing the dustpan and brush, I collected the broken glass and took it to the sink, washing it clean with bleach before disposing of it. By that time, Calin was back with the kit, squatting by the pool of blood and using a pipette to collect what he could into the specimen tube.

Once Calin collected what he could, he handed the tube to me. "Candied apple is not the scent I normally associate with blood."

"Most of the Angelis have a sweet smell to them. Haven't you noticed that about Mercury and Mathew?"

When Tommy came on Friday night, the scent of spun sugar filled the room and got stronger when he got closer. That's when I realized Spectra's sweet-tasting pleasure was a species thing. I hadn't realized until this moment it was the case for all their bodily fluids.

"Clean that up." I indicated the blood as I handed Calin the bleach. "I need to go check on her."

Broaching no argument, Calin took the bleach over to the stained floor. I grabbed my jacket and shoved the vial into my pocket. Pulling out my phone, I sent a message to Jacoby.

As I reached the landing on the second floor, Mercury stepped out of nowhere and followed me into the suite. We found Spectra and Cyn in the bathroom, rinsing the wound clean.

Mercury eased Spectra's hand out from under the running water, examined the damage, and then white light diffused the wounds. Spectra hissed and then exhaled hard. When the light retreated, Spectra's hand was whole.

Caressing our wife's cheek, Mercury kissed her forehead gently. "I have an hour or two if you want me to stay for a bit?" Mercury's hand drifted over her collarbone to the center of her chest, where he brushed his fingers back and forth, a faint glow following their path.

"Please," Spectra breathed, leaning into him.

As he comforted our wife, Mercury's eyes came to me, blue fire burning in them. I got the sense he could feel what had happened and was furious by it. He gave a slight shake of his head, then stepped back, taking Spectra with him, leading her to the shower. "Bay, can you turn the tap on?"

Stepping in, I pulled the lever. "Give me a second," I whispered then walked over to the sink and collected my bloodied shirt. "Thanks, Cyn. We've got it from here."

Eyes glancing at Spectra, Cynthia swallowed and left. Following her, I locked the door, went to the bedroom fireplace, and got it going. Once a decent fire was burning, I chucked my shirt on the logs and headed back into the bathroom. Mercury had undressed Spectra and himself, and they both stood under the hot water falling from the rainmaker showerhead.

Without asking permission, I stripped what remained of my suit and stepped into the shower, wrapping my arms around our wife and holding her from behind, just like Mercury was doing from his side.

"You were dressed for training." Mercury finally broke the comfortable silence, shifting his hand from Spectra's chest to her cheek.

"Mathew was waiting when I got home from work. Insisted on me working out with him for two hours," Spectra sighed.

"I'll tell him to give you a break tomorrow," Mercury assured.

Kissing behind her ear, I ran my nose into her hair to breathe her in. "How was the first week at Galaxy?" Spectra's entire body eased as she started telling us about her trial and caught us up on today.

Over her head, Mercury and I met each other's gaze. I wanted to believe the suggestion that it was all the training that caused tonight like Spectra was trying to tell us, but what I saw in the Angelis's pale blue orbs did not settle my concern.

After Spectra told us everything about her day, we left the shower and dressed. Mercury suggested Spectra have an early night, so we tucked her into bed. Once she was asleep, Mercury readied to leave.

"I'll walk you out," I offered, pulling my slacks back into place. Once we were out of the bedroom, I eyed the door to the suite. "How concerned should I be?"

"It was her tether with Alexander. This is the longest she's gone refusing his soul's need to be near him, and the strain of resisting it is what caused tonight."

"She needs to go to him?" I didn't want that to happen after he threatened her, but if it was going to hurt Spectra like this, I'd have to accept it.

"No. Spec can resist this. She needs to learn to shield herself from him just as much as she needs to learn to shield from an attack," Mercury assured as he pulled the door open to the suite, and we stepped out onto the landing.

"We normally learn our powers as children, but Spectra didn't have that option. Even as children, we get hurt learning to control our abilities. Spec is no different. She'll hurt now, but it will save her later."

"It felt like more than just the tether straining to me," I countered, remembering that weird sensation before Spectra's pain hit. "It was almost like an elastic band snapping back into place."

"I'm not all-knowing, Bay. Spec has always been a learning curve, but I have felt her try to resist the need to go to Alexander before, and this honestly felt the same, just a little more intense. If we keep her busy, she should be fine."

Accepting that Mercury had known Spectra a lot longer, I trusted his judgment. Agreeing to talk tomorrow night, I watched Mercury step out of sight. Taking out my phone, I noted Jacoby's response and started for my bedroom. I needed to change.

Luke was coming out of my office as I hit the third floor. "Is she okay?"

"Yes. Just exhausted. I have something I need to do. Can you keep an ear out in case Spec wakes up?"

"Sure."

As Luke headed down to his level, I went to my room, changed, and then used the ether to return to my office in the Pendant building. Scanning myself into the laboratory section, I was glad to see Jacoby already in his space, working on his computer.

When he saw me, he let me in and then followed me to one of his workbenches. Taking the vial of Spectra's blood from my pocket, I held it a moment, then met Jacoby's gaze. "No records of this addition to the serum. This won't be a long-term answer, but it may give us a better direction to improve the inoculation."

Jacoby adjusted his grip, taking the vial from my hand, and his brows drew together. "I can feel some strong emotions coming from this vial. There's almost a tugging sensation attached to it. Did this come from a siphon?"

"Double-blind, Jacoby. Let's just see what it does. I want to try it tonight."

Nodding, Jacoby started working. Taking out one of the vials of the existing antidote, he simply added one drop of Spectra's blood to it. It fizzed and sparked, then settled back to look how it did before. Using a dropper, Jacoby placed one drop under the micro-scope and frowned at whatever he saw. Shaking his head, he set the vial aside and grabbed another.

This time he spun a portion of the blood down and remade the antidote with her serum. I sat and watched every step of the process. I stood up when Jacoby filled a syringe and turned to face me.

"Time to see what it does?"

Jacoby nodded and collected the first vial to which he just added a drop of Spectra's blood. "If there is anyone you are willing to experiment on that you wouldn't miss, I'd be interested to see what this does to them."

There were a lot of creatures held down in the Vault I wouldn't miss, but I also wasn't inclined to torture others for the sake of experimentation. I'd gotten the antidote to a certain point before I even brought Jacoby on board, and then several more years of studies before we tried the inoculation on a living being. "You think it will be deadly in that form?"

"That's the thing. I'm not sure if it would be fatal or life-saving. The reaction I saw under the microscope changed the dynamics of the serum entirely. Still, I'm unsure if it was for good or bad," Jacoby admitted.

Taking the vial from him, I pocketed it and headed out to the elevator. I'm not sure what it was about Spectra's blood tonight, but the moment I was there beside her, I felt a difference. Like an epiphany.

The last sample of her blood I'd given Jacoby had been from when Spectra nearly died. There was very little to feel from it. But tonight, there had been magic in Spectra's blood. Remnant of the weekend, or a side-effect of something else, my curiosity immedi-ately activated. Heading to the Vault, I was about to discover what happened when you mixed Spectra's magic with mine outside of a bedroom.

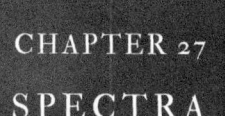

## CHAPTER 27

# SPECTRA

M<small>Y</small> <small>EYES</small> <small>OPENED</small> <small>WIDE</small> as my body slid across the bed. Sitting up, I looked around the room. "Bay?"

My heart raced in my chest as I took in the empty room. My senses told me there was no one here, yet I didn't precisely feel alone. My soul lurched, trying to yank out of the back of my body. Physically, I slid off the bed, whacking the bedside table with the back of my head as I went.

My soul and body snapped back together, leaving the sensation of a Chinese burn behind my sternum. Trying to get to my feet, I was barely standing when the tug-o-war happened again. I managed to snatch my phone from the bedside table but knocked the lamp to the floor as I was jerked another meter away from the bed.

Panting, I pressed Bay's number just as another pull hit. "Bay!" I screamed as I hit the wall beside the window.

Lifting the phone to my ear with trembling hands as I pushed myself off the wall, I received an automated message that the number I was trying to call was out of signal reach.

Hanging up, my thumb was moving to call Mercury when I was

thrown against the window, the side of my head striking the glass pane with force.

"Spectra?" Luke rushed into the room in just pajama pants.

"Luke," I sobbed and stumbled towards him. He was reaching for me as I was jerked back with more force than any other time. When I hit the window, the room tilted in my vision as it darkened for a moment.

"Calin!" Luke was yelling as he pulled me into his arms.

"I have to… go ghost," I panted.

"No. Hold on," Luke ordered. "Calin!"

"What is it?" Calin burst into the room, Gina behind him as the pull came again. With Luke holding me, preventing my physical form from following my spirit, I was stretched taut. My scream filled my head, stopping me from hearing whatever Luke was saying.

When the invisible force released me and my spirit snapped back into my body, I was ready to pass out. My fingers dug into Luke's shoulders, trying to keep myself together.

"I. Can't," I sobbed against Luke's chest where he held me.

"Just hold out long enough for Calin to get the tracker, Spec," Luke soothed, petting my sweat-soaked hair.

The force grabbed hold of me again, yanking me with such force that Luke came with me, both of us hitting the window, a smash reverberating where it struck my head, and Luke cursing. Stepping us back, Luke looked down where his arm had been cut open, then turned and moved us, pressing me against the solid wall a second before the force tried to pull me away again.

"Keep breathing, Spec," Luke urged.

But he didn't understand how painful it was to have someone try to rip your spirit from you repeatedly. Sagging against him. I sobbed, "I'm sorry." Then I exhaled all the air in my lungs.

"Spectra, no!" Luke yelled.

As the force ripped me from the room, I caught sight of Calin racing back into the room over Luke's shoulder. Relief flooded me, no longer being torn apart as I floated momentarily. Then I was drawn quickly away into the night.

Whatever forced me to go Wraith buoyed and carried me

through the sky. Exhausted from fighting, I relaxed into its hold and prayed I'd survive whatever this was.

Too soon, the sensation of flying came to an end. Opening my eyes, I took in my surroundings. A candlelit magic circle held me, beyond which all I could see were the shadows of tree trunks and darkness.

In the circle with me stood a lone figure covered in a black robe with the hood drawn up to cover their head which was bowed.

The candles flickered and then settled around us. The hooded figure lowered their arms, their shoulders rising and falling quickly as if breathing heavily with the strain of whatever magic they'd used to summon me. Refusing to inhale, I waited.

Slowly, they drew back their hood, revealing sweat-drenched brown hair sticking to the olive skin of his face. Then Alexander's sunken brown eyes fell on the space I stood invisible. He looked like he hadn't been sleeping and was just as exhausted as I felt.

"I know you're here, Spec. Please, show yourself." Alexander waited. When I stayed invisible, he sighed. "You're probably terrified right now. And likely very angry with me and unwilling to cooperate. So, I should point out that this circle will keep you here until I release you from it."

The pain of betrayal hit me. I sucked in a breath and released a sob as I charged at Alexander, shoving him hard as I materialized before him. "Why? Why would you do this to me?"

Grabbing my wrists, Alexander swayed under my impact but then put what remained of his strength into keeping hold of me. "You wouldn't come to me. Wouldn't talk to me when I asked. I tried, Spectra. I tried to find you and talk. I came to the church and asked you to talk to me, and you kept shutting me out. You left me no choice."

"So you tortured me and then trapped me with your magic?" I spat at him.

"Tortured you?" Alexander looked shocked.

"What did you think pulling my spirit from my corporeal body would feel like for me, Alex?" I yelled at him. "You repeatedly dragged my physical body into walls and windows until I gave myself up to your spell. It was the equivalent of being thrown around a room while you ripped me apart inside."

Alexander's mouth fell open as his eyes widened. He finally looked at me. His eyes noted first the white satin slip I wore, the black and purple bruises covering my body—the ones he just caused and the ones from training all weekend. When I touched the back of my head and winced, Alexander registered my fingers came back smeared with blood.

Holding those fingers out to Alexander, I pleaded my case. "You tortured me to get me here, Alexander. Why? Why do you keep hurting me?"

"Spectra." Alexander shook his head and moved closer, but I backed up. Alexander stopped, and his head and shoulders fell. "It was a soul summoning spell. I didn't know it would hurt your physical form. It's not like it was ever used on one of your kind before. I thought it would just turn you Wraith and bring you to me."

My stomach fell out at his words. "You used a spell to summon the dead on me?"

"I'm sorry. I thought, at worst, it might be uncomfortable if you fought it. I would never have harmed you like this on purpose."

Closing my eyes, his sorrow hitting me so hard I couldn't doubt the authenticity of it. Eyeing the circle, I lifted my gaze to Alexander's drawn features. "Well, I'm trapped here now. What is so important you'd torture me like this to tell me?"

Lifting his head, a spark of anger flared in all that despair Alexander was carrying. His eyes hardened as they met mine. "I was honest with you, telling you about Raquel, and you cut me off. As a lover, as a friend, as everything. I tried to do the right thing, and you left me cold turkey, knowing I needed you in my life. You hurt me first, Spectra."

Exhaling, I shook my head. "You broke my heart first, Alexander. Many times. Don't pretend you're some martyr because you were finally honest about planning to take another woman as your wife."

"Spec-"

"It's freezing," I cut him off, hugging myself. The sweat from fighting his spell and being outdoors in nothing but a satin shift in the middle of winter had turned my skin blue, and my extremities felt ready to fall off.

Not hesitating, Alexander took his cloak off and wrapped it around my shoulders. Covering me with the thick, soft fabric before pulling me tight against his muscular body. The material retained his body heat and quickly removed the ice from my bones. The problem was that it left Alexander in the nude with a giant erection.

"Why are you naked?" I balked.

"All sorcerers have to be naked performing high-level magic. The cloak is cleansed and bespelled for warmth."

"So, since you've trapped me here, one of us has to freeze until you say what you need to," I huffed.

"I'm happy to share the cloak if my freezing my balls off makes you uncomfortable." Alexander shivered. When my eyes drifted down, I noticed the cold wasn't affecting his hard-on. Alexander dropped his gaze and smirked. "It's the power high. Gets us hard as hell. Don't go complaining now. There were many nights I used the effects of casting to bring you repeated pleasure for hours."

My body heated at the memory, but I couldn't go there. "If you can behave yourself, I'll share the cloak until what needs to be said is heard."

The corner of Alexander's mouth turned up, but he gave me a nod as he released his hold on me. Taking Alexander's hand, I lowered myself to the soft carpet of moss on the ground, pulling him to follow, then laid down. When Alexander lay beside me, I adjusted the cloak to cover both of us like a blanket.

For a moment, we both just lay there side-by-side, letting the cloak warm us. Once neither of us was shivering, and the cloak's enchantment warmed the ground beneath us, Alexander took my hand in his.

"I've been in love with you since we were kids, Spectra. You're not my balance. I can accept that, but not having you in my life isn't an option. I've tried, just like you have, but I can't not see you or touch you. I at least need what we had before. I hated it, but I could bear that better than losing you entirely."

I chewed my lip, letting Alexander's words sink in before I reacted. It killed me to have lost our friendship. I knew Mercury and Bay were where I was always meant to end up in my heart, but Alexander was right; we had a connection even before the tether of our souls.

"I'm married."

"To a guy who you were seeing while still fucking me," Alexander countered. "You're not the sort to cheat, so he knew about me before you married."

"He did. But that doesn't mean he permits it to continue now that we are."

"He's sharing you with Bay Ryder."

My mouth fell open, and I turned my head to argue, but Alexander met my eyes and squeezed my hand. "Please don't take me for a fool, Spectra. I saw your Angelis put you in Bay's arms when I came to the house that night. You have an open marriage."

"No, it's-" How did I explain our situation? If I told Alexander I was married to Bay, it would reveal more than just the relationship. It would also no longer be a secret, and I didn't trust Alexander not to tell his father or note it in the file they kept on me in the NSIO.

Alexander propped up his head with his elbow, rolling onto his side, waiting for my excuse. "It's?"

"Agreed to. Between Mercury, Bay, and me. It's not an open marriage, but a polyamorous one."

Alexander drew his brows together as he considered me. Slowly, he caressed my cheek. "Are you saying I need to seek permission from the Angelis for us to remain lovers?"

"If that's what I wanted. Then yes." Taking his hand from my cheek, I squeezed it gently and freed it. "Alex, I didn't marry Mercury until we ended for good. I assured him we were done. I gave up on us. I can't just turn around and let you back into my heart and life and pretend it never happened."

Cupping my cheek, Alexander forced me to meet his eyes. "Spec, I can't sleep or focus. The guilt of losing you is eating at me. Please?"

"What about Raquel?" I asked, throwing this back at him. "Does she know you're here pleading to still have me as your sidepiece?"

Inhaling hard enough that his nostrils flared, Alexander backed off. "I have to marry and provide an heir. Raquel is strong enough to try."

"But she's not your balance, Alexander. If she was, you wouldn't be here with me. I know the stories of how it is for sorcerers when they meet their balance. It's an instant attraction, and there is no other woman for them once they recognize her as theirs. So for you to be here with me tells me she's not your balance, and it's what proved to me I was never yours. You would never have looked elsewhere if I had been."

Watching me, Alexander wiped beneath my eye, collecting a stray tear as he did. He leaned his forehead against mine and sighed. "I'm sorry I hurt you like that, Spectra."

"I'm sorry I was so hurt by you finding someone else that I cut you off without talking it through," I countered.

"I need you in my life."

"Alex-"

His lips pinched mine gently. "Please."

Putting my hand on Alexander's chest, I created tension, forcing his mouth back from mine enough to meet his eyes. "That is the tether in our souls talking. I feel it in me too. The need to join our bodies to make you whole, but we can't keep falling into this blindly."

"Tethered soul. Raging boner from the power high and a beautiful woman nearly naked beside me." Alexander shrugged with a naughty grin.

I wasn't as amused. "There is another woman in your life who believes you are monogamous to her."

Alexander lifted a brow. "Do you really think Raquel is that good? She's Lucifer's granddaughter. She has to feed the darkness inside her." Alexander caressed my neck and collarbone. "Not all Nephilim are pure in their heart like you."

"Alex-"

"I love you, Spectra. Do you love me?"

The pain of denying my feelings flooded my eyes. "I don't trust you anymore. Your behavior at Bay's house—"

"Was because my soul was being tortured by your absence."

"The church? You hurt me on purpose."

"Trust me, your husband ensured I paid for that," Alexander huffed his reply. Taking a breath, he met my eyes. "I just wanted you to feel what it's like for me. The pain of constant separation—"

"Was only excusable until I offered to get us untethered to save you that, and you turned vicious," I justified. "Then it became about the power you control by having me tied to you. How can I trust you now?"

Anger flared in Alexander's eyes, but he didn't act on it. Instead, his hand caressed the ball of my shoulder. "I'm not denying there are secondary motives for wanting you in my life, Spectra. But the first is and always has been my love for you. I can't help that your ability as a balance benefits me in other ways. I'm selfish enough to refuse to give it up, but that's not why I'm not sleeping or able to focus. I miss you."

Sweeping Alexander's hair back from his face, I stared into his eyes, getting a sense of the value of his words. "Then settle for being my friend. Being close like this is enough to satisfy the yearning of your soul for its missing piece, isn't it?"

Barking a laugh, Alexander fell back beside me. "Not really, no. It certainly isn't satisfying my cock." He stared up at the sky for several breaths. "But it's better than not having you at all."

Lifting his arm, Alexander encouraged me to cuddle into his nook.

"I need to tell Mercury and Bay that I'm safe. They'll be worried. Especially after the violent way you drew me here," I reminded, not moving closer yet.

Alexander considered me. "Say yes to being with me, Spectra, and I'll message your priest and tell him you're safe and that I'll bring you back tomorrow."

My mouth fell open, appalled Alexander would stoop so low. "If I refuse?"

Alexander shrugged. "This circle stays in place, and your lovers get to stress about what happened to you. But we'll have plenty of time to hang out together as friends while they search everywhere for you. They won't find you here, by the way. My sacred space is well hidden."

When I just stared at him, the side of Alexander's mouth twitched, then eventually cracked into a smile. "Fuck, the look on your face." Sitting up, Alexander shook his head. Getting up, he moved around the circle, muttering under his breath.

The drawing down of the circle was like water running off my skin. Shivering as the space got a little colder without the circle's protection, I watched as Alexander moved outside the ring of candles and pulled on his jeans and jumper. Then coming back towards me, he tapped the screen on his phone before putting it to his ear.

"Father Mathew. Spectra asked me to call and let you know she's safe. Can you pass the message to her husband?" Alexander listened a moment, then met my eyes. "I'll bring her to you in the morning. We need to talk things through without everyone else gettin' all jelly and interfering."

Whatever Mathew replied made Alexander's smile vanish. Without a word, he handed me the phone. Taking it, I put it to my ear. "Mathew."

"Spec. Are you okay?"

"A little worse for wear, but Alexander didn't hurt me on purpose this time. Summoning a Wraith isn't a practiced art."

"Idiot. Luke and Calin are freaking out about what happened to you. Bay and Mercury are searching the city. They've been to Alexander's place already. I'll let them know I've heard from you."

"And that I'm safe."

"Are you?"

Lifting my eyes to where Alexander had retreated and was drinking from a water bottle, I sighed. "I believe so, yes. As Alexander said, we need to talk. I ended things abruptly, and it had an effect."

Exhaling a long breath, I considered what we'd already

discussed and lowered my voice. "Mathew, if I can't resist temptation?"

Mathew was silent for a long minute. "Your souls are bound together. Your husbands will understand if physical connection eases what you both suffer. Do what you need to do to get home to them, Spectra. Confession can take care of the rest."

Closing my eyes, I nodded at his advice but didn't give my concerns any voice. The simple fact was that I would try to get through this night without submitting to Alexander's needs, but I couldn't deny that touching him still affected me. To the point his nearness made me want to reach for him.

"Thank you. Tell my husband I love him and will see him tomorrow." Mathew would know I meant both of them.

"I'll see you in the morning. Put L'Ordre back on," Mathew requested.

Holding the phone out to Alexander, he swapped me for the bottle of water he'd been drinking from. While I took a few big mouthfuls, he walked away with the phone, a smirk pulling at the side of his mouth. "It doesn't. This is very much about Spec and me. I'm a good son, but I don't subscribe to all of my father's ideas. I have no intention of handing her over to them."

Hanging up, Alexander dropped the phone on what looked like a backpack before returning to where I was seated. Laying back down and pulling the cloak across him, Alexander encouraged me to cuddle into him like we used to as teenagers. "So, tell me how the job hunting is going?"

# CHAPTER 28

## BAY

*"BAY!"*

Spectra's scream was an echo in my soul. I couldn't say I heard it, but I damn well felt it, along with her fear and pain. Our bond was getting stronger daily. I'd left Jacoby to monitor our test subjects and cut through the ether back to the estate.

Storming into Spectra's bedroom, I was shocked to find Luke near her smashed bedroom window, blood dripping down his arm despite the wound having already healed. Calin and Gina stood halfway into the room.

Gina stood covering her mouth with tears in her eyes. But as Gina's eyes found me, her hands dropped away, her eyes hardened, and she told me what I feared. "She's gone. Someone forced her Wraith and dragged her out of Luke's arms."

My heart thundered in my chest. Moving to where Luke stood, I saw the pain in his eyes. "I tried to hold her here long enough, but she was in so much pain and so exhausted from fighting them, she let go."

"Long enough for what?" I asked. My hand already moving, sensing the magic around him, getting a feel for it.

"This." Calin held up a fancy-looking syringe. I knew what it was without asking. "Luke thought if we could hold her long enough to inject her with a tracker—"

Nodding my head once, I let the magic drop from my hand. "It was a soul summoning spell usually used to summon the dead. He either didn't know what that would do to her or didn't care."

"He who?" Luke snarled. I hadn't seen him this worked up in a while.

"Alexander Williams."

Across the room, Gina gritted her teeth and turned and left the room without a word. Tilting my head, I wondered if Spectra saving her had built a stronger friendship than I had realized. Deciding it wasn't important right now, I focused on Spectra.

"Luke, I need you to search the places we know L'Ordre uses for rites. Calin, get our eyes at NSIO to let you know if they have Spectra there, and I want you to check out Henry and where he is. I'll call Mercury and go to Alexander's place. He'll want to take her somewhere private if this is about anything other than the NSIO."

As the others rushed to do what I asked, I pulled out my phone and dialed Mercury. He didn't answer. "Alexander Williams has Spectra. I'm heading to his place if you know where that is."

Hanging up, I used the ether to take me right into Alexander's living room. The place was dark. Empty. Central heating kept it warm, so I couldn't tell how long it had been since he'd been home, but the sense was not for a few days.

Since I'd never been in Alexander's apartment, I decided to put my time waiting to see if he brought my wife here to good use. Looking around the living area, there was nothing really personal on display. Not even any photos of his family. Strange, but he did bring women back here. Maybe he preferred his privacy.

But on the coffee table, next to a half-empty bottle of vodka, was a photo album. Picking it up, I flipped it open to find a book dedicated solely to Spectra. Photos of the two of them and Spectra by herself since grade school all the way up until she graduated only a few weeks ago.

The slight shifting of air around me alerted me to another presence. "Don't," I warned. "I am not in the mood for whatever you intend."

A sleek shadow moved near the doorway to Alexander's bedroom. While the hooded jacket protected their identity, I still recognized this de Sang. "You're one of her protectors. How did you know?"

"I always know," the cultured voice of a female responded.

In those three words, I knew this de Sang was young when she died, maybe in her late teens or early twenties. She was educated and came from money. Yet she stood here in ripped jeans and a hoodie that clearly came from an op shop. Most de Sangs didn't lower their societal class upon dying. They raised it. So this woman used her clothing to blend and be innocuous.

"You're Fantôme?"

"Do you know where she is?" the female asked, shifting to look over Alexander's desk.

"I know who she is with."

"But where?" the de Sang pressed. "Is she still in pain? Is he hurting her? What do you feel of her?"

Stilling, I eyed the assassin searching Williams' apartment while keeping me within her sights. "You know we are wed? How?"

"You left her blood on the floor after the Collector bled her." Her growl told me she wasn't happy I was wedded to Spectra and that she thought I was careless with her.

"I did no such thing. I ordered one of our men to clean it up. To bleach the entire place clean. I went back to check later, and it had been done."

The de Sang assassin paused. "I was there hours after Spectra was rescued, Mr. Ryder. I assure you, nothing was done to clean the site. Miranda and I cleaned it, including disposing of the Collector and evidence of Spectra's escape." The assassin's vivid green eyes glinted at me from beneath the hood as they met my angry gaze. "You have rats in your nest."

"When it comes to Essence, they seem hard to weed out."

"You are not the only beast master to walk the planet," the assassin smirked.

"No. But I am the strongest. I'll deal with the infestation. May I ask your name since we've encountered each other repeatedly?"

"Names aren't important."

"Yet, even Alexander knows you watch Spectra. You trusted him to protect her."

That snapped her attention to me, making her forget her search. Lifting a brow, I moved to the landscape photos on Williams' wall. "I was there in the church when you told him to deal with me." Observing another of the pictures, I realized we weren't going to find Spectra here tonight.

Stalagmites looked like tree trunks, walls so dark they looked like the night sky except where they reflected the camera's flash. There was only a small area of grass, or maybe it was thick moss on the ground. Perfectly sized and shaped for a protective circle.

"They're not coming here. Alexander's got her at his sacred space." I pointed to the array of photos.

The assassin's eyes flicked to the photos. "But sorcerers need to be able to see the sky for their magic."

"Only for high magic, and this cave does have an opening to the sky. It will probably only be the size of a well high above him, but these photos' greenery tells me sunlight somehow gets in."

Moving to the door, I stopped and glanced over my shoulder at the Fantôme assassin. "Spectra's the balance meant for me. I'd never hurt her."

"Nika," the de Sang muttered. "I'm Nika."

With a bow of my head, I stepped outside the apartment door. My phone rang as I was halfway down the stairs. "Mercury?"

"I just heard from Mathew. Alexander called him and let him speak to Spectra. She's safe. He just wanted to talk to her. He assured Mathew he would not hand her over to the NSIO."

"Where is she?" I asked. I needed to see her and hold her to know she was safe and unharmed.

"Still talking with Alexander. He promises to have her back in the morning."

"You trust him?" I doubted Mercury did.

"I trust Spectra. If she says she is safe, then I believe her. If she tells Mathew she needs the time to talk to Alexander, I trust Spectra knows what she is doing."

Mercury was right. Spectra had been alone in the world long before I came into her life. She knew how to handle herself or when to ask for help. "He does love her, Merc. She may not be his balance, but he loved her long before he knew she was a balance."

"I know, but that doesn't buy him a pardon or right to be one of her lovers after how he treated her," Mercury huffed.

"And what about Tommy?" I asked. Mercury fell silent. "I find it hard to believe you encouraged me to pay that debt, not knowing Tommy would want to do more than watch."

Mercury stayed silent on the other end of the line. Answer enough in my books. "How many other Angelis will want a taste of our wife?"

I could hear Mercury's jaw clenching on the other end of the line. Finally, he blew out a breath. "There was a pact. To protect her, initially, but slowly, we all developed feelings for her. Not all the same, and not all with the same intentions. I fell in love with her long before we ever kissed. I knew I needed to love her from the moment I saw her."

"Mathew?"

"Purely protection. Mathew's got that big brother love going with Spectra and just wants to keep her safe and teach her what she should have known. Tommy's is a little kinkier. He was just meant to be another protector. When you and Spectra had that moment in his club, his desire to watch her fuck became a fantasy that hounded him."

"Did it sate him?"

"Yes. But not permanently. Tommy's not balanced that thoroughly in decades. I'm afraid you just became his balancing act of choice."

"Of course we did," I huffed. "Any others I need to know about?"

"Just one. He's the one who saved Spectra, who created the pact. Who tied Alexander's soul to hers to keep her from converting."

"And what does he want with our wife?"

"His part in our pact is to keep her father away from her."

That got my attention.

"Why?"

"That, I'm afraid, is Angelis business that I can't disclose. I have to go, Bay. I'll let you know if I hear anything more from Spectra." He hung up, leaving me wondering what the hell else he was hiding from me.

Frustrated, I called Mathew. "Thank God I'd already given up on sleeping tonight. I gather Mercury called you?" Mathew answered.

The sound of spanking and a woman crying out, 'Oh father! Punish my sinful cunt!' came from the background.

"I gather that's the porn Spectra purchased for you?"

Mathew chuckled. "Abstinence sucks, as I'm sure you know."

"So, you're an actual priest?"

"This identity is ordained, yes. But that's not what you are calling about. I haven't heard anything more from Spectra."

"I know your kind has class structures. How much further up the power ladder is Mercury than you?"

"What makes you think he is higher placed?" The movie went silent in the background, and I could only assume that Mathew had turned it off.

"He's the son of an Arch, and I find you more forthcoming with information about my wife than my brother-husband."

"Ah! I don't think it's because he doesn't trust you with Spectra, Bay. More that the Angelis guard their secrets closely. In telling you about Spectra, he reveals himself to you. Does that make sense?"

Blowing out a breath, I pushed out into the chilly night. "Some. Can you tell me why the Angelis want to keep Spectra's father away from her?"

Mathew went quiet. "Mercury said that, did he?"

"He said there was a pact between four of you to protect her, and you all had a role to play."

"And Lincoln told Mercury he's keeping Michael ignorant of his daughter's existence. Interesting. Thank you for letting me know, Bay."

"You sound like there is subterfuge afoot."

"Well, let me put it this way. Either Mercury lied to you to prevent telling you something he didn't think you'd like to hear, or Lincoln is playing a different game to the one he told each of us we were part of."

"I'm not sure which of those I prefer," I answered honestly.

"Strangely, neither do I. I'll call you once I have Spectra." Mathew disconnected the call. Something told me I'd just unsettled the pact between the Angelis.

Giving up on this evening, not feeling any spikes of distress or pain from Spectra, I headed home.

Hours later, I was pacing my study floor when a sensation I'd never experienced passed through me. Pausing, I took a moment to assess what I felt, where it started in my gut and weighed heavy on my heart, and then I hung my head. "Oh, Spec."

Moving to the chair by the fireplace, I sank into it, the sensation of tears on my cheeks was surprising, but when I wiped them and found them dry, I realized again that it wasn't mine. So, I sat there, staring at the flames dancing, my bare feet buried in the soft fur of the bear skin rug.

Sunrise came and went. My phone stayed silent. I would be heading to Mayer Callisie's smorgasbord in a few hours, but if Spectra didn't turn up soon, I wouldn't go. Her well-being and safety were my priority, and I knew she would need me.

Unable to focus on work, I got ready for the party in the early afternoon. This proved worthwhile when I got the call I'd been waiting on an hour later. "Mathew?"

"Bay, I'm sorry it took so long. Spectra is fine physically, but well, she's a bit chaotic. I've heard her confession, and she has completed her penance, but now she needs to share her burden with the men she loves. Mercury has been here since he finished work. He's trying to soothe her, but it won't work without you."

"I'm on my way." Hanging up, I sent Luke a message to pick me up from the church, then cut through the ether to get to my wife.

Surprisingly, my sense of Spectra wasn't inside when I arrived outside the church. Following the sensation, I came to a small cottage and knocked on the door. The smells coming from the door were human. An aged male.

Mathew opened the door with a sigh and let me inside. "Whose place is this?" I asked straight away.

"Mercury lives here with our groundskeeper. Luckily, he's currently working," Mathew explained, leading me towards the back of the cottage. When we reached a door where I could feel my wife on the other side, Mathew turned to face me.

"She had intimate relations with Alexander," Mathew warned quietly.

"I'm aware."

"Spec is married to you and Mercury. So in Spectra's mind, she committed adultery. She needs reassurance, not your anger or jealousy."

Placing my hand on Mathew's shoulder, I squeezed gently. "I felt her guilt when it manifested. I am not jealous or angry with her."

Returning the gesture so that we squeezed each other's shoulders, Mathew nodded, then stepped back and opened the door.

## CHAPTER 29

## BAY

STEPPING INTO THE ROOM, I was surprised by how small it was. I think Spectra's walk-in closet at my place was more than double the size of Mercury's bedroom here.

"Bay," Mercury murmured from where he sat on the bed.

Spectra raised her tear-streaked face from where she was huddled against his chest and met my eyes. The guilt was eating her up. Exhaling, I slipped out of my coat, set it on the reading chair with Mercury's leather jacket, and then moved halfway up the bed. "Spec, come here."

Biting her lip, fresh tears escaping her eyes, Spectra crawled free of Mercury and came to stand before me. Her head was lowered, her shoulders folded forward.

"Look at me," I soothed, lifting her chin to meet my eyes. She did, those pale blues watering like crazy. "Your soul is tethered with Alexander. Your heart belongs to Mercury. Your body is mine."

Spectra whimpered. My thumb rubbed over her lips. "We love you. When I say we, I don't just mean Mercury and me." I waited as a sob racked her body. "Spectra. We love you. You cannot sin when you love us in return."

Another sob and the tiniest shake of her head. I tightened my grip on her jaw, enough to make her gasp as her eyes shot open wide to meet mine. "I love you. Do you love me?"

"Yes."

"Then being with me can't be a sin. Mercury loves you. Do you love him?"

"Yes, of course, but-"

"Then being with him is not a sin. Alexander loves you." Spectra cringed. I softened my tone. "Do you love him?"

Sniffling, Spectra closed her eyes and gave the slightest nod of her head. "Not enough. Say it, Spec. Do you love Alexander?"

"Yes." It was the barest of whispers, a breath with intonation almost.

Caressing her face, I breathed a kiss across her cheek to her ear. "Then you did nothing wrong," I soothed. My free hand skated down the front of her body, her nipples pebbling at my barely-there caress. "But we can arrange penance if you feel in your heart that you have transgressed and your confession to your god was not sufficient."

Spectra gasped, her eyes blinking wide as my hand found her bare thigh and caressed just where the satin slip ended against her skin. "Would that help, Spec? Do you think it would unburden your soul if Mercury and I take our pound of flesh?"

As we stared into each other's eyes, Spectra swallowed hard. Her tears had dried up, and her jaw trembled as she breathed the word, "Yes."

"Then confess your sin, and I will count the lashes?"

"Lashes?" Spectra's eyes rounded with surprise.

Smirking, I let my eyes slide to Mercury who was now standing behind our wife, his eyes on me with a sort of fear and utter reverence burning in them. "So to speak. Mercury, keep count." Mercury nodded behind me.

Slipping the spaghetti straps from Spectra's shoulders, I gave the slip of material a little encouragement, and it slithered from her body. "Did you kiss him?"

Frowning, Spectra nodded.

"Use your words, Spec."

"Yes."

Using my grip on her jaw, I dropped my shields enough to bathe her in my lust and kissed the hell out of her. When I finally pulled back, we were both breathing heavily. "That's one." Gripping Spectra's elbows, I pulled her torso forward and nodded at Mercury. He didn't even hesitate to spank our wife's ass.

Spectra jumped, eyes and mouth open wide as a yelp left her throat. Mercury massaged the spot, moving his neck until it cracked, a smile pulling at the side of his lips as he met my eyes and nodded once. Spectra moaned. Just a breath, her breasts brushed against my chest, and her ass pushed back into Mercury.

"Good girl," I murmured as I pulled back to meet her eyes. They were glassy with desire instead of tears now. Excellent. Let's see if we could appease her guilt and help her and Mercury find common ground simultaneously.

Dropping my hand, I brushed my palm across her firm tits, my thumb flicking her nipple, causing her to bite her lip and groan. "Did he touch and caress your beautiful breasts?"

"Yes."

"Did he ravish them with his mouth?"

"Yes."

"Two," I announced, then bent and ravished them, removing the taint of her sin. Two loud smacks filled the room in quick succession. Spectra cried out, her nails digging into my shoulders through my suit, but as Mercury massaged away the sting, her fingers eased their tension.

Dropping to my knees, my thumb brushed over her folds. They were already slick with her want, but she'd be dripping by the time I sank into her. "Here?"

Swallowing loudly, Spectra trembled. "Yes."

"Fingers?"

"Yes."

"Mouth." Silence greeted me. Spectra shook her head just a touch, making me grin. "Just one then."

Spectra jolted and cried out as I held her, then before she could recover, I covered her clit, licked it, then sucked hard.

"Oh. My. Fucking. God!" Spectra threw her head back as my lips released, and I licked her labia, tasting her arousal before I spread her lips open and took a sip from the source.

"That's it, baby. Grind all over his mouth," Mercury cajoled, his hands cupping and massaging Spectra's breasts. "Let him cleanse you, ready you for me. Because when I sink into you, I'll take the rest away, baby. You'll be ours again."

Spectra moaned words of agreement, of thanks for us cleansing her of her sin. It reminded me a little of what I heard of Mathew's nun porn last night, and I nearly choked on a laugh until Spectra tensed, her body getting ready to climax.

Pulling away, I smiled at the pout on her mouth when I left her hanging on the edge. Still, I kissed her so passionately that her whimpers were soon replaced with moans, her body rubbing all over me as I walked her backward. It only took two steps to reach the bed. Spectra caught between Mercury and me.

"You fucked him?"

"Yes," Spectra whimpered, and for a moment, the tears sprang back to life. "He didn't use protection."

Ah. That's what this was really about. Spectra had never given herself to him entirely, and now she had in a way that she knew was reserved for her husband. It didn't matter. I already owned her body. We were bound. No sorcerer could have that with her now. I wondered if Alexander realized that as he lay spent inside her.

"I'm so used to being with you and Mercury, I forgot," Spectra confessed.

My eyes met Mercury's over her head, wondering how he felt about it. The grit of his jaw told me he was a lot more pissed about this revelation. So, I raised a brow, turned my eyes to Spectra, and caressed her jaw.

"Everything else we could handle, love. Not that. That is for us only. You understand?"

A single tear rushed Spectra's cheek as she bowed her head in regret. Capturing it with my thumb, I sipped it from the tip, then tilted her face up and placed a tender kiss on her lips. Then I took two steps back.

Spectra's eyes widened, and she reached for me. "Bay—"

"Five."

Spectra lost her balance as the first smack hit. I caught her elbows and held her steady as Mercury spanked her bottom red, Spectra crying out with each slap to her inflamed flesh. When he dealt the five smacks, Mercury dropped his jeans, pulled his shirt over his head, and sat on the edge of the bed. Grabbing Spectra's hips, he yanked her back and onto him making her curse profoundly.

Not giving Spectra a chance to recover, Mercury started fucking her hard and fast. One of his arms wrapped over her breasts to hold her, the other giving him leverage on the bed behind him. Cupping Spectra's jaw, I locked her eyes with mine.

"You are our wife. We love you and will forgive you for seeking the comfort of the man who is tethered to your soul. It was never a sin. But the next time Alexander tries to bury that need in you bare, you'll remember this. Remember your husbands' love for you and what it means for you to give yourself so freely to another. Won't you?"

"Yes," Spectra whimpered.

Mercury was being too rough for her; I could see it in her eyes that she was fighting her natural instinct. Mercury hadn't balanced. That was the fear I'd sensed in him. His clenched jaw and the tension in his shoulders and neck showcased his fight against the temptation of getting rougher, of taking what he needed. But that wasn't fair.

"You gave Alexander what he needed. You can't do that for him and not your husband, Spec. Open yourself to what Merc needs from you. Give into him."

More curse words left her lips as Mercury became unrelenting. Inhaling, I exhaled and dropped my shields entirely, bathing them both in my power. Mercury barely flinched, but his thrusts evened out, and the bruising grip on Spectra's breast became a massage.

Spectra gasped, leaned back into Mercury, and grabbed a handful of his hair. Then she kissed him and rode him just as hard as he took her.

"Beautiful," I murmured.

Moving away, I kept my eyes on them as I slowly undressed. I couldn't leave Spectra and not have her one more time. I knew tonight was a trap. On the off chance I didn't make it home from the smorgasbord, I wanted to take the scent and feel of her with me.

Spectra screamed her orgasm as it came over her, taking the Lord's name in a way that I knew Mathew would be handing out more penance by tomorrow. Mercury grunted and stilled. Both of them breathed heavily.

Wrapping a hand around Spectra's waist, I lifted her from her Angelis and pulled her close, so she wrapped her legs around me. Then turned and pinned her to the wardrobe door.

Spectra gasped as I slid inside her. Slowly, I wound and rocked my hips in a dance of passion. She'd taken her punishment, siphoned Mercury's need, and turned it back on him. Now, I would love her. Gently. Carefully. I took my time, kissed, caressed, and let her feel how completely I was lost for her.

As we reached our peak and edged towards euphoria, I kissed her ear and whispered, "I love you. We love you. Whatever you do, if you do it out of compassion or love, we will always forgive you. Never forget it."

Spectra's eyes widened as I thrust a little firmer. Once, twice, she threw her head back, her body clenching and quivering as she climaxed. Two more thrusts and I was there with her, floating for those few critical seconds together before we plummeted back to earth.

Once the strength returned to my legs, I carried Spectra to the bed. Eased her down, kissed her, then backed away and dressed. Mercury was already retaking her, making love to her now just like I had done.

"I have to go," I announced, pulling my coat into place and checking my phone to see if Calin was waiting out front with Mathew. "Get her home safe," I told Mercury.

Breaking apart, Mercury nodded while Spectra reached for me. "Bay," she squeaked almost desperately. Going to her, I took her hand. "Thank you. For loving me. For—" she didn't say it, but her eyes shifted to Mercury and back to me, a blush filling her cheeks.

Giving her a wink, I squeezed her hand. "Stay safe, mon amour."

Outside, I took a deep breath of the cool night air. "Need a cigarette?" Calin asked from the shadows, both he and Mathew sitting at a small sun table there. "I needed one hearing it."

Smirking, I shook my head. "I'm going to be late. And snow is coming."

"Luke's waiting in the car." Calin pointed to where my sports car was parked in the driveway.

"Did you tell Mathew?" I checked.

"Yes," Calin answered. "They know to keep her safe if you don't come home."

Nodding, I met Mathew's eyes. "Thank you." When he tilted his head in acknowledgment, I shoved my hands in my pockets and headed toward the car.

"Bay," Mathew called. He waited for me to stop and glance over my shoulder. "Why do this? Why take the risk?"

"Because if I don't, they'll come for me another way, putting Spectra at further risk." Not waiting for further discussion, I accepted my fate and simply asked to make it home to my wife after tonight.

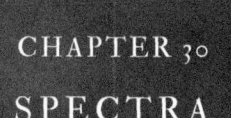

# CHAPTER 30

# SPECTRA

When Gina walked into the kitchen Sunday morning, she stopped and stared at me, a smirk pulling at the side of her mouth.

"What?" I asked, unable to hide my smile as I cooked breakfast for everyone.

"You're singing and cooking," Gina observed, her eyes flitting around the kitchen. She took in the set table with juice and toast piled on a plate warmer with a cover. "Are you making breakfast for everyone?"

"I thought it'd be nice to have breakfast together on a Sunday. You know, like a family," I explained, filling a bowl with scrambled eggs.

"Who's family?" Gina scrunched her nose.

Hesitating, I remembered Gina grew up in an entirely different situation to me. "I, ah… Before my sister died, we'd always eat breakfast together on Sundays before church. I know I'm not getting any of you to come to church with me, but I thought we could at least"—I looked at all the food I'd made and bit my lip—"I should have asked first. I'm sorry. It's fine. I'll eat and leave the rest for the others when they want it."

Taking the eggs to the table, I set the bowl down and looked out the window. Closing my eyes, I scolded myself. *They're a pack of predators. Of course they don't sit down and share a meal like a family.* I slumped down in the seat I'd claimed as mine because it had the best view out the window. It also happened to be the chair next to the one I'd realized Bay favoured.

A deep huff came from behind me. "I'll go get everyone. There better be coffee when I get back."

"On it," I declared happily. The side of my mouth twitched as Gina stormed out of the room and I raced over to get the coffee machine going.

When Calin and his wives pushed through the door, their noses leading them straight to the table, I was setting a pot of pitch-black gold out for them. Luke came through the door, and I turned with a smile expecting Bay to be with him. But he wasn't.

Tilting my head, I wondered if he'd had a late night or early morning. "Where's Bay?" I asked. "Is he still out running?" I checked the time on my phone because Bay was usually back from his runs long before now.

Luke frowned, looked at the time, then turned his head to Calin. "Do you know where he is?"

Eyeing me, Calin shook his head. "You cooked all of this, lil' sister?"

Confused by the sudden nickname, I smiled and nodded. That's when Mercury wrapped me in a hug and kiss from behind. "Morning, Angel. Sleep well?"

"Very. Have you seen Bay this morning?" I asked, enjoying his warmth.

"I just got home from work," Mercury answered, encouraging me to take a seat while he took Bay's usual spot.

"But Bay sits there," I whispered.

Mercury looked to Calin, shrugged a shoulder, and gave me a peck on the cheek. "You snooze, you lose. This looks amazing."

Unease settled in my stomach as I realized I couldn't feel Bay's presence. Being able to sense my husbands was something I still hadn't gotten used to. "Did he have an early morning? He's not here at the house and never came to bed last night."

"Did you sneak up to his room after I left?" Mercury asked. He'd put me to bed in our room, so it was a fair question. I shook my head. "Then how do you know he didn't sleep in his bed?"

"Because I can feel it," I snapped.

Everyone stopped, staring at me. Licking my lips, I sunk a little in my chair. "Sorry. I can just tell Bay hasn't been here all night."

"Didn't he go to the smorgasbord last night? Some fancy one uptown," Calin asked Luke.

"Yeah. The boss was using it to meet with some people he knew a few centuries ago. He told me to head home, and he'd make his own way back," Luke explained. "Maybe they made a night of it."

The words were honest, but there was something I couldn't put my finger on, which made my stomach twist. Everyone was eating, sharing the bowls around. I handed them on without taking anything.

"Aren't you going to eat any of this food you made?" Cyn asked when everything settled down. "Spectra?"

"Huh?" I looked around and noticed everyone was watching me again. "Um, I think I'm going to get started on my training and do my run before Mathew gets here." Rising from the table, I headed to the door.

"I'll come with you," Calin decided.

"You don't have to."

"Actually, I do," Calin replied, his eyes intent on me as he stood to follow me. "Plus, I haven't got my run in this morning." Calin glanced quickly at Mercury, and then we were heading outside and jogging out towards the forest.

I took the lead, setting the course Mathew had me running every weekend. I wasn't much for extreme exercise before this new training regime, but I got used to it quickly. Mathew said being Angelis was about having stamina.

"Why are you lying to me?" I asked when we reached the halfway point.

"I'm not lying," Calin defended. But in saying those words, he lied.

Picking up speed, I ran like something was chasing me. Why would Calin lie about Bay's whereabouts? It didn't make sense.

"Spec."

What could Bay be doing that Calin didn't want me to know? In my head, I heard heavy breathing. Could feel nausea rolling around inside me. Exhaustion and hunger clawed up my throat.

"Spectra!"

Hands grabbed me, and it just made the hunger worse. "Don't touch me!"

A flash of light. A grunt of pain. I blinked, and I was in the woods. Calin was meters away, sprawled on the ground, staring back at me wide-eyed. I was breathing hard, but I didn't think the run had been that strenuous.

Out of nowhere, Mercury appeared, took us both in, then turned to Calin. "What happened?"

Groaning, Calin got to his feet. "Spec started running faster than I could keep up on two legs. She freaked out when I tried to stop her and threw me off."

"Spec?" Mercury turned to me, wanting my version of the story, only I didn't have one.

Frustrated, I shook my head. "He's lying about Bay."

Mercury didn't even blink. "If Bay wanted you to know where he is, he would have told you. And since when have you been the clingy type?"

"I'm not. I just don't like being lied to." Annoyed, I shook my head and started back for the house. "I'm starving. I'm going back before there's no food left." Breaking back into my run, pounding my frustrations into the ground below me, I finished my run in record time.

Selena and Luke were just clearing the table when I got back. Going to the fridge, I grabbed a bottle of water and skulled it down.

"Wow, you've gotten fast. You might be able to keep up with Bay and me now," Luke praised while checking his watch.

Finishing the bottle, I refilled it from the filtered water tap. "Maybe. Is there any food left?"

"On the counter," Luke pointed at the bowls, watching as I proceeded to drink the second bottle before refilling it again.

Finally getting some relief from the dryness in my mouth and throat, I set the bottle aside. Grabbing a plate, I filled it with some cold toast, a strip of bacon, and the leftover egg and sat at the table.

"What's wrong?" Luke murmured to Selena.

"Her aura is different. Almost like it's filled with static. Something's not right with her."

I looked up to find them both watching me scrape my plate clean. I was about to ask why when Mercury and Calin arrived. My hunger sated, I took my plate to the sink and rinsed it before putting it in the dishwasher. I finished my glass of orange juice, then drank my third bottle of water.

"God, I'm so thirsty today." When everyone watched me warily, I huffed and refilled the bottle again. "Mathew will be here soon. I'm going to go and practice twirling a stick."

Calin followed me but kept his distance. Mercury headed to bed. When Mathew arrived, he observed me and set me on a task before having a quiet word with Calin. Mathew kept me busy the rest of the day, and I was so exhausted by the time we finished that I fell into bed with only a slight worry that I hadn't heard from Bay all day.

The following morning, I got up and readied for work. The hunger was gnawing at me again, so I made a big breakfast and drank four bottles of water before anyone else made it downstairs. Suddenly nauseous, I raced to the bathroom and puked everything I'd just eaten. Groaning, I stared at the bathroom wall.

Bay still wasn't home. Hadn't been home. I let that knowledge hurt me for only a moment, then I put it aside and focused on making a good impression for my second week at Galaxy. When I got home, Mathew was there and dragged me into the gym to exhaust me.

It was the same on Tuesday, Wednesday, and Thursday. Friday morning, I'd had enough.

"Where is he?" I asked quietly while Luke, Calin, and Gina had their morning coffee. No one answered.

"Something is wrong with him. I can feel it. I haven't had one hunger pang since I became a Wraith, and this week I've woken every day starving and thirsty. The hunger is now a constant ache." Everyone exchanged glances but stayed quiet.

Getting up, I walked out and down the driveway, not waiting for Miranda to arrive.

"What's going on?" Miranda asked when she pulled up to find me waiting with the guards at the gate.

"Bay hasn't been home all week, and no one will tell me where he is," I answered through clenched teeth. "I dream of him every night. He's either rolling around in pain with his hunger or has his fangs and fingers so deep in another woman it hurts me, but it doesn't sate him."

Shaking my head, I met Miranda's face, my eyes brimming with tears. "I haven't been hungry a single day since I died. But Bay goes missing, I dream of him starving every night, and then I eat until I puke every morning. Yet, everyone is pretending like nothing is wrong."

Miranda considered me. "I'll reach out to a friend and try to have an answer for you by this evening."

"Thank you."

Miranda put the car in gear, turned the music up like usual, and I turned my mind to my last trial day and all the questions I'd written down to ask last night before it was over.

On the way home, Miranda turned the radio down. "So, did they offer you a permanent role?"

"Not yet. Jack said it'd been great getting to know me. They have a few other candidates still to trial, but I should hear from them by the end of the month if I've been successful in getting the job," I answered.

"Great! So I have to keep working there for another month on the off chance you get offered a role because there is little chance I can just quit and then come back again." Miranda huffed and cursed under her breath. "Harvey isn't going to last another month. Maybe I can get a promotion before you come back." The smile Miranda threw my way was very telling.

Shaking my head, I turned my mind to home and licked my lips. "Did you find out anything about Bay?"

"Essence has him."

It was like an electric current zapped through my entire body.

Nodding once, Miranda continued. "They set a trap at a smorgasbord he was invited to. I don't know the details other than he is being kept prisoner by Mayer Callisie. He's come out of seclusion for the cure. And no, before you ask. We can't help on this one. He's just going to have to ride this one out."

Glancing at Miranda, my mind going a thousand miles per minute, the one thing I kept coming back to was that Calin and Luke had to know. "Why are they keeping it from me?"

"Because no one wants you looking for him, Spectra. If there is one person everyone fears Essence getting hold of worse than Bay, it's you. Bay may or may not know the formula to the cure, but he's also an ancient de Sang with a lot of magic at his disposal. He will survive this and make them regret it."

"In the meantime, I suffer and worry, and-" snapping my gaze to the side, I spotted a big SUV driving right at us at speed. "Miranda!"

The crunch of metal and glass filled my head, followed by darkness.

# CHAPTER 31

## BAY

My eyelids felt like sandpaper, my throat burned, and my heart and body ached. Rolling across the bed, the sheets tangled around me as the blood fever raged. I hadn't even been this hungry as a new de Sang.

The inferno inside me became too much to stand. Sitting up, I roared my rage, dropped my barriers, and flung my magic against every wall of my prison. The wards repelled my power, and the last of the gyprock exploded into dust and floated to the floor.

Falling back on the bed, sweating and panting, scratching at my throat in hunger, I whispered her name, "Spectra." The beautiful ghost who captured more than my lust. Every morning I feared losing her when I woke from the dreams haunted by her. But I could still feel her as if my hands held her.

My breathing slowed. The burn in my throat alleviated. Not entirely, but enough to cope. Closing my eyes, I gulped a breath and forced myself to sit. Observing my prison, I sneered at the wards engraved in the metal linings of the walls.

The room was once a luxurious guest accommodation. Over the week, my rage had demolished all the furniture except the bed. The uncontrolled lashing of my power had destroyed the illusion of the plaster ceiling and walls to reveal the iron and silver-laced barriers encasing my prison.

Nausea came like usual. Scrambling across the room and into what was once an ensuite but is now an exposed bathroom, I puked the toxic blood of last night's meal into the toilet bowl.

Sweeping a trembling hand through my sweat-soaked hair, I pushed to my feet unsteadily. I couldn't remember ever being this weak. At least the hunger abated enough that I could think clearly. That only made me worry for my wife. My balance. Siphoning a predator's need would have a nasty effect on her.

Every morning, I woke to the agony of hunger, but not long after the sun rose, it would leech away. Not all of it. But the worst of it. The pain worsened as the week wore on, and the relief became less effective.

It took me more days than it should have to realize why the hunger abated without my need to feed. Still, I didn't try and stop Spectra either. I needed her help.

Every day when Mayer Callisie came into my cell to use my weakness to give him the formula for the cure, I had my wits about me. I could think and respond clearly. Something that frustrated my captor. Only for him to send another poisoned chalice to me.

The first few nights, I tried to resist the allure of her blood, but the hunger gnawed at my insides, and it wasn't fair to Spectra to ask her to take all my cravings. So, I satisfied the women using my hand and fed on their toxic blood while they came. Blood that never sated me beyond the immediate ingestion.

It was a method of survival that couldn't last much longer. My control was slipping. Mayer wasn't stupid. Even when he entered the room, the door was locked from the outside. He used his phone and a particular predetermined code word that changed every day to indicate to the guard it was safe to open the door.

So, I wouldn't get out of here even if I tore the alchemist's head from his body. Mayer explained that I would be left here to starve and rot if I killed him.

What seemed like hours later, the door beeped and opened. A portable table was wheeled in by a de Viand while another carried two chairs and set them up in the middle of the room. A low-level de Sang brought a large tray filled with covered plates and supplies. Setting it down, he set the table like a five-star restaurant.

As the de Sang went to leave the room, I snapped into action. Wrapping a restraining arm around his chest, I grabbed his chin to turn his head. I bit deep, luxuriating in the untainted sustenance. It wasn't as fulfilling or nutritious, but it was better than nothing.

The clearing of a throat brought my eyes to the door where Mayer stood. Once he had my attention, he raised a brow. When I refused to give up my meal, he sighed and took his seat, waiting for me.

Finished with the bland meal, I released the de Sang, letting him fall to the floor unconscious, and took my seat. Clicking his fingers at one of the de Viands, he pointed to the drained body and poured red wine into each of our glasses.

"I should have known better," Mayer muttered as the door shut, leaving just the two of us.

Using the serviette to dab my mouth clear of any drips of blood, I then set it in my lap, ready to eat. "So, you're being hospitable now?"

"The definition of insanity is doing the same thing repeatedly and expecting a different result," Mayer explained as he removed the lids off the plates. "Starving you for a week should have had you begging for blood, willing to give me anything. That hasn't worked. It's time to try something new."

"Which is?" I raised a brow.

"Talking as civilized men who enjoy scientific discovery and research, and sharing good food."

Nodding my head, I followed Mayer's lead and started dishing food onto my plate. Juicy rare steaks and all the helpings you would expect as sides. But I didn't put a thing in my mouth until Mayer started eating, and then I followed his order, making sure I ate nothing he didn't touch first.

"You don't fuck your food," Mayer started, a subject entirely aside from what I expected. "Not that I wasn't aware of that for centuries, but I'd heard you were revived and preparing your own meals. Still, you don't have sex with them."

"No. I prefer to keep a clear delineation between food and lovers." I used only my hand or mouth to prepare my food when I fed. I didn't kiss them and would not give another woman my cock. Those two things I held back for my wife.

The poison chalice Mayer sent me was determined to seduce me last night. It took everything in me to resist breaking her slender neck when she dared to grope me.

"Why?" Mayer queried between mouthfuls.

"Does it matter?"

"I'm curious. I've never resisted feeding both my appetites."

Smirking, I took a sip of the wine. "It's just a personal preference."

Mayer raised an eyebrow. "I see." Finishing his meal, he sat back with his wine. "You're a very moral man, aren't you?"

That made me laugh. "Morality has a Likert scale. I just have a firm set of boundaries for my conduct."

Furrowing his brow, Mayer leaned forward, watching me earnestly. "So what made you go looking for a cure? Was there a particular enemy you wanted to use it against, or were you trying to wipe out a particular species?"

"Ah!" I set my empty glass down. "It's the first question everyone asks. Why? Interestingly, everyone always assumes it was to serve some nefarious purpose. To harm someone, or to take away some-one's free will."

"What other assumption is there to make?" Mayer conversed.

Picking some lint off my rumpled suit pants—I'd stopped wearing the shirt days ago—I sighed. "Too long ago, I learned that people's first assumptions about someone else reveals the character of the assumer."

"You say that because I suspect you of a nefarious mind, that I, myself, must have one?"

"After the last week, I didn't need your assumptions to define your character, Mayer."

Mayer grinned. "I guess not." Drumming his fingers on the table, Mayer considered me. "Who is Spectra Michaels?"

Narrowing my eyes, I sat back slowly. "An employee. What makes you ask?"

Reaching into his pocket, Mayer produced a phone and fidgeted with it. "She wouldn't happen to be the woman you came to my smorgasbord covered in, would she?"

The phone was the one I'd brought with me, but it was useless to them. It had no contacts or messages and wasn't linked to any accounts. It was the use of Spectra's name that concerned me. "Spectra's husband is an Angelis. You know as well as I do that anyone with two brain cells to rub together doesn't mess with an Angelis or his wife."

The side of Mayer's mouth twitched in unhappiness. "But she's the hacker Samus tried to take and ended up dead for." Placing my dummy phone on the table, Mayer removed his phone from his pocket. Tapping the screen a few times, Mayer then turned it to show me the footage of Spectra when she was being held by Essence a few weeks ago.

While I tried not to react, I knew I grew very still as I watched Samus pin my wife down and feed from her. The moment he realized she was a balance and how Spectra used it to her advantage.

The video played through. Samus losing his head. Miranda looked beneath the bed, then left. Then Mercury and Calin's team charged into the room almost too late, flipping the mattress and revealing Spectra exsanguinating on the floor.

Interestingly, when Mercury's power charged up, the sudden light between them took out the cameras in the room. Is that why Essence didn't know what happened to Spectra? Did Mercury's power act as an EMP? And if it did, how did he manage that at work?

"We know she lived. I gather the one who saved her is her husband?" Mayer paused and rewound the video to just before Mercury saved her and turned it to stare at Spectra lying all but dead in Mercury's arms. "How fortunate for her that she married a child of Raphael. But that doesn't explain why she lives with you."

"After Essence targeted my employee and tried to use her life to blackmail me, I offered her shelter. What was I meant to do? She was targeted because of her association with me."

"That was generous of you," Mayer challenged.

"As you said, I'm a moral man. And I don't want to be the reason why an Angelis loses his wife." Folding my arms, I relaxed back in my seat, eyeing Mayer, hating what I was about to do even more than the first time.

"If you are thinking of using Spectra to try and force my hand, I should warn you that Samus already tried that. So, I will tell you the same thing I told him before he tried to take an innocent. I like Spectra. She is a very resourceful young lady. While I would hate to see her harmed, especially considering what her husband is, Spectra is not worth compromising the antidote and having it fall into the hands of fascists."

Gritting his jaw, Mayer threw his napkin on his empty plate. "Well, Spectra Michaels' fate is out of my hands. Her skills garnered the attention of some of my colleagues, and you know what Essence is like once we become fixated. I just hoped she might be the stone by which we could shoot down two birds."

Frowning, I sat forward. "Who is the second bird?"

Rising from his chair, Mayer sighed. "It would seem Spectra Michaels has some very powerful allies. The other one that interests us is her best friend from childhood. Apparently, the poor boy is obsessed with her even though he can never marry her."

"L'Ordre?" I tilted my head.

Even without the confirmation, the glee in Mayer's eyes was answer enough. "A powerful tool to have in the belt of Essence arsenal, don't you think? We might not be able to get you to see things our way, Bay, but L'Ordre is said to be just as powerful."

Laughing, I stood to my full height, watching the smile vanish from Mayer's face. "You don't know."

"Know what?" Mayer snapped.

"Why you'll never get L'Ordre onside with you." Grinning, I shoved my hands in the pockets of my slacks and moved to stand across the room, enjoying this small win. "This means your little

Essence spy in his office either doesn't know or is twisting this situation to their selfish needs. Possibly both."

Watching Mayer's pupils narrow to pinpoints, I smirked. "Yes. I know you have someone in that office."

Hands curling into fists, Mayer quickly tucked them into his pockets, trying to portray relaxed confidence. "Pray then, do tell. What are we missing from our equations?"

"Spectra Michaels," I simply told him, enjoying the confusion that clouded his face. I let it sit long enough for a tic to form in the corner of his eye, a mannerism left over from his human days. "She isn't the reason L'Ordre will join Essence, Mayer. She's the reason he won't."

"Why?"

Glancing around the room, I let all humor fall from my face as I met Mayer's eyes. I glared into his soul, refusing to share my knowledge. The tic in Mayer's eye now included the side of his mouth on that side.

"What does that mean?" Mayer snarled. When I continued to meet his glare, Mayer lunged for me, but even weak as I was, I was faster, stronger. Grabbing his neck as I sidestepped, I used his momentum to turn him and shove him against the wall. Mayer screamed as the wards burned him for touching them.

"It means," I murmured close to his ear, the stench of burning flesh filling my nostrils. "That I'll happily explain to you why this ploy and the one to enslave L'Ordre to Essence were always doomed from the front porch of this building. And not a moment before."

Not letting up, I sank my teeth into Mayer's neck, taking my fill while he screamed and struggled against me. Stepping back, I flung Mayer away from me, letting him know that even weakened, I was much stronger than him, then resumed my casual stance.

Mayer stumbled, caught himself on the table, and panted as he touched his neck, checking it before turning wide eyes to look at me. I could have ripped his neck out, but I believed it would leave me to rot. The burns of the wards on the room were enough to get my threat across. He may hold me, but I can make him hurt.

"I'm done being your passive guest, Mayer. Release me or kill me."

Raging at my defiance, Mayer upturned the table, the crockery, and glassware smashing all over the floor. Pulling out his phone, Mayer typed in the password, then stormed to the door in time for it to open. "Clean it up," he ordered and stalked out.

Satisfied, I thumbed the stray drop of the alchemist's blood from the side of my mouth and casually moved forward. Collecting the dummy phone Mayer left behind, I put it in my pocket before the de Viands could enter.

A moment later, pain and fear breached my bond with Spectra.

*'Miranda!'* Spectra's cry echoed through the bond before everything faded. The sensation was reminiscent of when Alexander attacked Spectra at the church.

"Spec," I whispered, desperate to know she was safe, but nothing was there. The other end of our bond flapped free in the darkness as if it had been untethered. Having felt it before, I knew that wasn't the case, but it didn't stop me from worrying.

Eyes going to the door, I didn't need to wonder about the timing. Mayer asked about Spectra, telling me they knew she lived and where was obvious. Essence just made an attempt to retake Spectra. I just had to pray that Miranda was as good as the rumors of Fantôme suggested.

Gripping the phone in my pocket, I willed the de Viands to hurry up so I could call the burner I'd set up just in case I could stay in contact.

*'Stay strong, my love. I'll be home soon. I promise'.* I sent it through our bond. Even if she didn't hear the words, Spectra would feel the emotions behind them. I just had to hope she was there for me to come home to.

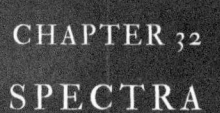

# CHAPTER 32

# SPECTRA

LOVE. Pure, unadulterated love swept me from the darkness and into my being. My head thrummed, my ears rang, and I wanted to vomit. Before I opened my eyes, I crept my hands toward my stomach, my entire body aching.

Slowly opening my eyes, I found darkness and shivered from the cold at my back. Above me were heavy clouds pouring rain down upon me. Confused, I turned my face to the left. Miranda's red vintage sports car was pushed off to the side of the road, looking untouched except for a blown tire.

From my perspective, I could see four pairs of boots and a woman's bare feet moving quickly on the other side of the car.

A loud grunt sounded, and knees joined one of those sets of boots, then the rest of his body as he collapsed to the ground, dead eyes staring toward me. The two others moved further along the roadside, continuing their battle.

Turning my head the other way was asphalt covered in shattered glass and bits of metal and debris. The SUV that hit us looked like it slammed into a solid cement wall at full speed, not Miranda's little sporty coupe, which barely had a scratch. Nearly the entire front of the SUV was gone, and the man in the driver's seat looked in the same state as the car.

Realizing I wasn't breathing, I filled my lungs with air, returning to corporeal form. As soon as I did, I started coughing. Rolling onto my side, I groaned. It didn't feel like I'd been injured, but I barely had the energy to lift my head.

Leveraging myself up, I got my hands on the ground and struggled to get my legs beneath me. My arms shook where they held my weight, and my legs felt like I'd been at sea for a month and couldn't handle the solid ground.

When I managed to get myself upright and stumble to the little red coupe to lean against, Miranda was striding towards me, looking all sorts of pissed off. "Are you okay?" she asked.

"Not feeling the best. Like I'm at the other end of a nasty stomach flu. What happened?"

"Well, you yelled at me just before these assholes hit us. There was a flash of bright light at impact. Whatever it was shielded our car and forced us off the road, but it totalled their car. When we stopped, you were gone, and the goons that survived the crash were trying to kill me and look for you."

"The air got knocked out of me with the impact," I explained my disappearance.

"Well, thank you for showing up. Let's get out of here before more Essence goons show up." Taking my elbow, Miranda helped me around to the passenger door and into the car. "Are you sure you're not hurt? Going Wraith doesn't normally affect you like this."

"I'll be fine. Nothing that a shit load of food and copious amounts of orgasms won't fix. At least that's what I did last time to counteract the effect."

Chuckling, Miranda tapped out a message in her phone. "Sounds like a cure I could get on board with. Why don't you order a few pizzas from that village pizzeria while I change the tire? Then they'll be ready by the time we are passing through." Shutting the door, Miranda raced to the back of the car. She'd changed the tire and started the engine by the time I'd completed the order.

Arriving back at the estate, Mercury and Mathew were waiting by the garage. As soon as the car came to a stop, Mercury had the door open, helping me out. "I ordered pizza," I told him, and indicated the back seat so they knew I was aware of what I needed. I was half asleep but trying to stay awake.

"What happened?" Mathew asked Miranda.

"Essence made a grab for her. They're all dead, and I made sure it was clear a de Sang killed them, but it won't stop them from coming for her. They know where she's living for them to hit us at that intersection on the way back from work."

"Which means you're not safe whenever you leave the estate," Mathew sighed.

"My trial finished today. It'll be a month before I hear if I was successful in securing the role, so I have nowhere to be for the next few weeks. Maybe that will throw them off," I argued half-heartedly.

"Maybe," Mercury agreed. His arm was wrapped around my waist, supporting me. Honestly, I was only still standing because of the pizza I'd already scoffed on the way home. "Thanks for getting Spec home safe, Miranda."

"Please! It was my pleasure. Who doesn't enjoy wasting Essence scum," Miranda cheered, then set her humoured gaze on me. "I'll maintain my cover at Galaxy until you hear about the job. If you need to go anywhere else and these two hotcakes aren't able to go with you, just call the usual number." With a wink, Miranda slid back into the driver's seat. "And thanks for whatever you did that protected my baby."

Mercury started escorting me inside when Miranda called out. "Umm, do you want the pizza?"

"I'll get it," Mathew offered.

"You know, if I learn to travel the ether, we don't have to worry about me driving back and forth to work," I told Mercury.

"We'll get there, Spec. You still have a lot to learn, but we should make good progress with you home for a month."

As I took my seat in the kitchen, Mathew arrived with the pile of pizzas and two bags of sides. "Did you order for everyone?" Mathew laughed.

"I did. Here, I'll help you sort it. I know who eats what," I directed.

Once we had our four pizzas and a heap of sides, we tucked into it. Cyn and Selena turned up pretty quickly, drawn by their noses, and sat at the table with us, joining Mathew and Mercury's discussion about the abduction attempt.

"Where's Bronwyn?" I asked as I finished eating an entire pizza to myself.

"She's working the afternoon shift on the perimeter today," Cyn explained. "They needed someone to fill in for one of the guards they had to take off the roster without notice."

"Why was he taken off the roster?" I asked.

"He was meant to clean up a mess for Bay a few weeks ago but left it there for others to find. It could have put people in danger. So, Calin stripped him of his shifts pending a full review," Cyn informed us with no emotion in her voice. "We'll have to take turns covering the gap in the roster until it's all sorted. Nothing to worry about. We've been patrolling this estate for years now."

"Luke, Calin, and Gina are home," Selena chirped.

Gritting her teeth, Cyn glared at Selena, but her newest sister-wife was too focused on the door. "Could you at least try and pretend your husband is your priority in front of others," Cyn snapped, getting Selena's attention.

Cowering, Selena whimpered and lowered her head. "I didn't mean anything by it. I called it by the order they walked through the door."

Sure enough, Luke pushed into the kitchen followed by Calin and Gina.

"Ooh, pizza." Gina breathed deeply, then moved quickly to the bench, finding hers and joining us at the table.

Just as everyone got settled, a phone started ringing. Calin pulled a cell from his pocket and stepped outside to take it. No one stopped to worry. It was polite to take the call out, but something drew me to Calin and that phone call. Which is how I found myself following him outside a moment later.

"... yes, but it wasn't successful. Spec's here and unharmed,"

Calin answered as he looked over his shoulder, his entire body freezing when he spotted me.

"Is that Bay?"

"It is, but he can't talk for long," Calin answered.

"I know. Just... he's okay?" I asked, gnawing on my lip as I waited for confirmation.

"He is. He was worried about you."

The door behind me opened, and Luke came out. "If that's the boss, tell him Jacoby from the lab has been trying to reach him all week but won't tell me why."

Calin kept his eyes on me as he listened to Bay's reply. "I'll tell him. Anything else? Do you have an ETA on when you'll be back?" Calin listened some more, nodding his head before answering. "Not great. It's taking a toll." With one more nod, he blew out a breath. "Okay."

Stepping towards me, Calin held out the phone to me. "Thirty seconds. Keep it impersonal in case they are listening."

Snatching the phone I stepped away. "Bay?"

"You're okay?" Bay's tenor washed over me like a warm shower after a five-mile run.

"I am. Miranda dealt with them. Did the same people who have you send them?" I asked.

"You know?" Bay huffed.

"I do. Tell me you'll be back soon."

There was a heartbeat of hesitation. "I'm not sure how much longer I'll need to be away, but I might need you to help at the office. I've asked Calin to introduce you to someone for me. I trust you to keep them in line for me."

Frowning at that answer, I was still muddling it over when Bay lowered his voice. "Keep up your training and stay close to those I trust." Then he was gone.

Swallowing, I dropped my face, forcing myself to keep breathing as I handed the phone back to Calin. "Bay said you need to introduce me to someone?"

Nodding, Calin glanced at Luke. "He wants you to meet Jacoby. Luke will take you on Monday, and you'll tell him that Bay has authorized you to know the results of the double-blind study. You're to make the call on what happens next."

"You want me to go to Pendant?" I checked with a cringe. Calin gave me a single nod.

"What's going on?" Luke stepped closer. "What did Spectra mean by the same people who have him? Where's Bay?"

"Essence has him. They set a trap at that smorgasbord he went to," Calin answered plainly.

"What kind of trap?"

"Contaminated food," I answered. "I've been feeling him starve and binge and purge all week. It's why I've been so hungry every morning."

"And why you've been vomiting and so anxious," Luke sighed. "You've been siphoning away his hunger, making yourself sick in his place. Spec, you need to stop. You can't satisfy his hunger."

"No, but I can alleviate it somewhat," I argued. "It took me a few days to work out what was happening, but I did, and I know it's helped him. I couldn't stop it if I tried. We are bound by our physical bodies."

Calin and Luke exchanged a look, but before either could say anything, Mercury stepped out the door. "I have to head to the city. Spec, are you okay? I can call out sick if you need me to stay."

Blowing out a breath, I rubbed the back of my neck. "As much as I appreciate the offer. You need to balance from this week, and I honestly just want to crash. But I'm going to go for a long run first and try and ward off the repercussions of using my power today."

"You don't look as bad as last time," Mercury considered.

"Honestly, it seemed to hit me a lot less this time. Maybe I'm getting used to it. Plus, the pizza helped. I think the greasier the food, the better my body copes."

Cupping my face in his palm, Mercury stared into my eyes, then nodded his head. "Don't go to sleep until you run. There is still enough latent energy to cause a backlash if you don't burn it off." Pinching my lips, Mercury kissed me tenderly. "I love you. Stay safe for me."

"I'll try," I answered, grabbed his shirt, went up on my toes, and kissed him passionately. Mercury groaned, then dropped one more peck on my mouth before he gave me a wink and headed inside. Surprising me to find we'd been left alone.

Stepping back into the dining area, Calin met my eyes. "Let me finish my dinner, and I'll run with you."

"I'll just go get changed then."

Too tired to bother with stairs, I exhaled all the air in my lungs, then floated up to my room on the second level. Thirty minutes later, I was running through the woods around Bay's estate, Calin keeping pace.

My mind kept going to the sound of Bay's voice tonight. How much I'd missed him. I needed more. Needed to touch him. Reaching for our bond, I thought about Bay and my need to feel his arms around me. To have his hands on me. To be naked with him.

My pace changed to match the tempo of the heartbeat I heard in the distance. Too far away. I needed to feel it. I stretched my gait to cover more ground. In my mind, I imagined I was running to Bay. That, if I could just run fast enough, I could run into his arms.

"Spec, slow down. You're pushing too hard," Calin warned, but I could feel Bay getting closer.

I ran harder. Faster.

"Spec."

Bay's heartbeat called to me. Drew me closer.

"Spec, wait!" Calin called from far away.

I raced into darkness, not caring I could no longer see the trees, the sky, or feel the cold of the winter night. My entire focus was on Bay. Needing to touch him.

Shadows blurred past me, and subconsciously I was aware that one of them stopped and stared at me, but my intention couldn't be hindered. Momentum pushing me through the darkness, calling me to Bay. He was so close. I could feel him like I did when he was at the estate, but not in the same room.

Dim lights flashed in the darkness, slowly forming symbols like lightning in a dark cloud. Coming and going from one blink to the next. Getting closer to me. And I knew with certainty Bay was on the other side.

Something caught me around the waist, lifted my feet into the air, and brought me to a sudden stop. The darkness shifted away, and suddenly I stood on a city sidewalk only a meter from a sandstone wall.

Blinking, I took a step back and took in my surroundings. I was down a side alley in the city. From the looks of things, I was in a federation residential area full of terrace housing in one of the old-style wealthy areas.

"That wall you nearly ran into is warded. You would have been badly hurt when you hit it," a man informed me, snapping my attention to where he stood beside me. The deep timbre of his voice seemed to resonate and awaken every erogenous zone in my body. The man stood hidden by a hooded cloak, but his closeness enveloped me in the scent of warm caramel.

"Who are you? Where am I?" I grew anxious, looking around. I wore my workout gear but was far from Bay's estate. "How did I get here?"

The hooded figure moved a step away, then turned to face me. "You used the ether to travel. I don't actually know where we are. I simply saw you running and followed, and when I saw the symbols of the ward flash in warning before you, I pulled you up to prevent you from hurting yourself."

The ether? Mercury told me it was too dangerous for me to travel like that yet. How the hell did I do that with no instruction?

Moving forward to the wall, I tentatively touched it. Nothing happened, but I could feel Bay on the other side. Exhaling all the air from my lungs, I pushed my arm through the wall, but immediately after the stone, I hit a barrier. It was indefinable and impassable. Like when I hit solid ground.

"As I said, it's warded. You can't pass through even as a Wraith," the hooded figure explained.

Pulling back, I turned to face him. "You can still see me and hear me?"

At this, he lifted his head enough for me to see the slight smirk lifting the side of his pretty mouth. "I can always see you, Spectra." He lifted the hood back with casual ease, just enough to reveal his

face. Caramel skin and hair, a handsome face meant to grace movie screens, and the most beautiful pale cerulean eyes I'd ever seen.

If I'd had air in my lungs, I would have blown it all out as that face came to me like the memory of a dream. "You're him! The one who made me like this."

"I am. Although I'm usually called Lincoln by my friends." Glancing around, he offered me his hand. "We should get you somewhere safe."

"Wait." Pulling back, I orientated myself, ran to the street, and spotted the street sign giving me the name and number of the building holding my husband hostage.

Lincoln stayed with me. Watching me. "What is it that brought you here?"

"My husband is being held captive in that house."

"Mercury is held prisoner?"

Freezing, I wondered if I should have admitted what I did. Lincoln seemed to pick up on my hesitation because he moved before me and met my eyes. "You can trust me, Spectra. I've been protecting you just like Mathew, Mercury, and Tommy have all these years."

Chewing my lip, I studied the Angelis before me. I may never have seen him, but there was a harmony standing near him I'd felt over the years. Usually, when I visited my sister's grave. "Bay Ryder is being held by Essence in that building."

Even frowning, Lincoln was gorgeous. "You wedded your body to him?"

"I'm his balance," I justified.

Flaring his nostrils as he breathed deeply, Lincoln rolled back his shoulders. "That's going to be problematic. I gather you're in love with Ryder?"

"I am."

Huffing, Lincoln pulled his hood forward again and offered me his hand. "Very well. We'll make that work. Come. I'll take you to Tommy. He'll keep you safe for tonight."

Hesitantly, I took Lincoln's hand and jolted when a familiar spark zapped me. The same sort of hit I got when Bay and I touched. We were back in the endless darkness from one step to the next. Two more steps after that, we were in the dark corner of Ténèbres, music pumping, and the clientele enjoying themselves.

"That seemed much better than running through the ether," I told Lincoln.

"For your first time, it was a good effort. The main thing is that you kept anchored to your destination," Lincoln explained as we moved towards the bar. "Make yourself visible."

Well, at least I found out where Bay was being held. Inhaling, I filled my lungs and returned to corporeal form. "I don't even know how I got there."

"You'll learn."

We were nearly at the bar, and Tommy turned towards us with a frown. When his eyes fell on the figure beside me, Tommy crossed his tattooed arms, hung his head, and cursed. Beside me, Lincoln laughed, and then he vanished, leaving me at the bar with Tommy, whose pierced brow jacked up in question.

"Can I get some water?"

Reaching into his pocket, Tommy handed me the same key he gave me last time. "Help yourself to whatever you need. You can tell me what happened when I close up."

Not questioning him, I took the key and headed into the staff-only area. Despite me being a regular, I was happy to go and hide. For starters, I was at a gothic nightclub in my active wear. Not a good look. And, to top things off, I'd run several kilometers before I jumped into the ether.

Grabbing a bottle of water from Tommy's fridge, I skulled it as I headed into his bedroom, undressed, and stepped into his shower. Once I was clean and no longer covered in sweat, I stole one of Tommy's Bathory shirts for a nightdress and climbed into his bed.

This day had sucked, and I was done with it.

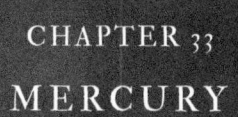

# CHAPTER 33

# MERCURY

THE SCREAM still echoed in my ears as I raised the flogger again. It wouldn't tear the skin, but the soft leather stung and left the flesh red. Twirling the wrist, I made the flogger kiss across her naked upper back, pulling another scream before the last had even finished.

When I first started using the flogger in a session, my masochist would moan. As the skin became inflamed, and her muscles ached from the stress position she was holding, what would typically be a tender caress was enough to cause agony.

The masochist's pain receptors were on high alert and over-sensitized, producing the optimal conditions for me to balance without permanently harming someone. The bonus was that while my scales were weighted by her screams and pain, in the end, she found pleasure and thanked me for it.

The scales of balance were like that. There weren't specific rules, just that the opposite was done to bring it back into alignment. It's why Spectra balanced without even trying. It didn't matter that she never went looking for her prey or purposefully caused that woman to run into the traffic and die the other week. All the scale cared about was that her actions put another life at risk or a person in harm's way.

Swinging my wrist again, I brought the flogger down on her bright red cheeks this time. Her cry was beautiful. The way she was bent over the spanking bench, I could see how wet her pussy was. How her lust was dripping down the inside of her thighs. The swollen red lips of her cunt glistened with need.

With one last twist of my wrist, I let the flogger kiss those lips and cracked my neck as the scream she unleashed eased the tension in my body. I never realized how tense I was until I balanced. Everything from this point was adding to the other side, buying me some extra time with my power before I needed to balance. Something over the last few weeks I'd needed for Spectra.

Thinking about my wife made my cock pulse with need. Tossing the flogger aside, I rolled on a condom, stepped up to my masochist, rooted my feet for maximum impact, and thrust deep. I wasn't small, and I knew it hurt for a woman to take me that deep without preparation. But this masochist loved it.

Wrapping her hair in my fist, I started pounding the hell out of her. With another cry, she was coming. Her cunt milked me hard as I drove deeper still, not letting up and forcing her straight into another climax as her screams cascaded through me.

How she knelt on the spanking bench forced her into an almost horizontal squatting position. It only took tilting her pelvis upwards to penetrate her balls deep. Deeper than I should without a warm-up, but after two orgasms down, she'd handle it better than straight out of the gate.

Grabbing her hips, I gave myself that access, and then I impaled the masochist and paused. Her screamed curse was a trickle of euphoria down my spine. It took my mind to last week when Bay urged Spectra to take me beyond her limits, and I balanced entirely with our wife for the first time.

"Fuck, yes!" I growled. Pulled back and thrust all the way again. Holding it deep for the count of five while my masochist cried out and tried to pull off me, but my grip held her tight. Her pussy squeezed around the base of my cock. The spasm of her muscles as both pleasure and pain worked through her. As she calmed, I did it again.

"Oh, God, Mercury. You're going to kill me," she whimpered.

"You know what to do if you need me to stop," I warned her. Giving her a moment, I watched her nails, trying to claw the leather of the spanking bench. A bead of perspiration raced down her spine, pooling in the dip I'd caused by forcing her body into this position. "Do you want me to stop?"

Her response was breathy, filled with lust, but also etched with discomfort. "No. Fuck, no."

Pulling out, I impaled her again with more force. There was much more agony in her scream, shifting my scale significantly. Pulling back halfway, I rubbed her back while she breathed through it. Once she'd calmed enough, I tried asking again. She wasn't using her safe word, but humans sometimes pressed their luck regarding bodily harm. Especially when the pain was their outlet, and they were having a bad week.

She had, of course. I always asked my masochists about their week and life before play started. It was essential to know where their head was just as much as it was mine. And mine was on a tightrope because Spectra was hurting with Bay's absence. I especially didn't like that it was physically taking a toll on her.

"Do you *need* me to stop?" I put emphasis on the word this time. There was a vast difference between want and need. She wanted to hurt, so she may not want me to stop, but her body may need me too.

A sob escaped her. I massaged her spine, spiking those pain receptors of her irritated flesh and soothing her simultaneously. "Do you need me to back it up or stop?"

"Back it up," she whispered.

Accepting the answer, I pulled out and released the cuffs that held her captive to the bench. Gently easing her to standing, supporting her weight because her muscles were sore and stiff, I helped her to the wall, and the Alexander's Cross. Pain slashed across her face, a hiss leaving her lips as I pushed her back against the padding and cuffed her wrists above her head.

Going to the shelf, I collected her favorite nipple clamps and smirked when she hissed as they cinched into place. Going to my knee, I sucked her clit hard without warning as I massaged her thighs. Once the tension eased, I stood and met her eyes, not bothering to wipe the tears that had ruined her makeup and left her looking like a hot mess.

Waiting patiently, I used a feather to trace her curves. Adoring her voluptuous breasts, rounded tummy, and generous birthing hips. All my masochists were heavier women. Healthy and curvaceous. That was my preference.

Spectra was toned and slim but not skinny. She had a lovely hourglass that, given time, might have filled out, but she'd been killed at age nineteen. An age before her body had fully matured from a young adult to the woman she would become. Spectra's beauty and my attraction to her was her heart and soul, not the physical casing. Though, I wouldn't deny all my masochists also had dark hair and pale skin.

Thinking of Spectra made my cock seep. Taking a breath, I lifted the masochist's thighs to my waist and niched my cock to her dripping core. "Are you ready?"

"I think so."

My eyes flashed to hers, but she corrected herself before I could open my mouth to check if we needed to stop again. "Yes. I'm ready."

With no tenderness, I drove my hips forward. I couldn't get as deep from this position, but she still felt me. The friction of her irritated flesh against the padding of the cross satisfied her need for pain, filling my cup of harm. I fucked her through another two orgasms before I'd backlogged more than enough and gave over to the pleasure.

As my cock jerked and released, my mobile started playing Lion by Saint Mesa. The ringtone I'd assigned to Calin.

"Fuck!" I snarled.

Dropping one of her legs, I caught myself one-armed on the

wall. I sent my mind down the bond to check on Spectra quickly, not getting any pain or fear, so whatever this was, Spectra wasn't in danger. That's the only reason I took the time to thrust once more, sending her into a final orgasm and letting the call go to voicemail.

Both panting, I eased away as she stilled around me. Removing the cuffs, I carried her to the chaise to recover, then went to my phone, the screen confirming a missed call from Calin. Putting the phone to my ear, I used my shoulder to hold it in place while I eased the condom off and disposed of it.

"Mercury, Spectra vanished on me. We were running, and she did that thing where she went really fast again and just disappeared in front of me. I'm running back to the mansion in case she shows up, but I'm not sure where to even look for her if she left the estate. I'll call Mathew if you can't get back to this quickly."

"Fuck," I muttered. Hanging up, I typed a message to Mathew and Calin, then turned back to my masochist. I had a duty of care to take care of her after a session, especially with her mental state this week. Before I could apologize for having to abandon her, a shadow moved across the room, then formed into a hooded figure I knew very well.

Crossing the room, passing straight through the furniture and the woman lying there, Lincoln's dulcet voice reached my ears. "I found her in the ether. I've left her with Tommy." He faded away as he walked through the wall and vanished. His ability to only let particular people hear and see him was rather handy at this moment.

Blowing out a breath, I let Calin and Mathew know Spectra was safe with Tommy, and then I put the phone aside and focused on giving my masochist what she needed. Starting with a relaxing bath.

SEVERAL HOURS LATER, I PULLED MY BIKE UP AND PARKED IT OUT the back of Tommy's place. I used the back entrance to come inside and make my way to the bar. Spectra was nowhere to be seen. I could feel her near, my eyes drawing to the staff-only sign on the door. Tilting my head, I turned my eyes to Tommy, who was wiping down the bar. It was nearing closing time.

Going to the bar, I gave Tommy a head jut when he looked my way. Coming to my end, he put a glass on the bar and poured me a few fingers of whiskey. "You're looking relaxed. Good night?"

"Finished work for a few days yesterday. Looking forward to spending my days off inside my wife," I answered honestly.

Scoffing, Tommy shook his head. "You just love that you get to call her that."

Lifting the glass, I gave him an evil grin. "I do." I sipped the whiskey enjoying the taste. "Lincoln made contact."

"He brought her here but didn't stick around. I have no idea how he got hold of her. Spec was dead on her feet and not dressed for the scenery, so I sent her straight to bed," Tommy confirmed as he filled my glass again.

"He found her in the ether. She stumbled into it by accident."

Bursting out laughing, Tommy arched his pierced brow at me. "Well, that explains why he made contact. She stumbled into his domain and all. You're lucky he brought her here instead of just taking her."

"She's not ready. Lincoln wants Spectra to learn to be Angelis before he starts teaching her the other stuff."

Tommy leaned his elbows on the bar. "You know as well as I do that walking the ether is one of the last things an Angelis learns to do. So, I'm calling bullshit. What is he really waiting for?"

Staring into the glass of amber liquid, I pondered that question, then met Tommy's eyes. "You had access to Spectra all these years. Yet, you waited until she got involved with the de Sang to make a move. Why?"

"She didn't understand what she was doing when she balanced. I wanted her consent to be understood rather than instinct. What made you finally make your move?" Tommy countered.

"I knew from the word go I wanted her heart. That meant waiting for the sorcerer to fuck up his relationship with her. I knew he would because she wasn't his," I answered honestly.

"You wanted her to love you, and she does. I wanted informed consent. Mathew?"

"He's only ever wanted to protect her. He's been in her life since she was born. Hell, he was there at her conception, I think. It was his altar Michael knocked her mum up on." I shrugged. As close as I was to Mathew, he never told me why he was in Spectra's life. He didn't need to. The answer was obvious.

"Kind of sweet," Tommy said with a wicked grin. "Daddy came to visit, seduced an elemental, and gave him a sister. No more wandering the earth alone for him."

"Don't start. You have more siblings and cousins than I can count in a hundred years. For a race meant to be voyeurs, your daddy sure does like to dip his wick," I teased.

Grin covering his face, Tommy topped up my glass again. "He never could turn down a good orgy. So, what is Lincoln holding out for? It's not love. Not informed consent. It's not about protecting her. At least, as far as not letting her convert yet."

Throwing back the third glass, I put some cash on the bar. "No idea, and you know he's not going to tell us until he's ready to act on whatever he's been planning. We can't get upset as long as he doesn't hurt Spec. He's the reason we have her in our lives to begin with."

Cocking that brow at me, Tommy took the money. "Again, I ask, why did Mathew never tell us or train her?" Tommy rang up the sale without waiting for my guess and then returned to serve his customers.

The truth is, I'd asked Mathew outright why he didn't try and train Spectra as a kid. He told me getting access to her would have been suspicious, and Spectra's mum was very protective of her girls. I hadn't moved here until after Spectra was already a Wraith, so I never knew her mum or sister. I always wondered what she was like before she lost everything.

Making my way out the back, I let myself into Tommy's apartment and dumped my jacket and helmet on his sofa. Crossing his courtyard, I stepped into the bedroom. Spectra was curled up and asleep. She looked beautiful, hugging the pillow. Undressing, I pulled back the sheets and slid in behind her, dropping a kiss on her shoulder as I took her in my arms.

"Merc," she sighed dreamily.

"Always," I promised her the unasked. Turning her face to me, I kissed her lips tenderly. My cock hardened instantly. God, I adored this woman. Spectra moaned as I guided my length between her thighs and then rocked against her, loving how she gasped as my hardness slid against the silk of her heat. She wasn't ready for me yet, but she would be.

Kissing her neck, I tapped and rubbed her prayer bead, loving how she squirmed against me with the stimuli. Tommy entered his room, his eyes brightening as he leaned his shoulder against the door jamb to watch for a moment. We made eye contact, he lifted his brow in question, and I nodded.

One side of his mouth lifting up in a naughty smile, Tommy yanked his shirt over his head before striding into his bathroom. By the time he showered, Spectra was slick and ready for me.

"Do you want me?" I whispered in Spectra's ear.

"Always."

"Can Tommy join us?"

Spectra, who hadn't opened her eyes yet, lifted her eyelids enough to see Tommy approach us with only a towel around his hips. "Just watching?"

"It's my preference," Tommy answered. "But if you need more, Angel, I'll happily join in. I'd love to eat your pussy and have Mercury watch you come on my face again." Going to his voyeur chair, Tommy took a seat, cracked a bottle of scotch, poured a glass, then sat back and took a sip.

Tommy rubbed a hand across the moisture on his chest and down his abs. Then, twitching his lips, he yanked his towel open, and his enormous cock bounced against his abdomen. Us Angelis definitely packed a punch below the waist.

"I've shown you mine," Tommy said.

Huffing, I nipped Spectra's neck. "Whatever you're comfortable with."

Biting her lip, Spec slowly pushed the sheet back, giving Tommy an uninterrupted view of what my hand was doing. Then she shifted her hips and slid over my cock, not stopping until I was filling her tightness. I groaned and gave an extra little thrust which made Spectra gasp for me.

"Fuck, you're something else, Angel," Tommy moaned and palmed his cock with his free hand.

Turning my attention to my beautiful wife, I forgot about the watcher. Spectra didn't, though. In every position, she ensured Tommy got a good view, and I have to say, seeing this freer side of my wife got me so hot. She made love to me and simultaneously put on a show for Tommy for hours.

It all came to a head when Spectra straddled me in reverse cowgirl and told me to make her come again. Then she made direct eye contact with Tommy. Licking his lips, Tommy picked up his drink, walked over to us, and stood right in front of Spectra, eye-fucking her as she rode me.

Tommy played with her breasts, taking a mouthful of his drink, then leaned down and kissed Spectra passionately. Grabbing her hips, I fucked Spectra harder. As she broke free of the kiss, Tommy threaded his fingers in her hair and led her mouth to his dripping dick. Spectra didn't hesitate to grab the base of his stem and suck and lick the hell out of him.

I nearly came just watching them. My focus on them meant I stopped being careful. Instead of making love to my wife, I was fucking her with an aching desire for all the naughty things I thought she'd never be into. Seconds later, Spectra was coming for me, her cries smothered by Tommy filling her mouth. Cursing loudly, Tommy groaned and held Spectra's head in place as he spilled down her throat.

The scene was so hot my back arched, and I prayed for God to save me as I filled my wife with my cum. Because if there was one thing I knew, it was that this couldn't be a one-time thing.

As Tommy stepped back, I could tell that one act with Spectra was enough to balance him. Which was a good thing, because Spectra floated around to lay on my chest, and then she was asleep on me seconds later. Finishing his drink, Tommy let out a large sigh.

I'd never seen Tommy look so relaxed, and I could tell he was already an addict from his first time with Spectra and Bay.

Chuckling, I gestured for Tommy to pull the cover-up and join us. Rolling to my side, I eased Spectra to lay between us and snuggled against her, ready to sleep. Just as Tommy turned out the light and I was drifting off to sleep, I caught the shadow of a hooded figure moving across the courtyard before it disappeared.

# CHAPTER 34

## SPECTRA

"ARE THERE STAIRS, MAYBE?" I asked as Luke and Calin led me to the elevator in Pendant's underground carpark on Monday.

"Could you manage them?" Calin teased. "Your legs must be sore after spending the entire weekend with them wrapped around the Angelis or two."

My face and chest heated as I covered my mouth on a huge yawn. "I've never had my legs around Tommy," I clarified. "He prefers to watch."

Calin and Luke shared a look, Calin openly smirking. "His eyes must be sore. You look like you've barely slept."

While Calin found it funny and enjoyed teasing me, Luke was disgruntled. "She needs food," Luke grumbled.

Mercury and I had stayed at Tommy's all weekend and spent most of it in bed, with Tommy watching or joining in much the same way he had with Bay. Despite what Luke thought, having Tommy there meant he made sure we ate between sexathons.

I had the impression Luke was more miffed about having to come to find me this morning. Tommy let them in, only for Luke to drag me out of Mercury's arms, promising to return me once I'd done what Bay asked of me. Then Luke had to wait for me to shower and dress. So, he was late for work.

Thankfully, Calin had Gina pick out some clothes for me to wear to the office today to bring with him. A work-friendly long sleeve black sweater dress that came to my knees was currently covered by my long black duffle jacket. It had snowed all weekend again, but that didn't stop Gina from packing black heels instead of my boots.

Arriving at the elevator, I chewed my lip. Luke jabbed the button with a huff. "I'll take the stairs." He blew around the corner before I could raise an opposition.

Sighing, Calin put his arm around my shoulders and hugged me to his side. "Don't mind him. He's worried about Bay."

"Aren't we all?"

The elevator arrived, and Calin stepped on, pushing two buttons on the console. "I'm more worried about you."

Wrapping my arms around me, I gripped my jacket hard and kept my focus on Calin. Maybe I could ignore it. I wouldn't notice I was locked in a metal box. "I'll be fine as long as we get Bay home soon," I whined. "At least they've stopped giving him poisoned blood, which caused me to vomit every morning."

"That's good," Calin agreed.

"Except they've stopped feeding him at all now. They're giving him solid food but no blood. He's pulling heavily on me. We can't control it."

"That's not good." Calin frowned. "You're trembling."

"Keep talking," I snapped before Calin could bring attention to the physical strain of my fear. "Bay's an ancient, right? They can go longer without blood. Do you know how long before it becomes perilous for him?" I asked Calin, hoping for something to bolster my hope.

Calin grimaced. "If they had just taken him, I would have assured you he could go up to a month. He has in the past. But because they fed him the toxic blood, I fear that any staying power his age provided him is undone."

That's what I was afraid he'd say. "Which is why they did it. They wanted him weak and desperate straightaway."

The elevator doors slid open. Luke waited in the foyer of what looked to be a research lab. I all but leaped out of the death trap. Focusing on my out-breath, I made it twice as long as my inhale.

"So, it's not just having a de Sang with you?" Luke raised a brow at me. The elevator doors had closed, and Calin left with them.

Glaring at Luke, I blew out a breath. "Normally, I'm just a little jittery, but I'm running on fresh air and sunshine here. I just want to go home to bed and sleep for a week. Or at least until Bay has returned home and had a good feed."

"Not a good idea." Luke frowned. "You may not wake up again."

My mouth dropped open. "You don't think he's going to come home?"

Avoiding my eyes, Luke typed a code into the lab door, then pressed his palm to the biometric pad. "Let's see what his plan is."

"His plan for what?" I asked, following as he opened the door, the sound of an air pressure lock releasing as we stepped into the antechamber.

"Do you think Bay would have had me drag you here for fun?" Luke admonished as we waited for the airlock to click back into place.

The second doors opened automatically, laminar air flow washing over us to prevent us from bringing contaminated air into the lab space. I mean, other than what was on our clothes. But we were still in the walkway between labs, all of which had lab coats hanging outside the doors.

"You think Bay sending me here will lead to his coming home?"

"I hope so, for your sake," Luke replied calmly, but the way he side-eyed me didn't settle my nerves. Stopping outside a room full of desks in cubicles, Luke rapped on the window. He gestured to a middle-aged man focused intently on his computer. "This is Jacoby."

The man's eyes widened when he looked at me. His mouth dropped open, closed, and opened again. He climbed out of his seat as if he was getting up to run from me, but instead came out into the hall, still gaping at me and reaching out to me like one does a spooked horse.

"Dead, but not dead. Buried rage just waiting to be unleashed," Jacoby muttered to himself. "My father told me your kind existed, but I never believed it until this moment."

Tilting my head, I caught the tendrils of spirit around the man. "Witch?"

"Empath. My father was a voodoo priest. He had the power to call the dead and give them a voice." Considering me a little longer, his focus eventually came to my eyes and became wide as saucers. "Oh, my. You weren't Nephilim before you died, were you?"

It was my turn to stare open-mouthed. "You can detect that?"

The man's cheeks turned red, and he lowered his eyes, looking suddenly younger. "An ex of mine was Nephilim. The eyes are unique if you get a close enough look at them. Especially when they're in the middle of a lust frenzy." Lifting a brow, the man looked from me back to Luke. "So what is so important you've dragged this poor girl from her lover's bed?"

"Lust frenzy?" Luke asked with an arched eyebrow.

"It's a known fact within their circles that when they give into the needs of the body, they do so frenziedly. Hours of back-to-back passion. I've heard the Angelis are even worse, taking days to sate their needs. Rather a cruel thing to settle on a race that only produces men."

Pretty sure my face was now bright red, I cleared my throat. "Bay sent me. He said you're to tell me the results of the double-blind blood study you've been working on for him. That I'd know how to proceed," I explained.

Frowning, Jacoby assessed me. "You're a haematologist or virologist?"

"Ah, neither."

"Jacoby, this is Spectra. She's an exceptional young woman. Bay gave her the power to determine what happens next with the study." Checking his watch, Luke huffed. "I need to get to a meeting. I'll leave you two to discuss whatever this project is. Spectra, call me when you're done, and either Calin or I will come and get you."

Not waiting any longer, Luke strode back towards the exit. Jacoby and I stared at each other for a long moment before he narrowed his gaze. "You must be close to Bay for him to trust you with this. He hasn't given another soul read access."

"You doubt that Bay gave his permission?" I understood his implication.

"You'll have to forgive that since I've not heard from him directly, I find it hard to believe a stranger's word," Jacoby justified.

Chewing my cheek, I couldn't fault his concern. I wondered what would be the right thing to reveal to earn his trust. "Bay's been abducted by Essence. They're starving him to try and get him to reveal sensitive information. He sent me to you, so I can only assume you hold the key to his freedom."

Taking a step back as if I'd slapped him, Jacoby looked shocked one minute and doubtful the next. "And how do you know this?"

This next one would be a gamble, but he'd understand if he genuinely had a Nephilim lover once. "I'm Bay's balance. His wife. I know they are starving him because I'm starving with him. You can call Calin or Luke, and they will confirm this, but this information puts my life in your hands. I'm trusting you not to breathe a word to anyone else." When Jacoby took another long minute to consider me, my eyes filled with tears. "Please, Bay said you could help."

Blinking at me like he'd expected any excuse except that, Jacoby licked his lip, then narrowed his eyes. "In stasis, but still alive. You're immortal, aren't you?"

Unsure about the change in topic, I hesitated. "I'm dead like a de Sang. And just like Bay, there is another death awaiting me. My vengeance was stolen from me. I'll never live again."

Considering me, Jacoby crooked his finger as he took two steps backward. "Come. I know how you can prove who you are to me."

"I can?" I frowned.

"Bay brought me a blood sample from a female a few weeks ago. He also gave me a sample of de Sang blood. When I combined the two, the de Sang blood started cell replication. I suspected the sample he gave me belonged to mates, but I could not identify the woman's species. I think if I take a sample of your blood, it will match that of the first sample he provided."

Using his palm, he unlocked the door to a smaller lab and started prepping a slide. Turning back to me with a needle, Jacoby asked for my hand, sterilized it, and quickly pricked my finger, collecting two drops onto the slide. While I held a tissue to my bleeding finger, Jacoby set the sample on a microscope.

Collecting a vile from a fridge of samples, Jacoby added two drops to the slide. While I watched, the blood drops clashed and looked like they wouldn't merge. "Wait for it," Jacoby gestured with patience.

In a blink, the two samples combined, and the dormant cells of the second sample started replicating. "Holy Hell!" I gasped, moving closer to the screen.

"I knew they were mates." Jacoby switched out the slides and started loading several onto different platforms, all taking up a corner of the screen. Grabbing his notebook, Jacoby pulled up a stool and gestured for me to sit. "Okay, Spectra. Let me catch you up on what I've been working on with Bay."

"You don't have to. I already know," I told Jacoby, staring at the screen and the four different samples loaded up. "You've been working on the cure."

Grin filling his face, Jacoby confirmed my suspicion, and then he told me his latest report. How my serum was the key, they were missing to make the cure work not only on de Viands but also on de Sangs.

"Bay was creating a cure for himself?" I asked, unsure.

"No," Jacoby immediately shut down that thought. "His initial interest in a cure was curiosity and for a de Viand. He started pushing to see if it could cure the taken by force for another reason." Jacoby turned a page, ready to continue.

"Which was?" I asked carefully.

Meeting my eyes without flinching, Jacoby cleared his throat. "I only have my suspicions."

"Which are?"

"When did you meet Bay, Spectra?"

Frowning, I did the math. "About a month and a half ago. Why?"

Placing his notes on his lap, Jacoby studied me for a long moment. "Bay only started expanding the use of the cure a month ago. When he bought me the first vial of your blood."

Unsure what he was suggesting, it took me a moment to realize where Bay first got hold of my blood. "The night I was nearly taken," I whispered. "He's looking for a way to cure me in case I'm taken."

Jacoby watched me, sympathy in his eyes. "He said it was for those who didn't choose to be like him. That it shouldn't be forced upon someone. They should have a way to take their lives back or die naturally."

A glob of fear and guilt was lodged in my throat. It was painful to swallow around it, but I found my voice with an effort. "Does it work?"

Tapping his notes, Jacoby sighed. "I created two inoculations. One I was sure would cure the patient, but the other, I wasn't sure what the outcome would be."

"And?"

"I want to preface this by saying the first sample of your blood didn't work. There was something different between the first and second that made your blood a viable unlocking component. Bay suggested the second sample was siphoning the patient's infection away. I'm not sure why it worked, not the second sample, but in the lab, yes. Both inoculations I made reversed the nature of the de Sang to their previous human self.

"We then chose two subjects for live testing. We didn't want to compare a new de Sang to one centuries-old, so we ensured they were both similar ages." Jacoby put photos of two de Sangs looking worse for wear on the screen. "Pre-inoculation." He then clicked his mouse, and another set of pictures of both patients came up. "One hour and then one-day post inoculation." Another set. "Five days after inoculation."

Pointing to one photo, I felt my jaw drop open. "Is he...?" The man was still a de Sang but looked fit and healthy and barely a day over twenty again.

"Yes. I gave test subject B the sample with your whole blood in it."

Blinking, I pointed to the final photo of the first test patient. "And this one?"

"He received the inoculation, which had your serum only."

"It doesn't work," I acknowledged. But then, a thought occurred to me. "Where was the injection site?"

"The arm."

Shaking my head, I considered the screen and the image of the slides with de Sang blood on it. "They have no cell replication, and their bodies are in stasis. I doubt the antivirus ever left their muscles. We should try injecting it directly into their hearts."

Both of Jacoby's eyebrows jumped to his hairline. "I'd like to do further tests on different age groups, but Bay is not the sort to subject living things to exploration studies. He prefers to have an idea of the outcome before he subjects anyone to it," Jacoby informed me. "Unless you can find a volunteer, our hands are tied currently."

"You can't use the same subjects?" I checked.

"Not without Bay to access to them."

My mind flipped through the details. Going to the sample fridge, I looked at all the different vials. "How many inoculations do you have to try?"

"Only two more of each." Jacoby indicated the rack which held preloaded syringes.

Nodding my head, I read the labels on them and then sighed. "I guess we'll have to wait for Bay to do further live testing, but you could probably simulate the effect of a direct injection to the heart."

Rambling some scientific terms that were over my head, Jacoby agreed—I think—and started jotting down notes. While his back was turned, I eased open the sample fridge, removed a vial of sample two, and put it in my jacket pocket.

"I'll head off then. Luke has my number to let me know how the sim goes."

"Yes, of course, thank you," Jacoby kept scribbling in his notepad. "You don't need a code to leave the lab."

Happy with that news, I left him with it.

Making my way to the elevator, I was too focused on my plan to fret about the enclosed space this time. Pressing the ground button, I took out my phone and typed the address I'd memorized into my map function.

As soon as I was out of the elevator, I went ghost, checking nothing fell out of my pockets, and then I was off on my mission.

Thirty minutes later, I arrived at the federation-style townhouse I knew held Bay. I could sense him still down that alley. Staying ghost, I let myself into the building, counting heads as I made my way to the basement and the room that held my husband.

There was a guard on the door, busy playing with his phone. Knowing the walls were warded, I tentatively checked the door. Sure enough, there was no way through. Which meant I couldn't just sneak in. I did, however, notice the lock they had on the room.

Ghosting back outside, I stood in the alley while I tried to think of the best way I could help Bay. He sent me to Jacoby, knowing he'd tell me about the cure. I could only hope that he wanted me to bring it to him. But why?

Taking the syringe from my jacket pocket. It was small enough to hide in the palm of my hand and the size of a pen. They'd likely take my jacket and possibly check me for weapons when I went inside.

Biting my lip, I slid the vial back into my pocket and pulled my hair up, twisting it up into a French roll, and used the inoculation to pin my hair in place. Using my phone camera, I checked that my hair covered it, then I took a deep breath and headed out to the street.

Climbing the stairs, I rang the doorbell. It took a minute before the door opened, and a relatively young de Sang stood there, eyeing me like I hid a yummy candy in my throat. "Can I help you?"

"I'm here for Bay Ryder."

Arching one of his eyebrows, the de Sang stepped back and opened the door wide. "Please, come in."

Taking a deep breath, I crossed the threshold. I was led into a parlor and left to wait for a few minutes. When the de Sang returned, it was with a much older one of his kind. His skin was tanned, with dark hair and chocolate eyes, and as he came closer, he barely came to my nose.

Looking me over, the older man smiled like it was Christmas. "Miss Michaels, I presume?" he asked with a thick Italian accent.

"It's Mrs. Raphangelis now," I corrected.

"Does your husband know you are here?" he asked.

"He's close by. He'll be able to find me," I assured. Mercury was in the city, so I knew if anything happened to me, he'd feel it and be able to locate me quickly.

His eyebrow arched. "You're bound?"

Lifting a brow at his interrogation, I didn't answer his question. "I'm sorry, you are?"

"Oh," he stepped back, looking distraught at having to introduce himself. "Forgive my rudeness. I am Mayer Callisie. An old associate of your employer." He bowed at the waist.

Bowing my head slightly in acknowledgment, I forced a smile. "Bay is just one of my employers."

"You care enough for him to come for him." Mayer came closer, then started to circle around me.

"Actually, he called me and asked me to come. That's how I found where you were." I hid the lie in the half-truth. "I gather Bay is still here?"

Peering at me, Mayer came full circle. "He is. He asked you to sacrifice yourself for him?"

Chuckling, I met Mayer's eyes. "No. He asked me to bring the information you were after to him."

"Information?"

"Yes. It's not my specialty, so I have no idea what it means. I am merely the messenger in this case. Apparently, you took an interest in me, and Bay thought it best not to put any of his people at risk."

The right side of Mayer's face ticked. "You don't mind him putting you at risk?"

Giving Mayer a sympathetic smile, I lifted my brow again and breathed out enough to stay visible but become insubstantial. "I'm already dead, Mr. Callisie."

Expecting him to test that theory, I was ready when Mayer grabbed for my neck, only for his hand to pass through me. I allowed myself to fade and then return to the whole vision but not be touchable. Mayer chuckled. "What a nifty ability that is."

"Indeed. Should we conduct business before my husband comes looking for me?" I asked.

Stepping away, Mayer nodded. "Of course. Please, take a seat. Tell me what information you have for me."

Did he think I was an idiot? Men! Honestly. I'd been dealing with abusive assholes and helping their wives and girlfriends disappear for years. Their biggest flaw was underestimating women.

"That's not how this will work. I don't understand the information; just carry it. Bay will need to be here for this to work. If you have him join us, we can get on with it." It was worth a try. Unlike Mayer, I didn't underestimate his intelligence.

"Ah, I see. Proof of life. Well, if you'll follow me." After nodding to the de Sang, who let me in, Mayer headed to the inner door. "Take her jacket and check for weapons, then bring her to see her master."

What did I tell you?

# CHAPTER 35

## BAY

THE LOCK on the door clicked. I didn't bother getting up. I was weak and starving, and I was aware that my connection to Spectra was the only thing sustaining me at this point. I couldn't keep draining her just to keep up appearances. God, I was so out of it I could almost feel her beside me.

"After you," Mayer's voice came from the door.

Yep. It was official. I was hallucinating. From my perch on the bed, I imagined my beautiful angel walking through the door, dressed in black as usual. Spectra looked like she just came from work or was ready to go on a date in that dress and heels.

"Bay, you have a visitor," Mayer announced as he stood behind the mirage of my wife, his eyes admiring her like she was a piece of steak. I wanted to kill him for looking at her like that, even if it was a hallucination.

The door clicked shut. Spectra shivered, her eyes widening as her head turned to the door, and she started worrying at her lip. Titling my head, I took in the dark circles beneath her eyes and the hollowness in her cheeks. She'd lost weight and looked exhausted.

As her pale blue eyes swung back to me, I could see the strain in her features, the slight tremble in her body. She was locked in a room she couldn't escape from with two de Sangs, and one of them was starving. Spectra's fear of enclosed spaces and predators steam-rolled down our bond as adrenaline surged through her system, breaking me free of my lethargy.

Getting off the bed, her fear energizing me, I stepped closer. "You came alone?" She wouldn't be so reckless. She was meant to get the cure and come with Luke, Calin, or maybe her Fantôme friends. Not alone. "Where's Miranda?"

"Who's Miranda?" Mayer quickly asked.

"I'm never alone," Spectra reassured. Her eyes narrowed as I swayed where I stood. Her hand moved to her stomach and clenched there as if my hunger gnawed at her. Taking two steps towards me, putting her halfway between Mayer and me, Spectra focused on me intently.

"You're too weak for this. You need a top-up to be any use." Her eyes flicked to her left shoulder, then met mine intently.

Mayer got between us, turning his back to me. "He can feed on you after I have the information I seek."

A polite smile bloomed on Spectra's face. "Oh, I wasn't suggesting he feed on me. Bay knows how I feel about that."

Before Mayer realized the danger, I was on him, my eyes all for Spectra as I sank my fangs deep into Mayer's throat. Precious metallic blood filled my mouth. It didn't matter that it tasted stale and was thick like a clotted milkshake. It was food.

Mayer struggled, but I quickly kicked the back of his knees and took him to the floor, gaining strength with every mouthful and Spectra's presence.

"Buy us time," Spectra murmured as she backed away.

With a snarl, I took long pulls of Mayer's blood into me, sucking and drinking until his blinks became slow and his heartbeat barely audible. When I'd consumed Mayer nearly dry, Spectra was standing near the door, tapping away on her phone.

Getting to my feet, I went into the bathroom, washed my face, and rinsed my mouth. As I came back out, I threw a kick at Mayer's body, satisfaction hitting me when a loud crack came from his ribs. "My love."

"What was your plan?" Spectra asked.

"You get the cure, using it to get inside, and then you and the calvary come and rescue me," I assured her. "What is your plan?"

"I have the cure, but he doesn't know that. It isn't reliable. The live testing was a fail."

I swore under my breath at the news. "We can't get out of this room without him."

Spectra scoffed and threw me a sarcastic look over her shoulder. "Did you forget what I do for work on the side? Honestly, Bay. Do you really think a digital lock could hold me?"

Of course, it couldn't. I should have realized that was no issue for someone of Spectra's talents. "You can hack it?"

Waving her phone at me, Spectra smirked. "Already done."

Moving toward her, I snatched my shirt and jacket from the end of the bed. "Then let's go."

Spectra's hand was suddenly on my chest. "If it was that easy, I would have told you to kill him." She gestured to Mayer. Caressing her hand up my neck, fluttering her fingers against my jaw, Spectra stared into my eyes, her concern still pulsing down our bond.

"There are a lot of predators in this building, and they have a security system that can lock the place down to stop you from getting out. You are weak and incapable of getting out of this house in your current state."

The love in her eyes was everything. I placed my hand over hers, where she cupped my cheek. My hunger for blood was fading, and the need for my wife was growing. The blood I'd taken from Mayer rushed to my cock. "Spec, what are you doing?"

"Taking your hunger and turning it into what I can use," Spectra murmured as she drifted closer.

"This isn't safe. I've gone too long without feeding," I warned, but I was leaning in for the sweet taste of Spectra's lips.

"I've gone too long without you. I'm starving for you, Bay. I need you. To kiss me, touch me, inside of me."

Growling as my need for her became painful, I hauled her against me and fed at her luscious mouth. As I yanked her dress over her head, our hearts were drumming in time. Her underwear fell to the floor and was quickly joined by my slacks.

Pinning Spectra to the bed, I shifted between her legs and drove into her without delay. Thrusting and pumping her body to the beat of our joined hearts. My hands caressed her ribs, waist, and hips, tagging all the areas where my absence had changed her form.

I snarled my disgust when my fingers bumped over the bony prominence she'd never had before. I did this to her. No, not me. Them. Essence. My eyes fell on Mayer's still form, his back to us, but I could tell he was already healing from my attack. Rage and violence filled me with the need to tear him to pieces.

Warm fingers touched my cheek, drawing my eyes to the angel beneath me, the sight of her staying my hatred. Allowing Spectra to lead me, I dropped my mouth to hers and kissed her with the same fervency of our bodies. I needed more, to be deeper.

I hooked one of her thighs to wrap over my hip. I loved the throaty purr that escaped Spectra and how her body arched and presented itself to me, urging me to delve further. A flutter in her core was all the warning I had before Spectra cried out her pleasure and milked my length.

The lust driving us backed off a little as her desire was fed. Spectra's eyes were glazed and her focus scattered as she panted, "More. Don't stop."

Grinning at her need for me, I nipped her bottom lip and wound my hips in a slow grind that had her making the most delicious little noises for me. "I didn't plan to," I assured.

Nipping down Spectra's throat, I rocked into her, then wound my hips as I withdrew before rocking forward to repeat the motion. My lips pinched between licks as I trailed my way to her firm breasts. Scooping them into my hands, I smothered them with my attention. Teasing with my tongue, flicking and pinching with my fingers, sucking so hard her body clenched around me and milked me in the form of small aftershocks of her pleasure.

As my hunger rose, Spectra tried to divert it to the lust of our bodies again. My cock throbbed and seeped, starving for the feel of her. Still, the desire for blood itched at the back of my throat.

Rising over Spectra, I took her hands above her head and held them with one hand. Caressing her face, I traced her lips with my thumb. My eyes closed, and a groan of wanton need escaped when she sucked my thumb between her lips. Tingles raced down my spine and zapped my balls, tightening them as more blood pumped into my cock.

"I can't hold back," I admitted. I wasn't sure if Spectra could feel her hold on my hunger slipping, but as she met my eyes and a single tear escaped, I knew she did. "I can't stop. It's too late. Please don't hate me," I pleaded.

As another tear fell, Spectra lifted her head, her lips brushing mine in such tenderness. "I am your balance. I willing give you what you need," she whispered.

"I love you," I susurrated, then delved my tongue between her lips, tasting her, thrusting into her as my yearning did her body. Grabbing her other thigh, I wrapped it around my waist and grabbed her ass as I started picking up speed. Thrusting harder and faster, the thirst became just as prominent as our need for each other.

Too soon, Spectra threw back her head and cried out her pleasure again. "God, Spec!" I groaned as my cock pulsed and throbbed before I spilled inside her. Grabbing her jaw, I turned and angled her head just how I needed it, and then I bit down.

Delicious, sweet, nourishing blood flowed into my mouth. One mouthful and every nerve in my body sizzled with life. A second, and I felt reborn. The third mouthful hardened my cock, tightened my balls, and had me pounding her tight body as hard and fast as possible, the desire to fill her with my seed overwhelming.

"Bay!" Spectra whimper-screamed as she plummeted into her pleasure again, dragging me over with her.

Releasing her neck, I roared the euphoria that spilled from my body. Biting my lip, I kissed her while our bodies still thrummed. Spectra suddenly fought against my hold on her, but I held her and shared my blood. Magic swirled around us, hers and mine. Our combined power tap danced down my spine, feeding our bond until it grew thick and juicy, flowing freely between us.

Dropping my head to the side, I licked over the wound on her neck, sealing it. I rolled, holding Spectra to my chest as she trembled. "You're okay," I assured. "We mated in the de Sang way, that's all. It won't hurt you."

Kissing the top of Spectra's head, I knew she was fighting the effect of my blood, but I wanted to reassure her that what just happened between us was good.

Rubbing my hand up and down Spectra's spine, I sighed. There was no gnawing hunger. For either of us. The bond was so much stronger now. My strength and power were replenished.

While Spectra recovered, I eyed Mayer where he still lay on the floor. We didn't have long now before he would wake and become a threat to my wife again. I wasn't sure how long he could be here before one of his people came to check on him.

Caressing my angel, I observed her. Already Spectra looked and felt healthier to touch. I wasn't the only one replenished by the blood exchange. Easing away, I caressed her face. She was still out to it, but I needed to have her ready for whatever came next.

Getting up, I dressed quickly, then redressed Spectra. As I gently put her clothing back on her body, her little simpers were kisses directed to my cock. I smiled quietly as I lay her back down, fully dressed and butterfly kissed all over her neck.

"Did you kill her?" Mayer groaned from the floor. He'd rolled over and was watching me mouth my wife's throat. "The Angelis will hunt you if you killed his wife. I knew you wouldn't be able to resist her when I brought her in, but I would have controlled you, prevented you from doing permanent damage had you not taken me out."

Glaring at the alchemist, I rose to my full height, collected my jacket, and slipped it on. "Thank you for your hospitality, Mayer, but it's time I go home."

From where he lay, Mayer laughed. The sound was deep and coming from low in his belly. "I miss the politeness of our age, Bay. The young de Sangs are always so crass and full of their own importance."

"They are no different to us, Mayer. They just don't hide it behind pretty words," I debated.

Grinning, Mayer pushed himself up to sitting. "Right you are." Getting to his feet, Mayer eyed me. "Her blood must have been good. You look healthier than I've ever seen you. I wouldn't have thought a creature like her could provide such nourishment. If I did, I would never have brought her down here."

We stared at each other for several minutes, a silent debate. My rage, which had simmered in the background while Spectra and I dealt with our immediate needs, started to burn hotter.

Spectra moaned and Mayer glanced her way, his eyebrows jumping into his hairline when he realized she lived. "You have more restraint than I presumed. But it changes nothing, Bay. You are not leaving here until I have what I need. Still, you can keep the girl for food. It makes no difference to me."

As Mayer made to move for the door, I got in his way, blocking his exit and driving him back up. My teeth ground together as power flooded my veins, feeding the flames of my temper. Mayer's pupils widened, his mouth opening and closing, his heart thudding in fear. "If you kill me, you will both rot in here."

I saw Spectra moving in my peripheral, but I kept focusing on Mayer so he didn't turn on her. "Her husband will come, and he won't be alone. Everyone in this building will perish. Let us go, Mayer, or I will slow your death and show no mercy."

Mayer's laugh was forced. Despite his bravado, I could smell his fear. "They may come and kill everyone. But they still can't free you if I am dead here."

The fool had no idea what a monster I could become when someone threatened my family. So few had encountered me when I truly let my anger go. The bear shifter whose fur now lay before my office hearth only one of three.

My eyes went over his shoulder to Spectra. She looked radiant, her hair flowing around as her glare bore into the back of Mayer's head. Recognizing there was a threat behind him, Mayer turned. He grabbed for Spectra's throat, the exact moment she thrust her hand up and exhaled simultaneously, causing her to blur around the edges.

Mayer jolted. His hand passed through Spectra's neck. Stepping to the side, I followed Mayer's eyes to where Spectra's wrist disappeared into his chest. As Mayer started to shake, Spectra floated back, her hand coming free just before Mayer fell to the floor.

"You should record this for your research," Spectra directed, offering me her phone from where she was sprawled on her ass on the floor. She was corporeal again, focusing entirely on the de Sang seizing in front of her.

"Are you okay?"

"Still a little off balance," she shrugged off my concern.

Frowning, I took the proffered device and recorded Mayer as bloody froth started forming on his lips. "What's happening?"

"I gave him what he asked for. The cure," Spectra answered as she crawled over to Mayer and started patting down his jacket.

That's when I spotted the vial still embedded in his chest. Spectra must have ghosted it into him when she went Wraith, but it was now a solid object. "I thought you said it didn't work."

"The way it was administered saw no effect. At least, not for this version. I suggested direct organ injection may prove more effective." Finding Mayer's phone, Spectra stood again. She swayed and stumbled, dropping her butt to the bed before she could fall.

"Spec-"

"I'm fine. I was the same when I first woke at your place after tasting your blood." Tapping away at Mayer's phone, she paused and lowered her hands to her lap as she looked at me. "Once you are ready, I'll unlock the door, and you can go deal with the zealots out there."

Mayer was still now, his breaths shallow and raspy. Keeping the camera pointed his way, I moved to Spectra and finger-combed her hair back from her face. "I don't want to leave you alone down here. Will you be able to go ghost and get yourself out?"

Eyeing me, Spectra cocked an eyebrow at me. "I escaped you, didn't I? And I was nowhere near as buzzed as I am right now.

There is a river of power racing through me. Once the dizziness clears, I'll have the energy to run a marathon."

I wasn't reassured, but Spectra caressed the wrist of the hand still in her hair and brought it to her mouth, placing the sweetest kiss on my palm. "Honestly, I've never felt this good since, well, since we married. My vision is sharper, my sense of smell too good because I can smell him decaying." Squishing up her face, Spectra covered her nose. "That's seriously rank."

She wasn't wrong. On the floor, Mayer was rotting like it was on timelapse. "The cure still doesn't work."

"Actually, I think it did," Spectra debated her voice nasally from where she blocked it. "De Sangs are in stasis. From what I saw in the research that's been conducted. This sample reactivates the cells, but it doesn't heal them. So, for an ancient, it effectively removes the freeze on their immortality. Their age catches up with them. I think the older they are, the faster their cells break down."

As Mayer turned into a putrid bubbling mass, Spectra shrugged her shoulders. "Of course, this isn't my field, and I'm guessing based on everything your friend told me this morning. Take him a sample and let him do his thing and he can tell you whether we cured him or killed him."

Rising to her feet, Spectra didn't sway or stumble this time. Meeting my eyes, she rose up on her toes, still blocking her nose, and kissed my mouth with such lasciviousness that I nearly dragged her back to the bed. Thankfully, the ridiculousness of her holding her nose had me laughing, Spectra joining me.

"You should call Calin and Luke, give them the address, and tell them to bring a team and come and get you," Spectra directed as she took her phone back. "I need to let Mercury know I'm okay and get out of here before that smell gets in my hair. I'm sure it's like the Bog of Eternal Stench and once it gets in the follicles, you'll never get it out again."

"Bog of Eternal Stench?" I chuckled as Spectra sent Mercury a text.

"Seriously? You never watched Labyrinth?" Spectra looked horrified. "Right. Next date night, I'm fixing this lapse in your knowledge. I reference that movie far too often for you not to understand it."

Her jest brought a smile to my face. I fell more in love with Spectra whenever she made me laugh. Being near her was the best and most addictive drug.

Shoving her phone back up the sleeve of her dress, Spectra picked up Mayer's phone off the bed. "Call your guys. I need to get out of here, and I can't open that door for you until the cavalry is on the way."

Doing as she asked, I gave Calin the address Spectra told me, then put my burner back in my jacket. Fisting the hair at the base of Spectra's head, I pressed our mouths together. Nibbling her bottom lip, I then slipped my tongue in to taste her deliciousness.

"I love you," I breathed across her wet lips.

Spectra's tongue flicked out, collecting the taste of me from her mouth. "I love you too. I'll see you at home." She tapped Mayer's phone screen, and the lock on the door clicked.

Pecking her mouth one last time, I released Spectra and left her there, pushing through the door and finally letting the rage of my incarceration free on the occupants of this building, starting with the guard at the door.

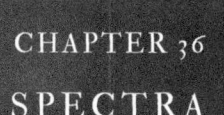

# CHAPTER 36

# SPECTRA

As the screams of dying men filled the building, I exhaled all the air in my lungs and floated out of the warded room. The body of the guard posted outside was torn limb from limb. Blood sprayed out over the surrounding walls, and his head was nowhere to be found.

A shiver raced through me as I floated upstairs. I found the guard's head here, at the feet of what could have been a burning effigy, except I recognized the face of the young de Sang caught in a scream of horror. Like the wind changed and froze him before Bay set fire to him.

The power Bay was pulling thrummed in my veins, so I had no doubt he was capable of this. I just hadn't realized how powerful Bay was before now.

"Holy hell," I muttered as the realization hit me. Even when we wed our bodies, I couldn't sense this, but now that we had mated, I couldn't ignore it. My husband was more than a de Sang sorcerer. How had he hidden this all this time?

Trying to shake off the shudder of conflicting fear and desire that wracked me at that moment, I navigated through various other scenes of the massacre. Eventually, I located my coat in the closet and became corporeal again to shrug it on. Upstairs, more screams rang out, and the fire alarm started sounding, but it couldn't cover the sound that followed.

The scream ratcheted in pitch with every passing second until it cut off with what sounded like someone spilling an urn of thick soup on the floor above me. I didn't need to see to know that it was nightmare fodder.

Yanking the front door open, I slammed it behind me and almost tripped down the stairs in haste to get out of there. There was too much for the brain to process as it was. Listening to Bay dismember others, no matter how evil, was not something I needed to add to my list.

I know I should have been disturbed by this side of my husband, but I wasn't. In fact, I counted on it when I set him loose on the men who had tortured and starved him for the last week. I only felt the need to protect innocence, and not one being in that house fit that category. Not even me.

"Spectra?"

Turning forward, Alexander stood on the footpath before me, leaving the car parked on the curb. His arms wrapped around me, concern filling his features as he took me in. "What are you doing here?"

"Alexander," I sighed. "Did you come to help Bay and me?"

"Bay's here?" Alexander tensed.

"Yes. Essence took him over a week ago. They came for me on Friday night and—" My voice fell away at the anger vibrating through Alexander's body. "Why are you here?"

"I was here for a business meeting."

Using his chest as leverage, I pushed away from him, disgust turning my stomach. "You have business with Essence?"

Alexander searched my face. His eyes fell to my neck, and his jaw tensed. "They fed on you."

Stepping back, I covered the bite with my hand, my heart racing as a new fear filled my head. "Did you send them after me? Is that what your business was here? You had them take me for you?"

"What?" Alexander blinked wide eyes at me. "No! Whatever

happened here, I had nothing to do with it. I was asked to come and meet with an alchemist. I didn't know he was with Essence," he defended as he reached for me. "Spec—"

"I need to go," I dismissed, pushing away from Alexander and trying to walk down the street.

"No, Spec," Alexander grasped my wrist, holding me there. "I swear to you, I had nothing to do with this. Let me take you home."

"I'm fine." I tried to pull away, but Alexander wouldn't release me.

"I know about you and Bay."

I froze on the spot. Slowly, I lifted my eyes to Alexander's. Anger and sadness were staring back at me. "What do you mean?"

"When we were last together, I didn't pull out. Yet your body isn't mine. The only other sorcerer you've been with is Bay. You wed your body to him. Why him, Spec?"

Closing my eyes, I rubbed my lips and fought to stay calm. "Why do you sorcerers always think females of my kind are only special to you?" I scolded, getting in Alexander's face. "My husband is an Angelis. When he claimed my body on our wedding night, the bond that you seem to think exists only for sorcerers was formed."

Alexander's mouth dropped open, then he quickly shut it, and his shoulders dropped along with his face. "Spec, I'm sorry. I don't know much about Angelis. I just assumed—"

"That's always been your problem, Alexander. You always make assumptions without fact-checking your ass." I went to turn away, stopped, and faced Alexander again. "I slept with Bay. I'm sure you already know that. But you want to know why it wouldn't matter if I bound myself to him?"

Narrowing his eyes, Alexander released my wrist and shoved his hands in his pocket. His shoulders tense and posture guarded. "Why? Why would he be a better option for you than me?"

"He can't have and doesn't want children," I answered. I waited for Alexander's brows to pull together and for the weight of what I had just said to settle on him. "The danger a sorcerer presents to a weak balance is carrying his child, not marrying. You need a wife to carry on your line. Bay doesn't. He couldn't even if he wanted to."

Stepping into Alexander, I cuffed his cheek and pressed my lips to his in a tender, public-appropriate kiss. "None of it matters because I'm not your balance, Alexander. I love you, but I'm not yours. Don't start a war with Bay over someone you can never have." Turning away from his heartache, I ignored the tugging in my soul and strode off down the footpath.

At the corner of the block, I looked back. Alexander was gone. Calin was exiting the black SUV that had just pulled into the space in front of Alexander's car. Several men in combat gear followed Calin into the townhouse. Luke stopped on the footpath and turned his gaze my way.

We met each other's gaze for a moment, and then Luke smirked and strode into the building. Pausing, I leaned on the wrought iron fence of the corner townhouse and bowed my head. Bay's rage was nearly wrung out. I was still struggling with what our new bond had revealed to me. How did he suppress this truth? Did Mercury know? Mathew? Surely, they would have mentioned it. Warned me.

The sound of a car horn made me jump and look around. Swallowing my fear, I checked my surroundings until I was sure there was no danger, then I turned and headed toward Tommy's bar. The church wasn't safe, but I knew I'd be safe at Tommy's. Plus, I could feel that's where Mercury was still sleeping.

"You left without your husband."

Spinning around, I eyed the hooded figure standing right behind me on the footpath. So close that I had no trouble inhaling his warm caramel scent. "Lincoln."

When he stood towering over me, only his pale cerulean eyes peering out at me from beneath his hood, I licked my lip nervously. I covered my tummy as it rumbled loudly. "He's safe now, but dealing with the Essence members who held him."

I jumped when Lincoln's fingers touched my chin, turning my head slightly to observe the bite mark on my neck. "I understand. We all have a temper when pushed." Bowing his head, he used his thumb to open my mouth and inhaled. Pulling away, he released me. "Hmm. Mated now too. That must have been a shock for you?"

My lips trembled, and my eyes filled with tears. I opened my mouth, ready to admit I still was trying to come to terms with it, but other than a whimper, I couldn't say it. Rubbing my lips together, I pointed over my shoulder instead. "Are you going to escort me to Tommy's?"

Eyes going over my head, Lincoln took a moment, then shook his head.

"So you were just watching Bay and saw me come out?"

"I sensed your distress and fear." Taking a step closer, Lincoln was almost touching me now. "It's time, Spectra."

My voice was a breathy whisper as I asked, "For what?" Everything about Lincoln made my body tingle. It was the same sensation I always got when I was close to Bay.

"For you to come with me to finish your training." Lincoln offered his hand.

I lifted mine automatically but stopped short of putting it in his. My bond with Bay tugged at me at the exact moment Mercury's also jerked. Something was wrong here. Pulling back, I shook my head. "No." Turning, I exhaled and concentrated on getting to Tommy's. I stopped short when Lincoln blocked my way.

"I told you before, your Wraith abilities don't work on me," he said as he floated closer. Offering me his hand again, Lincoln waited. "I will not hurt you, Spectra. I have waited patiently. Let you learn what you can, fall in love, and marry. Those tied to you have all claimed you except me. I have stood back, watched you draw us all to you, and waited for my turn."

"Your turn for what?"

His fingers caressing my jaw sent tingles through my body, weakening my resistance and drawing me into his body. "To teach you. To have you," the soft growl in his deep voice went straight to my ovaries.

I couldn't pull away from his magnetism. "I'm married," I pleaded. "I want to stay with my husbands."

"Mercury will know where to find you and will come to us."

"But Bay—"

"Is your mate. I need him to be part of this eventually, but first, you need to learn your truth, then you can learn his," Lincoln justified. His caress moved to my chin, lifting my face until I was covered by the cowl of his hood. "You feel our connection, don't you? You know we are bonded too."

We were. I knew that. But I just didn't know how that had happened. "How? We've never been together."

His humor was visceral, and my traitorous body swooned into his hold.

"Yet." His lips connected with mine, strong arms wrapping around me, pulling me tight to him, both of us feeling substantial even in our incorporeal forms.

Our lips merged as Lincoln danced us around. His tongue dipped in to taste me, and hot caramel fudge washed over my taste buds. I felt a shock of pain as he bit my lip and then candied apples mixed with the caramel, and my head became woozy.

"Wait," I panted.

Lincoln pulled back just enough to meet my eyes. His eyes seemed darker, and my mind flashed back to the nightmare of the angel looking back at me through the mirror.

"Oh, God," I breathed.

The side of Lincoln's mouth turned up, and then he was kissing me again. Darkness gathered around us and swept us away from the city street. Lincoln closed out the kiss and eased back from me as the world stilled around us. "We are already bound, but that does not constitute consent."

Putting distance between us, Lincoln moved to the side of a grand room, the walls all painted a deep blue, the old-style paneling on the walls trimmed in white, almost disguising the doors. In the center of the room was a huge bed which instantly gave me orgy vibes but in a very classy, almost heritage surrounding.

Pushing open a door, Lincoln revealed a beautiful pale gold and sky-blue marble bathroom. "I'm sure you need to shower. I dare say Mercury will be here shortly, and we can all eat dinner together to discuss the next few weeks of training."

"Weeks?" I squeaked. I'd just spent over a week away from Bay. I didn't want to wait weeks to see him and ask him everything running around my head.

A caress along my jaw brought me back to this room. The Angelis, who was far too sexy for his own good in front of me. "How long you are here will depend on how quickly you learn, Spectra. Frankly, I'm happy to give you longer and divide our time together between training and pleasure."

The kiss he bestowed on me was all tease and zapped straight to my clit, making me squirm and press my legs together to find relief. With a chuckle, Lincoln allowed enough space between us to meet my eyes.

"I'll go get us some food. I've left a robe in the bathroom for you. Your clothes carry a waft of putrefied flesh on them," he revealed as he scrunched his nose a little.

With one last peck of his lips, Lincoln moved to another door and opened it to reveal a grand hallway that seemed to go forever. "Make yourself at home."

"Where the hell are we?" I asked, feeling slightly agoraphobic by the length of that vast corridor outside.

"My home. The castle of souls in Purgatory."

"I'm in Hell?" I squawked, my arms wrapping around me protectively.

"Not quite." With no further explanation, Lincoln stepped out and shut the door.

My only relief was the sound of a lock clicking into place. I just wasn't sure if it was locking things out or me inside. I cursed, then immediately apologized to Mathew in my head. Taking my phone out of my sleeve, I checked it and cursed again when there was no service.

"Come on! How can Hell not have cell reception in this day and age?" Huffing, I dropped my phone on the bed. Then catching a whiff of the putrefied alchemist, I headed for the bathroom. Just because I was in Hell didn't mean I had to smell like it.

CHAPTER 37

# MERCURY

My PHONE BUZZED on the bedside table, drawing me from my dreams of Spectra. She was screaming in fear one minute and moaning as I took her body hard, only to turn back to her cowering in the dark in fear as Bay showered in the blood of his enemies. Shaking my head at the weird thoughts, I rolled over and grabbed my phone.

SPECTRA

I'm okay. Heading back to Tommy's now.

Sighing, I threw back the sheets and went to the shower, cleaning myself with the intention of getting dirty as soon as Spectra got here. It took a lot of control to let Luke and Calin drag her away from me this morning.

"Spectra on her way back?" Tommy asked.

Wiping the water out of my eyes, I found him leaning against the bathroom counter, chugging a bottle of water. Squirting shampoo into my hand, I lathered up my hair. "Yeah."

"It's strange, right? We can fuck for days without sleep, but once you blow your load in her, she near passes out," Tommy considered.

"Oh, Spectra is always raring to go, and she keeps up, don't you worry," I assured. "Just remember, she's not like us."

"Because she died," Tommy checked, then nodded his head. I tilted my head back and rinsed off the shampoo. Tommy put the lid on the empty water bottle as I finished the shower. Standing straight, he looked at his watch. "We should eat when she gets here. How far away is she?"

"She was in the city and not far away." Wrapping a towel around my waist, I finger-combed my hair back from my face, then focused on Spectra to see how close she was. I faltered when she seemed to be nowhere and everywhere. Frowning, I concentrated, but my sense of her bounced around empty space.

Tommy was suddenly in front of me. "What is it?"

"She's gone and yet here," I answered. I tried to draw on our bond to determine if she had gone Wraith to access the building without disturbing us, but... "She was just on the other side of town, and now she's gone."

When my eyes met Tommy's, he clenched his jaw in anger. I knew immediately what I was feeling. "He's taken her," I scowled. "That selfish son of a..." Snatching up my clothes, I started yanking them on.

"I warned you," Tommy reminded me.

"Yeah, yeah. Let's not tell Mathew until I've spoken to Lincoln and figured out what he's playing at."

Tommy snickered. "Come on, Merc. He wants what we all want. A female of our kind we can balance with."

"That was never my goal, nor Mathew's. Spectra won't balance me, and I'd kill Mathew if he even tried to use her for that."

"Do you doubt it's what Lincoln wants?" Tommy challenged me.

Lincoln put all of this into play. He sent me here to watch over Spectra after he found her, with the job being to keep her from converting. He always had a plan for Spectra, but none of us knew it.

The simple fact was that he balanced when he made Spectra. That's why he created Wraiths randomly. Not all innocent souls murdered before their time were given the chance of life by taking their vengeance. Lincoln only did it when he was desperate to balance.

So, what was his long-term goal with Spectra? Gritting my teeth, I pulled on my boots. "No. I don't." Getting to my feet, I grabbed up my jacket and pulled it on. "I'll be back."

Focusing my thoughts on Spectra and Lincoln's home, I disappeared into the starlight of the ether, the space between the Celestial and Epoch realms. With my focus locked on Spectra, the Castle of Souls, Lincoln's home flashed ahead, as if lightning slashed the darkness to give me a glimpse of where I was heading.

Storm clouds filled my path, and I was standing in the grand foyer, the resting place for souls waiting to be reincarnated. It was a combination of those who were not yet ready for their final destination or elected to return to the epoch realm and leave their afterlife.

The Castle of Souls was nearly the size of a small city. Thankfully, moving around here was much like the ether. Closing my eyes, I focused on my bond to Spectra, then opened my eyes and found myself in front of an apartment door. Knocking on the door, I waited. Nothing.

"Spec, it's Mercury."

The door opened, and Spectra was in my arms, clinging to me like her life depended. Holding her to me, I stepped back into the room and shut the door, making sure it latched before I relaxed.

"Okay, shh," I soothed the angel in my arms.

Rubbing my hand up and down her spine, I carried Spectra to the bed and sat down, arranging her so she sat in my lap and could stay cuddled into my chest. Spectra's long, lean legs were smooth under my hands as I continued to soothe her. I folded her robe to cover her just in case Lincoln turned up. He didn't need a key to get in.

"You want to tell me what happened? How did you end up here?" I queried, since Spectra wasn't crying or trembling. She seemed disturbed more than anything else.

Exhaling hard, Spectra told me how Lincoln found her on the street and kissed her, and then she was here. There was some indication there was a conversation where Lincoln told Spectra she needed to finish her training. Still, she didn't go into detail.

"How can I be bound to him when we've never been together?" Spectra finally asked.

This, I could explain. "All Wraiths are bound to death. Or whichever death angel made them. It's what stops you from crossing over if you are human. When the Wraith gets their vengeance, it releases their bond and returns them to their human existence."

"But it feels like my bond with Bay," Spectra replied.

That surprised me but wasn't hard to believe. "That makes sense. Your body is bound to Bay in much the same way as your corporeal form is bound to Lincoln to hold it in stasis for you."

Waiting for Spectra to say more, I finger-combed her hair. It was knotted in the lengths, so I had to be careful not to catch them. "Lincoln claimed you first, Spectra. The rest of us were drawn to you later. And I'm not going to deny that he is ridiculously alluring for a child of death."

Spectra snorted a laugh. "Right? What's with that? Death was meant to be scary, not make you want to throw yourself at him."

"If you think Lincoln is bad, just imagine his father. Azahel can get women and men, that way inclined, to jizz in their pants with nothing more than a smile. I see him and his offspring all the time around the hospital. It's good they rarely show themselves to humans, or people would die while their caretakers were busy panting over them."

Chuckling in my arms now, Spectra tilted her head back to meet my eyes, her humor sparkling in her pale blue irises, but that's not where my attention went. Lifting my hand, I brushed the nasty hickey on her neck and had to grit my teeth.

"That doesn't look like Lincoln's kiss."

Flinching, Spectra pulled out of my arms. Moving to the head of the bed, she set her back against it, pulling her knees up to her chest, tucking the robe around her legs to prevent flashing the room.

"Okay, there is obviously more to your day than just Lincoln abducting you off the street with a kiss," I opened for Spectra.

"Bay fed on me," Spectra whispered. "I let him. He was too

hungry to release into the world and only needed a small amount of my blood to be back to full health. Honestly, it was finished before I even registered he'd bitten me.

When did Bay get back? "Why don't you tell me what happened between you leaving with Luke and Lincoln finding you." Because I should have linked that something must have happened before now. There is no way Bay would have let Spectra walk back to Tommy's alone. Not while Essence was targeting her.

Flicking her eyes to me, Spectra hugged her knees tighter, then she inhaled and told me what had happened. Starting with meeting Jacoby to Bay, massacring every soul present in the house when he escaped.

"… that's when I ran into Alexander," Spectra told me. She continued to explain how she thought Alexander had joined Essence for a moment.

As Spectra talked, my mind went back to the dream. To Spectra's fear of Bay. Was it just seeing his rage unleashed that scared her, or his feeding on her?

"… that's when Lincoln found me," Spectra finished. She wasn't looking at me but staring across the room, and I sensed that her mind was still back there and whatever psychological trauma she had endured.

"What can I do?" I asked gently, trying to coax Spectra from wherever her mind had taken her. It left her chewing her lip and staring at nothing as if it may attack her at any moment.

Blinking, Spectra turned her spooked gaze my way. The tension left her body, and she crawled back into my arms. "Tell me we can go home."

Kissing her temple, I sighed. "I'll speak to Lincoln."

Spectra sighed as she nuzzled her face into my chest. "My body is buzzing and wanting you, but my head just wants to sleep."

Laying down with her, I cuddled Spectra against me, then slid my hand between her legs, brushing her folds tenderly before sliding between them to find her heat. "How about I do all the work, and then you'll sleep soundly?"

A moan was all the answer I needed. Releasing the belt of Spectra's robe, I rolled her onto her back, and then I made sweet love to my wife. Taking my time, making sure to build her pleasure so that her climax was a whole-body experience. Then she fell asleep in my arms.

"I'm guessing she won't be eating."

Turning my head, I scowled at Lincoln, standing by the small table in the room as he placed a tray of food down. Ensuring Spectra was covered with the blankets, I pulled on my jeans and moved to that side of the room, keeping my voice down.

"What the hell, Linc? You just abducted her off the street?" I hissed.

Rolling his eyes at me, Lincoln continued to set out the food. "You make it sound like it was a traumatizing experience for her. I assure you, she was traumatized when I found her."

"Which time?"

Giving me his trademark smirk, Lincoln gestured I take a seat. "No point letting the food go to waste. I'll make sure there is more waiting when Spectra wakes up. Is there something specific she likes for breakfast?"

"Protein. Eggs, Bacon, and Spinach. If you really want to impress, croissants." Picking up the knife and fork, I started eating. "She's not herself tonight," I prodded, hoping Lincoln might have an answer for me.

"Bay mated her."

Barely restraining an eye roll, I picked up the glass of wine. "That happened ages ago."

"No, the first time he wed her body to his. This time he mated as de Sangs do with a blood exchange. Where beforehand their bond was like a walkie-talkie that lost its power with distance, it's now a living breathing thing that no amount of distance can dampen."

Lincoln's explanation made me nearly drop my glass. "Well, fuck!" I huffed, putting the glass back on the table. "So, I'm seeing her reacting to feeling Bay so intently?"

Nodding his head as he chewed his steak, Lincoln tapped the stem of his wine glass while throwing a glance Spectra's way. "She would have felt every ounce of his rage and power as if it was her own. That violence probably sickened her and fed the Wraith's need for vengeance."

"That was still a messed-up thing to do to her," I scowled at Lincoln.

Raising his eyebrow at me, Lincoln didn't even flinch. "All Angelis become Celestials on their death in the Epoch realm and join their fathers. Would you have preferred I let her convert and be at the mercy of our fathers? She had no idea who she was or her power. You know what would have happened had she suddenly showed up in Machen."

"What makes you think she'd end up in Machen? Why only the fourth level of Heaven and not the seventh where our fathers reside?" I asked.

Lincoln smirked over his wine at me. "Each of our fathers, as one of the seven Archangels, serves upon the Throne of Glory in Araboth. But like my father rules here in Shehaqim and your father rules in Raquie, Michael rules over Machen. We go to our father's realms when we are granted our metaphorical wings."

Taking a mouthful of his wine, Lincoln set it aside and sliced another piece of his steak ready. "She's not going home with you, Mercury. Spectra has come close several times over the last two months. Either by using her powers or by one of those fanged bastards hoping to take her from us—"

"You are not meant to have a prejudice against any souls of the Epoch realm," I lectured. "And despite folklore, de Sangs are not soulless."

"Doesn't change the fact they've been hunting a soul I've given my protection to," Lincoln growled. Setting his cutlery down, he put his elbows on the table and leaned in to keep his voice down. "Cover her absence from her other husband however you must, but don't share her whereabouts."

"Bay would never hurt her." I rejected that idea immediately. He might be a de Sang, but he loved Spectra.

"I know. It's not Bay I worry about, but the power he used today brought the interest of others their way. I wasn't the only one outside that house to see Spectra emerge. Trust me, they took note.

We need her trained before they come sniffing around and discover who she is."

"Not just Essence?" When Lincoln met my eyes, his flashing sapphire with the seriousness of this conversation, I started to dread who else could have taken an interest in Spectra. "Who?"

Pursing his lips, Lincoln looked to the bed and kept his voice low. "Do you know Bay's lineage?"

Frowning, I shook my head. Bay was born so long ago. Sorcerer's blood was so watered down that it was often hard to determine from which choir they even originated, let alone the actual great-grandfather.

"A watcher, but not a low order. Bay's bloodline traces to the fifth Heaven and its Archangel Samael."

My cutlery dropped to the table. "The dark servant. His great-grandfather is Samael?"

"Samael is not Bay's great-grandfather but Kabaiel, the star of god."

Kabaiel was Samael's grandson.

"So, Kabaiel has kept tabs on his bloodline and discovered Spectra?" That wasn't as bad as Samael discovering her. Kabaiel was a protector and abandoned his choir to become a leader of the watchers. A celestial who turned his back on his born nature and chose instead to pursue the counter-balance was rarely heard of. It would take a great deal of control and will-power to manage.

"No one has seen nor heard from Kabaiel since the holy war," Lincoln educated.

Huffing, I glared at the descendant of death opposite me. "You can be damn infuriating to have a conversation with, Linc. Just tell me who."

"Kabaiel's father, Kushiel. He has never forgiven his son for leaving Machon, for choosing to protect mankind instead of punishing the wicked."

Staring at Lincoln, I don't think I blinked for several minutes. One of the seven angels of punishment was drawn by Bay's power. And now a dark servant was taking an interest in my wife.

"Now you see why Spectra must stay here to finish her training," Lincoln relaxed back in his seat and started eating again.

Swallowing this new information, I set my gaze on Spectra. How peaceful and beautiful she looked in her sleep. "Don't get too comfortable with my wife, Linc."

Giving me a slight nod, Lincoln observed Spectra. "I know the effect I have on women. I will ensure her consent is true and not a complexity of our bond."

Inhaling deeply, I blew out my breath and picked up my knife and fork again. "Well, I guess I better pack a travel bag. It looks like I'll spend my days off work in purgatory."

# EPILOGUE

## BAY

Snow was falling again. There had been more snowfall in the two weeks that Spectra had been missing than in the entirety of winter. My computer dinged, but I couldn't take my eyes off the view outside my office window. "Where are you?"

The bond between us pulsed, and my vision washed into a long corridor that seemed to stretch forever. Sitting forward, I pushed at the connection. "Show me where you are, my love."

Turning her head to the side, a mirror on the wall cast the reflection of a figure in a thick black hooded robe. None of her features were visible, but I knew it was my wife. What I hated was the fear I felt in her whenever I connected with her now.

"Spec," I mourned. "You have no reason to fear me. You never have."

Stepping closer to the mirror, Spectra's pale face and eyes became visible. Her silky black hair was braided and hung over one of her shoulders. "Bay," she whispered, touching the mirror as if she saw me in her reflection.

Desire and love warred with her fear of me, and I was doused in her longing for me. She missed me just as much as I missed her.

"Soon," Spectra murmured, and then she was heading down that long hallway again.

The door to my office opened, and Luke stepped inside. He looked drawn. A week ago, Luke admitted he saw Spectra leaving the townhouse. I think he blamed himself for her disappearance.

Pausing, Luke assessed me, sighed, and took the seat across from me. "How is she?"

"Exhausted. Spec misses us but is also terrified to come home," I offered. "Of me. She's scared of me." I'd told Calin and Luke I'd fed on Spectra and strengthened our bond. They believed her fear of me was that I bit her. I knew better. "I don't know how to set her at ease."

"Did Mercury offer any help?" Calin asked, following Luke in.

"He assures me once Spec has learned to control her powers in a safe environment, she'll come home," I replied.

"It's not like he went with her. He's missing her just as much as you are," Calin defended.

"Except that Mercury knows where Spectra is. Who she is with. And can go to her anytime he wants to," I snapped.

"Well, there is that," Calin agreed and dropped down in a chair. "I have nothing. No one knows about a building where the corridors seem to go on forever."

When I turned my attention to Luke, he slid a photocopy of a painting onto my desk. Picking it up, I looked at the blurry image of a hall that went on forever. "It's the right perspective, but the one in Spectra's eyes looks a lot more luxurious than this."

"Look at the date of the painting. That probably was considered luxurious," Luke argued.

He was right, but I couldn't be sure it was the same place. Between the way the walls blurred and the ghostly figure lingering further down the hall, it may not even exist.

"This is from an old Roman text. They call it the Land of Death and his Friends. Or at least that is the translation I managed to find," Luke explained. "It was originally drawn on papyrus, and the accompanying text has been translated multiple times, so I can't be sure what it was originally meant to say."

My computer pinged again. With a sigh, I clicked on the reply and then stood up. "I'll try speaking to Mercury again tonight, but I have a client meeting right now, and they've requested discretion."

As Calin and Luke got up, I walked to the door. "It's a good lead, Luke. Thank you, both of you, for trying to find her."

"You're not the only one who cares about her, Bay," Calin muttered before stepping out.

Luke paused by me. "While you were away, Selena worried about Spec a lot. She said her aura started to change. That your suffering was tough for Spec to endure."

"You think she's doing this as revenge? I can assure you she's not," I worried.

Squeezing my shoulder in reassurance, Luke met my eyes. "What I mean is that Spectra changed. Has been changing since you entered her life. Look at everything she's been through. Maybe she needs this space to find who she is again." Striding through the door, Luke didn't look back.

Blowing out a breath, I couldn't deny there was some truth to Luke's observation. Spectra had already lived through so much pain. In the last two months, she'd learned who her father was and what she was, and she'd had some very traumatic experiences.

On top of everything, our courtship was very short. Two weeks from meeting to married. I wasn't ignorant that it was heavily influenced by Alexander Williams breaking her heart. The same could be said of her quickie marriage to Mercury.

Understanding that time away while she dealt with this other new part of her reality didn't take away my longing or concern for my wife. Spectra had feared me since we met because I was a de Sang. Ironically, mating as a de Sang had made her fear me more, but for an entirely different reason.

"Mr. Ryder." Claudia caught my attention. She waited for my eyes to meet hers, then gestured to the woman approaching the door. "Ms. Nika Bailey."

The woman who stopped before me was striking. A pale face, grass-green eyes, and straight pale blonde hair pulled back in a

French roll. Her clothing was fashionable and appropriate for a business meeting, right down to her Louboutin kitten heels.

What was the most impactful about this woman was not her looks but the awareness that I knew this de Sang. The Fantôme who watched over Spectra. "Lovely to meet you face to face, Nika. Please come in."

Stepping back, I waited for her to pass, then shut the door after her. "I'm guessing this isn't actually a business meeting."

"You've been elusive the last few weeks. Only going from your home to your office and back again. It has made making contact with you via my usual means difficult," Nika replied in her cultured voice. "Even today, I normally would have sent Miranda since she has a face you already know. But her cover was blown here, so that option was also unavailable."

Moving to the lounge seating area of my office, I gestured for Nika to sit. "Please. Can I get you a drink?"

"I'm sufficiently hydrated. Thank you." Nika lowered herself into the sofa and crossed her ankles, angling her legs in the refined way young ladies were taught. This woman carried herself like another young lady I knew well.

"I can understand you keeping a low profile these last few weeks. After the Essence abduction," Nika continued, letting me know she knew what befell me. "I'm surprised L'Ordre let your massacre pass without issue, though."

"Spectra escaped just before me, and he saw her state and her distrust of him being there," I revealed. "He was upset that I left him no one to dismantle to relieve his temper."

Nika held her back straight, her posture near perfect as she watched me. "Essence took Spectra? How?"

"She knocked at the door, actually, but L'Ordre doesn't know that. His conversation with Spectra on her escape left him thinking their attempt on Friday night had been successful," I answered truthfully.

"Okay," Nika considered. "Then where is Spectra now? She's been strangely incommunicado since you resurfaced. At first, I thought you were making up for lost time, but as I hear it, Spectra is missing."

"Missing for some," I clarified. "Spec's Angelis protectors know where she is, but are unwilling to share her location with me."

Narrowing her eyes, Nika barely showed the way she suddenly tensed. "Why?"

"My understanding is that Spectra is being trained in the way of her kind."

"But why are they hiding her from you?"

"They aren't. I can see where Spectra is and what she does at any time. I know that she is safe. I just don't know where they've taken her." Shifting, uncomfortable with what I was telling this de Sang, I knew I could trust her with Spectra's truth, if nothing else.

"Apparently, she needs to learn how to control her powers in a safe environment. I gather Miranda told you about what Spectra did on Essence's last attempt?"

"She did," Nika confirmed.

I'd expected as much. Luke filled me in on Spectra shielding Miranda's car from damage. "So far, Spectra has learned many of her abilities when her life is in danger. She has no control over them, and that has had a significant impact on her. She needs to learn that control or her next encounter with Essence might make her more of a danger to herself than the enemy."

"Yet, you search for her?"

"Understanding doesn't stop me from worrying. It is an instinct for me to find Spectra and try and protect her."

"I guess we have that need in common."

"I guess we do." Relaxing a little, I asked a question I'd been burning to know the answer. "When did you start protecting Spectra?"

"When her mother died."

That was interesting timing. "Spec's mother put Spectra's life at risk in her desperate attempt to find Spectra's sister."

Nika tensed again and couldn't meet my eyes. "I'm aware."

Studying the woman opposite me, I realized that while they had different colorings and different facial structures, they had one thing in common. "Strange that her mother chose to end her own life after Spectra was attacked by the de Sang she was servicing," I alluded, testing her reaction, and I got it.

"Be careful which stones you lift to find secrets, Bay. It doesn't take much for one of those to fling up and hit you in the eye," Nika warned.

"I would have killed her had I cared for Spectra then like I do now. The woman was so caught up in her grief for her eldest daughter she forgot her younger daughter even existed and still needed her."

Nika glared at me when I leaned toward her and added, "I wouldn't have left her bled out in the bathtub for Spectra to find, though. That only further traumatized an already suffering innocent girl."

Breaking eye contact, Nika pursed her lips and picked at an invisible piece of lint on her dress. "The body needed to be found, and the death not suspicious for Spectra to collect the life insurance policy."

Relaxing back in my seat, I huffed. "The insurance policy expired when Spec's mother failed to make the payments. Spectra struggled to keep a roof over their heads and food on the table. She had to choose where to spend money, and insuring things like her mother's life was not something a fourteen-year-old girl prioritizes."

Nika's eyes flashed to mine, pupils dilating a moment before her shoulders sagged. "I was a newly minted agent when I was sent to deal with that woman. Her behaviors and actions were careless and brought the wrong attention to the community."

"I guess a professional businesswoman——a high-flier——not showing up to work would be suspicious enough. Attending elite parties and sporting multiple bite marks would draw further attention," I agreed.

Sadness passed through Nika's eyes. "I didn't mean to cause Spectra more trauma. I was still there when she came home. The way she stood there looking at her mother in the bathtub, it was obvious the poor girl wasn't sure whether to be relieved or fall apart."

Silence filled the room. I didn't have to imagine what it was like for Spectra. I'd seen her eyes the night she told me about those years. Her heart was forever scarred by her mother's actions. I decided that since Nika wasn't in a hurry to leave, I should try to find out more information from her.

"Can I ask, were you taken with the sole purpose of Fantôme?" I wanted to know how the assassin squad chose their members these days. What was it about Nika that made them take her?

"Recruited for Fantôme, no. Inducted into them, yes," Nika clarified. "I was attacked in my college dorm by a de Sang, and he took me. When I awoke and realized he'd killed me, sentenced me to this life, and stolen me from my family, I repaid him in kind."

Well, that was interesting. "You killed your sire?"

"I did. He was a young de Sang looking to build himself a college harem. An idiot, really." Nika had no remorse for what she had done. "Fantôme found me after that and recruited me. They were created to protect the de Sangs against anyone exposing them to humans. Weeding out the stupid and those whose egos made them dangerous to their own kind. That is not what they stand for anymore."

"They are assassins for the highest bidder," I confirmed.

Nika bowed her head. "Some of us still hold to the old ways."

My eyes traveled to her ankle. "Hence the lily. You and Miranda are Lilium faction. I should have realized sooner."

Nika's jaw dropped open. "How do you know that? No one knows there is a separate faction."

Smirking, it was my turn to pick at invisible lint. "Oh, that's not true. Those of us who were members of Fantôme when they became divided know that Lilith Lotus refused to be an assassin for hire and created her own splinter cell."

Nika's eyes were wide saucers now.

Enjoying her surprise as she considered me through a different lens, I eased back further in my chair. "Several walked away when the divide happened. Choosing other ways to protect. I always believed it wasn't just de Sangs who needed protection."

"That makes sense. You are a sorcerer and a master of beasts," Nika fathomed.

"That was when the idea of Pendant was born." Leaning on my knees, I kept eye contact with the assassin across from me. "We are on the same side, Danika. Whether it be your cause as a Lilium or your love for your sister. We want the same things."

A swell of emotion filled the de Sangs very green eyes. "You know?"

"I had an inkling when you were at the wedding, but I recognized you from the photos Spectra keeps in her room the moment you stepped through that door." I waited to see if she would threaten me for revealing this secret. I continued when Danika gave me a small smile of happiness to know Spectra kept photos of her around. "If we want to protect Spectra, we must pool our resources."

Tilting her head in a predatory manner, Danika assessed me. "What for?"

"They are not going to stop coming for her. We can't afford to always be on the defensive. She'll lose eventually," I suggested.

"You propose going on the offensive?"

"I do. More specifically, I propose we find whoever is calling the shots and who put Spectra's name on their list, and then we take off their head."

A smile slowly bloomed on Danika's face. "You have a thing for decapitation, don't you?"

I shrugged because I was aware she was referring to how I dealt with the Essence scum at Mayer Callisie's townhouse. "It's quick and effective. No need to drag things out."

Rising out of her seat, Danika waited for me to stand and then offered me her hand. "I believe working with you will be an enjoyable experience, Bay. I'll send word when I have a few leads."

"I'll chase down some leads on my end and keep you updated on Spectra's well-being," I offered in return.

Bowing her head slightly in acceptance, Danika pivoted and left. Waiting for the door to close, I moved to my desk and picked up the phone.

"Boss?"

"Calin, forget the search for Spectra and meet me in the crypt in ten minutes. It's time to question our newest acquisition." Not all of the Essence members died at that house. Even with my temper at its worst, I knew not to destroy a good lead.

After hanging up with Calin, I dialed another number on my burner phone. My stay with Mayer wasn't a complete waste. His blood revealed a key player in Essence to me. Someone I knew well.

"Grandad? How goes married life?"

"I'll tell you all about it when you arrive. It's time to deal with your son."

Sighing, my grandson took a moment. "I'll be there in two days."

To be Continued in Angelis.

# GLOSSARY

**Nachtwelt**

The supernatural world (Nocturnal world)

**Predators**

Those who prey on others to live or for pleasure. They may hunt humans, animals, or other Nachtwelt. It is the hunt that makes them a predator, not the type of prey.

**Predator de Sang**

Predators of blood

**Changeur de corps**

Shapeshifters (also referred to as De Viand).

**Predator de Viand**

Predators of flesh. These are the predators who hunt to eat the flesh of their prey. While most shapeshifters can also be referred to by this term, not all De Viand are shapeshifters.

**Syphons**

Feed off people's emotions or energy (syphons who feed on lust are known as Succubi and Incubi).

**The Tolerant**

Those with power, divine or otherwise. They are called tolerant because they are willing to tolerate the existence of others, or behaviours, they disagree with. This does not in any way insinuate they are peaceable.

### Celestial

Different species to humans. They possess the powers of the divine and are able to cross the veils between realms. They are created, not born, they are all male and physical perfection personified. The Celestials are ranked within triads. The ones humans know most about are the first triad, the most powerful and the closest to God. The Archangels rarely involve themselves with a human, and so it is rare to meet the offspring of an arch. But there are many more in the second and third triads who entertain the company of human women frequently.

### Angelis

Children of Angels. Angelis are the offspring of a Celestial and a human woman. Again, only males, they will possess some of the powers of their fathers and, though ageless and able to live for centuries, they do suffer mortal wounds and deaths just like their mothers. On dying, an Angelis will convert to become a Celestial.

### Nephilim

Grandchildren of Angels. Nephilim are the grandchildren of Celestials. While Celestials are extremely virile, they only produce male offspring. Therefore, for the Angelis to reproduce, they must also take human women as their lovers.

### Balance

Female offspring of Angelis and Nephilim are very rare, but they happen. The odds are one in one hundred. Female offspring are known as balances. When trained, a balance can syphon the emotions of another and turn it into something that person needs. They are also able to shield themselves from the powers of the Nachtwelt. They can identify creatures of the Nachtwelt by their powers, because each power runs on a different frequency. For this reason balances make excellent trackers.

### Sorcerer

The offspring of two Nephilim or a sorcerer and a balance. While it is rare for a female Nephilim to be born, when they are, they tend to reproduce with their own kind. Sorcerers will carry some powers of their great grandparents. Their power usually burns across many frequencies and they must learn to shield others at a young age to prevent harming innocents around them. In order for a sorcerer to reproduce, he must find a balance strong enough to withstand his power, or their child would kill the mother before it could be born. For this reason, every sorcerer spends their lives searching for their balance.

**Empaths** (Clairvoyants / telepaths)

Those who can share another person's emotions, and thoughts. Some may be powerful enough to breach the barrier between the living and the dead and able to divine with spirits.

**Elementals** (Witches, and illusionists.)

People who embody the power of nature.

# JOIN THE BEAUTIFUL AND DEADLY

## Join Ebony's Mischief List

Sign up to Ebony's mailing list for the following perks:

- latest news on new releases
- heads up on upcoming promotions
- exclusive freebies like coupons to read Ebony's stories on Radish for free
- first chance at Giveaways
- get a free book

Go to https://ebonyolson.com for more information

# DARK FANTASY / PARANORMAL ROMANCE BY EBONY OLSON

### STANDALONE BOOKS

Of Shadow and Light

Boundary

Silver Rogue

Halos

The Grave Keeper: All Hallows

### ANGELIS SERIES

Spectra

### HIERARCH SERIES

Succumb

Numinous (March 2023)

Masked (June 2023)

Exodus (September 2023)

Burning Immortality (January 2024)

### OREY GELUS SERIES

Orey Witches

Edge Gelus (Mid 2023)

### RAVEN'S WING TRILOGY

Phased **(Radish Fiction Exclusive)**

### MER TALES

Indigo Shores **(Radish Fiction Exclusive)**

# ROMANCE SUSPENSE BY EBONY OLSON

## Hotel Series

*HOLLY CLAIRE TRILOGY*

Holly's Trilogy: Books 1-3 Hotel Series

(Compilation of Henderson, Cassidy, & Holmes)

*JESS BUTLER TRILOGY*

Best Sunset: Books 4-6 Hotel Series

(Compilation of Best Man, Best Layover, & Best Knight)

## Standalone Books

Black Mark: The Complete Saga

Calypso

Rain: A Dark Past Romance

Protective Instinct

# ABOUT THE AUTHOR

Ebony lives in Sydney, Australia, with her husband, daughter, and six rescue cats. She loves to read fantasy, thrillers, and paranormal romance, spending most of her free time with her nose in a book or writing.

Having always possessed an over-active imagination Ebony spent her younger years regaling friends with fantastic stories, holding her audience captive with the passion and suspense of her characters plights. In adulthood, she shows no signs of stopping her imagination from spreading across as many pages as it can find.

Website: http://ebonyolson.com/
Ebony's Mischief & Mayhem Peeps
Ebony' Mischief & Mayhem Discord Server

facebook.com/EbonyOlson.Author

twitter.com/Ebony_Olson

instagram.com/ebony_olson

amazon.com/author/ebonyolson

bookbub.com/authors/Ebony_Olson

goodreads.com/Ebony_Olson

www.ingramcontent.com/pod-product-compliance
Lightning Source LLC
Chambersburg PA
CBHW070200120726
47909CB00001B/191